I0603976

For mum, without her this story wouldn't exist, thank you
for all the trips to scotland and the tales of folklore.
Without your support this wouldn't have surfaced, thank
you mum, I hope you love this.

Prologue

Kelpie started his day like any other. Wake up, start getting dressed.
His day was very much the same every day except this day there was
something that was going to throw him out of his usual routine,
whether he let it change him was up to him to decide.

***

Kelpie had a strong, well developed trim body that was clothed in a
long-sleeved shirt that was untucked and carelessly buttoned,
revealing a smooth, well-built pale moonlight coloured chest. He was
always dressed in plain black trousers and shoes, with a loosely tied
leather apron that was placed over the top of his clothes to help
protect them from anything the clocks could dish out. He'd learned
his lesson with the clocks, they had a separate personality, some were
more mischievous than others. His hair was long and curled slightly
at the ends, sweeping mainly to the right-hand side with a little curl
on the left. His hair was always funny to him for it curled like the
ripples in a river, all stuck up in any direction falling slightly over one
eye. His skin had always been paler than the average human, but that
was because he wasn't human, he was the mythical folklore water

spirit. To some cultures he had been labelled a kelpie, hence his name. He learned from an immature age the best way to hide was in plain sight, having his human name as what he actually was couldn't have hidden him more. For Kelpies it was normal, in their human form for their skin was the same colour as the moonlight. The fact humans thought he was named after a kelpie for his pale skin made him laugh, humans were so gullible when it came to myths.

***

Opening the shop Sprites and Spirits was always the last thing on his agenda. To everyone the shop looked like any other on the old, cobbled street from the outside and unless you believed in magic and folklore the shop would appear as any other, but to anyone with belief and knowledge of fairies and folklore knew differently, for the very doors of the shop itself were filled with magic. When someone first walked into the shop the first thing you encountered was a massive tree situated in the middle of the shop, the previous owner had designed it like that to hide the pillar in the middle to anyone or anything that could see it. The floor itself was an old rickety wooden floor that creaked and cracked with every step, but when others saw the floor what encountered them was a lush green grass meadow filled with flowers of every kind, honeysuckle encircled the base of the tree. Myriad items of magic or magical properties were placed lazily around the shop, little enchanted tools made for fixing the clocks as well as little orbs of fairy light made to illuminate every little crack and corner of the shop, to everyone else these would just appear as normal overhead lights. He could tell if a non-believer walked in, he could never put a finger on how he knew, the shop just felt different, less alive when they were here. Stairs were hidden behind the tree giving access to the top of the shop which housed the living quarters. Shelves filled with various bits and bobs of strange colours and shapes covered one wall while books of every language both human and other filled the remaining wall both behind and beside the workbench. What Kelpie loved most about this shop was that if you headed through the leaf covered archway it led to a room filled with clocks of every colour and style of course these were not ordinary clocks, no, these clocks led to different realms, realms filled with magic and wonder. Every clock led to a different world, these four belonged to the four biggest and well-known realms in the magical world. In being the four biggest worlds, they had a doorway which was bigger than any other.

***

These four realms were that of The Brownies, The Selkies, The Kelpies and the most elusive of them all was the realm of The Fairies. Some of the doorways were hidden in plain sight for them to pass into the human world, these however were hidden inside intricately carved

clocks. Some of the clocks had been found in the worlds that

accompanied them and others, people had brought in to be fixed, not

knowing what they were. In which case he kept the original and

replaced it with an identical duplicate. Sometimes the ones people

brought in were so obviously magical without them knowing as they

had lost their belief in anything outside the world they could see, little

did people know that ancient clocks, one's people normally confused

with the free-standing grandfather clocks as the humans named them,

the type that were always hidden away out of sight of everyone for

either being too old or too dusty, held doors with secret passages to

different worlds. And this story starts with one such magical clock

that led to a magic filled adventure of love, memory, and gaining

overall confidence within oneself.

Chapter One

New Beginning

The day started like normal, nothing unusual. People came in to walk around looking at the clocks for sale that were on display and walked out again. He knew many of the villagers all wondered how he remained open, but it wasn't his job to fill them in. Kelpie could tell who could see the shop for what it was and who saw the fake, it didn't surprise him when a lot of children usually walked past with their parents and begged them to let them go inside to see the big tree, surrounded by flowers and lights he always thought that being a parent would mean being able to see things the way your child did but that wasn't always the case. The parents would look in and see the fake shop then tell their child that they have to stop making up lies about things that weren't there. He guessed it made sense that the amount of people that actually believed in him and others of folklore and myth had gone down, if this was how they were being treated, being told to stop believing by saying they were lying made them forget in a sense. It made him wonder what was going to become of this world when all belief was gone. Many people whispered about his shop, the strangeness of it being open despite nothing coming in or leaving being the main one, that was until today.

***

Kelpie came back from his lunch to find someone had left their amazing clock outside his shop doors. Carrying this thing in was not going to be easy, it was taller than his six-foot eight frame. Kelpie looked around his store front, whoever got it here could still be around to help. After a while it seemed whoever dropped it off was long gone. He turned to unlock the doors before gradually and carefully walking the clock back into the shop, he could have picked it up but that would cause too much chatter among the town's folk. Once behind the safety of the store with its doors closed Kelpie picked up the clock not even bothering to look first, there was something magical about this clock and he was going to find out. Placing it carefully in the middle of three other massive grandfather clocks that held the doorways to the Selkie, Brownie and Kelpie realms. He spotted an envelope tucked in between the detail at the base of the note that read.

Dear Sir,

I found this clock in an abandoned house that I am restoring. It looked a little worn down and broken. If it can be fixed, please feel free to find it a new home through your store. It looks like it needs to be loved a little, somehow to me it felt sad which I know is a strange thing to feel about a clock. Maybe you can help it find happiness again.

He placed the note back down onto the counter. Before returning his attention back to the clock in question.

"Hmm. This isn't like anything I've seen before. Even if every magical clock is different. Whoever wrote the note was definitely right; it feels safe. How could it feel like something? Whatever it is, it's definitely a magical one. "

Kelpie inspected the clock for he was confused if it was even a clock at all, for it looked like a tree. The clock itself was a chestnut brown with beautifully carved details at the top, with intricate Celtic patterns. Although it still had three of its original branches, on one sat a carved and painted little bird which sat on the left-hand side painted with different shades of orange, red finished off with a little blue tail. Inside it had four weights and a pendulum which were situated below. There was blue forget me nots, rocks, and mushrooms all along the bottom. All the different flowers were open and blooming wildly, all except one.

"It's a beautiful clock but definitely feels sad."

Kelpie carefully moved it into place next to all the other big grandfather clocks, while he worked on an order that was due for pickup that day, so it was all ready and completed for the gentleman who dropped it off a couple days prior. By the time he had finished it the sun was setting indicating that the day had ended, the setting sun had hit the newly positioned forest clock and the positioning against the sun had caused it to start to glow. The branches started to grow little wooden leaves, and that one little flower that was shut had started to open. With his arm crossed around his body and his fingers rested against his temple, he pondered what could have made such a peculiar but interesting clock.

"Even more peculiar, this is definitely magic if I wasn't sure before now, I'm definitely sure. Maybe it could lead somewhere maybe not. Maybe it's only a world available to pass thought at the setting of the sun."

***

Kelpie turned around walking to his bookcase to grab the book of magical doors, maybe he could find where and if it led anywhere or any other information about it the book itself was small, small enough that if you did not know what you were looking for, you would pass over it. For only in the hands of someone from one of the four magical realms would the book expand to its full size unveiling its invisible content. Kelpie had added to this book bit by bit when he had ventured through the doors and seen, tasted or experienced things that were different or unique to that realm. The book itself when enlarged looked like a door itself, an old wooden door with a few splits and a silver knocker on the left-hand side. A garden vine grew up the spine and over the right-hand side of the book, it curled slightly covering a few sections of the door. At present time green ivy leaves covered the vine making the cover look as enchanting as the content within. Kelpies' favourite thing with this book was that it changed with the seasons. Within the books there were chapters on Selkies, Fairies, Brownies, and his race 'Kelpies,' he loved putting air quotes around that it made him laugh but the name stuck with them which made his name his favourite joke Kelpie of the Kelpies. His chapter in the book had all the known names of his race Kelpie being the most used, but there were also chapters on all the known doors to the other realms. Every door had a different image representing the worlds it led too. What always surprised him was how detailed the doors were even though they were inside the clocks he had. Each page had a picture of the clock and the door which lies hidden within. He brought the book over to the clock that was in front of him, to see if he could match it to one of the documented doors.

***

He opened the book, while perching against the counter. The first chapter was on Selkie doors. The Selkie door was as blue as the sea with a black and white emblem of the Selkie on the front. It had a woman with long black hair that blended down into the fins of a seal. This door was found in his shop, it had ocean-like qualities for the clock itself looked like waves crashing down.

"Hmmm it's not a Selkie door, for its not blue or has anything to do with the ocean anywhere on the front."

The next was the door of the Brownies, it did not match this chapter either as it was not chestnut oak or squeaky clean. The Brownies door was a dark old oak, with brooms and rags on the front and if you looked ever so closely you could see a tiny Brownie popping his head out from behind the broom on the front. The clock from which it was hidden, was a tall dark classic grandfather clock that was never dirty or dusty. For the Brownies inside kept it as clean as a whistle.

"Hmm not this one either."

Turning the page it was his chapter. He knew the door did not belong to his category as it was not dark as the midnight sky and there was no horse to be seen. The concluding chapter that was written was his world, the Kelpie realm, to which he was the prince, thankfully his father let him be the guardian of the doors for the time being. Until it was his time to take the throne and find a wife. His door was simple, it was a dark midnight blue similar to the Selkies oceans, the only

difference was the fact it was a darker blue and the main detail on this

cover was a stunning long-haired pitch-black horse with white swirls

for pupils. Which was the Kelpies true form. Although they could

take the form of a human this was the form, this was the form they

were most comfortable in. Sometimes he visited through the door to

his homeland just to reminisce and run along the long winding river

that led through the country. For you see Kelpies had the power to

cleanse and purify all water they touched, a power he had used well in

the human world. For there were many lakes and rivers which he

frequented there. Doing this made him feel like he was at home again

and gave the humans a better life with clean unpolluted water.

"This is definitely not a door of my realm, or the Selkies or even the

Brownies. Which means it belongs to only one."

The last door that was registered in the book of doors, was the door of

the fairies. All that was known about Fairie's door was they

resembled that of a forest with either flowers, trees, or ivy.

"The door has all the characteristics of the fairy realm. Ivy, flowers,

and the clock itself is shaped like a tree." Kelpie shut the book as he

was certain it was a door to the fairy realm. In fact, the book of doors

was originally made in the fairy realm. That realm had never been

before so there wasn't much known about the world that was inside or even how to enter the world. As he was about to put the book back on the shelf, he noticed that the flower that had previously been closed was starting to open slowly till it stopped its bloom.

***

Kelpie lowered himself down to where the flower sat, he waited for a while and the flower was no closer to opening. He noticed that the sun had gone down; he supposed it must only open when the setting sun was on the clock. He realised he would have to wait till the setting sun tomorrow to see if it would open anymore. The days continued for Kelpie like that for a while, each day the flower opened a fraction at a time, till on the last day he looked, and the flower had opened completely and inside the flower lay a tiny wooden fairy. He carefully picked up the tiny fairy and placed her upon a leaf that was on his desk. She was so small with delicate lace like wings that sparkled in the setting sun, her dress was the deepest peridot green similar to her eyes that sparkled like gems. Everyone said the colour green was associated with fairies. Her dress had flowers along the top which in turn created sleeves for her, while her dress itself was a split dress at the side with a multitude of colourful flowers inside creating the effect of flowers following her wherever she goes, a matching headband encircled her hair which was a beautiful caramel colour that ran down to her hips. Her skin was so pale she looked like a porcelain

14

doll, she was a beautiful carving which someone had spent a long time on to make her extremely detailed, she must have been so loved while being created. Kelpie always believed that when something was created with love, it had a life and a soul.

"Maybe she has a soul. I've always said when someone creates something with all of their heart, then that creation is given a soul." The sun had not fully set yet which allowed him to see her in all her glory as carvings always looked their best in the setting sun. The sun hit her peridot eyes which caused a strange occurrence to happen. She started to glow from her eyes travelling down to glow from the inside. Kelpie gently placed her back down on his table and left the room as the light was getting so bright. The light grew brighter and brighter and brighter till all of a sudden, the light ended.

***

Carefully he re-entered the room to find the carved figure had become a real person. She sat on her side propping herself up on her arms, her wings drooping as if she was sad. She lifted her head slowly to look over her shoulder at him. She looked so sad even to the point it looked like she would cry. Kelpie slowly approached and lowered himself down to where she was.

"Are you okay?"

She looked at him with wide, heavy eyes. She placed a hand on his

15

chest then to her own, almost as if she were trying to figure out if she was the same as him.

"Here let me help you up."

Kelpie extended a hand to her, and she looked at it as if she had never seen one before. He smiled a gentle smile trying to reassure her everything is okay.

"It's okay. I won't hurt you."

She looked at him once more through her hair which had fallen over her eyes creating a slight curtain, giving him a gentle tiny smile, she placed her hand in his. This very action caused him to smile.

"There you go. Everything is okay. I guess we can take this as a new beginning for you."

Kelpie smiled as he gently lifted her up off the cold floor. He sat her down on his stool next to the fire while he went across the room to grab a warm blanket from his work stool in the other room to wrap her in. Being careful of her wings that were still drooped and laid against her back.

"There you go everything's going to be okay. Can you tell me your name?"

She looked up at him and smiled while slowly reaching her hand up to his face to let it rest against his cheek. When she did that Kelpie realised she felt so cold to the touch. Placing his hand upon hers he smiled back at her reassuring her everything is safe.

"It's okay you don't have to speak. We can sort everything out together. Well to a new beginning."

She just smiles in agreement towards him.

" Let's get you warmed up."

He walked to the kitchen bringing her a hot drink, Kelpie placed an arm around handing her the warm beverage.

Chapter Two

Aerwyna

Kelpie sat her down on a little stool by the fire he had started. Placing an iron cauldron of water over the fire to warm it up for a brew.

"You can stay here for a while. While I go warm some water for a bath for you"

She looked at him quizzically, maybe she had not heard of a bath before. Kelpie assumed that fairies could have bathed in a stream or a river in the forest. Either way he dashed upstairs and started warming water for a bath for her. When he descended the stairs to bring her to the bath, he wrapped an arm around her shoulders and showed her a place where she could stay until they could find a way to bring her back to her own world or until she remembered. Kelpie showed her all the things she could need for a bath before leaving her a spare set of clothes which were his own as he did not have any women's clothes in the house. It would be one thing he would have to do; she could not walk around in the same dress all the time. After all this Kelpie descended the stairs once more to make the brew to warm her up that little bit more.

***

Kelpie flitted around the room picking up and taking different plants and throwing them in a glass bowl near his teapot. The teapot was so intricately made with blue roses which made up the top of the handle a decorative side and the holder of the lid. A blue and yellow butterfly decorated the side along with the blue rose. Green leaves were placed at the bottom of the handle bringing the whole teapot together. Six similar glass tea cups sat around it each with its own blue rose and leaves. After he had thrown everything in the bowl, he realised that the Fairy was standing in the doorway wearing the clothes he had given her the best she could. She looked like a child who tried to dress themselves for the first time, it made him laugh at how cute she looked at that moment. She had both her legs in one trouser leg, he did like his trousers baggy, but he never thought they were that baggy. The shirt he had given her was one that was small on him, it had small buttons on the front which she had put on backwards. The look made Kelpie laugh which he felt a little guilty about, he slowly approached her helping her out slightly. Once he was done he rolled up the trouser legs a couple of times. It was then he realised the height difference between them both, as well as rolling up the sleeves he noticed how small her hands were compared to his. Being raised around sea fae everyone was of equivalent size so seeing someone so small and delicate made him a little nervous. He walked behind her, gathering her hair up in his hands and pulling it out from under the shirt.

"Beautiful. It's like caramel."

This caused her to look down with sadness on her face. Maybe she did not like her hair or maybe what he said made her sad. He was not sure but seeing her sad was not what he wanted. She raised her head up and he was beside her once more. He told her that he had made tea and it was beside the fire. Kelpie placed his arm around her shoulder directing her towards the stool situated beside the fire. Upon the table was the teapot he had pre- prepared for them, all he had to do was add the ingredients to the pot and pour in the water. Kelpie bent down to man the fire, keeping it at a safe level.

"Im...Imagination?"

Kelpie turned from taking control of the fire to see his fairy guest pointing at the blue roses on the teapot. He had always assumed that the fairies knew all flowers and their meanings as well as all plants and their benefits. Kelpie placed dried chamomile, dried Liquorice root and dried ginger root in the teapot one by one each time asking her.

"Do you know what these are?"

She pointed to the dried chamomile taking it from Kelpie's hands, taking a deep breath.

"Chamomile helps sleep."

 She lifted the lid of the teapot and gently placed it down on the table,

placing the chamomile inside. Next, she took the dried Liquorice root,

bringing it to her nose and took a deep breath.

"Liquorice root helps the stomach."

She again gently placed it in the teapot. Last was the ginger root to

which the same thing happened. She brought it to her nose taking a

deep breath before placing it in the teapot with the others.

"Dried chamomile, Dried Liquorice root and Dried ginger root when

together overall effect calming."

***

Kelpie smiled and hearing her speak gave him peace of mind. She

was okay but something was making her sad. He walked back over to

the cauldron grabbing some water with a ladle filling up the teapot.

They sat in silence while the tea brewed. She looked round the room

that was filled with wonders that Kelpie had got or got given from the

other realms. There were brooms and pans from the Brownies realm

the intricate designs upon then fascinated him. There were seashells

from the Selkie realm. But what intrigued her more was the

beautifully carved figure on top of the fireplace. Getting up slowly

she walked to the fireplace that had the intricately carved figure.

21

"This is beautiful, what is it?"

"It's a kelpie."

He said from the stool just behind her. Her fingers followed the indents down the tail towards the fins. The carving was as detailed as the real thing, which she could remember someone telling her, she had not seen one for herself. Its hair flowed around its body and its legs. While fins followed down the tail.

"It's beautiful."

Kelpie got up and stood next to her, it was then again, he realised just how small and slight she was compared to him. Her features were illuminated but the low glow of the fire, emphasising the beauty and delicate nature of her. Her eyes were illuminated by the fire in such a way that they seemed to glow similar to how they were when she was a tiny doll, while her lashes casted a slight shadow that fell over her cheeks. Her hair glowed to a rich deep caramel colour than he had seen before. It was beautiful, she was beautiful; he could see how she was a fairy. He was always told fairies were small, delicate, and extremely beautiful people. That one look from their eyes could captivate anyone. Much like how kelpies struck fear into people and led them into traps. Fairies could enchant people with beauty and lead them to safety and good fortune. For they made people feel safe when they were around as if nothing could harm them. She turned around examining the room once more now that she was standing the fire illuminated every inch of the room making what once hidden visible. Nearly every flat surface has either a finished clock or something to do with clocks covering them.

***

 Clock faces with filigree designs, clock hands, gears and a small little clock with wooden animals, birds,rabbits and a small little deer. It reminded her of her home.

"Home?"

She pointed to the small clock turning herself towards the clock. Kelpie turned to follow her line of sight which had landed on his newest creation, a little woodland clock.

"Forest. Do you live in the forest with animals like theses.?"

She nodded her head. So, she was a forest fairy. That would explain the flowers in her hair and on her dress. The green she was wearing made everything fall into place only someone from the forest would wear green and have the most enchanting green eyes which he was drawn to more than he cared to realise. Kelpie walked to the book of doors which was still in the adjoining room, he'd left it there when she changed from little wooden fairy to a slightly bigger non- wooden fairy, him heading there to record information he'd found resulting in her following him. Peering around him she saw the clock with the hidden door to her world.

 "Home. Home"

"Yes, that is a fairy door."

"One of them."

She replied to him. Was there more than just one fairy realm from what she said implied there were more. Maybe when she was better, he could find out more about the other realms. Did all transpire in the same realm therefore used the same doorway or did they have different entrances if that was the case there were more doors that they didn't know about there for were left undocumented. It was at that point in the array of thoughts that he realised she had no idea who he was. He had not told her his name or anything. "Sorry I've never introduced myself, have I?" He set the book back down on the table to the right-hand side of him and turned back towards her.

***

With one hand placed behind his back and the other in front while he bowed as low as he could as he introduced himself to, his beautiful new caramel coloured haired Fairy.

"The name is Kelpie, that's what the humans call me, my real name is…..."

He paused and threw it while maybe two names would confuse her

more. Maybe if he stuck with his human given name for now.

"It's of no importance, my dear fairy. I am the prince of the Kelpie

world and I'm pleased to make you acquainted."

 Taking her hand in his, placing a gentle kiss on the back as he

bowed, he turned his face upwards towards her to see her smiling as

she started to curtsy.

"Hello dear prince, my name is Aerwyna. I'm not sure how I came to

be here but thank you for taking me into your humble abode. it's a

pleasure."

She couldn't remember anything of how she got here. Has she lost

her memory? At least he knew her name now. Aerwyna was such a

beautiful name and it matched her perfectly. She smiled up at him

now that he had released her hand and returned to his full height. She

held parts of clocks from the table in her hands.

"Are you interested in clocks.?"

She smiled and nodded her head. For Aerwyna had not ever seen a

clock before or that she could remember. All she could remember was

her name. Her smile faded every time she tried to remember anything

other than her name, Kelpie could tell when she was unsuccessful as

the sadness that never left her eyes slowly covered her face.

"Come on. Let us sit down and have some tea and I'll tell you how you came here to me. In this shop."

Kelpie offered his hand to her to lead her back to the stool she had vacated a little while ago, she placed her hand in his, allowing him to lead her back there. When her hand was placed in his it just felt right like her hand was moulded to fit his, like it was made to hold his. The thought both terrified and intrigued him. They sat and drank their tea as he explained how the clock had got left in his possession. Once he got to the flower opening up the look on her face got increasingly sad. Finding out she was turned into a carved figurine must have been a shock for her. It was strange that she was a figure in a clock. Most everyone who used them as a gateway passed through the pendulum tower and out the door which was hidden behind creating the illusion of the grandfather clock, and the folktale of grandfather clocks being magic.

***

After they had drunk their tea, everything was explained up until now. Kelpie showed Aerwyna back towards the room that she could use. The room was a basic room with basic furnishings. She had a bed with a warm covering on top, a place to store her clothes and belongings. Placing his hand on the door handle not wanting to intrude into her space, he thought she would need a place to escape to after what she had been through. After explaining where everything went to Aerwyna, he said good night and closed the door walking down the short corridor towards his room, which was directly opposite Aerwyna's. Sitting on his bed he went through the events of the day, Aerwyna coming to life in front of his eyes almost, the feeling that she was starting to ignite within him was what was causing him the most worry, holding someone's hands no matter how small and delicate and suited for his in very way shouldn't have done that. Even to a Kelpie, he thought they were immune to such things. He also knew he would have to go out in the morning and get her some other form of clothing seeing her on his wasn't helping the situation at hand with the feeling he was suddenly feeling. He would have to find something to cover her wings. People in this village didn't believe in fairytales and or folklore.

***

Waking up in the middle of the night was as easy for him as the sun rising. It was when he performed his purification of the waters that the village used for drinking water, he loved that by doing the medical task everyone seemed healthy, it gave him pride in being a Kelpie. It was easy for him, similar to blinking, but it amazed him every time. Approaching the door, he looked on the landing before starting his descent down the stairs, when he reached the bottom of the stairs, he placed one hand on the edge of the tree he peered up the stairs to where Aerwyna was sleeping, maybe protecting her was his new task, keeping her safe was now a top priority. With this he quietly opened the door enough for him to squeeze through and out the shop before shutting it behind him, walking to the river situated behind his home. The purification process was simple enough, all he had to do was nip his finger enough to draw blood, for Kelpie blood even a small amount was enough to purify anything, even make a whole river clean. The blood fell from his finger dropping into the water with a tiny splash, it rippled throughout the river. Seeing the ripple travel continuously up the river informed him that he now knew this job was done at least for another week.

Chapter Three

A Memory

The first few days went by in peace, Kelpie showed Aerwyna how to fix clocks by changing the gears and replacing certain parts, he even showed her how to make her own. Aerwyna had started making her own to the best she could, she started to carve the Celtic pattern from the Centre which in turn started to create a flower Centre, from there a Celtic pattern encircled the flower. Carving circles upon the outside giving the illusion of raising the number from the main clock. She placed the main clock on a square back where Aerwyna then carved Celtic corners to finish. Kelpie looked over her shoulder just as she was finishing the last corner.

"Wow you picked that up fast. It looks beautiful. Now we just have to varnish, and we can hang it up."

She smiled. She was starting to smile much more now than the first few days. The first day was a distressing day for Aerwyna.

*** The first day ***

Kelpie left early that morning to get her some clothes from the local market. The market was only a short walk from his shop and yet it contained everything you would ever need. He would bypass all of his usual stalls and go straight to the clothing side of the market he thought. The scenery from his shop to the market was his favourite thing about going. The way he walked was just over a bridge. It took longer to get to the market, but it was the most beautiful. The bridge was suspended over a little waterfall which fell over a rock. He liked how the rock split into three which created the little waterfall in three littler waterfalls. The bridge was surrounded by trees which diverted the sun all over the woods in little rays of light. Green moss and ivy covered every rock, up the side of the bridge. Every now and then he would stop on the bridge and just look over the side watching the waterfall flow into the river below. He paused there for a while before he remembered, he had to get Aerwyna some clothes that would match well with the people here but also work at hiding her wings. Kelpie thought that dresses would be easier for her being loose enough for her wings and comfortable enough to walk and work around the shop in. When he got to the market, he quickly located the women's stall for clothing. The first one he found for her was a sleeveless deep purple with a string fasting all up the front with Celtic knots running alongside it. Aerwyna could tighten the dress at the back with the corset style fasting making it easier for her to keep her wings covered yet comfortable for them. Kelpie's favourite one that he found for her was a dark moss green off the shoulder dress with long flowy sleeves with Celtic patterns running across the top of the dress as well as along the waist. The skirt of the dress had to layers a solid green player and a lighter green more flowy thin layer, making the dress cooler to wear during day-to-day tasks on the hotter days as well as being able to layer for the colder days.

"Perfect."

Kelpie picked up a few more dresses for similar style in the colours deep blue like the sea which reminded him of home the dress itself was had a white long-sleeved dress underneath with a blue overlay on top which tied up on the body leaving the skirt to flow free around her, the thought of him seeing her in this one made him happy. A lilac button-down dress was one he was attracted to instantly. The colour would match her wings and highlight her hair perfectly and against her skin tone it was perfect. The sleeves were sheer lace so it would show off her delicate arms enhancing all of her features. The last dress he picked up for her was a plain button-down dress with no sleeves and in patterns which would be perfect for her around the workshop. What attracted him to it was the fact it was a deep ruby red colour. Although Aerwyna had five dresses in total to swap around with, he thought to also grab her some shoes, an apron for the workshop as well as a cloak in case they decided to venture to the town or villager together. He found the cloak stall easily, on display they had many colours ranging from purple to red but the one that grabbed his attention the most was a cloak in a peridot green to match he eyes Celtic knots ran down the full length of the sides, two strings which could be tied into a little bow was what closed the clock which in turn added the feminine touch to it, shoes, and some smaller tools for her, the thought came to him when he saw the small tool that he could teach her to carve a clock maybe she could find some happiness within that , he would try anything to get her to smile. If he got her the tools, he would have to get her a small apron as well she wouldn't want to ruin her new dresses, he could imagine her face when he arrived with all the small parcels all for her face would light up and she would smile her biggest smile, she had a beautiful smile.

***

Kelpie came back a couple of hours later to find Aerwyna standing in front of the clock. She emerged from humming a selkie lullaby, she was still wearing the clothes he gave her, seeing her wearing them and the fact he rolled them up several times made him smile. She looked like a little child who had taken adult's clothing. Kelpie stood at the door for a while just listening to the lullaby she was humming, could it be a way for her to get her memory back, the thought occurred to him that only people associated with Selkies would know a Selkie lullaby, maybe she had a Selkie friend. This thought gave Kelpie an idea. He had friends in the Selkie world, maybe if he wrote a letter explaining everything that had happened, maybe someone who remembered her or maybe someone knew how she ended up in that tree. It was at that moment he heard a crash from the next room.

***

Aerwyna had fallen backwards over the stools with a face of fright looking towards the tree. He ran frantically into the workshop upon seeing Aerwyna on the floor looking petrified staring up at the clock in front of her.

"What happened, is everything okay?"

Kelpie dropped down to the floor beside her as she clung to him in terror. Hiding her face in his chest. He looked at the tree then back down at her wrapping his arms around her trying his best to make sure she felt safe and secure once more. She removed her face from his chest to look at his, tear stained her face and she spoke with a shaking voice.

"I... I found out how I ended up in the tree."

They sat there on the floor for a while till she had calmed down. Kelpie kept his arms wrapped around her until he could feel that she had fully calmed down. After what seemed like hours trying to keep her calm Kelpie helped Aerwyna off the floor and directed her towards the stool in the other room by the fire, which was slowly becoming her stool, to calm her down more with warmth from the fire and a nice calming sweet tea. Kelpie thought explaining the new tea to her would calm her that bit more seeing as it was something she did often here.

"Todays a new blend. Maybe it should help calm you a little more. It is calming and a little bit sweet as well. It's dried hibiscus, dried cherries, dried orange peel, dried rosehip, and vanilla bean."

Kelpie smiled at her pushing the ingredients towards her, encouraging her to have a look and a smell just like she had before, it worked much to his surprise and delight. Aerwyna slowly reached her hand out towards the ingredients and one by one brought them to her nose and placed them in the teapot.

"Antioxidants, Vitamin C and Calcium, helps Inflammation, helps Immune, and a little bit of Sweetness. Overall, a sweet but relaxing brew."

Kelpie placed his hand on top of hers, concern so prominent on his face. Worrying about her had become second nature to him now.

"Can you tell me what you remembered?"

Aerwyna took a deep breath and sighed. For she could see or hear much. Taking some sips of her tea she spoke.

"I saw someone who was dressed similar to me, only she seemed different somehow. She had brown hair with green sections that looked like leaves. I couldn't see her face clearly, but she said I would spend eternity in this tree until someone who could teach me to learn to love both myself and others appeared but that would never happen as I'm unable of such feelings as love."

Aerwyna placed her head in her hands. She had gotten placed into a tree as a carved wooden figure so she could learn to love, but at the same time was unable to love. That was definitely a strange reason to be put in a tree, with no hope of reemerging. Kelpie deep in thought placing his fingers against his temple. That was until he remembered that the sound she was humming could help her with her memory a little more.

"Hey now, I did find out one thing, you were humming a Selkie lullaby, maybe you have a friend in the Selkie world. We could even go to the Selkie world if you would like, maybe see if someone recognizes, maybe that would help."

Aerwyna raised her head from her hand a few tears staining her face, but there was a tiny hint of a smile appearing ever so slightly on the corner of her lips.

"You would do that for me."

Kelpie could hear the sadness in her voice, she was in a place she did not know, with a person she did not know. Now she found out someone had purposefully put her in a tree. Kelpie just smiled to reassure her and place his hand on her shoulder. She smiled her biggest smile ever as She leant forward to wrapping her arms around him in a hug.

"Thank you, Kelpie, you're so sweet."

She placed a gentle chaise kiss on his cheek before pouring him another cup of sweet tea.

Chapter Four.

Selkie world

The next day Kelpie and Aerwyna got themselves ready to venture to the world of the Selkies. Aerwyna wore her original dress of peridot green with the waterfall of flowers along the inside of the back, along with her flower head-dress, as they both thought it would possibly help people recognize her more. Kelpie loved her in that dress the colour matched her perfectly, the flowers around her head just accentuated the colour of her hair. As they approached the Selkie clock, the free-standing ocean blue clock curved just like the ocean waves up the sides towards the main face of the clock. The pattern painted upon the door was a midnight setting moon against the ocean, this was the secret hidden door of the Selkies. To access the door was easy, opening the door was a little more difficult because you had to open the main front of the clock and reach around the pendulum to where you would shrink down to the side of the door and just walk through a small tunnel which would lead you, their world.

***

Taking Aerwyna's hand Kelpie opened the door and the smell of the sea hit you straight away. The light smell of sea salt mixed with the darkness of the tunnel was a trip to the senses. The smell made you imagine that you were standing on the beach with your eyes closed taking in the scents and sounds of the sea. Kelpie walked through first while Aerwyna followed closely behind. Once they made it through the tunnel the scenery that awaited you was breath-taking. They emerged from the door on a beach at low sunset. The sky was half lit with stars and half with the setting sun. The tide low with bioluminescence plankton casting the shore in an illuminated blue, which was only visible when the sea was moved or when waves rippled towards the sand. They walked just next to the sea leaving little illuminated footprints in the sand. The beach was surrounded by a forest, slightly reminding Aerwyna of her home.

"Wow this is beautiful."

Aerwyna let go of Kelpie's hand running towards the sea, Kelpie's hand felt cold without her in his anymore, he didn't think that just by the removal of her hand from his could make him feel so empty. Aerwyna stood at the edge of the ocean staring out in amazement at the sights, the sound even just the feeling of being next to the ocean calmed her tremendously. Kelpie was getting used to Aerwyna being around, the thought of her leaving both worried and scared him a little. The thought of him being on his own again in the shop made him sad the thought of it being quiet and not seeing her sitting by the fire making a new brew for him or even just relaxing the fire, just did not seem right anymore, she had even taken up reading the books in the workshop to learn anything they would let her, she was mostly interested in the book of doors, he thought it was because she wanted things to talk to him about, but he was never sure. Kelpie stood behind her their hands at their sides nearly touching, he thought if he reached just a little, he could hold her hand. Kelpie slowly moved his hand closer to her ever so slightly, just enough for her to realise it was there, the possibility that he could take her hand in his again was driving him crazy. Aerwyna sat down on the beach turning her head to look at Kelpie standing there all alone. She offered her hand to him causing him to smile and laugh brushing his hair away from his eyes, Kelpie took her hand taking a seat next to her. Sitting on the beach made Aerwyna forget about the tree and everything else that had been troubling her, just sitting here with Kelpie beside her made her happy at the same time, like she felt at home here. It was at that moment that the ocean started to make a small wave. The bioluminescent plankton hugged every curve of the wave, which also helped illuminate what was inside the wave. A small pure white seal was within the wave heading straight towards them.

"Saoirse?"

 Aerwyna said in recognition. The wave kept coming closer and closer and closer to the shore, making Kelpie and Aerwyna stand up on the beach.

"You recognize her?"

Kelpie was shocked because this little seal was not just a little seal, it was a Selkie. The Selkie princess. Could she have been a princess from her realm? It would make sense with her dress and her magical peridot eyes.

"Yeah for some reason."

The wave curved up to an amazing height before it curved so much it pointed straight at the sanding floor before it crashed on the beach leaving behind a woman standing on the edge of the sand half on the beach half in the ocean. Kelpie was always surprised with Selkies for they were always bone dry when they came out of the water. She was a tall woman compared to Aerwyna but still smaller than Kelpie she had black hair and eyes with a white fur coat with hood resting upon her head, the coat hung off her shoulders revealing her dress. Her dress was long and flowy just like the ocean with ruffles along the bottom overlapping at the front creating an elegant yet uncomplicated design. The sleeves hung off the shoulders just like her coat. Her hair finished at her chin curling ever so slightly at the end, it is glistening just like the surface of the sea. She looked every bit like the ocean.

***

 "Aerwyna, what are you doing here?"

Saoirse slowly approached Aerwyna and Kelpie taking one illuminated step at a time from the sea, seemingly confused as to why they were both here. Taking a seat next to Aerwyna Saoirse could not believe her eyes, she had been missing for years, and now she was suddenly here. Kelpie drawing Saoirse's attention once more explained everything that had happened up to now.

"So you're saying someone with brown and green hair turned Aerwyna into a wooden figure and locked her within a flower on a tree That leads from the fairy realm to the human realm you presume? Have I got that bit correct."

Kelpie slowly nodded his head looking out towards the sea, he thought facing her would make it all seem more real than it always was.

"And Aerwyna has no memory but of that and her name?"

Both Kelpie and Aerwyna nodded for there was not much more they could say. The thought made Aerwyna look out towards the sea and the never-ending sight it held. Kelpie turned his line of sight away

from the sea to look at Aerwyna, she was a slightly behind his so he

had to turn himself as a whole to be able to look at Aerwyna, but he

couldn't see her face, but he could tell she was sad just by looking at

her. The fact that there was nothing she could do hurt him more than

he cared to realise. Saoirse racked her brain. There was only one

person who had that amount of magic and matched that description.

Elvina.

"Aerwyna, do you remember me, or anything else?"

Saoirse asked, sitting on the beach with both of them. Saoirse looked

toward Aerwyna, but she found there was already someone looking in

her direction. A knowing smile made its way on Saoirse's face for she

could tell that Kelpie had something toward Aerwyna that neither of

them were willing to admit. She could tell by the look in his eyes, she

had been told that Kelpies had very stern looking faces; they never

showed their emotions, but by looking at his face all of his emotions

were plain as day. She couldn't help but smile, maybe something

would happen, maybe nothing would but at the moment that was of

no importance, whether they had to help Aerwyna feelings or not. But

once this was settled and she had her memory back she was finding

out all about that one way or another.

***

Aerwyna continues to look out at the ocean trying, hoping, praying to remember something, anything happy. Anything that was not someone curing her to be a wooden doll till no one knew when.

"I can remember your name, some…something that was pink. But other than that, and knowing now that I was once a little wooden doll not much. I'm afraid"

Kelpie's face fell in sadness as well as Saoirse's. Exchanging looks they knew they had to do something. There must be something that they could do to help her or even make her smile.

"Princess, please If you have any information that could help us in any way, anything at all, even something small. We would be thankful"

 Kelpie pleaded with Saoirse. He would try anything to help her even if it meant her leaving him and going away. If it made her happy, he would do it. Saoirse had a smirk on her face for she had deduced that Kelpie was indefinitely hiding a secret of his own, what she didn't know was whether he realised it himself. Saoirse looked at Kelpie, her smirk deepening. She could tell by the look on his face.

"don't you think It's funny how we wake up each day and never know if it'll be the one that will change your life forever, isn't that right Kelpie."

Kelpie gulped. He knew what Saoirse was getting at. The smirk said it all, and he was slightly starting to understand himself, whether what he was thinking and what Saoirse was thinking was the same he would never know, but a Kelpie and a Fairy it was never heard of before. Besides he was a prince of a different realm he could not do that, plus it was different from normal Kelpies married Kelpie and Fairy's to Fairy's. That was how things were done, breaking them now wasn't right and marrying a Fairy was preposterous. He shook his head which presented him with a concerned look for Aerwyna and a knowing smirk from Saoirse, he came to the conclusion that he would have to be incredibly careful with his actions and words when around her.

"Aerwyna, let's have a talk."

Saoirse held out a hand to her to take a walk along the beach. She explained all that she knew that Aerwyna was a princess of the fairy realm, the spring realm to be precise, she also explained the four realms that resided with the fairy realms had sent out search parties for her, but they could never find anything, the four princes searched for ages as it was said whoever found her could have her hand in marriage. That resulted in a grimace from Aerwyna. Saoirse laughed but she continued saying that there were some people who never gave up the search for her, they knew she had to be somewhere, and all the while there was a chance, she was out there they wouldn't give up.it had been several years since then and even her father was starting to lose hope, they never found any trace of her, there wasn't much more they could do they search all realms, she even explained that they went to neighbouring realms such as hers in case she appeared there. After searching all the realms and still no trace they didn't Have much of a choice but to give up their search, it had been two years since then and now even her father presumed her dead. Now she had figured out why. The fact that she had been in the tree for years shocked her, what shocked her more was the fact so many people searched for her for many years, and she was right there under their noses. How many people must have passed by here when they went through the doorway? She was so shocked that all she wanted now was Kelpie at her side. Walking back to the sea and towards Kelpie calmed her and made her smile. Just seeing him made her forget all about her worries of the past, but it gave her new worries for the future. It's had not been long since she arrived back here once more and the fact that the feelings her had for him just kept growing frightened her, Aerwyna decided it was best for her and Kelpie if she didn't think about them at present and just live in the moment, for you never knew what was around the corner, beside she didn't have many memories, but she thought the idea of a Kelpie and a Fairy was unheard of. Seeing the look of happiness and worry on Aerwyna's face confirmed Saoirse's idea, they both had something, some feeling for each other whether it was just because of the situation they found themselves in or real feeling she didn't know but at the moment it didn't matter. When things were better she thought there were many things she could do to bring such a couple closer together. From her memories Aerwyna was very stubborn when it came to offering her feeling she never thought she was worthy of love or anything else for that matter, maybe Kelpie would be the one to bring her out of her shell, and show her that she could be loved. Saoirse thought that had to be the case for if Aerwyna had been inside that tree for many years and it only now opened when she was inside Kelpies shop that had to mean something it was either that or it was just pure coincidence, "Kelpie."

 Aerwyna ran towards him, arms open wide in a hug, a huge smile on her face. Seeing this caused a reflection of the same expression on Kelpie's face. Hugging Kelpie close gave Aerwyna comfort, the comfort that nothing could hurt her, nothing could challenge her. She felt safe right there in his arms. Kelpie wrapped his arms around her which was not a challenging task to do for her being so slight compared to him, but in his mind, she fit perfectly in his arms.

Stroking her hair, he started to hum a lullaby his mother sang to him, when was the last time he had hummed it wasn't in a long time, at least not since his mother. That fact in itself shocked him and she made him feel comfortable. Aerwyna looked up at his face, causing his smile which once covered his face dropped in an instance. Aerwyna looked frightened and this in turn frightened him.

"Kelpie, Saoirse says I'm the princess that can't be true I can't be a princess."

***

Aerwyna was a princess that explained so many things that he had noticed. Why she knew the Selkie princess, how she poured tea so delicately and politely. How she knew all the benefits to flowers, herbs, and roots, including which ones to use for different ailments. That was beyond a normal fairy's knowledge, they knew the properties of certain plants but the knowledge for aliments was left to the higher-class and high-class fairy's such as royalty and healers. Saoirse asked Kelpie a couple things. The main thing she wanted to know was how he knew to bring her here. Kelpie explained that he had heard her humming a Selkie lullaby when she was standing by the tree she emerged from and thought that maybe she would have a friend here or at least someone who would recognize her. It turned out

47

he was right on that front. After a while of answering the questions that she had involving Aerwyna, Saoirse thought it was time to ask a personal question to Kelpie.

"So, what's going on with you and Aerwyna?"

Saoirse did not think Kelpie could blush at all but the look on his face proved that wrong so very well. She was learning a lot about Kelpies, many things she thought they couldn't do, she had always been told that they were unsociable beings, but she had never seen someone go so red before. She found it sweet and a little bit funnier than she probably should have.

"I ... I have no idea what you are talking about." The redness that covered Kelpie's face only darkened at his statement. He knew all too well what Saoirse meant and if he could avoid the conversation then he would do anything in his power to do so, for the time being.

"Kelpie."

Saoirse sighed looking at Kelpie she could see that he genuinely cared about her, even though he was denying it with all his might. But with Aerwyna's memory gone and Evalina out for her, she had to be careful and make sure that he had her best interests at heart even if it meant he was not in the picture.

"Look, all I need to know is that you won't hurt her, by the sounds of it she's gone through enough and at the moment you are her source of comfort because she has me now. I need to know that you have her

best interests at heart even if that means you're not in the picture. So,

give me one reason why I shouldn't keep her here in a place she

knows with someone she knows rather than in a strange world with

someone she only just met a couple of days ago for the first time."

Saoirse didn't want to be the bad guy or girl in this case, but it was

such a peculiar situation that she didn't really know what to do all she

could think of was Aerwyna, she had to exclude their feeling for each

other at present, by the look of it they were already denying their

feelings for each other, maybe they thought it was strange to feel so

strongly for someone in such a little time. But Saoirse knew so many

people who knew near enough straight away that they met the person

they were meant to spend forever with. But for the safety of

Aerwyna, feeling couldn't matter at the moment, not with Elvina

about she never really did like her, but she couldn't put a finger on it.

She looked over at Kelpie who had turned his head back taking a look

at Aerwyna with her feet in the sea looking as happy as could be, her

dress getting a little wet from her crouching playing with some fish in

the sea. But what made him smile the most was seeing how much she

smiled when she saw him. Her smiling brought him joy now, the

thought that she would not be there made him sad, but he would do

anything to keep that smile on her face even if it meant he wasn't there. That fact that he would not see her again made him sad more than he thought it would but for her he would do anything, keeping her safe was the main and best thing that could be done. Maybe one day he would see her again, and that day would be the best day of his life. Kelpies smiled and fainted a little, turning his face away from her and back to Saoirse.

"For her I would do anything. If it meant keeping her safe. Meeting her was fate, becoming her friend was a choice, but falling in love with her was beyond my control. Even if I were blind within my heart, I could still see the beauty that is her. If her staying here is best for her, then so be it all I ask is that I could come by to see her please. Just being near her brings me joy. Being able to see her every now and then is all that I ask. Please do not take my joy from me." Kelpie's smile grew bigger and bigger the more he talked about her. Saoirse didn't think that he even realised what he had said, the fact he unintentionally said he was falling for her was strange and unordinary for his race, Saoirse had never seen a Kelpie fall for someone, anyone, let alone a fairy. This was a once in a lifetime thing, that she would be silly to destroy, maybe them falling for each other was what was meant to happen. Saoirse stood there and pondered that she had heard that Kelpies were the best at protecting as when they feel for someone, they never let anything happen to that person, and Elvina

wouldn't go to the human world Saoirse knew she wasn't fond of.
Maybe Aerwyna would be safer with Kelpie than here.

***

Kelpie started to walk towards Aerwyna, his smile growing bigger
and bigger with each step he took. Aerwyna's smile was dazzling, it
was bright and cheerful, so much more cheerful than what Saoirse
had seen when she saw Aerwyna back home. This was definitely
what was best for her, Saoirse knew in her heart that Aerwyna staying
with Kelpie was in her best interest.

"Kelpie come try, this feels amazing. And look at the little fishies.
I'm going to call them unicorn, fairy, and rainbow."

Kelpie peered into the sea looking at the fish that she had re-named.
The fact that she had named them after their appearance was a sign
that she had no memory of her world, seeing as these fish were native
to there. Kelpie knew what he had to do, Aerwyna had to stay here,
try to regain her memories, anything that she could regain herself was
what would be best for her. Kelpie's smile dropped as he began to tell
Aerwyna that she should stay here for her benefit to keep her safe. It
was not what he wanted to do, he wanted to just pick her up run for
the door and keep her safe with him. Aerwyna's smile dropped as he
said that. Thoughts ran through her head, he did not want her there
anymore she had become a nuisance. He didn't like her. She had

51

become a burden to him. He explained it was because he was worried
for her safety and that she should stay in a place that she knew with
someone she knew. But all that ran through her head when he was
talking was the fact, she was a nuisance to Kelpie. Her face dropped
to the fishes in the sea, dreaming of being one and not being able to
bother Kelpie or anyone. Kelpie smiled and let out a little chuckle.

"This is why people worry about you."

 Kelpie placed a hand on the side of Aerwyna's face cupping her
check in his hand. She lent her head further in his hand looking up at
him through her lashes.

"Are you worried about me?"

Aerwyna looked at him pleading with him with her eyes to let her go
back with him. If he said he was worried about her maybe she was
not as much of a nuisance to him as she thought, she was. She loved
the thought that she found Saoirse again but staying with Kelpie was
what she wanted the most right now. From where Saoirse was
standing, she could see a look of utter adoration on both their faces,
she could tell that even if they refused to see and believe it, they both
loved each other deeply.

Kelpie gave her a gentle little smile.

"That goes without saying."

Kelpie turned towards Saoirse, taking Aerwyna's hand in the process. "Saoirse even though you are her friend, and she loves you. I cannot let her stay. The person that put her in the tree is still out there and will probably know you are her friend. For all we know they could be checking here. Please let me take her home. With me."

Saoirse smiled at them both taking Aerwyna's and Kelpies free hands. Seeing as he refused to let go of her other hand much to Saoirse's delight.

"That's all I needed to hear. Just write me a letter to let me know how you're doing."

 Pulling Aerwyna into a hug involutory made her release Kelpies hand much to his dislike. Saoirse didn't realise how hard it would be to let someone you cared about go. Even though Aerwyna was not that far away it felt further than ever before. Seeing how she lost her memories it became harder and harder to let her go with each passing minute. She knew but only one thing that would keep them together, Saoirse whispered the lyrics to amhran na farraige saying it might come in handy for her.

 "Don't be a stranger. That is to both of you. And Aerwyna if you ever feel lonely trying that and if it does not work you're always welcome through the door just be sure to let Kelpie know where you are going so Kelpie does not panic."

She looked at Kelpie over Aerwyna shoulder and gave him a wink, causing him to blush slightly again, he lost count of how many time his emotions had shown on his face, his father would disapprove but his mother would say that it was perfectly normal to show emotion when around people you cared for.. With that said and done Saoirse walked them to the door that connected them back to their world, hugging them both one more time.

***

She had to get back to the ocean as she had been away too long. It was then that Kelpie realised that Saoirse had a stripe of white hair at the front, which only happened when Selkies spent too long out of the ocean, spending a long time out of the ocean had always had Selkies ill, there was a way that they could spend time out of the ocean for an extended period of time, but it was not something Kelpie knew about. After hugging Saoirse one more time and promising for what felt like the hundredth time to visit again and to stay longer. Aerwyna stood at the edge of the sea and watched Saoirse disappear under the waves of the sea only to see her jump above the water as a small pure white seal. Aerwyna turned back towards Kelpie with tears in her eyes, she smiled a small sad and gentle smile knowing everything was all right and she knew there was at least one person out there who knew who she was. She also knew that no matter what she had Kelpie beside

54

her, and she knew that he would never leave her, no matter what happened.

***

Kelpie and Aerwyna left the beach side to walk up the small sand hillside towards the cliffside to where the door was located. Walking back through the door was strange for Aerwyna; the smell of the ocean was not there anymore, instead all Aerwyna could smell was wood and wood polish; it was the smell of Kelpie's workshop. Aerwyna took a deep breath at the smell in the tunnel.

"Home."

Kelpie smiled offering his hand to Aerwyna once more, resulting in her gently placing her hand in his and a spark ignited between them. Aerwyna knew what this meant she felt something, but still could a Kelpie and a Fairy really be together, she didn't know if he felt the same, she was never able to read him even though Saoirse said he made it extremely easy to see what he was thinking. Looking up at Kelpie all thoughts disappeared from her mind.

"That's right Aerwyna. We're going home."

Kelpie looked down at their entwined hands for a moment thinking about Aerwyna and how easily it would be to stay like this forever with her. Though for a moment he thought about the future, waking up with her beside him, even the thought of her agreeing to marry

55

him came into his head. It was at that moment that he realised

Aerwyna had been looking at him with the same look in her eyes, was

she thinking the same he didn't know but he could have fun figuring

it out. He looked down at her, her lashes casting a shadow over her

eyes

"Why do you say my name all the time?"

" A name as beautiful as yours deserves to be said as much as

possible for it matches its owner perfectly."

Aerwyna looked to the ground with a slight blush on her cheeks.

"Come on, we're nearly home."

Kelpie reached ahead and opened the door to what was now home to

the both of them.

Chapter Five

Brownies

The days after seeing Saoirse went by easily. Waking up in the morning to the smell of breakfast, his favourite bacon and eggs, she always added something to them, she called it her secret magic ingredient. Freshly brewed tea was always necessary beside the breakfast making his mornings heavenly. Walking down the stairs to see Aerwyna was like a dream seeing her in the kitchen wearing her handmade apron, she made herself out of old clothes she found in a box. He did not know that he had female fabrics in the back. His father used to run the shop before maybe they belonged to his mother. Aerwyna's apron matched her hair; it was a light sky blue with clusters of pink roses with leaves surrounding them. She had added pockets for ease in the kitchen, lining all the seams of the pockets with a darker pink border. Seeing her in it was a highlight of his day. In the mornings she would pick the herbs and flowers from the jars she had nested against the wall and placed them in her pockets, bringing them to the teapot and cups on a tray with the breakfast beside the fire. They would wake up, sit beside the fire and drink Aerwyna's new brew she had created. It seems to have become their

new normal. Which, he wasn't complaining about it suited him
perfectly he wouldn't have changed a thing. The smile on his face
said it all.

"Today was earl grey tea leaves, dried lavender. Rich in antioxidants
and calming."

He loved that she felt she always had to explain her brews to him in
detail. He had never liked his mornings before she came here, now
his morning was his favourite time of day because he got to see her.

***

Fixing clocks together had become his new normal, and it had
become one of the many highlights of Kelpies Day for she was
always beside him. Although today was not like any other for the
Brownies had come to visit. The Brownies liked to visit Kelpie for he
always had things to clean. Being a clockmaker who left all gears and
hands around the place, they found much pleasure in re-arranging the
workshop neatly for him. They loved it even more when he was
carving a clock, they would collect the shavings one at a time as he
carved and placed them in a bag by their clock, they usually took the
shavings back with them, Kelpie had no idea why. Normally they
would come in to clean and just disappear without Kelpie knowing
they were there. But today was different because they had Aerwyna to
talk to. While they cleaned, she carved little cups and saucers for

them as well as a little kettle with spoons. She asked each Brownie for their names because it was always the same three that came to clean. The oldest Brownie wore a little green hat with ribbon tied around the middle at different angles, a coat with a little golden button. Their trousers were ripped at the end, and they never wore shoes. Little parts of brown hair poked out from under his hat. What always surprised Aerwyna is their eyes were always green like hers.

"My name is Arion. It's a pleasure, your highness."

Arion said gruffly bowing ever so slightly to Aerwyna. It was obvious the Brownies respected the fairies and knew their princess well. The Brownies were on good terms with the Fairies so they knew the royal families, so they said to Kelpie knowledge that confirmed to him there was more than one royal fairy family, he still didn't know what the other Realms where call and if they resided within the same Realm with the same door or if they had separate doorways. Maybe they had a transfer system on their side to transport between each realm. He had many questions about them but none that matter as much as now they knew the royal family which meant all of its members including Aerwyna. Aerwyna blushed for she had not ever been called her highness that she could remember.

"Oh, please just call me Aerwyna."

She places a small amount of lavender and earl grey tea into a small jug for the Brownies to drink after they had finished. It was strange for Aerwyna. She never made such a small amount of tea, or carved such a small jug. It was a little difficult, but she enjoyed the challenge.

"If you wish your high… I mean Aerwyna. Allow me to introduce my sons. This is Kano"

He waved his hand over the Brownie wearing yellow. He was dressed similar to his father, although the shirt was different being it had no button but a collar. "And this is my youngest son Cas." Again, he waved his hand to the Brownie wearing pink. This Brownie was dressed the same as the other son. His shirt had a slightly different collar as he had a deep pink strip running along the middle. Again, they all placed a hand in front and bowed ever so slightly towards Aerwyna, this made Kelpie laugh seeing how Aerwyna got embarrassed when they bowed to her. Aerwyna laughed and waved it off, she engraved their initials into the cups that she had carved for them. The letters themselves were elegant like fairy writing. They curved at the top creating a wind like style of lettering. Arion's was a strong based letter with a curved for the middle. Cas's had an extra curve through the middle adding a wisp of magic to the side. While Kano's was a strong letter with half a circle within the letter. Carving theses in their cups gave them a sense of belonging that they did not just have to come clean and disappear anymore they could stay, drink, and talk just like everyone.

"Boys, if you're done come and have a cup of tea. That means you are Kelpie too."

Kelpie laughed, Aerwyna stood by the fire with her hands on her hips waiting for them all to make their way over to the fire. She always made sure he had a tea break during the day. He loved his little breaks. Aerwyna held her hand out on the counter by the clock display, so the Brownies could hop on. But they thought otherwise and just jumped down off the table and ran along the floor just like little children with their arms in the air, resulting in a little laugh from Aerwyna. Aerwyna poured her and Kelpie's drinks while the Brownies admired their cups that Aerwyna made them. Their little faces made Aerwyna smile for she could tell that they loved their little cups. She got up from her stool and disappeared into the kitchen which she had banned Kelpie from entering all morning.

***

A few moments later she re-emerged from the kitchen wearing her apron resulting in a big smile from Kelpie, sometimes she would love to know what went through his mind when he saw her, two trays were in her hands one quite small which he assumed was for the brownies and the other of normal size.

"These my dear friends are sugar plum fairy cookies. I remembered the recipe this morning and I thought I would give it a go. They turned out very well if I do say so myself."

Aerwyna set their tray down which made the brownies just jump up with joy at the sight of cookies for no one knew how much of a sweet tooth they had. They clasped their hands in front of them and let out a big smile showing off their little pointed teeth. The cookies were completely covered in sugar and were pink, purple and beige making them look like they had just come out right from a fairy tale. Which made them laugh because technically they had.

***

Aerwyna had made enough big cookies to last Kelpie the rest of the day for he had a bad habit of snacking while he was working. Which always made Aerwyna laugh as she kept the plate beside him stocked up with treats. It seemed sugar plum fairy cookies were now his new favourite. The Brownies plate was piled high with cookies as she made a little extra for them to take home. They all sat and drank their tea and ate their cookies. The Brownies were sitting on the windowsill looking out at the people passing by unknowing what magical stories and items lied within the store. Before long, the sun started to set, and it was time for the Brownies to go back home.

Arion ushered for Aerwyna to come down to him, to which she placed her hand on the table and ushered him to hop on her hand so she could bring him up to eye level.

"Aerwyna it was a pleasure to meet you. If you shall ever need our help in any way, blow on this whistle and we will come to you with as many Brownies as you need, and if needed we'll bring you back to the Brownies realm till it's safe for you to return."

the whistle Arion had given her was a slightly smaller version of one they had seen around the shop, Kelpie used to carve them when he didn't have, much to do, but unlike his theirs was exceptionally clean no rough un-varnish edges and it was smaller as well, small enough that she could keep it in her pocket, and no one would be any wiser. She looked over and both Kanos and Cas nodded their heads in agreement. She lowered her other hand to the table so they could hop on, and she raised them up for her as well.

"Thank you all so much, you are so amazingly sweet."

Aerwyna places a small kiss on each of the Brownies, making their littles face so red as a rose. Their reply to that was a small little peak with their hand splayed against her cheeks causing her to smile . They were like little children even though she was sure they were older than her.

Aerwyna lowered her hands back down to the counter to let the Brownies go home. She told them to feel free to visit at any time for the door would always be open to them. She placed their cups and their jug in the cupboards with hers and Kelpies proving they always had a place here always. And with that the Brownies bowed one more time to both Kelpie and Aerwyna, before running again with their little arms splayed out back towards the Brownie door back towards their world.

Chapter Six

The Pink Forest

Aerwyna was in the dead of sleep, dreaming of walking down

moss-covered concrete stairs with a rail made of an old tree log and

branches twirling their way up from the ground, entwining

themselves around the log. Bushes with vibrant pink Camellia

flowers cascaded down both sides of the path, some encircling the

branches covering the railing and flowing over the edge cascading

back towards the ground creating a sort of curtain. The stairs led

down to a pathway which widen at the end the closer you got to the

water, the path which was suspended upon the water was encircled by

a railing which like that path before was covered in camelia encircled

the entire path was suspended over the water, the lake spread out in

front of her eyes, it sparkled and shone like it was made from every

blue gemstone known. She felt like she could just stand there forever

just taking a breath and staring out into the lake, it gave her peace.

Trees covered with the same shade of pink leaves as the Camellia

flowers behind framed the lake all around every side. She continued

walking along the path, her hand trailing along the railing in-between

the flowers, taking in all of the beautiful scenery this world had to offer. Her favourite was that the sky was always at sunset casting a purple haze over the sky which reflected the smooth surface of the lake. Following the path around Aerwyna found a waterfall at the end, with no more path in sight. The turquoise water reflected everything like a mirror, the trees, flowers, and the leaves surrounding it casting the reflection in a haze of pink and purple. The waters crashed over the edge of the falls casting a small rainbow over the moss-covered rocks at the bottom, the rainbow reflected against the water giving the appearance of two rainbows over the falls. The further Aerwyna walked through the forest the more she recognized it. That was until she came to a dark part of the forest. All the light and bright colours had faded from existence, trees at the border where part alive and part dead the further in she went the more the trees had lost their lustre, lost the leaves lost everything that made them beautiful the further she went in the more they seemed to have died in this part it, creating a dark haunting area of the forest. A voice continued to echo through the woods, it was too far away for Aerwyna to understand what it was saying. Until the forest turned to night. The chill of the wind rose the deeper and deeper she walked in, the further in she went the lest the light could touch. Aerwyna came to a tree that she remembered; it was the tree Kelpie found her in when she first came to his world. A big gush of wind came up from behind her forcefully pushing her into the tree.

"You shall stay here little princess, till you can find someone to love you. Oh, there's only one problem, there's no one here that would miss you or even love you so it's best you never come back dear sister." The sinister laugh was the last thing she heard before she woke up screaming.

***

Kelpie came rushing into the room to see if Aerwyna was all right. The scream frightened him more than anything. Many thoughts ran through his head on what could have happened to her. He had never heard her scream like that, and he never wanted to hear her scream like that again. The fear it sent through him was indescribable. The terror that propelled his body forward up the stairs as fast as his legs would carry him, getting him to her side.

whatever it was that scared her he would find it and fix it and if necessary, destroy it. Kelpie found her huddled in a ball on her bed with tears flowing down her face, the bed covering was splayed all over the floor whatever it was that scared her wasn't in the room, it was in her head, it had to be a nightmare. Placing his lamp down on the bedside table he realised he was still in his day clothes as he had just come back from the river when he heard her scream, he prayed that she would not notice that was the last thing she needed, knowing that he left her alone at night in this house, on her own. He perched on the bed making sure to mind her legs which she still had tucked near her. Wrapping his arms around her he stroked Aerwyna's hair he had come to learn that one of the one ways of calming her down was to stroke her hair and sing the lullaby. He was thankful to Saoirse at that moment that she had given him a letter with the lyrics on so he could learn, it took him a while to learn the Selkie tongue but for Aerwyna he would do it. It was one tongue he didn't learn as a kid even though his father made him learn every language when he was younger, he didn't know if he was going to get this right, but it was worth a try if it brought her even comfort. He reached into the pocket of his midnight blue cloak pulling out the piece of paper inside. Giving it the once over he started to sing the Selkie lullaby.

Idir an is idir as

Idir thuaidah is idir theas

Idir thaiar is idir thoir

Idir am is idir ait.

As an sliogan

Amhran na farraige

Aerwyna breathing slowed back down to normal, looking at kelpie through tear-stained lashes she smiled. He had learnt the song just for her. He could not have been sweeter. She placed her head back on his chest, relaxed her arms, legs and mind and snuggled down close to him falling asleep. Kelpie wiggled around slightly readjusting himself so they both were laying down as flat on the bed as he could manage. Before he both knew it, they fell asleep right there in each other's arms.

***

Daylight broke the darkness in the room hitting Kelpie eyes first as he had fallen asleep with his back resting against the bed frame. Even after all his wiggling he could get completely flat against the bed not with Aerwyna resting against him. Squinting against the harsh light he yawned but could not move. He looked down to see why to find Aerwyna still fast asleep on his chest, Aerwyna was snuggled down in the crook of his shoulder, avoiding the light of the sun. It made Kelpie smile. She obviously didn't move in her sleep, he thought maybe it was because she felt safe beside him. Kelpie half debated pretending to be asleep just to see how she would react but the other half that was more sensible thought about sneaking out before she woke up. Before he even had a chance to choose an option Aerwyna started to stir. She lifted herself up with one arm rubbing her eye with the other. The moment she saw Kelpie a smile covered her face. She smiled up at him, a smile that Kelpie had never seen before. A smile of content and love.

"Good morning."

Kelpie felt a sharp twang through his heart, placing a hand over his chest he looked down at Aerwyna the moment she locked his eyes with her, another twang. Was he ill, this had not happened to him before, but he didn't mind, he had Aerwyna she made everything better. He thought if he was ill, he probably had one of the best people next to him to take care of him and nurse him back to health.

***

At breakfast it was kelpie's turn to make it, so they had French toast with summer berries and syrup, it was new to Aerwyna she never had either French toast or syrup before. Kelpie said it was something he had often when he was back home but since being here hadn't fancied the effort in making it. They pair that with a fruit tea made with crushed summer berries. Kelpie said it was often what his mother would serve it with. While eating Kelpie asked about what had woken Aerwyna up last night. As she explained about the stairs surrounded by pink Camellia flowers and trees, with the amazingly turquoise blue waterfall, reflecting the purple sunset sky. Kelpie had a thought about where she could have been in the dream. The main place he thought of was the fairies' forest, which explained the pink Camilla and the trees. The question left unsolved was which realm of the fairy's she belonged to; he knew it was the forest but which forest remained to

70

be answered. The only thing they had left to solve was who put her in

the tree.

Chapter Seven

Choices

Kelpie had an idea of something he could do, but he was not sure if it was what was best for Aerwyna. That was all that mattered, what was best for Aerwyna. The idea he had was that he could take her to the fairy forest to see if that triggered any memories, but he had seen how she had reacted to the previous memories that she discovered. The last thing he wanted was to cause her any more pain or any pain at all. "Aerwyna."

Kelpie took a deep breath rubbing the back of his neck with one hand, giving her the choice was the best thing. If she wanted to go back there then he would support her, but if she were not quite ready, then he would wait for her to be ready and be ready to go with her whenever she was. Kelpie signed to remove his hand from behind his neck, he had no idea how she was going to take this but there was only one way to find out.

"If you wanted, I could take you to the fairy forest. We could go through the tree door and see if it triggers any memories for you. Maybe we could see what happened."

***

Aerwyna didn't know what to say, should she go or should she stay. If she went did that mean she would have to stay and never see Kelpie again. Looking at the fire she remembered all the times she had with Kelpie. Teaching her to make clocks, having tea with Arion, Kano and Cas, finding Saoirse again. He had even brought her new clothes which she loved. He had thought about her when buying them, she didn't want to let all of that go. She did not want to leave Kelpie's side. But then again, she would know who she was, if she had family, friends and find out why that fairy pushed her in a tree and called her sister. She had all these questions left unanswered but if answering them meant leaving then she would rather not remember. Aerwyna clung to Kelpie's shirt which was slightly dusty and dirty with wood scraps and oil from the gears, he was so caught up in his thoughts he forgot to put on his apron. Aerwyna found the smell comforting, it was the smell of Kelpie he had always calmed her down while she was here.

"I don't know. I want to find out who I am. But if it means leaving you, I will rather not know. Leaving you gives me more fear than I ever thought possible. I'm not sure what that means but I would rather stay here with you. If that's okay with you."

Aerwyna looked at him through her lashes, it was her only way of seeing him when she was close due to the height difference between fairies and Kelpies. Kelpies were six foot eight while fairies were just five foot two. Kelpie placed his arms around her comforting her in the only way he knew how. Embracing her. They stayed like that, which to Kelpies didn't feel half as long as he wanted before she moved, which resulted in him feeling half empty, as if he were missing something. Placing a hand on top of her hair Kelpie said.

"Always believe in yourself, for if you do this no matter where you are, you'll have nothing to fear."

Aerwyna smiled up at him hugging him once more. She wanted to go, and she thought it was best but to her Kelpie was what was keeping her here, keeping her safe.

"Can I think about it and let you know. I'm not sure what is best for I don't want to leave you or our little house."

Hearing Aerwyna call this little shop their little house made him feel all fluttery inside. The thought that living with him here was comfort to her to the point she did not want to leave, made him happy. He had not felt like this before he did not even know if Kelpies could feel like this. It crossed his mind that there could be a possibility of it seeing his father and his mother together. Maybe he thinks it could be possible. But something about Aerwyna was making him feel happy and he did not want to let that feeling go or let her go.

***

A couple of days went by and Aerwyna had not said anything else about going to the pink forest. Kelpie was not going to push her to a decision; it was her choice whether she wanted to know about herself by going to the forest. Although she had not said anything, she was happy as it was time for Anion, Kanos and Cas to come again. Talking to them always made her smile. Maybe they could help her to decide. Anion had not changed in the entire time he had been coming here, he was grumpy when he first started coming to the shop and he was grumpy now. The only change that could be seen in him was when he was with Aerwyna the grumpiness in him would disappear for he always smiled a lot more when she was around. They would talk for ages after they had cleaned. Sitting next to her on the table drinking from his handmade cup, it always made Kelpie's blood boil that he had a cup from her, and he had not. He thought several times of asking her to make him a cup, but it would not be the same, the Brownies never asked for theirs. Kelpie thought that Anion knew this somehow. Kanos and Cas were no better as they always raised their

75

cups to him with a cheeky smile upon their face, he had heard

Brownies were cheeky, but he did not know that for sure. Till now.

"So Aerwyna how have you been getting on living in this world with

him."

 Anion gave Kelpie the up and down, making sure he knew where he

stood and if he hurt her or made her cry in any way, he would have

him to deal with. Brownies were small but they were mighty.

Especially when it came to people they protected, and for Kelpies

lucky Aerwyna was very well protected by them, sometimes even

from, himself. Aerwyna must have seen this for it caused her to smile

at him and laughed a little. She mouthed to him not to be grumpy, this

resulted in a huff from him, how could he not be when he had the

most beautiful woman living with him, but she was being taken from

him by three small and he repeated small little bugs. Too bad she

didn't know any of this as Kelpie would never say any of it out loud.

Kelpie just laughed a very sarcastic laugh while being the hot water

over from the fire, filling up their tea and Anion and boys as well.,

Aerwyna had carved a little ladle making it easier for them to pour

the brewed tea into their little jug. The Brownies were currently

sitting in his chair, so Kelpie took a perch on the arm of Aerwyna's

chair. He didn't mind having to do that; it put him closer to her and

gave him a one up on the Brownies. When Kelpie had walked to town one day to gather some items for the kitchen as well as some more ingredients for tea. He passed an old antiques stall and decided to take a look. He thought if he could find Aerwyna a chair, she could keep perching herself on that ratty old stool. After browsing through the many, many shelves in the store he came to the last aisle to which held the furniture section. Right at the very end of the bare aisle was a padded sky-blue chair decorated with a lace like pattern. Kelpie knew this would be much more comfortable for Aerwyna than the little stool she was currently sitting upon, and it matched her perfectly soft and gentle with a delicate touch. He himself had a wooden chair that he made himself so all he had to do was purchase some cushions and right next door to the chair was the perfect cushions to make it a little more comfortable for him. They were a dark midnight sea blue, he looked at them when at himself it matched his alias as well. He laughed a little when he saw Arion, Kano and Cas sitting on those exact cushions now, while he was perched next to Aerwyna. The look on their faces made this moment all sweeter. He placed his hand on the back of the chair to keep him steady. This action resulted in glancing between Kanos and Cas who could obviously read him by the big blush that slowly crept across his face.

***

When it came time for the Brownies to leave, both Kelpie and

Aerwyna were sad it was always lively when they were here. Mostly

coming from them tormenting Kelpie and him tormenting them back,

which always made her laugh, they got on so well even with them

tormenting each other all the time. Once seeing them back through

their door Aerwyna looked over at Kelpie who was looking at his

own world's door with sadness on his face. Was he missing home?

Maybe they could go to his home just for a day or two. That was

when Aerwyna had an idea. She would pack a picnic and take Kelpie

back home for a day, maybe that would make him feel better. Little

did she know this would cause more trouble for her than she would

realise.

Chapter Eight

Surprise

Aerwyna packed Kelpie's favourite items she had discovered over her time with him. Including her as he stated famous sugar plum fairy cookies. His favourite brews of tea with water in a wooden cup for insulation. Aerwyna had not told Kelpie of her plan for she wanted it to be a surprise. Kelpie was still asleep as it was the rare occasion as the shop was shut for the day, which made it all that easier to surprise him as he was treating himself to a lie in. Aerwyna slowly snuck up to Kelpie's room, opened the door and jumped on the bed startling him awake. Kelpie let out a loud scream of surprise from Aerwyna jumping on him once his eyes were open he started laughing at Aerwyna who was now clinging to him to stop her falling off the bed, after he jolted himself up out of his comfortable lying position on his warm bed. The more he moved the more she clung to him, he turned in his bed, so he was in a sitting position, causing another laugh out of Kelpie as Aerwyna clung to stop her headfirst over the side.

"Well good morning to you too."

***

Aerwyna left his room allowing him to get dressed but not before telling him she had a surprise for him downstairs. This left Kelpie to ponder in his bed what on earth could be the surprise, he hadn't had a surprise before and by the way his mind was going he didn't favour them. It was the not knowing that seemed to annoy him as he tried to think of every possible thing. This left Kelpie sitting up in bed rubbing his temple with his fingers. What is it that she could have done to surprise him. She didn't know how to get to the market as he had not taken her there yet, so it was not that she could have made him a clock or cup without him noticing. Kelpie was left without any ideas she really had found the way to surprise him, she hadn't banned him from entering any places of the shop. He was completely without ideas. Kelpie made his way down the stairs to be confronted by Aerwyna standing at the door to the Kelpie world with a basket ready.

"Where are we going?"

Aerwyna smiled, debating whether she should tell him or blindfold him and make it even more of a surprise. Thinking this made her smile and laugh. Kelpie took on a mischievous look upon his face, if she were not going to tell him he would have to tickle it out of her.

"If you don't tell me, I'm afraid I'll have to tickle it out of you." Kelpie raised his hands ready to tickle, taking a step closer to her

making Aerwyna drop the basket and run to the next room. Kelpie
quickly ran after her chasing her hand poised ready to tickle.
Aerwyna kept running between the three rooms that made the
downstairs trying to escape the tickles she knew she would get. What
she didn't count on was for Kelpie to go in the opposite direction.
Aerwyna ran into Kelpie hard chest at first, she thought she had
misjudged her direction and ran into the lounge wall it was one when
kelpie had his hands wrap around her making her unable to escape.
Kelpie started his tickle attack around her waist, working his way up
to around behind her ears; she was always more ticklish behind them.
Aerwyna squirmed to get away, but Kelpie had a good hold of her. It
didn't matter how much she wiggled or tossed and turned she couldn't
manage to break away. All she managed to get his hands away from
behind her ears and they came to rest on her waist.

***

Looking up and him made her heart flutter, the look on his face was
all she needed to smile. But there was something else in his eyes this
time, it was more of a darkening a longing she thought, she didn't
know what would happen but before she knew it, Kelpie was placing
his hands on the side of her face slowly bringing his face closer to
her, they were so close that if she moved just the slightest bit their lips
would be touching. She had to admit several thoughts passed through

81

her mind: would she let him kiss her, would it disrupt all that they had built between them now, or would it lead to something more.

Aerwyna couldn't say that she wasn't tempted to just move slightly to make a light brush against his lips but before her head could help her make a decision her heart made its move, she found those two never listened to each other. The lightest of touches happened and it just felt right, like this was meant to happen, like it was written in fate to happen, that everything up until now had led to this very moment.

Pulling back ever so slightly to see his face didn't last long before he slowly snaked his hand behind her head under her hair, taking a little and gently pulling her head back, his hand coming to rest on the back of her neck. He looked in her eyes and smiled

"You're beautiful inside and out. Don't ever forget that okay. If you do, well I'll just have to find a unique way to remind you."

Biting her lips, she smiled. Whatever was in his eyes before only got darker after the slight brush, she wondered if he would be brushing his lips against her again, would he take control this time, or would he let the matter drop. She prayed with all her might that he didn't let it drop. She released her lips from her teeth running the tip of her tongue over them wetting them slightly.

"Okay."

His eyes darted down to her lips, of all the things she could do, she had done the one thing it seemed she couldn't resist. The temptation was there for the taking with his hand in her hair and his other snaked around her waist pulling her as close to him as he possibly could. If this were the surprise, she had planned for him by all means she could surprise him every single damn day. He came to rest his eyes on her once more, taking in the many shades that seemed to dance around, he never knew there were so many different shades of green, but it seemed she had every shade known to the man and others within her eyes. He could get lost in her eyes, the longer he stared at them the deeper they seemed to pull him into their trance. Without a second thought he loved his head ever so slightly at first, he wanted to test the waters if her eyes closed then he knew that she wanted it as much as he did. Aerwyna's eyes flickered up from his lips to his eyes and back again. The slower he moved the more eyes seemed to flick between his eyes and lips. This look in her eyes practically begging him to kiss her once more made him smirk. He knew exactly how to make her feel wanted; the question was could he make her feel loved

Once again, his lips were placed on hers and fireworks erupted in him, he felt like this is what he was supposed to do. At this point it didn't matter that they were different, it didn't matter that they were a

Kelpie, and she was a Fairy, if this were the way they wanted to go then, by God that's the way they would go, and anyone that stood against them, they would know his opinion on the matter. Aerwyna slowly moved her hands from gripping the bottom of his shirt to slowly moving them up the flat length on his stomach and over the curve of his chest before coming to rest on the back of his neck, in doing so she deepen the kiss by pulling him closer to her while he tried to snake his hand around her waist more feeling she wasn't close enough to him, that she would never be close enough to him. He held her like she was the most precious, most breakable thing in the world. His hand released the gentle grip on her hair and slowly slid down the length of her spine. Resting his hand on the small of her back He pulled away slowly Aerwyna slowly gently pulled her lip back in-between his teeth once more which resulted in Kelpie pulling it from her teeth and saying if she did that again he would have to repeat the process of what happened. The very move drove him crazy. After a small laugh escaped her lips, they came to rest their heads together while staring in each other's eyes. Things felt so right in that moment, he thought if the world ended at the very moment, he wouldn't have a regret in the world. Things were going perfectly right now, and he would do anything to keep things as they were.

"What was the surprise you had for me? If it was that, then I will take

that surprise whenever. And wherever you wish"

He smiled, placing a light kiss upon her lips once more, seeing the

small blush that slowly crept on her face and the realisation of what

they did. Her face turned the most beautiful red to him. He thought

then that it didn't matter what surprise she could give him, anything

would be amazing if it came from her, he knew he would love it. She

always put so much thought into everything she done. He knew that

from the way she treated the Brownies she didn't need to make them

cups and a jug, but she had much to his dislike, but she didn't have to

know that.

"I packed up a picnic for us when we go to the Kelpie world. You

looked sad yesterday looking at the door to your world. So, I planned

this as a surprise."

She twisted out of his grip running towards the basket she had

momentarily dropped when the tickle fight broke out. She reached for

it and spun around so she was facing him once more. With her arms

open wide she yelled.

"SURPRISE ."

Aerwyna still had her hands raised in an attempt to surprise Kelpie, but when she opened her eyes, she saw his face had dropped.

"You did what?"

Chapter Nine

Kelpies' World

Kelpie took a few wobbling steps back towards the stool beside the fire. Did he really look that sad looking at home? It was a welcome surprise but if he took Aerwyna there, it wouldn't be long before others of his kind tried to take her from him to keep her even worse, he could even think what they would do if somehow she was lost from his slight.

"It could be dangerous for you; you see kelpies have the power to seduce women. Of all races human and otherwise. I fear if I take you there then it would only be putting you in danger"

She was beautiful, many other kelpies, some that he would know and others he wouldn't, would try to seduce her there. Guaranteeing her safety would be hard but she planned all this for him. Maybe he could keep her safe if he took her to the royal garden, she would be safe there within the grounds, no one other than those who resided there or worked there dared enter the place. It was an idea but he would have to warn her though he would have to transform to his original form and to some people that were scaring them and that was the last thing

87

he wanted to do. But by transforming into his original form, it would get them there faster and the faster they got there the safety she would be. He weight up all the pro and cons of this journey, the cons definitely out weight the pro, but it was something she wanted to do for him, and he could not take that away from her, she done this just because he looked sad towards his world, it was true he hadn't been home in quite some time.

"Okay Aerwyna but we are going to have to do this my way okay otherwise I can't guarantee your safety. kelpies like to seduce women, especially ones that are, how do I say this…. Beautiful and unattached."

Kelpie explained everything to Aerwyna how he would have to be in his original form, he explained what that would look like hoping to frighten her in any way, he also explained the fact that she would have to sit on his back so they can get to safety faster, this caused a blush to creep up her cheeks. He told her for the safety of both of them the picnic would be in the castle grounds and that his father would be there, this got him a quizzical look. She could understand how it would be for her safety but his. He thought to himself it would have to be there for her safety and the safety of everyone else if anyone even tried to go near her with impure intentions. For all they know she was his and only his. Upon hearing that his father would be there to frighten her a little, she didn't know much about kelpies, she did not know if they like fairies or anyone for that fact. When she had met Kelpie, he was on his own then as well. Maybe they were solitary creatures, if they were she couldn't blame them, but she thought that must have been a very lonely existence if that was the case. Even though Aerwyna was scared she wasn't going to let that stop her. She could see from his face Kelpies missed his home.

"That's okay. In a way it will be fun to meet your family."

Kelpie could hear the slight terror in her voice, but her face just made him smile. He rolled his eyes.

"Right okay fine you win, let's go but you listen to me the entire time okay."

Aerwyna's face lit up when he agreed, and the biggest smile played on her lips. She was so happy to say anything, so she just nodded.

***

With that they packed the picnic with a little more food just in case Kelpie's father wanted to join with a deep breath from Kelpie they were on their way through the Kelpie doorway. The air inside the tunnel was as fresh as she had read in the book of doors that Kelpies can purify water at a touch. Walking through the tunnel was vastly different from walking through the Selkie door, where it was slightly illuminated by the stars, Kelpie's tunnel was dark. There was no light at the end of the tunnel. The world on the other side once they passed through that dark tunnel was in the dark of night but it was illuminated by the light of the moon. The doorway led them out through a massive weeping willow, its leaves and branches creating a curtain around the magical doorway effectively hiding it from Plain sight. The willow itself was situated beside a massive river that flowed through the middle of the grass enclosed by trees on either side. Both Kelpie and Aerwyna sat alongside the river just in front of the willow itself, its leaves gently blowing in the wind for a little while allowing Aerwyna to take in the beauty of the Kelpie world. Her eyes flicked over everything from the gentle flow of the river so gently it looked like it wasn't moving at all, the moon that illuminated everything in a gentle glow. Aerwyna glanced at Kelpies his eyes had always fascinated her but in the kelpie realm they wherever more beautiful, his eyes were dark with small white swirl in the middle but here they were bigger and brighter than ever, it was like the moon illuminated them more allowing them to see everything more clearly. She found herself thinking that she could spend hours looking into his eyes and never get bored.

"Are you cold at all Aerwyna? The temperature here is always a little colder than where we stay."

She was a little cold, but she did not want Kelpie to worry. So, she told him she was fine, but he did not believe her in the slightest, he could see her shivering, Kelpies had good eyesight to begin with but in their world they were enhanced even more. He had made a little seat of grass and told her to stay here so he went and got a blanket. Some kelpie women along the river made blankets out of the grass that grew here, thankfully he knew of where some were kept. He got up and told her to stay not to move only if someone who wasn't him came towards her, she was to hide within the willow and go back through the door, if he couldn't find her then he would know where she went. Aerwyna sat down with the picnic basket beside her. While Kelpie ran off to find her a blanket much to her surprise even in his human form, he was able to run atop of the water. She hadn't read that in the book she thought they could only do that when in the original form. She guesses it must be something about him being back home that he could do that. He had told her only in his original form could he walk on top water in the human realm. It had only been a couple of minutes before Aerwyna heard a rustling in the trees behind her, she hoped it was Kelpie, but he went along the river he wouldn't suddenly be behind her. Kelpie had told her that there were many kelpies that roamed around here looking for lost women of any race to seduce. He told her if it was someone, she didn't know to run through the door, but he had said what to do if the doorway blocked.

"Kelpie is that you?"

" I'm a Kelpie but probably not the Kelpie you're looking for."

***

The stranger's hair was dark like Kelpies but a lot shorter. She would not be able to play until the end with her fingers. His eyes even though the same as every other kelpie seemed menacing to her. Aerwyna didn't know what to do. She couldn't leave and he blocked the entrance to the door. He stood with his back towards the willow. She didn't dare leave as Kelpie would not be able to find her, but she couldn't stay here, she knew what Kelpie had told her about his race, but he was starting to creep her out. She had to find a way to make him leave.

"Could you please leave, my friend will be back soon."

Aerwyna tried to be as polite as she could be but her fear and worry of him was growing every second, she prayed it didn't show in her voice, if the Stranger caused a hint of her being afraid it would probably entice him more. He sat down beside her closer to her than she liked. Aerwyna shifted away to her left a little, but it didn't work moving away only made him place his arm around her bringing her closer to him. Effectively stopping her in her tracks

"Oh, don't worry, we Kelpies like to share the unattended."

He leaned in closer to her as if he were going to try to kiss her, she screamed for Kelpie, but it came to her mind that it was his human name not his real name shouting that would amount to nothing, but bringing more of his kind to her. she knew he was not anywhere near her; she knew shouting the name would bring help but she had to try something. She couldn't allow herself to be entranced by this disgusting thing in front of her.

"KELPIE."

Aerwyna screamed and screamed and screamed until her throat was rough. She tried to scream again but that one resulted in the beast covering her mouth with his hand silencing all sound from her.

"That's it, keep screaming."

The glint in his eyes scared her more she knew if she didn't get out of this quick it was going to be the end of her.

"I like it when they scream, it makes it more fun."

He traced his tongue up the side of her neck running it along the line of her décolletage. He jutted her head side to side as quickly as she could. If she could just free herself from him maybe she could get away. Pain shot through her back; the evil bugger had his measly arm on her wing pulling it in a painful direction. Her arms were pinned between his legs as he towered over her, but he had forgotten for the most part she still had full use of her legs.

"GET OFF ME YOU BLUNDERING DOLT, KELPIE I'M HERE, KELPIE."

The smile on his face hastily disappeared as Aerwyna brought her knee up landing on a very precious part of him, but he didn't have much time to worry about it, before she knew it a hand was placed on the stranger's shoulder yanking him off of her in a flash.

***

Kelpie stood there holding him by his collar. Dropping him on the floor he falls with a hard thud. Moving to Aerwyna's side placing an arm around her he spoke looking down at the fellow kelpie sitting on the floor.

"Listen carefully, you lowlife, she is my woman, do not touch her. Tell that to all the others as well, if they touch her, they will have me to deal with."

The fellow Kelpie bowed as best he could, being in pain in two separate areas. He stood and ran off down the river in the opposite way to Kelpie. Kelpie found Aerwyna on the floor for her legs had given away from fear once he had let her go. He crouched down to her side and pulled her into his arms. It was then and only then that she realised just how afraid she was, once kelpie held her all the feeling came out and she started to cry. It felt like she could not stop crying all the while Kelpie held her.

***

After a while, her crying slowed down, and Kelpie pulled her back so he could see her face. Wiping away a tear from her check he dropped it into the river, and it created the most magical water display of a horse running along the river side dancing and spinning. Seeing how beautiful Kelpie could make water appear, made her smile, it showed her that he was not afraid to be himself here and that made her happy. When Kelpie saw that she was smiling it put him at ease. It caused him to laugh.

"Remind me not to get on your bad side."

The slight fear in Kelpie's eyes made her laugh. She tried to assure him that she would never in her dreams do that to him. He laughed again pulling her towards him once again.

"I guess I'll just have to take care of you for a lifetime."

This resulted in a small slap to his arm which he pretended caused him immense pain. He laughed again and found himself laughing more and more each day. Kelpie raised his hand to brush some hair that had fallen over Aerwyna's face behind her ear. He loved that by doing this it allowed him to be able to see her more clearly for who she was. She was beautiful inside and out. He had no worries about that. He didn't have to worry about the other Kelpies now, news

would have spread, and no one would dare to even go near her now.

All he had to be worried about now was… his father.

Chapter Ten

Kelpies Father

Once making sure Aerwyna was calmed down fully from the ordeal

earlier. Kelpie transformed into his original form, which was a

majestic pure black horse with a long flowing mane and tail.

Aerwyna had never seen anything or anyone so beautiful, seeing

Kelpie in his true form was truly magical. It was rare to see a Kelpie

in their true form, so this was one of those rare occasions. Standing in

front of him Aerwyna rested her head upon his muzzle but what

would be his forehead if he were human. Closing their eyes to enjoy

the moment of feeling connected without words. Kelpie bent his front

legs to allow Aerwyna access to his back then. She tried with all her

might to get onto his back, but he was still too high as when he was in

the original form, he was still six foot so even when he was bent

down, he had to drop his back legs as well getting as low to the

ground as he could. It was a struggle for her, but she was finally able

to situated,herself on his back but she had forgotten the basket.

Turning his head slightly to look at her, making sure she was safe on his back, he started to rise up off the ground but stopped when he saw the basket and bent his head forcing Aerwyna to jolt forward wrapping her hands around his neck and mane. He picked up the basket in his teeth, turning his head to give her the basket. After a while she was all settled again after a few glances at him when she found out he may or may not have bent his head to get her to hold on to him tighter. She made sure she had a picnic basket tucked in the crook of her elbow nice and tight so they wouldn't lose the lunch.

***

Kelpie started to walk towards the river. He could feel Aerwyna tense up her hold on his mane which made him smile internally. It didn't take him long for him to start walking towards the water, when near the edge he turned his head once more waiting for Aerwyna to say she was ready. She was too frightened to speak, the thought of running on water was strange for her, all she could think was they were going to   fall and sink to the bottom. She took a deep breath and closed her eyes. When she returned her breathing back to normal, she nodded to Kelpie letting him know she was ready. Placing a hoof on the water one at a time he could feel that she was scared he could tell by the grip on his mane. Once he had all four hooves on the water he stopped and just stood there waiting for Aerwyna to open her eyes. If she saw that they were on the water and they hadn't sunk maybe she would relax a bit more. It took a little while for Aerwyna to open her eyes. It took her to realise they weren't moving to open them and to her surprise she found they were standing in the middle of the river, the willows and tree surrounding them dragonflies hoovered all around them fluttering all around. It was beautiful the moon shone on their wings making them look like little floating lights all around. Kelpie turned his head; he knew at a glance she loved the river and was falling in love with his world. He let out a huff in a way to check if Aerwyna was ready, she leant forward hugging his neck she nodded once more, and Kelpie set off running on top of the water which caused Aerwyna to cling to him for dear life. After she realised that all was safe, it didn't matter how fast he ran she didn't budge she was completely safe on top of him and she knew that she would be, knowing that she lifted her head from him taking in the beautiful sights of the kelpie world that could be seen from the river. Aerwyna could see everything the little homes the Kelpies made for themselves, what she found surprising was none of them were undercover, most had a grass bed with a few essentials plotted around. The surprise didn't last long on her face when they were reaching the end of the river which coincidentally houses Kelpie's home and the royal palace.

"I have never seen a palace so big."

Aerwyna was in shock at the height of the walls and the number of guards there were along the river. The closer they got the more she seemed to lean back nearly in the process. She quickly caught herself. The castle of the Kelpies was magnificent, tall walls with archways at the front that only allowed anyone kelpie on the river to walk into the place at a time she assumed it must be for security reasons. Ivy hung from the top cascading down creating an ivy curtain over each archway. Kelpies walked straight through the ivy curtain revealing the palace itself, Aerwyna helped parting the ivy curtain with her hands although this did not stop the look of wonder on her face. The palace was covered with magnificent ivy which fell from the turrets on top of the towers cascading down the walls, Water lilies of every colour grew all around the bottom of the place, and the river turned into a mini lake with the palace walls. They had every colour pale pink with a hint of yellow, dark burgundy, fuchsia pink. But what surprised her was there was only one pale blue almost lilac one, she would have to ask Kelpie about that when he was human again.

***

Kelpie bowed his head and lowered himself down allowing Aerwyna to slide off his back, he rose up to his full height standing on his hind legs which allowed him to transform back into a human. Water swirled up all around him, lowering as he transformed. Kelpie was now standing at his full six-foot eight height wrapped an arm around Aerwyna's shoulders taking the picnic basket from her in the process. This action resulted in a few sideway glances from anyone in the courtyards as well as the guards standing at the entrance. They wore no uniforms, only shirts with the Kelpie emblem upon the front, the emblem was slimier to the one that was displayed on Kelpie mantle, and plain black trousers and shoes slimier to Kelpies. Walking through the main door of the castle was amazing, Wisteria hung all around the entrance and walking through the archway of Wisteria was amazingly beautiful. Passing through the main entrance door Aerwyna was face to face with painting all over the walls of Kelpie's family relatives. As well as a grand staircase was the centrepiece of the whole foyer. It curved off to the right disappearing at the top to reveal the landing of the upper floor. Midnight blue carpet covers the middle of the stairs while. The same colour roses covered the rails of the stairs framing it perfectly. Aerwyna shock grew increasingly more the further she walked into the foyer.

***

"Prince Cailean."

A deep voice boomed down the staircase. Standing at the top was a man who looked like an older version of Kelpie, slowly descended the stairs, hands clasped behind his back. Aerwyna assumed he must have been related to Kelpie somehow. This was how Aerwyna presumed Kelpies looked although he looked similar to Kelpie there was something about him that seemed profoundly serious and stern. Slowly he descended each step pausing slowly in a sense it was like he was owning the stairs each step one at a time. making Aerwyna's heart skip a beat in fright.

"Your home."

Kelpie lowered his eyes and he knew out of everyone his father would call him by his name and not the human name that he had told Aerwyna. His eyes narrowed in on Aerwyna who was clinging to Kelpie's arm hiding behind him

"And this prey tell is? Who have you brought with you."

By this time, he was near the bottom of the stairs. She knew Kelpies were tall but this one was even taller than her Kelpie, she had to crane her neck up even more than normal to even look at his face. He tilted his head down towards her making her feel even smaller than she already knew she was. Kelpie placed his arm around Aerwyna's shoulder, once more getting a quizzical look from the tall stern man. The stern looking man's eyebrow rose ever so slightly at Kelpie movement, Aerwyna hoped he didn't jump to conclusions there was nothing between them that she knew of, yes, they had a kiss but that was nothing was it?

"This father is Aerwyna, she is the Fairy princess. And presently she is living with me in the clockwork shop. We have come for a picnic as she thought I was homesick. You can join us if you wish."

This was Kelpie's father, Aerwyna thought they had to be related to someone due to looking remarkably similar, Kelpie msu7t have taken after his mother more his father had very stern features while Kelpie had quite soft features, compared to his father anyway. Maybe this is what Kelpie would look like when he gets older. Kelpie's father sneered down at Aerwyna, sizing her up in a way.

"So, you're the Fairy princess that went missing, I suppose you've gone back home and told your father that you are all okay and well, if not I do hope you've at least written him a letter."

Aerwyna gingerly shook her head for she hadn't been home or written a letter yet or even had a thought about going home.

"No sir I have not, I don't want to leave Kelpie's side."

The sneer on his face didn't let up. He asked who this Kelpie was that she mentioned as there were only the three of them and neither of them had that name.

"My dear I think you'll find there is only yourself, me and the prince Cailean. In the present of us. There is no Kelpie as you seem to say."

Kelpie rolled his eyes his father knew that Kelpie was his human name he had forgotten the mean streak that his father had, worry played on Aerwyna's face she didn't know what to say or what to do at that moment. Kelpie smiled down at Aerwyna and gave her arm a squeeze; an action that did not go overlooked by his father The sneer that was previous upon his face turned to a little smile. Which in turn did not go undiscovered by Kelpie, his father never smiled at anyone let alone someone he just met.

"I'm deeply sorry, your highness, I didn't know Kel… I mean prince Cailean real name. you see I lost my memories and Kel... I mean Cailean thought it would be easier for me to only know his human name so as to not be confused. I apologise if I have caused any offence. "

The smile on his father's face grew bigger and he could have sworn he heard a little chuckle from his dear old father. What was he up to, it was then that he realised he introduced her to the Fairy princess. His father always had something with the fairies but he never said what.

"You know. Yes. Maybe I will join you. If the invitation is still offered."

Aerwyna just smiled and said of course it is.

Chapter Eleven

Picnic

Kelpie had a bad feeling, he knew his father was up to something, it was his favourite pastime to either make jokes or to make his life as hard as possible, but what his father was up to he didn't know.

"We can have a picnic in the royal garden. I'm sure"

Kelpie's father had to take a break because he couldn't remember her name.

"Sorry my dear, what was your name again?"

Aerwyna looked up at him, before looking to Cailean, the name suited him why he hadn't told her before she didn't know, she was gaining her memories but by bit these days. His father still scared her, but she was getting used to him, she thought he might just be miss understood and maybe deep down he was a kind man. She smiled up at him, which she had to do as he stood so close to her that she had to bend her neck all the way back to be able to see him properly. This action of hers caused his father to take a step back. She could even see a little smile in the corner of his mouth, when he smiled it made his features softer.

106

"My name is Aerwyna Sir. May I ask what yours is?"

This surprised him; few people ever asked for his name in a long time, everyone here in the palace and out just called him His Highness or Your Majesty. Cailean tried to stop Aerwyna asking but to no avail, he had started to come to the conclusion that once she had an idea in her head there was no stopping her. With his head in his hands, he looked to his father, he had no idea what the man was going to do. To his surprise he cracked a smile and even gave her a little chuckle.

"That you may my dear"

He raised a finger in front of her face, the slight smile growing bigger by the minute.

"But I shall not give that to you yet. You will have to wait till next time, or we can play a game where you can get a chance to guess each letter. What shall it be, my dear?"

***

The idea of playing a game to find out a name, both excited and intrigued Aerwyna. Few people around wanted to play games and Cailean and the Brownies were always far too busy for such silly things. She looked over to Cailean who had a look of dread on his face, which made her smile and want to play the game all the more, if not just to torment him a little. Aerwyna asked how the game would be played. His father explained that as they walked around the palace, he would tell her the number of letters then he would show her clues that were situated around the castle. But then he would ask her at the end of the picnic what her answer would be and if she got it correct, he would give her a prize, but if she got it wrong then she would just have to try again next time.

"The first hint is right here."

He pointed down to a small patch of dark purple flowers which were situated just outside the back entrance of the castle. The flowers themselves had plenty of butterflies fluttering around it.

"This is called Common dog violet."

  It is quite a Common flower around here. Caileans' father said as he slowly bent down and plucked a flower from the cluster before turning slightly and handing it to her, with a small hidden smile on his face. The action caused Cailean to roll his eyes at his father, always the flirt, you could take the man out of the Kelpie world, but you couldn't take the Kelpie out of the man. Taking the flower from his much bigger hand than hers, Aerwyna took a deep breath; she could see why the butterflies were so attracted to it for it smelled so sweet.

Walking a little further into the garden Caileans father decided to take them through his personal garden. He showed her Alpine bistort a tall, stemmed flower with a small white bucket shaped flower only at the top. Again, similar to the last he bent, plucked just one and handed it to Aerwyna. Next, he pointed to the Ivy that covered nearly the entirety of the back of the castle. Once again one leaf was handed to her, she was starting to realise what he was doing, the flowers and plants he was handing her were the hints to his name, all she had to do was figure out what it was. Lastly, he showed her one that he explained he planted for Caileans mother, which was called Nigella which meant love in the mist. If her memory served her correctly, she couldn't be sure, but she was halfway there to thinking she had that right. To which once more he bent and plucked a flower, but unlike the others he brought it to his lips first before handing it to her. She understood at that moment that he must have loved his wife very much to be reminded of her just through a flower. The thought of Cailean thinking of her just by looking at a flower made her smile, he was loved that much, she thought how amazing that must be. After walking through the most beautiful garden Aerwyna had ever seen they came to a stop just beside a little lake that had a small water just towards the edge to which Caileans father decided was the perfect place for their little picnic. The mini waterfall right at the back of the garden, under a tree which parted in the middle creating a skylight with the full moon being framed right in the middle, to were the men laid the blanket for the picnic. Once they had sat down on the blanket

that Caileans had brought so it made her laugh to see it was made of

fabric rather than grass like the rest in the Kelpie realm. Aerwyna

placed her flower from his father on the blanket for turning to dish

out the food and beverages that she had packed that morning.

Caileans father ran his hand over the hints which lay in front of him,

before turning to them both to run over them once more. Aerwyna

had placed them down in a random order. There were four different

specimens of plants in front of her.

"Can you give me one more hint, just to make sure that I'm not

missing anything at all?"

Her plea cause his father to smile, he had always been such a tease

and if he had given her the letters, he was sure to make the hint

encrypted

"Of course, my dear the first letter of each makes up my name, now it

may just include them once or it could include them multiple times,

the answer is up to you to find."

With that he bent his head and wished her luck on her challenge.

Caileans knew that he had made it really easy for Aerwyna to guess

for he had said plants which the first letters made up his name., but

then he had to throw a riddle in the works and say it could include

them more than once. It made him smile that he thought that she wouldn't be able to find out, Cailean knew that she had read the book

of door and it had his name in there but unfortunately it had smudged

but it was easy to see how many letters it was and that it started with

the letter c, from there finding the answer was easy. The very idea

itself that he made it so easy meant somewhere within him, he liked

Aerwyna, and that made him happy.

***

Aerwyna looked deep in thought throughout the picnic, Caileans

father loved the tea brews that Aerwyna made for them all, making

her promise to bring some for him to keep next time, but she had to

admit it took her awhile of swapping the plants around trying

different layouts to see if that could be his name, tried repeating the

same plants again but she couldn't find one that had worked. She

found loads that made sense but when she tried to put that name and

pair it with him it just didn't match. She had tried names such as

Cian, Cianan, Cain, and Cainin. There were the only four that she

could think of including the first letters he had given her. She thought

maybe it had something to do with the meanings of each name,

maybe that could help her decipher which one belonged to him. The

first she started with was Cian which meant Ancient, she looked over

at him and shook her head that one didn't seem to fit, so she removed

that one form her mind the next she thought of was Cainin which to

111

her knowledge meant loving change. Again, this was a good match for him, but it just didn't feel right to her. She tried Cianan which meant possessor she shook her head immediately this was on where near a suitable match which meant her last choice was Cain which meant acquired spear. This she could see matching him for a spear could be useful when used correctly but also it could be used against anyone it wished. Caileans father smiled at her as she was moving the flower around in various places making up different names with them, every time she got it right, he gave a little giggle, just before she moved it on to another. Kelpie just rolled his eyes. His father obviously loved Aerwyna just like he was starting to. His train of thought stopped at the moment he just said he loved Aerwyna. That could not be because he had not known her long enough for him to feel like that. He found that at that moment taking a look at Aerwyna next to his father that it didn't even matter now no matter how much he tried to stop himself he found himself on a road with no end in sight, he found he was just going to have to ride it out and see what happens, he thought if that kiss earlier was anything to go by, he wasn't as far away as he thought. He would let it pass for now he did not have time to think about that. Just seeing Aerwyna smiling at her father like that made him smile, his father had not smiled like that since his mother died. Aerwyna went over the hints aloud.

"So, it was Common dog violet, Alpine bistort, Ivy and Nigella."

The look on her face said it all Cailean could tell that she had figured it out.

***

Aerwyna glanced to the side at Cailean then back at his father.

"I have an idea now but I'm not completely sure how I should go about it."

Caileans father tried to look shocked because he knew he made it in a way that he had made it extremely easy. He smiled and waved his hands at the hints in front of her and told her to either use the flowers or just say whichever name she thought it was. Aerwyna smiled at him once more before saying her guess.

"Is it Cain?"

His father just laughed as well as Cailean. Looking at Aerwyna she knew she had it correct which made her happy for the name suited him well.

"That is correct my dear. As for your prize I'll have to retrieve it once back at the palace."

Aerwyna smiled at both Cain and Cailean realising at that moment their names suit each other as well. They both started with the letter C and they both matched them perfectly, she wondered in that moment if his mother also started with a C. if fact, she wondered his mother

113

hadn't joined them and neither of them had mentioned her, she wondered what happened was she ill or was she no longer around she hoped it was neither and that she was just caught up in some worked that required her attention, or that she didn't know that they were here and would be awaiting them at the palace. In light of her mind this was turning out to be the best picnic she ever had. If she could do this again, she would be happy because they were brilliant company. After a little while they all packed up the picnic even though both men would not let her pick up a thing or even carry a thing, or even roll up the blanket, Cain had caught a glimpse of Aerwyna's wings when she attempted to pick up the picnic basket, but in the end, she just stood there with her hands on her hips looking at them both, they glance between themselves before shrugging their shoulders and heading towards the place. Cain whispered something into Caileans ear before turning back to Aerwyna and offered his arm to escort her back. When she had taken his arm, he leaned down, so he was able to whisper to her that they glistened like the sun. this caused Aerwyna to jump to shoot her eyes to him, he reassured her that everyone her had no problem with fairies or anyone of their kind, he told her that all the while she was here, she wouldn't have to worry even after what had happened earlier, he apologised for sword had been spread around the realm that she was not to be touched and no one was to attempt anything by order of the king. Cain told her that he loved the sun and seeing her wings and brought such a rare thing to his realm as people here saw it often but not in the Kelpie realm, he told her that he felt most pleased by them as even though he was the king of the Kelpie he never really saw it often, for as he was the king of the kelpies and had to stay at the palace.

***

Once back at the palace Cain had gone straight up the stairs to fetch Aerwyna's prize. Someone showed both Aerwyna and Cailean into the lounge to take a seat in front of the fire. While Aerwyna poured what was left of her latest brew of black tea leaves, dried rose petals, cinnamon, ground ginger and whole clove. Adding the cinnamon and ground ginger gave a subtle flavour to the tea creating a relaxing warming tea. She turned to Cailean, smiling ever so slightly before saying.

"So, your real name is Cailean huh. Means one who is triumphant. Seems to suit you well."

He was about to answer when after a couple of minutes Cain walked back down the stairs and into the lounge.

"Here you go my dear, I hope you like it."

Cain winked at Cailean, and he didn't understand until he saw what his father had handed Aerwyna. What he had handed her was a

115

locked rock which only Cailean had the key to, but he knew there was no way Aerwyna would not know that was unless his dear old dad told her, as he knew as well what the dear box held. To Aerwyna it looked like a rock with a rose shaped, rose gold coloured clasp with a heart shaped padlock on the front. Even though Cailean was worried, the look of confusion upon Aerwyna's face made him forget. He was confused at the rock but with her being a forest fairy she knew the difference between a normal rock and anything else that resided in a rock. Her smile was so big, she was that happy at just receiving what she thought was a rock.

"It's a geode isn't it."

Both Cailean and Cain looked at each other. They were shocked that she knew it was different so quickly, they knew that they shouldn't have been that surprised considering but that didn't stop them.

Cailean wondered what she would be like if she knew what it held, or if she could tell there was something hidden within.

"It's beautiful. Thank you, Cain."

Aerwyna passed it to Cailean; he couldn't hide the little look of being a little frightened while placing it in the bag ready for them to go home. Cain sat down in his seat to have one last drink with them before they started to head back home. After a few more minutes had passed and the teas were drunk, that chat had been chatted and everything was packed ready for home. Cailean sent Aerwyna to the front door ahead of him as she wanted to take one last look at the waterlilies before she went home, which left enough time for him to ask his father why he gave the geode to Aerwyna.

"Why did you give Aerwyna the geode of all things?"

His father just smiled obviously knowing something that his dear son didn't realise yet or refused to notice.

My dear son, you have the same look on your face as I had when I met your mother. You have it there for when you are ready and by the looks of things that will not be far off. I bet by now you have even protected her and called her your woman, just like I did at your age, once you meet the person you're destined to be with all sense goes out the window. Cailean just follow your heart it'll lead you in the right direction.``

Caileans face said it all. He had done that when she was by the river and another kelpie had tried to make his move on her. He didn't like the thought that she could go to someone else or belong to anyone else. But it had not been long since she met him. It had only been a month or two no one could fall in love that quick with someone. His father smiled knowing full well what was running through his son's mind and placed a hand on his sons' shoulder.

"Love can come slowly, or it can hit you like a train when you least expect it. All you have to know is that if you love her that much that the thought of her leaving or not being able to see her again frightens you. Then you love her true and true. If that's the case then I'm afraid she is your heart's flower and there's nothing that you can do about it."

He sighed looking over at the picture of his late wife over the mantle above the fire and sighed.

"It happened to me once with your mother and I knew that she was the one for me in a month remarkably similar to you, my son. Just know that she would want you to have it and give it to your heart when you were ready. That is why I gave it to Aerwyna. She can have a little fun trying to figure out what it was or what's in it. It seems that the dear girl loves a puzzle or two."

That sounded more like his father than the riddle maker. Getting up from the chair they had retaken when their little talk commenced, he smiled at his father and gave him one more hug before leaving to meet Aerwyna outside. Walking through the lounge he stopped at the front door for he saw Aerwyna had stopped in front of a portrait of his mother. She was an elegant soul with long black hair that was as black as night. It curled slightly just like Caileans did, it made her smile knowing that this was slimier to him, her eyes were all that was different about her to other kelpies for, she was a human. She assumed she was a human that his father had tried to enchant but failed, maybe she was able to enchant him first. She thought that maybe He fell for her at first sight but refused to admit it, she couldn't tell much from the portrait, but she assumed that they were happily wed and that the rest was history after that. Cailean placed an arm around Aerwyna's shoulder causing her to jump a little.

"Are you ready my dear."

Aerwyna smiled up at him, placing her hand over his. She asked him to explain why only one waterlily was different out in the river. To which he explained that his mother was an avid flower enthusiast, so she brought flowers from everywhere she went and raised them here. He explained that that water lily was the last flower she planted and that was why it was the only one of its kind. Aerwyna asked that one day when he was ready if he could tell her about his father and mother, they seemed so in love even now. It was something she wanted to be loved like that, loved like you was the most precious thing in the world. She gave his hand one more squeeze before looking back up to his mother and said.

"You don't have to worry; I'll take diligent care of him. Thank you for bringing him into this world."

Cailean looked up at his mother and knew that if she was still here, she would have loved Aerwyna, his mother never cared what race people was she always said that if you were ever going to fall in love with someone fall in love with their eyes for, they are the window to the soul and they never ever change, so if you fell for them, you'll forever be in love. He didn't know how but he could feel his father smiling from behind the wall still sitting in his chair no doubt listening in on the conversation. It didn't take long after for his father to join them in the corridor and walk with them out to the gate to see them off. With all the goodbyes said and Aerwyna promising to come back and visit again soon, Cailean transformed back into his original form, bowed picking Aerwyna, which didn't last long as his father had wrapped his hands around Aerwyna's waist lifting her up onto his back and handing her the basket. Aerwyna smiled at him and placed a chaste kiss on his father cheek which resulted in a slight shocked blush on his part, leaning back up into a seating position Aerwyna passed a small jar to Caileans father which had the remainder of the tea they had at the picnic in assuring him that she would bring him more when she came to visit again. With all said and down Cailean was up and running across the river to take Aerwyna home.

Chapter Twelve

The Letter

Getting home that evening, so many things had changed, she didn't know what she should call him. Did she call him Cailean, his highness or did she go back to before and call him Kelpie, so many things had changed that things at home didn't seem real. It shocked her that Kelpie could turn into a horse, and he looked majestic as anything but seeing the change in real life with all the water swirling up around him then suddenly, he was either human or horse was truly magical. She didn't know if fairies could do anything the same or if they even had any magic at all but him changing was the best thing she had seen. Seeing his world, she realised there was no way she would fit in there and possibly no way he would fit in her world but where they were now would never really fit them. She knew in her heart that he belonged in his world, and she belonged in hers, But the very thought of her going back, she didn't want to entertain the thought, for it meant that she went to hers for she was scared. Going back to her world meant accepting who she was and whatever responsibilities she would have. It also meant the possibility of losing

121

him forever. All these thoughts ran through Aerwyna's head. Leaving Cailean, going home, facing the family she did not remember. The very thought terrified her. Placing the picnic basket on the kitchen counter, she found the rock that Cain had given her, and it made her smile. It was only a guess as to why it had a lock on, but it made her smile and to her at this moment it was all she needed. Aerwyna placed it in the pocket of her dress so she could take it upstairs to her room, maybe seeing it would bring her joy if she placed it on her drawers then it would be the first thing she saw every morning. Slowly walking up the stairs she could hear Cailean in his room pacing up and down along the floor, something must have been bothering him. If he wanted to tell her to ask for her opinion on whatever matter disturbed him, he would have done, and she would be there to listen when he was ready. Sitting down on her bed she held the geode in her hands. She thought to try the lock, but it would not budge. She thought about asking Cailean but his face when she got it originally told her otherwise. She thought maybe that would be something for another day, Placing the geode on her dresser she changed into her night clothes snuggled under the covers and drifted off to sleep.

***

Aerwyna's dreams that night were similar to all the others she had, they had her walking through the pink forest that was incredibly beautiful, till the darkness came and she got trapped in a tree. Although what made this night's dreams so different was it started off different. She was dressed in a pure white long flowing dress. The sleeves fell off her shoulder tying in a bow in the middle of her chest, the top of her dress was fitted to her while the skirt flowed down well past her feet dragging along the floor slightly. The top layer was slightly seen -through revealing delicate light pink lace flowers underneath cascading down from the waist. Looking around the room flowers were everywhere up along the rope that held the bed within the air creating a floating swing effect. Vials every size and shape held different coloured liquids of all different quantities. She didn't have a long time to look around the rest of the room as the door opened causing her to jump. A man walked into the room wearing a thin white shirt which hung low on his body, the sleeves pointed down at the end. His hair was blonde and long and flowed down well past his waist. The length of his hair itself helped enhance his pointy fairy ears and delicate features. A crown sat upon his head which was made with autumn leaves which sat around his head entwining with berries and pinecones. He held his arms open walking towards her to embrace her in a hug.

"My dear you look beautiful"

Taking her in to hug he released her just enough to take hold of her hands in his, he released on hand raised her other above her head before he spun her around getting a better look at what she was wearing.

"Hmm…you're missing something?"

Taking a step back he placed a hand on both of his chin leaving a finger to tap at his lips debating what she was missing. The man stayed like that for a while before he clicked his finger, she assumed this meant that he figured it out.

"My darling you've not got a tiara on. That is what is missing."

Walking over to what Aerwyna assumed was the dresser, he opened it. A drawer to reveal several different tiaras. There were ones of all shapes and sizes, but the ones that caught her attention most looked almost handmade compared to the others, they all had different shades of leaves on them ranging from gold to silver to even autumn green. Some had berries on one did not, each had its own design but at the same time felt the same, what made the so different is they all had a different centre, one made a pure moonstone that both waxed and waned. One had a pure silver stag with a clear quartz dangling from the crown itself while the other had the bigger most pure ruby in the middle followed by a smaller ruby hanging below that she had ever seen. But that one that caught her eye the most was in fact the one the man decided on. After a while of deciding he picked up a tiara full of jewels that sparkled like the sun, it pointed up in the middle and flowed down over all creating three separate points which only in turn helped to enhance the style of the tiara. The tiara itself was a rose god filled to the brim with both diamonds and moonstones. Three marquise cut moonstone created the first point in the tiara which were framed by a three-pointed leaf either side covered in diamonds' flowers created the centre point at the base of the crown before it curved in a small under curve towards the next points on either side. This was followed by five smaller round moonstones flowing on top alongside. Further marquise shaped moonstone dotted themselves around the points of the tiara followed by further three pointed leaves and flowers, she found that the main point of the tiara seemed to be copied on the further points. She loved that the base of the tiara itself seemed to flow like a ripple in the water, the very thought reminded her of Cailean which made her smile. The man plucked the tiara in question from the array that seemed to live in that dresser and walked over placing the beautiful article upon her head completing the look.

"There you're already."

He placed his hand on either side of her face tilting it down bringing his lips to her forehead placing a kiss upon it. It was then that Aerwyna awoke this time without a start for she had a beautiful, kind, caring feeling dream. One that made her feel warm inside, Aerwyna wondered who the man in her dream was, whoever he was he seemed kind and loving towards her.

***

Aerwyna got dressed in her favourite purple dress that Kelpie had brought her from the market. She looked at the geode she received yesterday and instantly smiled. When she got herself ready to go downstairs, she thought about what kind of tea and breakfast she should make. She also realised that she would have to make extra it was time for the brownies to come again, she found they were coming increasingly more often since she first arrived here. Once she was in the kitchen, she thought about what she could make for the brownies to take home with them after they finished. A loud sound startled her from behind, the first thing she thought was maybe there was someone at the shop front and knocked to either buy or hand a clock in. when she moved the curtain that covered the window to find there was on one there, a puzzled look crossed her face. The knock sounded again only this time she was closer to the room that held the

doorways. The knock sounded as if it came from one of the doors.
She thought that she should wait for Cailean to wake up, but what if it
was important. What if someone needed their help? Against her better
judgement Aerwyna slowly approached the room of clock trying in
an attempt to figure out which door the sound came from.
"Hello?"
She said cautiously. Slowly she started approaching each door,
peering inside each. She approached the Kelpie door first, slightly
opening it, wondering if his father had decided to pay them a visit but
there was no one there. Turning around slightly to the left she
approached the Selkie door, she thought maybe it would be Saoirse.
Opening the door revealed nothing but a dark tunnel. Only two doors
were left which were the Brownies door and the Fairy door. At this
time Kelpie walked down the stairs causing her to jump again at the
creak of the staircase.
"Oh Cailean, Good morning. I'll fix your breakfast in a minute. I just
have to find out where a knock like sound came from."
Cailean looked at her quizzically the thought that she heard a knock
sound that was strange, on one really came here other than the
Brownies but they never knocked, they would just turn up randomly,
so he thought someone must have knocked for a reason, not many
people knocked unless they wanted passage through to the human

realm, but he knew not many wanted to come to the human world to

if was indefinitely strange. He asked which doors she had tried

already, in which she explained that she checked the Kelpie and the

Selkie door with no Advil. Cailean took it upon himself to check the

other two doors. When he checked there was nothing behind the

Brownies door, not even the tree annoying Brownies themselves, it

left only one door to check the last door, the Fairy door. The one door

that neither of them wanted to go through at the moment. He

approached the last door, opening it slightly to reveal nothing, he

opened the door completely to reveal nothing, no one was standing

there, there was nothing but a letter on the floor just inside the door

addressed to Aerwyna.

***

Cailean handed a letter to Aerwyna which made her happy, she never

had a letter before. Looking at the time she realised that the Brownies

were near arrival. She placed the letter in the pocket of her apron

which she always wore when she was baking or making her amazing

tea concoctions. He loved seeing her in her apron. She looked like a

little housewife which he loved the thought of. The thought made him

smile to himself, not realising he was smiling for real, which caused

Aerwyna to look over at him quizzically.

"Cailean? Is everything okay?"

128

He just kept smiling and started walking towards her pulling her into a hug. Her hugs were like sunshine, they were warm and always made him smile. The day passed like always, they had their tea and sugar plum fairy cookies with Anion and the boys. Cailean showed her some more skills at making clocks, which in turn got some disapproving glances from Arion, Kano and Cas as well, he had to admit that fact was a bonus to being able to be close to Aerwyna. Her carving had got a lot better over the time she was here, it made him proud that he could teach her a new skill, in a way it made him think that if there was a time that she had to go away, or he had to leave then at least she could do something that would remind her of him. He didn't know if it would come in handy her being a fairy and all, a fairy princess to be precise but it made him feel like they were connected in those moments. Especially when he was showing her how to carve a contemporary design, which meant an evening spent sitting close at the work bench these moments were his favourite. Aerwyna was nearly finished carving her own clock, which was a big task for her, she made it her task to create an entire clock herself without his help, he had normally helped her but this time she was being stubborn about it, she wouldn't even let him see her project he could only assume that she wanted it to be a surprise for him, for letting her stay here with him this whole time, not that she needed to give him anything, her very presents beside him was enough. The day passed quite quickly considering everything that happened recently, regaining memories, finding Saoirse, visiting his father, much to his dislike on that last one, Kelpie didn't like to share, and he was still sour that his father had received a kiss from her. Although Aerwyna liked that day, it was a much calmer day compared to all the others.

***

Aerwyna went to tidy the kitchen after dinner, drying her hands on her apron. It was then she remembers she had the letter in her front pocket. She perched herself against the sink and opened the letter, it read

My Dearest Daughter,

Saoirse wrote to us explaining what happened to you, and I cross my heart we are trying everything in our power to find the person who trapped you in that tree. She explained you're staying with someone named Kelpie. We hope he treats you well. We understand that it could be hard coming back seeing your betrothed again after staying with another. But whenever you're ready we shall all be here waiting for you. Just remember a flower does not think of competing with the flower next to it. It just blooms. Always be yourself and you will be fine. You are brave, strong, and beautiful. You never have to prove yourself to anyone. Remember that for us. You are always in our hearts.

We love you dearly,

Love your Mother and Father.

Chapter Thirteen

Caileans Letter

Kelpie walked in the kitchen to find Aerwyna still propped up against the sink, her hand covering her mouth while tears slowly spilled over the rim of her eyes and flowed down her cheeks. Cailean dropped the basket in his hands and walked over to Aerwyna, praying, hoping that nothing was immensely wrong. He dropped to his knees in front of her his hands on her arms searching her face for any answers on what had happened. Aerwyna dropped the letter on the floor and fell to her knees and started hugging him in the process. He wanted to read the letter but taking care of Aerwyna was first on his list. He stayed there next to her on the floor hugging her as long as she needed, until night fell. She was still clinging to him, but it was getting too cold to stay in the kitchen. Scooping her in his arm, she fit so perfectly but that was not what he was thinking at this moment, something was written in that letter to cause all this crying.

At present time keeping her warm and letting her feel that she was safe was what mattered. Cailean walked them over to the already lit fire and tried placing her down in her chair, but it didn't work. Her

132

hold around his neck was too strong. He tried placing her down into the chair before then attempting to pry her hands off of his neck but again to no avail. He tried a few more times but he came to the conclusion that she may be small, but she could have immense strength when needed. The only option he had left was to take a seat and place her on his lap.

***

It took a while for Aerwyna to stop crying, she had not even realised that she was sitting on Caileans lap. It was what he thought she needed, being able to know that there was someone there, that she wasn't dealing with this alone. Cailean started to stroke her hair slowly rocking her humming the Selkie song to her. After a while of humming the lullaby, it did not seem to be calming her down. Then an idea popped into his head.

"Hey,"

He gave her a nudge with his shoulder trying to bring her attention to him.

"Can I sing you a song that my mother used to sing when I was sad?"

This caused her to raise her head, he hadn't really mentioned his mother at all to Aerwyna. Although she did not say anything her eyes said it all, they were tear stained but they glistened like jewels. He took her silence as a yes, snuggled her into his shoulder wrapping her in a warm blanket and an embrace and started swaying side to side, singing the lullaby his mother sang to him.

My love is like a red red rose,

That's newly sprung in June,

My love is like a melody,

That sweetly played in tune,

And fair art thou my bonnie lass,

How deep in love am I,

And I will love thee still my dear,

Till all the seas run dry,

His voice was soft and gentle, with the swaying that he was doing it did not take long for Aerwyna to stop crying and slowly drift off to sleep. He didn't need to look down to tell that she was asleep, his mother was a proud Scottish woman and she always told him the best way to stop someone crying was to sing this. She had called it her lucky charm for the day when Kelpie used to cry as a child. He could not thank his mother enough calming Aerwyna down was his main task that night, the other was finding out what started it all off. Taking her up to bed that night was easier than every other night. She didn't want to be apart from him because she was scared of her dreams. That night however he hoped that singing that song to her would give her sweet dreams, but just to be sure he placed a bit of his blood on her lips effectively cleansing the area from all things bad. She knew what he had done as he had done this before at the river. Where she had asked him what it would do, after he explained she asked for it every night to try and help. He prayed it worked for her dreams, she deserved beautiful dreams. Cailean tucked her in making sure she was nice and warm, moving stray hairs that had fallen over her face, she looked like an angel. Turning around he started to tip toe out of the room when his eyes came to rest on the geode that his father gave her. His curiosity got the better of him, slowly he took a hold of the geode and continued to tip toe back to his room. He wondered if his father truly put that inside the geode, if he had then Kelpie needed to make sure that Aerwyna could never get in this until the time he decided what he wanted to do. Once he got back to his room, he realised he still had the Aerwyna letter in his trouser pocket. He had to find out what had made her so sad. Maybe there was a way he could fix it and make her happy again. Cailean lit the lantern in his room, and sat down on his little stool in the corner and started to read. He found out that in her world Aerwyna had a betrothed, but he knew that things like that could be ended easily if one found someone who their parents and everyone approved of. They also had to be either of the same social standing, or higher he knew he was of the same social standing but what he couldn't count on was the fact he was a Kelpie,

they could at the right time say that he had bewitched her to fall for

him and therefore agree to marry him if he so choose to go down that

way. It was a tricky situation being of different races no one ever held

it against people but to some it was frowned upon. He looked at the

letter again, could that have been the reason she was so upset about

the fact she had a betrothed. The thought made him sad, if she went

home then there was a chance that she would rediscover her feelings

for her betrothed if she were the one that picked him, which would

mean she would have to leave him. He knew that if that were what

had to happen and was fated to happen then nothing he could do

would help him. It was then he decided once a day he would write her

a letter explaining everything he thought about her, what he thought

of every menial thing she thought she did that he loved so, so that if

that day came when she had to go then she would be able to take a

part of him with her.

***

Cailean walked to the desk under the window and opened the draws

taking out some paper which Kelpie royalty always wrote upon, it

had dark blue corners with leaves rising up one side. It was his

favourite paper to write upon as they had matching envelopes and it

came in many other designs. Over time he thought he would use them

136

all, writing her a letter, it was something that his father did for his

mother when he was enchanted with her beauty, it seemed fit to

continue the tradition. Laying out the colourful paper out, he dipped

his glass pen in the ink, his mother had given him this pen when he

came out as the Prince of Kelpies, it was something they done, the

children of Royalty stayed hidden from the eyes of the public till they

were essentially and adult which his mother told him in human years

was eighteen. What he loved about this pen was that his mother had

included all his favourite colours within the glass before it was

gripped at one end and twisted in theory, trapping the rink within the

spiral. It had the colours of the rainbow but what surprised him now

was the majority of the pen had more shades of green than any other.

After he dipped the pen, he started thinking how she should start.

There were many things he wanted to say to her, but never found the

time. Although now he had all the time to get everything and

anything he wanted out on paper for her, he had no idea on where to

start. What felt like hours went past before the idea hit him, she was

curious about his mother and fathers meeting, which could be the first

letter the story of his parents meeting.

Chapter Fourteen

Caileans Mother and Fathers Story

Caliean thought about how to start the tale for it was exceptionally long. He started to walk around the room bouncing the pen off of his lip, which he forgot he had already dipped in black ink, pondering what to write. How could he go about it? His father starts the tale of them, with him going to enchant women like a typical Kelpie. Kelpies like to enchant women and bring them back to his world, sometimes it was to wed them and sometimes they ended up trapped in their world as servants to whichever Kelpie had enchanted them. His father went in search of another servant but ended up being enchanted by his mother instead, or so his father told him. Kelpie supposed the only way to start was at the very beginning, so that's what he did. He sat back down at his desk, re-dipped his pen this time remembering not to put it against his lips, and he started to write.

My Dearest Aerwyna,

You once asked me in the Kelpie realm how my parents met, It's a long story so I'm afraid it might be a long letter, but here's the story for which you asked. My father had always told me that Kelpies went to the human realm to enchant women to either become their brides

It was then that he knew that his grandfather must have been a stubborn, stubborn man, very much like his father. At least now he figured out who he got that from. He had extraordinarily little memory of his grandfather as sadly he passed away when he was way younger. His grandfather never really liked the fact his mother was a human, but he begrudgingly accepted her when he was born. Kelpie was told that his grandfather doted on him, giving him everything he wanted, although he had no recollection of it. His grandfather must have loved him very much. Cailean had a feeling writing this letter was going to bring up many memories for him, especially about his mother, he hadn't sat down and thought about her for a long time, he prepared himself for all the memories that would resurface and pulled himself out of his thoughts and continued the letter.

***

My father didn't want to disappoint him so he decided if this next woman didn't agree to come with him willingly, he would have to use his powers. He had everything set up, his plan was to try and woo the server at this little café he frequented when he was here on this side of the realms. The only problem he had encountered here was her shifts were unreliable. So, he came up with another plan: he would have her come to him. My father found out that she was in charge of this big carved grandfather clock in the corner of the shop. He hadn't got a good look at the clock, but he had a feeling he could use his powers to somehow disable the clock so that she would have to get it fixed. And at that point he was undercover in the shop that we are staying in right now, which was the only shop in the part of the realm there were, in he thought in theory they had no choice but to come to him. It didn't take long for her to come to the shop and ask for his help, the problem that he had was he didn't have enough time to enchant her,

for her pure beautiful heart had already started to enchant him. My

father took a long time to fix the clock in the shop, just so he could go

there every day and catch a glimpse of her. She had truly got his heart

although he refused to believe it, everyone could see. He told me it

went on for months before he even acknowledged it to himself that she

had some hold on his heart.

Cailean stopped and put the pen down he went to go check on

Aerwyna, she hadn't made a sound, but he just wanted to make sure

she was okay for his own peace of mind. Before he checked on her,

he tip-toed downstairs grabbing himself a sugar plum fairy cookie

and a cup of Aerwyna brewed tea, he knew he still had a lot to write,

and he needed some fuel for the rest. Walking back upstairs he began

to realise how similar everything was to his parents meeting. He had

met Aerwyna by a clock or technically in a clock. He was even

refusing to admit things he didn't want to happen or not happen just

yet. He reached Aerwyna's door which he had left partly open just in

case and leant against the door frame. He was getting used to having

her here, so what if she had a betrothed, he was a prince as

well, and if she felt the same towards him then it could be cancelled.

But that meant him admitting many things for which he wasn't ready.

After confirming to himself that she was okay he trudged back across the hall to his room to continue the letter for Aerwyna.

***

After a few months he had finally acknowledged to himself that my mother had enchanted him through and through. Now my father realised the only obstacle that was left was trying to persuade her to come back with him. He could only think of one way that he could attempt, that was to tell her the truth, he didn't want her to be his servant, he wanted her as his wife. But another obstacle presented itself, her betrothed. He was a slight man, in my father's words not much to look at. But that wasn't the problem with him, he didn't love my mother, he just wanted to marry her because her father owned the only café in the town. Skye, my mother, was the true beauty of the island. She was always told that if folklore were true, she would belong to the Kelpie clan. For she had long wavy hair that curled at the bottom, much like how mine does. Her eyes were what enchanted everyone as they were as blue as the ocean. My father knew what he had to do, he had to steal her away only then would she be safe from her betrothed and could have the possibility of being happy. He planned to change to his true form and appear in front of her with a letter stating that he could take her away from all of this with the geode attached around his neck. For the only way he could take her

142

Cailean leant back in his chair, the thought that his mother was never

able to return to her world did make him sad, but he could remember

that she told him she never regretted her decision to marry his father.

He had given her everything she wanted, a family that loved her and

her freedom. He couldn't imagine what a love like that would feel. A

love where even the thought of never being able to return

didn't bother you as long as you could be with them. A love where

you would lose everything just to be with them. Kelpie wondered if

Aerwyna could imagine ever doing that. He knew his mother would

have loved her if she ever had the chance to meet her. The problem

they had was that she was human, and humans had a much-shorter

lifespan than Kelpies. It was foretold that a human that was in possession of a Kelpie heart lived longer, but the Kelpie would still outlive its partner, it was sad to think of but what made it sadder was that once a Kelpies heart was possessed once his partner passed so did their heart and their ability to love another. He sat there and remembered his mother and everything she used to do, having a mud fight was her favourite when he was but a young boy trying to help her garden. He laughed to himself while looking at the ring box she would have wanted him to have it and pass it on along with her memory. He continued the letter getting to the part he loved the most.

***

The thought of leaving her world never scared his mother once, she just took it as another adventure. She agreed to come with my father straight away, leaving with only the clothes she was wearing, and the geode held close to her heart. She hopped on my father's back hiding her face when it came to him running on top of the water, much like how you did. And she left to start her new life with my father in a world in which she did not know which people she did not know, but she was never afraid for she knew he would protect her at any cost. He had given her his heart and she had given it right back. Months went by and my grandfather still didn't approve of my mother, but she made his son happy and over everything that was what was important. My parents spent a lot of time in the garden under the moonlit tree we had our picnic under. It was her favourite place for my father to strum his guitar. He had brought himself into the human world while my mother sang her favourite poem, it was one thing she had which could calm both my father and later on myself down whenever we were sad or scared. Coincidently I sang it to you, and it calms you down enough you feel asleep. It was under that tree that my father unlocked the clasp of the geode revealing the rainbow geode inside. In the moonlight it reflected the light in colours of blue and purple. She loved the box it came in but what it held was so much more precious to her and much more beautiful than she ever could have imagined.The ring that was inside held a Alexandrite stone in the middle encircled with rose gold, the band itself was thin but four small diamonds were encapsulated within the band giving it a subtle hint of their realm. my mother always said that the colours of the Alexandrite and inside the geode enhanced the diamonds. It didn't take her a lot of time to answer him

as she knew the answer from the moment she got here. Their wedding was quick because they found out shortly after that I was on the way. And that my dear Aerwyna was the story of how my mother and father met, fell in love, and ultimately lived happily ever after. There are some similarities between their story and ours. If our story ever turns out as magically as theirs did, then I know that we'll be happy for all

our life.

All my heart

yours always

Cailean

He finished off the letter sealing it away in a similar envelope to the paper writing Aerwyna name on the front. The first of many letters were done, he just hoped she liked it. His parents' story was one of his favourites. He had the thought that if he were going to write many letters to Aerwyna he would need a place to keep them safe till he was ready to give them to her.

"Maybe a trip to town is in order."

He thought about taking Aerwyna to town with him as she hadn't seen the town yet, he knew that the café his mother worked at was still in operation. Maybe they could have their lunch there. It was all decided, with that he ducked out back to sort out the river before tucking himself in to sleep dreaming of the day Aerwyna would open the geode.

Chapter Fifteen

Town

After the hard day that Aerwyna had yesterday Cailean decided to treat her for a change. Cailean woke up especially early that morning. He knew she always woke up early so he woke up even more early in an attempt to beat her. He wanted to make her breakfast and a cup of freshly brewed tea. So, he snuck downstairs as quietly as he could. He stood at the kitchen counter and pondered for a while debating what to make her for breakfast, then he remembered when they had French toast how much she loved the syrup. He decided it was time for her to try waffles with syrup and maybe as an even bigger treat he would add strawberries. He had never made waffles before, but he was willing to give it a go. He rolled up his sleeves ready to give it ago, there's a first time for everything he said to himself. It didn't take him long to realise that after several attempts at making the batter, that baking was not one of his strong suits. He turned around to grab for ingredients to re start the batter until a sound startled him. Turing around slowly hands and clothes covered in flour at the sound of a chuckle.

***

Cailean found Aerwyna leaning against the doorframe covering her mouth with the back of her hand, a little bit of a smile peeked out from behind her hand. A smirk worked its way upon his face, at the corner of his eye he spotted the bowl of flour he kept there so he didn't have to keep walking over to the over side to retrieve more. When an idea popped in his head. Dipping his hand in the flour he had an idea.

"Are you laughing at me?"

He pointed at Aerwyna with a smirk hiding his hand behind his back, it seemed he wasn't quick enough before Aerwyna clocked the flour in his hand. She took a slow step backwards obviously realising what he was planning to do.

"Cailean Don't you even think about it."

The smirk on his face just intensified. He slowly crept closer and closer to Aerwyna. Unfortunately for Aerwyna she wasn't fast enough. Cailean flicked his fingers forward, throwing the flour right in the middle of Aerwyna face. Aerwyna wiped the flour from her eyes, and Cailean knew he was in trouble. Aerwyna made a quick dash for the bowl of flours grabbing a handful in the process.

"Cailean, you are so in trouble,"

He dashed around the room narrowly avoiding Aerwyna's futile attempts at throwing flour on him. He loved that the ground floor of the house above the shop was only divided by only one pillar in the middle and doors between each room, which gave him lots of hiding places to catch Aerwyna in the run of things. It didn't take him long to catch Aerwyna in his arms while she was trying to find him, little did he forget she had the flour tucked in her hand. It didn't stay there long before it ended up in his face.

"I should have remembered that."

Cailean blew out a big breath creating a cloud of flour smoke in the process. Causing her to laugh, they looked at themselves covered in flour and decided before anything they should wash up. They both walked to the bathroom washing their faces to remove the flour. In the process Aerwyna asked what he was trying to do. In which he said he wanted to make her waffles and tea, but it hadn't turned out very well. This caused Aerwyna to laugh. It was so sweet that he tried ,few people did, that's when Aerwyna decided that Cailean needed some cooking lessons.

***

They both started towards the kitchen, Cailean washing his hands while Aerwyna struggled in trying to tie her hair up. He dried his hands off on his shirt and took one of her hair ribbons off the side, placing his hands under her hair he gently gathered all of Aerwyna Caramel coloured hair up. His fingers gently grazed the back of her neck sending shivers down her back. Every little graze, every little touch, every little brush of his fingers gave her goosebumps. Aerwyna hadn't even realised that he had finished putting her hair in the sky-blue lace ribbon which matched her dress that day, a blush crept onto her face turning her nearly the same colour as her hair.

"So… I… let's get on with the baking shall we."

Her sentence came out in a stutter, making her blush only increase more. The first instructions she gave Cailean was the fact he needed an apron so he wouldn't get his clothes dirty, well any more dirty than he already had. It was at that moment that they realised he only had his clock making an apron which was on its way out anyway.

"Well, we don't have any spare aprons. So, it looks like I'll have to go into town to get some more. While I'm there I may as well get some other items as well."

 Cailean peered down through his hair looking at Aerwyna, her face said it all. He was tempted to say that she couldn't go just to see her face, but he concluded that was too mean.

"Do you want to come with me to town, Aerwyna."

Again, her face said it all, he was able to read her like a book, he loved that she was so open with her expressions. He didn't even have to say anything before her apron was off and she was running up her stairs to get re- dressed, ready to go to town. Once they had left the shop with their capes and shoes on, making sure that Aerwyna's hair was down, adding extra cover for her wings. They set off for town.

***

As today was an absolutely gorgeous sunny day Cailean decided to take Aerwyna the scenic route to town instead of the back way through the woods. He knew that Aerwyna hadn't been to town before she would find it magical. For the place he lived looked like it came right out of a fairytale, for he lived in the outskirts of the town of Llwyn, the very same town his mother grew up in. Llwyn was a small town on the edge of a lake in Kirkessie, Kirkessie was a massive loch that many little towns sat alone beside it. Many little rivers that flowed throughout every outskirt town had a river and a source of water; thanks to Cailean the water was even clearer than it had been. The walk to town took them past beautiful half grass covered rock which just added to the beautiful route of the town, the path was lined with little rocks letting people know that was the path. The sun was passing the cusp of the highest point casting little rays of light shining down as it emerged over the top. Several bushes and little trees covered both the massive rock and the edge of the path. Little steps made it possible to walk halfway up the massive rock allowing you to peer over the edge taking in the beautiful scenery this town beheld. Cailean thought he would have to take Aerwyna up there one day and

151

show her all the splendour this realm held. His favourite part of walking to town was coming up over the horizon, he didn't know if it had a name, but he called it the three-hole bridge. He looked down to see Aerwyna gazing, mouth opened at the sights ahead and realised she must have seen the bridge already. The bridge was situated over a river that ran in the middle of a grass field. The river itself was as pure as water could be even without his help. Little rocks and mini boulders sat at various places along the side and in the river, some creating little waterfalls and other little dips in the rivers, making the water turn white with movement. The thing that he always loved about this river was when the moon reflected upon it making it wax and wane, just like the moonstones in the ring his father had given his mother. His mother always said the scenery here was the best in the world. By the look on Aerwyna's face she thought so too. She ran forwards towards the bridge, her hair floating along behind her. She looked perfect, her cape and her hair twirling around with her as she spun in circles on the bridge taking in the beauty, sunshine and fresh air the place had to offer. When Cailean joined her on the bridge they stood just taking in the beautiful sight over the river. The mountains that encircled then added to the aesthetic allure the place offered anyone who crossed it. The only thing that was fairly new was the bridge itself. The three-hole bridge was a man-made structure making it easier for the townsfolk to get across the river. The cobbles of the bridge's walkway were made of all different stones but in the eyes of a believed the bridge which was made of cobble was actually made of crystals, each crystal was placed by a different person holding their wish within the stone. His mother told him that once the wish was completed the crystal lost its shine. But in doing so allowed anyone who stood on the bridge to have their wish accepted by the bridge with the chance of it being fulfilled, as everyone who wished was fulfilled and dimed it allowed someone else's wish to take a place. Even though Cailean couldn't see the crystal bridge he believed it was here. He lent his arms on the top of the bridge holding his head up upon his hand, it didn't take long before he was turning his head down slightly to see Aerwyna. She blended so well into this world, so well into his life, maybe a lifetime with her wouldn't be so bad, his thoughts went down that line once again making his imagination on the subject go wild. After standing on the bridge for a couple of minutes they continued on the journey to town.

***

"Welcome to Llwyn "

Cailean raised his hand in the direction of the town. The town itself was breathtaking. It was a small harborside town running along the edge of a loch. Several boats were out on the water both big and

153

small, sails and no sails. Everything was new to Aerwyna. Cailean decided they should walk along the harbour side, which was lined with houses and shops of every colour. To Aerwyna it looks like a fairytale little house painted in bright shades of pink, blue, white, and yellow. It didn't take her long before she was running down the path between the houses and the harbour heading down towards the beach path where she could reach the water. Trees lined along one side added some shade during the summer months. Across the loch you could see right across the loch to the other side which displays the pure beauty of Llwyn. Vast open plains covered the entire side and a few houses could be seen in the far distance. What he loved most about town was the fact it was secluded which helped it remain pure. What he loved most about this town was every morning it would be taken over by a market which sold everything from food to clothing, utensils to work tools. If you ever needed anything, Llwyn market was your place to go. They spend their time walking around the market as Aerwyna's eyes were getting caught by everything that was taking her attention. She stopped at the dresses, cooking equipment and everything in between. The main thing that had caught her eye the most was at the male clothing stall. They had a midnight blue royal suit which she imagined would look amazing on Kelpie.

"Excuse me sir, can I ask about this suit?"

She placed her hand on the sleeve thinking it would suit him perfectly. The suit entailed a cape with elegant details of swirls and pearls running up along the seam, a few pearls hanging off the top of the cape around the front enhancing the detailing of the entire cape. The two sides were connected with a gold chain that hooked onto a gold button on the opposite side, three of these connected the cape together. An almost black top sat underneath adding the contrast against the midnight blue of the cape, silver buttons ran up the middle acting as the fastening, matching silver piping covered the seams of the entire top along the top, bottom and sides adding a fine detail to the dark top. The grey trousers matched the top with the silver piping running down the side of the legs disappearing into black calf high boots the silver piping followed down onto the boots adding an elegant design to them. Ruffles of white fabric were added to the sides with a silver button adding movement to the entire outfit.

"Ah you have a good eye ma'am. This is a suit inspired by the folklore of Kelpies. Hence the dark colours."

Just the sound of his human name made her blush in memory. She could vision him in this, it would make a perfect gift for him. Her blush didn't get past the old gentle merchant.

"Ah, is it for your loved one?"

He winked at her, making her blush deepen. Which made the old merchant laugh.

"Ah I can remember being in love when I was your age my dear wife was remarkably similar to you. You were able to read her like a book."

Aerwyna looked at the suit again then around to Cailean who was at the food stall just a few stalls up behind her. This didn't get past the merchant.

"I take it, it's the tall dark-haired stranger at my wife's stall."

Aerwyna didn't say anything and just nodded. The merchant agreed that the suit would match him perfectly.

"I'll tell you what my dear. I'll give it to you at half price okay."

Aerwyna remembered that when Cailean had sold one of the clocks that she made he gave her the money from it, she just hoped it was enough to get the suit for him.

"May I enquire how much it shall be dear sir."

The merchant was surprised that someone so young was so formal in her speech. But it made the merchant smile as he went around back working out some calculations for her.

"Well, my dear it would normally be 973 Suruna normal so with the little discount for you my dear that comes to a total of 773 Suruna please,"

Aerwyna grabbed her purse from inside her cloak being careful not to show her wings in the process, Cailean had told her to be careful as many people were frightened of people from the fairy and folklore realms if they believed in them at all. She wasn't sure how the money worked in this realm because it was different from the money she had back home. She asked the gentle merchant if he would help which caused a glance at her in amazement.

***

"Ah so you must be from far out of town then, everyone in these parts uses this currency. But if you're new it can be tricky to wrap your head around. I'll give you a hand."

The merchant walked around the stall just as Aerwyna emptied her purse onto the stall countertop. It didn't take long for the merchant to realise why she couldn't work the money out, for as Aerwyna bent to empty her purse the edge of her wings dented the side of the cloak revealing the outline. The merchant was always a believer in fairies and folklore alike, so he felt privileged the serve a fairy, or anyone from the different realms, even if he didn't say anything. he explained that the currency they used came in different values, them being hundred Suruna, fifty Suruna, ten Suruna and finally one Suruna. He also explained that these were easily identified by the pictures engraved on the face of the coin. The village although many didn't believe in folklore engraved their coins with the designs of the Kelpie which was on the hundred Suruna, Selkies which was on the fifty Suruna, a thistle was on the ten Suruna and the one Suruna which had a little bird engraved on the face

"So, my dear what you need is seven Kelpies, one Selkie, two thistles and three birds,"

The merchant explained it in the most understandable way they he could find. Aerwyna sorted out the correct number of coins while the merchant packed up the suit for her. She handed the coins over to him just in time for Cailean to walk over to her.

"Ooh, what have you brought?"

Thankfully, the merchant also sold women's hair ornaments. Mostly likely made by his wife. She explained that she was just looking at the floral hair clip. On that she could use when she was at the shop to keep her hair out of her face when she was carving or making treats and tea. One that had caught her eye was one filled with roses. It had both white and dusty roses with leaves and smaller rose buds surrounding them.

"I'm just looking at this hair clip."

Cailean picked them, he found one that was the same but just a fraction smaller before he started rolling up part of her hair, he placed one on the left-hand side just above her ear. And the other just above her right the contrast against her cameral hair matches perfectly, in fact in his eyes it enhanced her features and hair perfectly.

"How much my dear man."

The merchant looked over at Aerwyna, her hand hovering over the hair clip, a blush slightly showing on her cheeks, and he smiled. Looking at the gentle man in front of him he noticed his eyes and understood why his secret fairy visitor was so fascinated with the Kelpie suit, seeing them together reminded him that things beyond what we could see still existed and sometimes the pairings could surprise you, if you only knew where to look.

"For you, my dear sir. It's free for the lovely little lady."

He looked over at Aerwyna and winked. They both thanked the merchant, and he passed the box to Aerwyna all wrapped up so he wouldn't be able to see what it was. The last stop they made before heading back home was visiting the café where his mother worked.

Chapter Sixteen

Waffles and Memories

They reached the café where Kelpie's mother previously worked

before she left her world to be with his father. His mother told him

that she always loved the folklore of Kelpies, so she worked at a café

that had a name related to them. She told him it was called The Misty

Moon. It was a small café hidden out of the way behind the market,

because it was hidden away. It was like a treasure few people found.

The café itself blended in perfectly well with the surrounding

buildings in Llwyn, it was once you got inside that the magic became

apparent. Once you walked through the arched doorway you were

surrounded by walls filled with every book in every size and colour

you could imagine. jars filled with amazing things covered a little

table at the front, the colours caught Aerwyna's eye.

"Cailean, Cailean what are these."

Aerwyna had already dropped down to the table with jars of every

size and shape, looking at the contents they held. Cailean couldn't

help but laugh as he knelt down next to her and started to explain that

the smaller jars were filled with jams of assorted flavours, to which

Aerwyna said they should get some for breakfasts and maybe they could have it with their breakfast one day. So many different recipes

ran through her head, the first being that both she and Kelpie could

make jam tarts to go with their tea when they got home.

"Cailean we could use this for baking, right?"

He nodded, picking up three jars once with purple blackcurrant jam,

another red with strawberry jam and the last was orange with orange

marmalade. The part of the café that Kelpie loved the most was the

ceiling. They had covered it with artificial moss and hidden little

lights within, so it looked like little fairies or as most believed lights

were in the sky. Arches of elder wood could be seen in between the

moss adding to the enchanting feel of the café. At the back of the café

stairs ascended to the viewing deck cafe that sat up above the shop

part of the café. Walking up the stairs the railing was covered with

leaves of every kind entwining themselves up. Some had said that the

leaves changed depending on who walked up them, others just

thought it was a trick of the light. Once you emerge from the curtain

made of purple and lilac flowers it reveals a garden café. The floor

was covered in grass and small daisies, every table was decorated like

toadstools, strings of fairy lights hung in the trees and bushes.

Flowers of assorted colours were scattered in-between the bushes

which decorated the walls creating a magical looking garden. The

menus which sat upon the toadstool tables stated everything they had for everyone to order. The menu was printed on watercolour paper with images on opposite corners sealed in an almost see-through envelope sealed with a moon and star seal, it matched the café perfectly. The café had told Kelpie that since the café was so small, they were able to put every little detail in that they wanted to match the allure the café had. Aerwyna definitely agreed that the menus, the little toadstool chairs sat upon the grass covered floor as well as being surrounded by flowers and bushes everything matched the allure of the café.

***

Taking a seat near the railing at the front of the second floor of the café, taking in the beautiful large windows that allowed people to take in the beautiful view of the harbour situated in front of the café. Aerwyna sat there looking at the menu for a long time, there were so many things on there she wanted to try. She looked at Cailean who just rested his head on his hand looking at her and giving her a little chuckle. He had been here before, so he had tried nearly everything on the menu. After about 5 minutes waiting for her to decide with her eyes flicking all over the menu and back again, Cailean decided it was time, he helped her out a little.

"Do you want a hand in deciding what to get? It can be a little overwhelming if you haven't been here before."

162

Aerwyna just nodded at him which made him slide his toadstool next to her sharing the menu. He was so close which made Aerwyna's face turn slightly pink. Being near him allowed her to get a whiff of him, he smelt like pure fresh water, like it had just rained. The smell after it rained was her favourite smell and now, he smelt like that. After careful consideration Cailean called over a waitress who was dressed in a dark purple short sleeved top with two tails hanging down the back. Little silver buttons ran in two lines up the middle of the top adding a little bit of sparkle along with the two buttons which sat on the small of the back. A white collar sat at the stop connecting to the back of the top. A white ruffled skirt with a purple stripe sat on her hips. Knee high socks with purple lace up flats finished the ensemble. She had her hair tied up into two bunches on top of her head. What made Aerwyna smile was that her hair was the same colour as the waitresses' uniform.

"Hello there, my names Karin and I'll be your server. What magical items can I get you both today?"

They both decided on the cinnamon and nutmeg waffles with Aerwyna having the sky-blue hot chocolate and Cailean having the colour changing lemonade. Karin walked down the stairs to place their order, while Cailean had spotted the box the Aerwyna was trying to hide with her cloak.

"What have you got there? Did you get something at the market.?"

Aerwyna tried to hide the box better with her cloak, but it didn't help he had seen it and was asking her many questions trying to find out what it was. Aerwyna didn't give in to any of his questions, she got it for him to be a surprise and that's what it was going to remain as one till the time she was ready to give it to him. Aerwyna was thankful when the waitress Karin came back up the stairs with their order halting Kelpie from asking any further questions. She placed the waffles in front of Aerwyna. The waffle had all types of fresh fruit which Aerwyna loved, strawberries, grapes, and bananas drizzled with a little syrup just to finish it all off. The face Aerwyna made, made Cailean laugh, her eyes grew big, and her mouth dropped open looking at the delicious dessert in front of her. She was so happy that she hadn't even realised that Cailean was still right next to her. All her focus was on the waffle and now on her sky-blue hot chocolate. She had the straw between her lips a look of pure bliss on her face, he knew that nothing we would say at that moment would reach her. Aerwyna was so happy with the waffle that she couldn't wait to eat it, she was so eager that she had gotten the whipped cream on top of the waffle on her nose. Cailean sat there drinking his lemonade and enjoyed the moment of bliss with her. She wasn't worried about the fact she lost her memory, or the fact her parents told her she had a

betrothed, he liked that she wasn't worried about anything at home.

Just the fact that she was enjoying her time right here right now was

what mattered.

Chapter Seventeen

Fireflies

Walking back from town with all their spoils was a handful. Aerwyna decided that using the last of her money she would buy some jam and snacks from the Moon Magic café. Unsurprisingly the part that did shock him whatsoever was where most of her money went to was from their tea stall in the market. The stall had a dark purple star patterned cloth decorated with little jars full of colourful tea and herbs. Colourful lights hung from the top draggling down casting a low luminescence glow over the items for sale. Thankfully for Cailean each little jar had a tag tied around the top explaining what was inside and its benefits, making it easier for him to understand why Aerwyna was hurriedly grabbing jars at random. But of course, she knew what was in them with just a glance, that was the power of a fairy. He stood beside her taking any and all jars she was handing to him, she was like a child in a candy shop. He couldn't help but laugh which caused Aerwyna to look up at him, making him stop abruptly. Aerwyna had grabbed teas made of blueberry and hibiscus as well as the love potion that they served in the shop. She didn't believe it was actually a love potion, but she did love the ingredients it held. She explained to him that the love potion included hibiscus, dried apples, dried strawberries, coconut, lemon, and a little bit of cinnamon. The flavour combination intrigued Cailean making him tempted to walk back to the café and get a cup now, but he knew he would have to go home with Aerwyna soon. It didn't take long for Aerwyna to have ten different jars filled with tea and some other kind of dark blue liquid. Aerwyna smiled up at Cailean staring at the jar with curiosity he smiled at the jar, he didn't know what she was up to but whatever it was he was sure to love it.

***

 After leaving the market they had enough things in their bags to last them ages, as well as enough tea to last them a decade.

"Why did you get two of the same tea?"

He was curious because she had gotten two jars of the tea made from black tea leaves, dried orange peel and cinnamon. It was one that she had brewed before, maybe it was one that she bought for someone else. Aerwyna looked up at him and smiled, it was then that he realised who she had brought the tea for.

"Let me guess. That ones for my father."

Aerwyna didn't say anything, she just smiled, and he knew he had it right. She did say that she would bring him some tea next time they went to visit. He guessed it had been a while now, it had been a few months since Aerwyna was found in the tree that first time. The longer she was with him the harder he was finding it to let her go. His hand rested by his side along with Aerwyna's thoughts ran through his head about taking her hand in his, feeling her touch against his. He wondered what it would feel like, who ignited sparks just like that kiss, would it bring her closer to him, would he get a chance to kiss her again. The thought of it all made him smile, it seemed like she had the same idea as a few seconds later he felt a tiny hand wiggle into his. Aerwyna had taken his hand first, which was rare for her as she was still a little worried about most of the things at home. Every time she saw the tree a look of sadness wormed her way onto her face even though she tried to hide it from him. Cailean had seen many things that made her sad at home; the recent one was when he would catch her looking at the letter her parents sent her. He hoped in his heart that there was something he could do to make her happy again, her smile to him was all the joy he needed. It seemed to him at that moment with her hand in his, her by his side maybe was all she needed to be happy, he hoped that just being near him was enough. If that was all it took, then that would be what he would do.

***

Cailean decided to take the long route home as he had something special to show Aerwyna in hope it would make her smile. He took

168

her up the firefly path. It was a cold dark path, but it became a magical paradise at night. He wouldn't tell her why; Cailean just took the bags from her hands and took her hand once more making sure he had a firm hold on her. Cailean took her up step by mossy step, moss had started to grow over the beams that lined the staircase slightly covering the stairs up to the field. Trees arched over the sky shielding them from the stars and the night sky that was starting to build. A few rays of light made their way through the treetops casting the path in an ambient glow. It didn't take long for him to put the bags down and stop in the middle of the steps.

"Why did we stop?"

He didn't say anything, he just smiled and told her to wait and see. Aerwyna of course being small thought something was going to happen up in the sky, so she bent her head backwards her hair nearly touching the floor which cause Cailean a gather it all up wrapping it around and tie it with a bow at the bottom of her head so it wouldn't get dirty, he didn't want his little caramel to get her hair dirty, he had gotten used to calling her his little caramel even though his never said it to her, or even said it aloud, to him that what she was, his little caramel fairy. She turned her head and gave it a little shake loosening her hair a little which cause Kelpie to give her a stern look, she had found over the last couple of month that she like to torment him, and she knew that best way to do that was while he was putting her hair up yet again. She knew he liked her hair and didn't want it to get dirty, so she found great fun in tormenting him with it, it was the only thing she found that she could use against him. It was then that her smile dropped to a wide-open mouth gaze. He guessed at the moment the surprise he had for her finally raised their sleepy heads. Because Aerwyna's head was looking up at the sky she hadn't noticed the fireflies rising up from the long blades of grass that sat below the trees. The fireflies floated all around them illuminating the enclosed path they were in. Cailean raised his head looking up at the fireflies filling the enclosed space before tilting his head down and seeing Aerwyna looking at the in wide eye amazement.

"They're beautiful."

Aerwyna turned her head slightly looking at Cailean who was already looking down at her. Life couldn't get much better than it was now he thought he had Aerwyna beside him every day and seeing her in the mornings was pure bliss for him. She looked back to the fireflies that were floating all around them, not quite hearing Cailean speak.

"Yes, you are."

She turned her head to him and shook. She didn't know if she had heard that correctly, but she hoped she did. Aerwyna looked at him with wide eyes instead of the fireflies had he just said she was beautiful. she was at a loss for words how did one respond to that, if that was even what he said, did she ask him to repeat it he hadn't ever said anything like that to her before. Aerwyna didn't know what to say or do so she grabbed a loose section of her hair and started passing it through her hands. Cailean had seen her do this several times before when she didn't know how to react to a new situation. Cailean placed his hand on her shoulder, he raised a hand to her chin bringing her eyes to him. He could see she was trying to find a way to reply to what he had just said to her.

"If you're at a loss for words, you don't have to force yourself. That in itself is a form of comfort."

She smiled at him a little more at ease now. That was what Cailean wanted, her to be happy and to smile a lot, seeing she confused and sad broke his heart a little bit every time. She was still nervous most of the time, either when someone walked into the shop or a loud noise happened, she would hide herself away. He knew where she would hide away until she had calmed herself down, he found it ironic that her hiding place was under his desk, she always said she felt safe there because it reminded her of him and the fact he would never leave her. It had always made him smile thinking of that, but at present showing her how amazing this world could be was what made everything so much better. If she enjoyed the fireflies, what he had in

store up the path was going to truly shock her.

Chapter Eighteen

Meteor Shower

Kelpie took Aerwyna's hand once more leading her up to their next

destination, walking up the illuminated path and away from the

fireflies. The further they got away from the fireflies the darker the

path became, and the tighter Aerwyna's grip was on Caileans hand.

Walking up the path in the dark was difficult for Aerwyna because

unlike Cailean who had Kelpie eyes, her eyes wouldn't adapt to the

dark. Cailean felt Aerwyna grip tighten quickly as her foot slipped on

the moss-covered stairs quickly, he dropped the bags he was carrying,

pulling her up and into his arms. His arms came to rest under her legs

and her wings had fallen out of her cape spreading themselves to their

full glory, it was the first time Cailean had fully seen her wings, they

were beautiful the low glow of the fireflies illuminated certain parts

making them shine, his hands themselves rested under them on the

small of her back her hair had fallen free from the bun he had placed

it in earlier allowing it to fall free down over his arm and down her

back, in between her wings. Her arms wrapped themselves around his

neck bringing her face closer to his than it had been in a while. The

look in her eyes said it all, if she kept looking at him the way she was, everything he had kept hidden for such a long time was going to come out. He didn't know if Aerwyna was ready for everything he was thinking or feeling yet. But when he thought about putting her down it didn't feel right. It felt like she belonged in her arms right where she was. He moved her around a little, so she was sitting on the crook of his one arm while he crouched down picking up the bags her arms had come to rest on his shoulder and around his neck given the support she needed to balance on his arm. With his other hand he collected the bags, not allowing Aerwyna to wiggle her way off his arm, even though it would have been easy to do.

"It's probably safer for me to carry you up the stairs."

Aerwyna just nodded her head snuggling down on her arm against his shoulder, it surprised her how warm he was seeing he was a water spirit, she thought they would be cold blooded and therefore feel cold to the touch, but Cailean was much different he felt so warm, and she felt safe in his arms. It didn't take her long before she was falling asleep against him.

***

Cailean realised that she had fallen asleep and manoeuvred her to rest against his chest so she wouldn't fall, looking down at her when he reached the top of the stairs to find that Aerwyna had moved herself to lie in the nook of his shoulder and fallen back asleep once more, she had awoken a little when he had readjusted her position, but it looks like it didn't take her long to fall back asleep once more. Cailean didn't know what was best to do, leave her to sleep or wake her up to see the magic that was going to happen, he chose the latter. He sat crossed legged on the cool grass resting Aerwyna between the nook of his legs, still keeping her head rested against his shoulder. He left her there for a while looking around at the tree enclosed field they were currently sitting in. This field was one place he came to when he first arrived in this world, it reminded him so much of his home. The trees enclosed around only letting in some rays of the low moonlight through while they never grew in the middle leaving an accessible area where people and others could see the clear sky on a good night. It looked similar to the trees by the waterfall where they had the picnic at the palace. He felt a small hand come to rest against his cheek he hadn't realised a tear started to run down his cheek and Aerwyna had woken wiping the tear away.

"Sorry I didn't mean to wake you up. Sorry for crying as well." Aerwyna's face dropped, it hurt her to think he had to feel sorry for crying in front of her. To her and her people crying was a sign that you had been strong for far too long and needed a shoulder to rest upon. Aerwyna wiggled out of his lap and onto her knees wrapping her arms around his neck pulling him into a hug, it didn't take him long before he swung his arms around her pulling her as close to him as he possibly could. It was at that moment that the sky lit up the field with thousands of meteors shooting though the sky. The sky was clear of any and all clouds leaving a sky full of stars, the Nexttron galaxy was even visible which was rare for this time of year. It sat on the left-hand side of the sky illuminating the entire field with all its stars. The meteors shot across the sky right in front leaving the sky in a hue of blue and purples. Aerwyna sat there, her arms still wrapped around his neck, who was now enjoying the sight that all in this realm beheld for them in front of his eyes. The sight of the meteors and stars behind Aerwyna illuminating her caramel hair made his heart flutter. She spun around on her knees resting her head against his chest, his arms came around enveloping her in a hug keeping her close and warm while they watched the meteors shoot magically across the star covered sky.

"Doubt the stars are fire, doubt that the sun doth move, doubt truth be a liar, but never doubt I love."

Aerwyna turned to look at Caileans face smiling, she placed a chaise kiss upon his cheek which resulted in Caileans face turning so red she could see it in the dark of night. He got embarrassed with Aerwyna looking at him so, so he turned her back around resting her back once more against his chest, while his arms were tucked underneath her arms keeping her safe, and close to him.

***

Cailean propped himself up with his hands against the cool grass Aerwyna tried her hardest, but she had fallen asleep not long ago, Kelpie sat there looking up at the sky enjoying the cool night air and the stars a little while longer. Aerwyna had turned onto her side resting her head against his shoulder with one hand resting on his chest and her legs tucked up in the nook of his legs. He rested one hand on her hair running his fingers through the lengths. Her hair was soft and smelt like wildflowers, it was quickly becoming his favourite scent. He quickly figured out a way to carry both her and the bags of shopping all the way back home. He scooped her up in his left arms once more resting her head against his shoulder while one hand came to fall behind his shoulders. Because she was of a small stature, she was easy to carry one handed. Cailean took one more look at the stars and galaxy as well as one more look at Aerwyna's sleeping face before trudging along through the forest towards their home. Walking back down the stairs the fireflies still illuminated the stairs making it easy to follow down and find the exit back towards the main path. The main path wasn't that long from where they diverted off of, a few moments more up the main path and over the bridge and they were

177

back to the house back home. Walking through the door he placed the shopping bags filled with every kind of tea and jam he thought existed as well as the mysterious box that Aerwyna had so carefully tried to hide from him, the temptation to open it was strong, but he resisted with all his might. He just shook his head and smiled knowing what she was like. She had brought something that she didn't really need to buy., but had brought anyway. Walking up the stairs he removed Aerwyna cloak and shoes and placed her into bed, Cailean was surprised that he made it all the way back home and she hadn't woken up since she fell asleep in the field. He tucked her in, making sure she was all snuggled up and warm before waking back down to put the jams and teas away, that was when he noticed a letter on the floor in front of the Fairy door Aerwyna emerged from at the very beginning. He bent to pick it up seeing it had no addressee on the front, He decided to open the letter in case it was important, there was no name he thought maybe on the start of the letter it might say who it was for. He had a feeling it was for Aerwyna, but many things had

changed and surprised him numerous times. It was then he saw the seal of the Fairy royalty and assumed it was from Aerwyna's parents. Cailean opened it just to check but what he found surprised him the most. It was a letter from Aerwyna's betrothed.

Chapter Nineteen.

Prince Aelfdane

Kelpie sat by the unlit fire and read the letter by moonlight, if he were writing to her, it couldn't be good, he hadn't contacted her once since she re-awoke from the tree, Saoirse even told him that he didn't worry when she disappeared originally, if he was her betrothed it must have be a political matching if he didn't worry when she had disappeared for several years, but surely some part of him must have cared if he waited all that time for her. As he read his worst fears were confirmed as his heart sank. There was no love or even a caring thought anywhere in this letter, it was completely political, he must have waited for her for some reason but what it was he didn't know. But he knew one thing there was no way he was going to hand her over to someone so cold and heartless. He refolded the letter and placed in back inside its envelope before walking back towards the kitchen so he could put away the shopping. Aerwyna woke early that morning earlier than she had done before, maybe it was because she fell asleep much easier than normal for, plus she was tired from walking around the town. She plodded downstairs after changing her dress and brushing her hair before she platted it down one side. Once she reached the kitchen, she gathered up all the ingredients she needed for the tea that morning which was the love potion she had got from the market yesterday which included dried hibiscus, dried apples, dried strawberries, coconut, minced dried lemon and a little bit of cinnamon. Reaching the front room, she filled up the cauldron with water from the kitchen and set it over the fire. It was then that she saw the letter on the side where Kelpie had left it the night before. She turned it over in her hands trying to find who it was too but to no avail, so she done what she thought was best she looked for the addressee on the inside. So, she Opened the letter

***

Dear Princess, Aerwyna

I am writing this letter to you to tell you that I have chosen the right partner for my life and that is you. It took me a lot of thinking and after that I have come up with a decision. I thus propose you become my better half. I am sure that you would be perfect in every way for me. It has been quite some time now and we have been talking to each other.

She wondered if he had the right person, she thought how he could have been talking to her when she was in the tree for so long, did she emerge from the tree before and no recollection or did she talk to him before she even went in the tree. She covered her head with her hand, trying to remember hurt her head but she had to know so she continued to read.

Also, the meetings that we have had in the past are moments to cherish. Thus take this letter as my marriage proposal, once more, also, now that you have my question, I will be eagerly waiting for your reply and decision on the same. Please reply as soon as possible as I will be eagerly waiting for it. Your parents already gave their blessing and consent so all you have to do is come back and say yes.

Thanking you,

Yours truly,

Prince Aelfdane

Aerwyna covered her mouth with her hand, everything her parents said in their letter was true, she had a betrothed, and it meant she was a princess with responsibilities. Could she still stay here with Cailean even if she were a fairy princess? She thought that maybe if she wrote to her parents and explained the situation of her feeling that maybe they would cancel this betrothal. She looked up and saw Cailean leaning against the door frame.

"Sorry I was going to tell you this morning so you wouldn't have to read it alone, I came in last night and it was on the floor in front of the tree. I'm not sure what he meant by it but if you want to go back and sort it out then I'll go with you, but I'll support you in any decision you make."

Aerwyna dropped the letter just as fast as she picked it up running towards him wrapping her arms around his waist and burying her face in his chest. After calming her down with the tea she had pre brew for them and the remainder of the food from the town yesterday, they began to speak about all the things that were worrying her. Aerwyna told Kelpie that her dreams still haunted her. Mainly the one where she ended up in the tree, but others had started to make their way into her mind. Aerwyna assumed they were her memories, which scared her, the person she was in them wasn't who she was now seeing how she was she could understand why she was shut away in the tree.

"I was such a horrible person that I even put myself in a tree."

It was the first time that Cailean didn't know what to do or say to help Aerwyna or to stop her crying, all he could do was place an arm around her and hope she found comfort in that. Seeing Aerwyna cry was horrible. All she could think about was how much she hurt people to the point they wanted to get rid of her. What worried her the most was if she went back home would she revert back to that person once more. Almost knowing what she was thinking Cailean said only one line before walking down the second staircase towards the store. What he had said was enough for Aerwyna to realise that even if she went home who she was now that was all that mattered, from what she saw she was completely different and that had to account for something. Aerwyna grabbed a pen and some paper writing down the words by yourself. An original is so much better than a copy. The words Cailean said to her, she would hold them close to her and whenever she felt down, she had them to look at and hopefully feel more like herself once more. Aerwyna walked to the bathroom washed her face over removing any evidence of her tears before walking downstairs to help open the shop.

***

This day was a little different to most other days, many people had walked down from the town and were browsing in their shop. What surprised them was many had left with handmade clocks or had brought their clocks in for repairs. It surprised Aerwyna seeing so many people in the shop. Many people were buying both her and Kelpie's hand carved clocks. Which surprised her as she didn't think anyone would buy any of hers. After a couple of hours, the shop had quieted down quite a bit with only a few people still browsing around. Aerwyna removed her oil covered apron and walked to the kitchen to make a cup of tea and some snacks for Cailean, he was busy rushing around tending to the other patrons. Aerwyna made a brew of loose black tea, peppermint, dried orange blossom, pink peppercorns,

183

cloves, and to add a little sweetness she added a tiny amount of chocolate. It was one of her favourite blends she created . It smelt like the holidays, the type that made you all warm and feel loved. She paired that with a few, sugar plum fairy cookies and walked into the workshop to place the tray next to him. When she got in there the workshop and shop was completely empty all of the patrons had left with their spoils. Aerwyna was thankful that the workshop had emptied out; it was a lot quieter, and she didn't have to be so conscious about hiding her wings from anyone. After letting her wings loose, she felt Kelpie come up behind her trying to sneak a cookie from the tray without her seeing. Aerwyna pretended not to notice she just shook her head and gave a little chuckle, turning her head to look up at him he gave her a coy little smile.

"Thank you, my fairy."

Cailean bent his head placing a light kiss on top of her head. He had started to call her his fairy recently since going to town, he didn't know when he started it, but he couldn't be bothered to stop. He still had to be careful to call her his Carmel fairy; he thought that might worry her too much. He enjoyed these little moments they had together. In these little moments I seemed like time stopped, and everything was on pause, everything could just remind how they were with him and her being them. That was until a cough was heard behind Kelpie who's back was faced towards the Fairy realm tree.

"Ahem, I'm looking for someone, would either of you be able to help?"

The sound caused both Cailean and Aerwyna to turn around and look towards the tree to find a tall well-built slender man standing in front of the tree. He had pure white hair that was parted in the middle and swept back a few strands escaping falling over his eyes. His eyes were blue but there was something Cailean didn't like about how dark his eyes looked, there was something menacing about them. He was pale skinned similar to both him and Aerwyna, but something seemed off, he wasn't as pale as a Kelpie and was more tanned than a fairy, he was clad in a white low cut laced up short sleeve tunic, which was half covered with a dark green armoured arm piece which was laced up the left-hand side with as strap under the right arm keeping the piece in place. Several dark green belts of a similar style were draped around his waist, Criss-crossing over his midriff. a darker green bet hung low on his hips holding his arrows on the small of his back, his bow perched over his armoured left arm. White fabric was wrapped tightly around his forearms shielding his arms from the impact of the bow string. The green trousers he wore finished off his ensemble with similar dark green calf high boots. What drew Aerwyna eyes to him was his pet bird he had perched on his right forearm, it was a magnificent bird of blues and greens, long feathers made up its tail floating down, his head was similar with feathers that flowed down its back like hair that led to its small dark blue face and beak. Aerwyna recognized it from her realm; it was an Ophelia bird, she hadn't seen one this colour, but it was beautiful. Ophelia birds were frequented in all four forests of the fairy realm, Aerwyna had remembered that her realm was split into four those being the summer, spring, autumn and winter. She herself was from autumn which didn't explain all the green she wore and the flowers, when the man in her dream which she presumed was her father wore oranges and reds with autumn leaves around his head. Aerwyna looked at him trying to see if she recognized him as male fairy were able to conceal their wings unlike female fairies.

"Umm, yes of course, we shall help in any way possible."

Aerwyna had once described to him what they were like when they hid their wings, they could conceal them that all the better than females due to always going to wars and fights. Cailean stared at the stranger; he didn't like how he was looking at her. Aerwyna couldn't shake the feeling that she knew this person from somewhere, but she invited him into the lounge while Kelpie grabbed another cup from the kitchen. The stranger explained a brief description of the person he was looking for. Which piqued the interest of Cailean as the description he gave was remarkably similar to Aerwyna, in fact, it was almost exactly like Aerwyna, but there was subtle differences like her personality and her eyes, which didn't seem like her he told them that who he was looking for didn't care about other people's opinions and would make sure that they knew that she didn't care and make them feel meaningless. The only things that he had said that sounded like her was that she had long caramel coloured hair and she disappeared wearing a green dress with a floral head ring crown. He told them it was a gift from him to her on the eve of their engagement, but she had disappeared moments later. He had just presumed that she had run off not wanting to marry him but was too scared to tell her parents. The sound of his voice proved that he cared extraordinarily little in the fact that she had run away from him that day. Which made Cailean curious as to why he was here now looking for this mysterious woman. The only way Cailean thought this could be settled was to ask who he was looking for and more importantly find out who this stranger was.

"If you tell us the name, we might be able to help you …"

Cailean added extra time on the you part he asked, hoping, praying that the stranger would get the hint and give up his name.

Thankfully for him he got the hint, he rose from the spare stool which was normally used for the Brownies. Placing one arm in front around his midriff and the other on the small of his back as he bowed, his Ophelia bird flew up onto his shoulder.

"By my word, excuse my bad manners, I'm looking for my fiancée, a princess of sorts she would be hiding in this realm I suppose. My name is Prince Aelfdane of the Samhradh forest, a part of the Fairy realm. Pleased to make your acquaintance."

He offered his hand up to Aerwyna, seemingly to place a kiss on the back of her hand similar to most princes. She looked back at Cailean, her eyes pleading with him to tell her what to do. Should she take his hand or leave it and turn away.

Chapter Twenty

Recognition

Cailean didn't know what the best cause of action would be in this situation. Aerwyna's fiancée was here, in their house, looking for her. He looked down at Aerwyna whose face was white as a sheet she had obviously realised who was standing in front of her. The fear struck her almost immediately, he was here, and he was here for her. Aerwyna looked up at Cailean pleading with him with her eyes on some advice on what to do. It seemed to him that this prince hadn't recognized Aerwyna yet, so they were safe for now, but he didn't think it would be long till he found her out.

"Of course, we can help you out. We don't have any rooms that you can stay in around here; the closest is in the town. It's not that far from here. I can give you a map to help you. Maybe they might be able to help you. Bit of advice for you though, maybe keep the wings hidden when you're there. People here are not really fond of our kind, or yours although there are some exceptions."

Cailean placed his arms around Aerwyna to bring her to his side and away from the prince. The further she was from him the better it was, there was a feeling he was getting from this Aelfdane, and it wasn't good. He lent down and whispered in Aerwyna's ear telling her to go upstairs and stay there until he came to her. All Aerwyna could do was nod her head so many things were running through her head, she had been found and if he found out who she was she would be dragged back, and made to marry him. The prince's eyes followed Aerwyna as she walked past him and up the stairs, he could see there was something about her that was intriguing to him, but he had a mission to completely find his bride and bring her home to marry her, and no little human distraction although similar were going to distract him. Aerwyna sat upstairs hiding in Kelpie's room for she felt the safest there. She hoped this prince wouldn't think to start looking for her. She had changed a lot since she was last there and since he last saw her. She hoped and prayed that she had changed enough that he wouldn't recognize her.

***

A long time had passed since she went upstairs to hide Aerwyna hope Cailean was okay everything had gotten so quiet. She peered out of the door to hear footsteps start walking up the stairs growing louder and louder. Fear struck her again he realised it was her and was coming for her, she scanned the room looking for a place to hide. The room was bare; she was stuck with nowhere to hide and nowhere to go. She ran to a corner and pressed herself up against the wall as best she could, praying that she could make herself small enough that he wouldn't notice her hiding just behind the door. The door opened a little bit more as heavy footsteps entered the room Aerwyna held her breath trying to remain as still and silent as possible. The footsteps stopped just inside the door Aerwyna held her breath for what seemed like ages to her, that was until she heard Caileans voice from down the stairs calling up.

"The bathrooms down here if you're looking for it."

The prince let out a loud sign. Scanning the room once more, he had checked all the other rooms up here and she wasn't in any of them.

"I was sure she could have been her; she had the same hair colour. I wouldn't forget that dirty rust coloured hair anytime soon. Her features were not anything to put a rose to if anything she didn't look like a fairy at all. It would have been better if she had never resurfaced at all, then all the kingdoms could be mine."

With that he left, and the loud footsteps made their way down the stairs getting quieter and quieter as he went. Making sure she was safe Aerwyna unwrapped her arms from around his midriff unable to stop the tears from falling. His words hit her hard. He was right, she was rusty and nowhere near as beautiful as a rose. She couldn't stop the tears from falling. Closing the door, she turned and went to sit on

Caileans bed. If she stayed here, she would just cause him more trouble with things similar to this. It was obvious people were going to try and find her now that she was free. Aerwyna looked up at the ceiling trying to stop the tears from flowing, she thought of her day in town with him and how perfect that was, if all her days could be like that, she would be happy. She wondered what would be best to stay here with him but have the constant worry that someone would come for her and possibly endanger Cailean and everyone else in the town to get her, or just go with him now and end all of this now. Aerwyna knew she didn't have much time to make her decisions, but there were so many facts to consider with each decision. It was at that moment when she was the most down, she had heard her mother's voice give her some well needed advice to give her strength. Beauty begins the moment you decide to yourself and decide your own future. Confidence is radiance and loving yourself is beauty. Just by remembering that she had all the strength she needed to face this prince, he couldn't just come here and try to bring her back when he didn't even know her, he couldn't define her by the colour of her hair or even have the audacity to compare her to a rose, he was not the person who could define her only she could define herself, no one else could do that, and she wouldn't let them even try.

***

Aerwyna threw off her cloak revealing her wings, she wasn't afraid of anything he was willing to or had already tried. If anything, Cailean would have her back, there was no way he could harm her or even get near her before he stepped in. She marched down the stair's determination plain on her face she was going to give him of piece of her mind and tell him that she wasn't going to go back with him, she wasn't going to give up her kingdom to him and there was no way he was going to define her because only she could do that. She realised in that moment he would be the prince of his own kingdom why did her need hers so bad and why did he want all kingdoms, there was something that just didn't make sense about it all, but she would find that out later when she talked to Cailean he would have something in his multitude of book to help her. Right now, she needs to shut down an obnoxious asshole of a price. Approaching the doorway Aerwyna placed a hand over her heart feeling its rhythm taking a slow deep breath she said to herself, you have all the power you need if you dared look for it, with that she marched into the lounge. She stormed into the lounge where they were when she left, ready to give this stuck-up prince a piece of her mind. Storming into the lounge took more courage than Aerwyna thought she had once she was in there. The prince had already left for town to search for a place to spend the night until he found her. A sigh big enough for Cailean to hear escaped her lips before she fell to the floor landing on her knees on the floor, all the courage she had left her in that one moment, replacing itself with relief. Cailean knelt beside her, placing a hand on her shoulder.

"Everything will be okay. I won't let him take you away. No one should have to do something they don't want to do. There's no way he will be able to hurt you in any way, especially while I'm around. I will never let anyone hurt you not now, not ever"

Caileans arms enveloped Aerwyna in a deep warming embrace hoping that in some way his embrace would help her forget all the trouble and worry in the world and just think of him for this moment for as long as it calmed her. Aerwyna couldn't help but make herself cosy in his embrace. Just being within his arms helped her forget, forget that her idiotic betrothed imbecile was just in the town, that her parents wrote her a letter letting her know, all of it was building up near spilling over what she could handle. All of it was instantly forgotten the instant Kelpie held her in his arms.

***

She told Cailean about what the douche had said in the room which cause his temper the runoff the charts, one for even having the nerve to go upstairs sand entre her room without knocking or even gaining permission to enter from the occupant of the room, to calling her most beautiful caramel hair rust. But what confused him the most about what Aerwyna had told him was the fact he said then all the kingdom will be mine, in order for him to do that he would have had to either win a battle with the neighbouring forests or inherit them through marriage like he was trying with Aerwyna. If he were already married surely her parents wouldn't allow him to be betrothed. It was all very peculiar, and would be something he would have to research, who was this Prince Aelfdane and what did he want with Aerwyna.

Chapter Twenty-One
Time

It dawned on Cailean that now that Prince Aelfdane was here, it was only a matter of time before he found Aerwyna. Which now meant their time together was limited, there was so much he hadn't shown her yet and now he wouldn't get a chance to, unless he found a way to extend their time together. Cailean ransacked his vast bookshelves from all the different worlds hoping praying there was something that could help them. Every book he went through held no answers, anything that would half help them was either lost for all eternity or stolen away to another land which had no door. He knew within himself that he wouldn't give up until he found something to help. He was down to the very last book when Aerwyna strolled into the room with a tray of tea and his favourite cookies.

"Cailean it's time to put the books down now and have some tea, today we've got raspberry rose tea and of course your favourite cookies."

He couldn't help but smile, Aerwyna was dressed in her favourite purple dress, the long sleeves complimented her long slender arms the colour complimented her hair in the best way possible by making itself a perfect backing for the multitude of different shades of caramel that intertwined themselves within her hair. Her wings even though slightly transparent radiated the different hues and shades of both her dress and hair. He wouldn't ever forget how they shined along the firefly path. He couldn't help but smile. It made him laugh how she didn't even have to do a thing to make him smile. His smile increased even more before he pushed himself up off of the desk before making his way over to where she had set up the tea. It didn't take long before Kelpie decided to torment Aerwyna a little, he reached his hands towards her waist knowing she was the most ticklish there.

Aerwyna saw what he was doing from the corner of her eye.

"You wouldn't dare?"

The smile on his face turned into a wicked grin as he crouched down holding both hands up in the air where she could see them making himself looked armed and ready.

"Oh, wouldn't I?"

Aerwyna saw the wicked glint in his eyes before she ran at full speed out the back door, she knew that once he got a hold of her, he wouldn't let her go. The wicked grin grew before he was clambering out of the nearby window onto the low wall before jumping to the ground just outside. Just as Aerwyna had rounded the corner looking behind thinking she left him in the dust. When she turned her head, it revealed Cailean leaning up against the wall on the other side smiling like a devil.

"O-oh my god! H-how are you here?"

Confusion was all over Aerwyna's face that was flushed from running away from him the best he could.

"Did you teleport here, can Kelpies even teleport, it is not normal to be able to get her that fast you were just there and now you're here. It's not normal."

"You're cute when you say what's on your mind, why are you running away?"

Cailean looked at the ground and slowly ever so slowly took the distance between them away step by step getting closer and closer to her.

"Y-You know exactly why I was running away. I saw that look in your eye and that can only lead to one of two things."

Every step he took closer towards her she took two back, but she was running out of room for you to see the river at the back of the house was fast approaching her.

"What look are you talking about? Describe it to me?"

The wicked glint in his eyes only intensified as Aerwyna looked to the ground realising this wasn't working which caused Cailean to smile more, that was until he realised that in two more steps Aerwyna would end up in the still calm river behind her.

"It's an honour to know that I leave you speechless."

"It's good to know that you know."

Aerwyna tried to keep her voice steady as he continued to approach her. Aerwyna's face deepened to a shade of red that Kelpie didn't know a face could go. Aerwyna looked up at his eyes for only a second before looking back at the ground again. She started to walk back again but Kelpie's reflexes were quicker he grabbed her arm and pulled her back. Kelpie looked down at her and the wicked grin turned soft.

"This isn't enough."

"What's that?"

Aerwyna quickly pointed over his shoulder hoping he would look, giving her a chance to run away but to no avail.

"I'm not fooled."

He ran his hands down her arms taking her hands in his.

"Please stop rejecting me. Do you know how many times you've rejected me?"

He gave a gentle tug on her hands bringing her a tiny bit closer to him.

"I have to hear whether or not you will accept this confession, so Please don't run away."

Aerwyna looked to the ground again, her hands still within his.

"I understand I'll listen to you so let go of me and we'll talk over tea. Okay?"

"Really"

He slowly let go of her hands, but as he did Aerwyna smiled and turned tail and ran back inside the house. Cailean turned to the door and couldn't help but smile. He knew she would be sitting by that fire and would listen to everything and anything he had to stay, whether they felt the same about extending their time was yet to be seen.

***

Aerwyna's scream could have been heard from everywhere, the instant sound of it sent fear and terror straight through Cailean. Grabbing a log of wood that was perched against the wall he ran back inside to see to his amazement wind of a multitude of colours whipped around the room doused the fire out, threw things around the room a few things falling and breaking, the power of the wind nearly was able to push him back out through the door, but he was too stubborn and grabbed hold of things that were nailed to the ground pulling himself closer and closer to where Aerwyna was holding the book he was previously looking at. Her eyes changed colour, they had an almost ominous glow about them when she was holding the book like it was talking to her and her to it. When Cailean reached her, he could hear the chant she was uttering.

"Seall dhuinn na tha sinn a 'sireadh, na tha sinn a' feuchainn ri lorg. Cuidich sinn le bhith a 'lorg na h-ùine, an àm airson ar lorg. Lorg sinn clach Myrios."

Cailean quickly grabbed some paper that was tucked under a rock to write down what Aerwyna was saying. All he could pick up so far was Show us what we seek, what we seek to find. Help us find the time, the time to find us. Let us find the Myrios stone. Almost like someone was speaking through Aerwyna the rules of the stone were given.

"Rach gu fàinne na sìthe, chan fhaigh ach an cridhe agus an t-anam as fìor-ghlan clach na truaighe. Nuair a lorgar cleachdadh a-mhàin nuair a tha cruaidh fheum air an ùine fhèin tha e mì-chinnteach. Aon uair 's gu bheil thu aig an fhàinne-sìthe, coimhead airson an soidhne sìthiche aig dol fodha na grèine gus a' chlach a lorg, ach bi faiceallach mu iomadh cunnart air an t-slighe. Feumaidh tu a bhith treun agus làidir; feumaidh tu a bhith an urra ri chèile gus an obair agad a dhèanamh.

chan eil an seo ach aon de cheithir, lean a' chiad boillsgeadh gus

leantainn air adhart chun ath fhear gus clach Myrios a lorg."

Cailean barely had enough time to finish writing before Aerwyna let

go of the book, halting all wind and talk radiating from the book, it

wasn't long before she dropped to the fall, Cailean being just slightly

faster catching her before she hit the floor with full force. After

placing Aerwyna on the soft bed in another room Cailean went to

look at what Aerwyna had said from the book. Looking at the paper

in hand he read.

"Go to the fairy ring, only the purest of heart and soul will find the

Myrios stone. When found use only when desperately needed time

itself is uncertain. Once at the fairy ring, find the fairy sign only at

sunset to find the stone, but beware of many dangers along the way.

You have to be brave and strong; you have to depend on each other to

do your job. This Is just one of four, follow the first clue to continue

to the next one to find the Myrios stone"

Unfortunately, he wasn't able to write it all down, he hoped that

Aerwyna would be able to fill in the blanks. He looked up the stairs

and he thought about Aerwyna how dangerous the fairies ring could

be, he couldn't risk taking her through one, he wondered if there was

an easier way to extend their time before she was taken from him

forever.

Chapter Twenty – Two

The Myrios Stone

Over the next couple of days both Aerwyna and Cailean looked at

what was noted down what she had said while holding a book and

attempted to decipher what it meant. Noting down each clue

separately they started to work.

"Go to the fairy ring,

Only the purest of heart and soul will find the Myrios stone,

When found use only when desperately needed time itself is

uncertain,

But beware of many dangers along the way,

You have to be brave and strong; you have to depend on each other to

do your job,

This is just one of four,

Follow the first clue to continue to the next to find the Myrios stone."

Looking at a section at a time Cailean tried to think where the nearest

Fairy ring was, he hadn't seen one in the area when on his little

adventures to town and back. Maybe it was further than town, further

than he had already explored on his own. Rising from the chair he

walked over to one of the hidden cabinets pulling out a single slightly yellowing page. Cailean carried it over like it was the most delicate

thing in the world, unrolling it with the gentlest hand it revealed itself

to be a map of the area. The isle of Kirkessie, was a small isle in itself

but once on the isle, it went on for mile and miles, this map also

included all the hidden entryways on and off the isle both magical and

other. The walk around the isle would take weeks, if lore filled people

didn't use these hidden ways. To find the fairy ring was going to be a

challenge to his memory; there were three different fairies' rings in

and around the isle. Finding which one was going to be the challenge,

searching all of them would take them valuable time that they didn't

have. The prince was here searching for her any time they wasted

brought him closer to finding her, and Cailean didn't want to think

what he would make her do if he found her. He couldn't let that

happen; he wouldn't let that happen. Turning his head slightly to the

left he saw Aerwyna wide eyed staring at the map, it was most likely

the first time that she had seen a map.

He knew that the fairies' realm didn't have to have any form of maps

to see where they were going; it was all just laid out in front of them.

It wasn't hard to find your way in their realm. He could imagine that

flying high above the clouds seeing the world all at once was a once

in a lifetime thing, one that they got to experience every day. It was

easy on the ground as well. Aerwyna told him that the trees changed depending on which forest season you walked into. He could imagine that at first it would be strange to walk from summer to autumn and winter to spring, but he imagined it would be the most beautiful thing.

***

Looking deeply at the map there was only one fairy ring that he thought the riddle made the most sense about, but there were two problems: one it was the other side of the isle the other they would have to go through the valley of the Banshees. He had heard many stories and tales of the valley of the Banshees, none of them good. He had heard they were used to warn people that death was near, if her wails were heard the louder they were the closer to death they were. In the valley of the Banshee, they used the echoes of the mountain side to lure unexpecting people into danger. Her wail would echo of the mountains, led them to danger in hope of guarding the valley, what the Banshee didn't know what that at the end of their valley was nothing it was just an empty field, but they never left the valley so they were never aware, he didn't like that fact that they never listened to anyone either, it didn't matter how many times they tried to tell them or justify their case to be allowed to walk through, nothing worked. His father had told him that many Kelpies had been lost to the Banshee; he hoped that they wouldn't add to that total. They could avoid the valley, but it would take them three times as long either way around to get to the fairy ring, which was a different challenge on its own. You see the fairy ring, he thought it could be on its only island just off the coast of Kirkessie, to get there would be a challenge in itself as he didn't think there were any boats or modes of transportation there, in that unadopted area. He knew from his books that when a fairy's wings got wet, they couldn't fly and escape any dangers that followed them, they had to rely just on their legs to escape dangers. He knew that it would be dangerous to go through the banshee valley, but he couldn't think of any other way. Cailean looked over and Aerwyna once more saw her smile with amazement at the maps and all the different places made him smile, for her he would risk it all. He found if he had to be the one to carry her all across the ocean with her on his back so be it, he would do it, he didn't care that it would exhaust him. He would risk everything but her. Travelling through the valley could endanger her more than anything he had to figure out whether it was worth the risk.

***

Packing up the unusable maps, placing them back within the safety of the tree. Cailean realised that night had fallen over them. He would have to work out a plan eventually, finding the fairy ring was only one part of the riddle, he came to the realisation either way Aerwyna would have to go with him, it was common knowledge that Kelpie

206

weren't really welcomed around fairy wings unless they had someone

to speak for them that they were there for good and not for trouble or

worse. It didn't escape his mind that the riddle had physically told

him that in order to finish the mission he would have to bring her

along, and that brought along its own challenges and problems but on

the plus side he got more time with her, that was what they were

doing this for, for time together. For her he would defend her against

anything his challenge had in store for them.

Chapter Twenty – Three

Adventure

Once packing all supplies they would need in one big backpack that

Cailean held, Aerwyna ran all over the shop collecting practical

things such as spare clothes and shoes and things like cloth that they

could use for bandages if either one of them got hurt. She also

collected impractical things such as glass jars of tea, Cailean didn't

think that she realised that they wouldn't have a kettle to boil them

into brew. The idea did cross his mind that maybe there were certain

things in the tea that could be used for medical purposes. Once she

put in everything, she could possibly think of, she bent to try and lift

the tiny pack that he had given her, but it didn't last long as he had

reached down that much quicker than her and picked it up adding it to

the massive pack he carried, as even though she tried with all her

might to get him to let her carry it, he wouldn't let her carry a thing,

much to Aerwyna's annoyance. He had packed everything from

salted meats and long-life biscuits She thought if he wasn't going to

let her carry anything then she was going to pack everything else they

needed such as, book, maps, paper extra provisions, and anything else she could think of. The very idea of travelling around intrigued her, being able to see all this world had to offer, but at the same time, she feared the unknown. How people would see them, how they would see her if at any point her wings were spotted. The fear of people's reaction was what was at the forefront of her mind. As much as Aerwyna tried to push the thought away they kept rising to the surface showing worry on her face, that was until he walked not the room, it was as if just his presents in the room made her relax and the thing that was worrying her didn't seem so bad anymore. She was able to smile again and laugh whenever he was around, maybe this adventure would be fun and maybe it would bring them closer together.

***

"Aerwyna, do you have the maps and the snacks? If so hand them over you're not carrying a thing, you hear me."
Cailean yelled through the shop running around collecting the final few things they needed before they set off. Aerwyna had never seen him run around so frantically. The very sight of him becoming so frantic about so many tiny things made her laugh, he wasn't the frantic type otherwise she would have spent the whole-time chuckling to herself. Propping herself up against the counter she watched him run from one side of the shop to the other and back again, up the

stairs and down the stairs, and everywhere in between. Watching him run around was starting to hurt her neck, she didn't realise he could run so far so every time she tried to follow him, she had to whip her head in another direction just as fast. She placed her hands on the back of her neck trying to release some of the pain that had started to accumulate there.

"Have you finished running around like the Dullahan?"

That cause him to stop in his tracks

"I think you'll find him a lot more attractive than Dullahan. Thank you very much. I have everything: food, drinks, tea and maps but most importantly…"

He wandered over lazily towards Aerwyna, placing a hand on either side of her pinning her between the counter and himself.

"Most importantly?"

He moved one hand from the counter to cup her chin in between his finger and thumb bringing her eyes up to him. The action caused Aerwyna to swallow hard. The close proximity of them was causing her heart to do strange things she hadn't experienced before. Though she found that when he was around her heart did strange things on a regular basis. Her heart was beating so fast she thought it felt like it was going to explore. Cailean picked up on her reaction causing him to smirk, he was sort of glad that he was so much out of practice that he could still make a girl or a woman nervous just by being in his vicinity. She loved his smirk, only one side of his lips tilted up when he did, and it made him look like he wanted to devour her heart and soul. She wouldn't mind if that was want, he wanted to do, if fact she thought that she would rather enjoy being devoured by him, the thoughts in her head maybe her pulse quicken, she placed one of her hand gently on his cheek cupping his face, the action made him lean his face into her hand, his hand snaking around the back of her neck cradling it within the warmth he felt there. His other hand that was once   on the counter rose to rest on top of her hand bringing it to his lips before placing a gentle kiss on her fingertips trailing down her hand and up her arms effectively bringing him closer to her. Cailean raised his eyes to look at hers before he bent his head placing his lips ever so close to her neck his breath was hot on her skin. She could feel his smirk against her skin.

"Most importantly…. I have you."

Cailean nipped at her neck a little before he placed a gentle kiss on top before moving away to pack the bags. Suddenly the air felt cold around her and Aerwyna missed his warmth. Everything was packed and closed down, all the light had been snuffed out; all fires killed the shop was now closed with a sign allowing anyone who would visit the shop the knowledge that it was closed for the foreseeable future but will open again. With all done they set off with maps in hand to find the Myrios stone.

***

Walking along the path to town was as beautiful as it ever was; the bridge was covered with moss and flowers; the river and waterfalls underneath flowed freely creating the most wonderful sound as calming as nature could be. Since the time they walked to town someone had added a wooden rail along the sides, she thought that maybe someone had fallen over and they were put there to prevent anyone else getting hurt, she hoped that whoever had fallen wasn't too badly hurt. The birds were flying around tweeting away singing their songs. Walking around seeing Cailean in front of her reminded her of walking through the woods of Foghar with her mother. The feel, the smells, the safety she felt, she couldn't help but hum along to her favourite lullaby as they walked. This drew Caileans attention; he was loving and fascinated by how much she had changed in such a short time with him, she was still nowhere near what that asshole of a prince said she was like, and he couldn't see how anyone saw her like that. When she first came out of that flower, she wouldn't even speak to him or anyone and now she was walking here beside him humming away, yes, he supposed he didn't know what she was humming but whatever it was sounded beautiful. It made him relax and feel more at

212

ease, there was no mistaking that the very thought of this failing and them having to split up worried his mind, Just the thought of her having to go back to that damn silly bumbling prince was bad enough it made him even more demined, but he found with her humming it wasn't what was at the front of his mind at that moment.

"What are you humming there, Gradh milis ?"

Aerwyna's humming abruptly stopped, she looked at him quizzically like she didn't even realise she was humming. Instead, she just looked at him and smiled.

"Me humming, nope not me."

His smile quirked again, she loved his smile. He tried and tried again to try and get her to start humming again but nothing worked, leaving the bridge they walked through the town picking up anything else they may have forgotten or not had back at the shop. When they reached the far end of the town and looked out to the fields that followed Aerwyna reached for Cailean and Aerwyna was now approaching unknown territory, the fact scared her immensely but knowing he was right beside her made it not seem so bad. They both took a deep breath and took their first steps into the unknown.

***

Aerwyna's face dropped at the sight that was in front of her, the river that flowed beneath the bridge rounded them leaving a bigger

213

stunning river in its stead. The sun had set, casting a purple hue of the sky and the river below.

"We should camp here for the night. I don't want to travel at night, I'm not sure what lurks around here when the sun has set."

Aerwyna was extremely glad when Cailean said that she didn't know that carrying tea and food around in a bag would be so draining, and she couldn't think of a more perfect place to spend their first night than by the most beautiful river she had seen in this realm under a purple sky. It didn't take her long to drop the bag and collapse on the ground by the river. Cailean glanced over his shoulder and found her sprawled on the floor looking at the star slowly appearing in the sky. It didn't take her long to start humming again, except this time she included some words.

"oho oho oho mo leana,

Oho mo leana, is codail go foill,

Oho oho oho mo leana,

Mo stoirin ina leaba ina chodladh gan bron."

"Gradh milis, what do the words mean?"

Aerwyna opened her eyes slowly, turning her head to him as he slowly lowered himself down to lay beside her. She turned her head back to the stars before he reached the ground. Aerwyna's eyes never left the sky as she spoke about the song and its meaning relating to her mother.

"It was my mother's favourite part from the whole lullaby. Her favourite line was Mo stoirin ina leaba ina chodladh gan bron which means "my sweetheart in her bed asleep without sorrow."

Aerwyna's sadness could be heard in her voice as she spoke about her mother, it seems like she either wasn't around anymore or things weren't the same at home. It made him sad that she wasn't happy at home. He hoped that by him being with her it would offer some comfort. He wrapped his arms around her and pulled her closer to him, placing a chaise kiss on top of her hair, hoping it would offer some comfort.

"Come Gradh milis let's set up the tent and get some sleep. We've got a long day tomorrow. If we're going to reach the fairy ring by night fall"

Aerwyna raised herself up onto her elbows resting her head on one facing him, she smiled leaning over to place a light kiss on his cheek in return.

"Let the adventure begin."

Chapter Twenty-Four

Lunaris

After a restless night sleeping on the hard damp ground, Aerwyna woke with a start. Many animals had come out during the night to investigate who they were. She presumed that they must have come into the animals' feeding ground as many deer and fawns had come, she woke up many times to see them drinking by the water where she joined them to look at the stars. They had many deer in her realm but because she was from the autumn forest most of the fawns had grown by then, so it was new to her to see them so young. She glanced over at Cailean several times throughout the night he slept so peacefully. She had to stop herself a couple of times from running her hands through his hair, she knew if she did, he would wake up. It was going to dawn soon and she just sat at the edge of the river taking in the beautiful sight of the sun rising, beginning a new day, with new possibilities.

***

Aerwyna tried her best to start a small fire with bits of wood that she found lying around, but it seemed being stuck in a palace for most of her forgotten life was catching up to her. She sat there and rubbed two

216

sticks together vigorously to no avail, she thought she must have been trying since sunup, her challenge didn't last long, until two strong pale arms reached around her taking her hands in his as they both worked to light the fire together.

"You know a lady shouldn't be doing this, you should have just woken me up if you were cold, or even better have cuddled up to me I would have kept you warm all night."

That got him a narrow-eyed glance from her, as she slowly turned her head around to face him as best she could. After a few minutes their fire was lit and Aerwyna was now happy to defend her case to him, she spun around as quickly as she could. What she had factored in was they were both balancing on the legs in a crouched down position. The abrupt turning made Cailean lose balance which made him automatically reach out to grab the nearest thing to him to be able to steady himself which in this case was her. The result was Aerwyna trapped in Caileans arms and somewhere from his crouched position to falling on the floor he had turned pinning Aerwyna between him and the ground. The fact of this didn't go unnoticed by either of them. This had been the closest they had been since their kiss and near kiss just before leaving, Aerwyna hoped that he couldn't hear how fast her heart was beating. She didn't know whether it was better to continue looking at him, turn away or close her eyes to see what he would do.

She opted for the latter. She closed her eyes waiting to see if he would do anything, by closing them all her other senses were heightened she could hear his breath increase, hear the wind gently blowing the blades of grass, the smell of him oh how she loved how he smelled. She waited for what to her felt like ages, she could feel how he gently brushed his fingers against the side of her face moving some hair away that had fallen, how his hands snaked his way around the back of her neck pulling her up to meet him. She held her breath waiting for what she hoped he would do, but it never came instead she was assaulted with the cold air wrapping itself around her as he moved away from her. She opened her eyes to find him heading over to where they left the bags last night she thought to retrieve their breakfast. She pouted a little, she couldn't figure out what had changed since the last time when he kissed her, what was she doing, was she doing something wrong, did he not have any interest in her any longer. She sat there looking at him and she came to the decision by the end of the day she would make him want to kiss her again, and she would be the one to reject him, see how he liked it. She found then that she had a slight mean streak when it came to him, which made her laugh. She didn't really know how she would get him to kiss her, but she knew she would have fun finding out.

***

After they had their simple breakfast of porridge with a few bits of fruit and some pre-made brews that Aerwyna had brought from the market. They sat by the fire to study the maps to plan their journey to the fairy ring, much to Caileans disappointment there was no other way to go than through the valley of the Banshees. He didn't know if she knew about Banshees, so he had to think of the best way to inform her of their quirks with a lack of better words to describe them. He had to tell her to avoid their screams as best she could, if they were heard far away then it was still bad but if they were heard close up then it was deadly. He had read up a lot on the Banshees when he found out that they wouldn't have much of a choice, he knew they had a sonic scream that could shatter glass and therefore cause blood vessels to burst, they were able to pass through solid objects and move much fast than an average could walk he wasn't sure if they could move faster than a Kelpie and a fairy, but he prayed that he didn't have the time to find out. The two that they had to be the most careful about was the fact that they had the ability of invisibility and the most dangerous one was their death touch, it had been proven by the people who had written the book, but it was said that their death touch had fatal effects on the living some could immobilise you and some could be deathly fatal. He had to be thankful that whoever had written the book had also written some hopefully effective weaknesses of theirs, which when he looked

included iron, salt, magic. He made sure that they brought iron with

them. He made sure that Aerwyna was wearing an iron bracelet so if

any got near her, she had some hope in deflecting them.

"Aerwyna, you need to wear this iron. It's only one of the three things

they are supposedly weak too, the others we don't have access to. I

need to know that you are safe, we don't have, and magic and we

don't really have a lot of salt not enough to fight off Banshee's"

Aerwyna looked up at him. She could see the worry in his eyes, and

she knew that he wanted to keep her safe, but all she could think

about was how he was going to be kept safe in the process of her

being safe. She took a hold of the bracelet placing it on her arm

making sure that quickly after she grabbed a hold of Caileans arm,

she had to have some knowledge that he would be safe as well as her,

she had to have some comfort in knowing, if it was a dangerous as he

told her, he needed to give her at least that knowledge.

"And how are you going to be safe? How will I know that if I'm

wearing this iron, how will you be safe? You owe me at least that

much. I need to know you'll be, okay?"

He looked down at where her hand enveloped his arm and looked at

her. The worry in her eyes spread all over her face, she was genuinely

worried for him, and he didn't know how to comfort her in this, he didn't know if either of them would be safe, but he couldn't let her

know that. He knew he had to reassure her somehow, but he didn't

know how. It was the first time he didn't know how to reassure her

and that scared him, even more than he was already scared. Banshees

were not someone to be messed with and looking at the map the

valley was fairly long and not that wide.

"look Aerwyna, I'm going to have to be honest with you, and this fact

scares the hell out of me for two reason, one being I've never been

this honest or ever told anyone that I'm scared and two I'm not sure if

I can guarantee safety for either of us, that fact scares me more than I

care to know. There not a lot known about Banshees; they normally

stay within their area and us in ours, if exceedingly rare that they two

cross paths. So, I need you to listen to me the entire time we are in

there, at least that way I know that you'll be safe if the worst comes

to surface. So please wear the bracelet and keep it on until I tell you

otherwise. You don't have to worry, I have one as well, mine is under

my clothes. So, you have to trust me, is that clear?"

In the process of speaking to her both of his hands had come to rest

on her upper arms holding her safe in between them. Aerwyna didn't

know what to say, it looked like he was as scared for her as she was

for him. There wasn't much they could do; it was like the riddle said.

"but beware of many dangers along the way. You have to be brave and strong; you have to rely on each other to do your job. It's like the riddle said there will be dangers along the road, but we must rely on each other to complete the task, we must be strong and brave. I trust you Cailean more than you think."

He smiled looking at her, it made him happy that she trusted him, but of all the times to admit it, it had to be when they were about to embark on a journey of which they could or couldn't come back from. After their little talk after breakfast, they packed up their belongings and packed them all up, securing them in their packs, Cailean making sure he had the heavier stuff compared to Aerwyna. They set off towards the valley and hopefully not to their death.

***

Whoever had drawn the map however many years ago had obviously not walked the directions to the valley. When he looked at the map and double checked the distance he was sorely mistaken at where they would be by nightfall. In theory they would only be about halfway to the valley of the Banshees so they would have to find another place to stay for the night otherwise if would be sleeping on the ground once more, and with Aerwyna wings Cailean didn't want that, he checked around the map to see if there were any nearby villages or towns and there was only one. The village of Lunaris, he searched to see if there were any other villages around but that was the only one. He rolled his eyes, that was the only option which caused Aerwyna to look up at him. She was the one who would have to be most careful in this village, no one was bad here or hated their kind in fact it was the opposite they were infatuated with their kind, his father had always told him stories about this village and how they tried to find doorways to trap Selkies by taking their coats and trap fairy's by clipping their wings together therefore enabling them unable to fly away and with not knowing where they where they couldn't walk off in case of getting lost or worse walking to Banshee territory. His father never told him what they'd done with Kelpies, and he prayed he didn't find out. The fact that he had to explain to Aerwyna that he had read the map wrong and that they were going to have to stay in something called an inn which he explained was like staying at a house by you rented it for the night and left, you didn't stay for long, she sort of understood what he had meant but he wasn't sure that she hadn't fully understood. But he had to hope that she did as they wandered into the village.

***

They past many different inns but they all gave off this feeling that Cailean just didn't trust, many you could see through the windows and see the men's enslaved wives while their coats hung just out of

223

their reach taunting them of a place they could never go, the fact he

now knew Saoirse seeing this hit him deep deeper than it would have

before. Knowing things like this happened to her people was

disgraceful. It took him a while walking around the village looking in

all the windows of the nearby inns seeing how disgraceful there were,

till one up ahead hidden away from all light from the street was a inn

that had a sign outside that stated

'no fairy trappers or enslavers here.'

He knew looking at that out of all the inns her had seen this was

probably going to be their safety bet, especially with Aerwyna in tow

with her wings any slight glance of them here and he had the feeling

he would be in a lot of trouble with all the villagers when he beat

them to a pulp for trying to touch her. The only problem that he found

with the inn was that in smaller writing under the warning was a

saying that read

'only married couples welcome here'

He knew there had to be a downside to this, for them to stay here it

meant they would have to pretend to be married therefore they would

have to act as a married couple if the need was there. Cailean tipped

his head back wondering how he was going to explain this. He rolled

his head to the side when he heard a little chuckle from Aerwyna's position. She was squatting down looking at the sign out front of the inn he stood at, pointing at the line he dreaded most.

"Cailean. It says here only married couples can stay."

He didn't like how she air quotes the word married. If he knew then what the evening would entail, he would have opted for sleeping on the ground another night. His head dropped into his hand as he knew that the only way they were going to stay in what he assumed then was comfort was to pretend. He didn't like the look that was on Aerwyna's face.

"Yes, if we want to stay here, we're going to have to pretend that we are married."

The further along that sentence he got the quitter his voice got. Aerwyna took the chance and closed in on him, raised up on her toes ever so slightly to bring her face closer to his, she remembered her promise to herself earlier this morning it looked like the opportunity had just presented itself to her. She placed her hand under his chin like he had done to her many times before.

"If it looks like we want comfort, we're going to have to pretend to like each other."

He opened his mouth to protest that they wouldn't have to pretend but he thought better of it. If the look on her face was anything to go by, he thought it safer to play along.

***

They walked in through the front door of the inn to find a little old lady sitting behind the desk, if was then they both realised why the sign was so prominently against trappers and enslavers, the innkeeper herself was a fairy, her wings we more coloured than Aerwyna were, but it made everything so clear to them. Aerwyna had whispered to him that fairies from the forest of Geamhradh, she told him that they were extremely strict on relationships with each other they didn't spend a single night in the same house until all vows had been read, only then would they even step foot in the house of their partner. If he wasn't nervous already, he definitely was now, he had never been exceptionally good at lying, maybe if he left it all up to Aerwyna it would work better. He bent down so he was level with her ear and asked if she could take control of this one, they needed a room with two rooms, or one with a sofa at least. Aerwyna walked up to the counter and asked the lady if they could have a room for the night with two beds, which resulted in the lady peering around her to look at Cailean. Her suspicions rose when Cailean stayed behind her rather than stood beside her like a husband should have, she retracted her silent statement when she saw that he had all the bags and was probably staying back so as to not trip his wife. Aerwyna explained that they were newly married, and her husband was still nervous around her, she whispered something that was just out of his hearing which caused him concern. But whatever she said worked, the lady handed Aerwyna a key to whatever room she was able to secure them. Before walking over to him and ushering him down to her level. Leaning down he was cautious; she had a look in her eyes he hadn't seen before, and he was a little worried. It didn't take her long to place both her hands on either side on his face pulling him closer to her, she pulled him so close that her breath tickled his lips.

"She doesn't quite believe me, so I have to make her, do you trust me?"

Cailean couldn't do much more than nod when she was this close to him all reason seemed to ooze out of his mind, and he lost the ability to speak. He nodded his head saying that he trusted her with whatever she needed to do. With a smile on her face, her eyes flicked to his lips to his eyes then back again before she gently ever so gently placed her lips on his.

Chapter Twenty-Five

The Inn

All rational thought left Caileans mind when her lips were on his, it didn't take him long to drop the bags he was holding to wrap his hands around her back pulling her closer to him. His hand snaked around her waist while the other slowly moved up her spine causing little goose bumps to form along her arms the higher up his hand went before it weaved its way into her hair taking a hold of a section enabling him to manoeuvre her where he wanted her to either deepen or lighten up the kiss as he saw fit. He chose at that moment to deepen this kiss ever so slightly before he removed his lips from her to trail them down her neck coming to a stop in that little dent between her shoulder and her neck that he loved so much. He stopped when he heard a small cough, the little old lady that sat behind the desk had a smirk on her face, whatever she thought before she definitely didn't think now, if her face was anything to go by. Caileans face instantly blushed, but Aerwyna's just looked smug like she got what she wanted. Which in her way she had he just didn't

know about it. Yet. Aerwyna winked at Cailean as she turned and
waved to the lady before she told them their room was up the stairs at
the end of the corridor on the left, room 73.

***

The room was small and filled with the bare essentials, things like a
wash basin, sofa, sideboard space and the one thing he worried about
the bed, the one single extravagant things in the room filled with
plush cushions, linens and pillow the only problem he found was it
was only one. One double bed for the both of them, how would he be
able to do this stay in the same room but even worse the same bed.
He liked a challenge, but this one may be the hardest he ever faced.
"I'll take the sofa, I'm shorter so ill fit on it better than you will."
Before he even had a chance to say he would take the soda she beat
him to it. It was late in the evening, but he tried to argue but she
wasn't having it. We kept going till it was really late in the evening,
but she was still not giving in. finally he gave in much to Aerwyna
relief, she was tired of both arguing with him and from the day's
journey. Cailean left the room and stood outside the door so she could
change into her night clothes in private. He rubbed the back of his
neck. What was he going to do, he couldn't sleep in the bed while she
was on the sofa, for one his mother would have killed him, and two

229

he was raised to be much more of a gentleman than that. He turned

around and faced the door once more before knocking.

"Aerwyna, are you dressed ?"

He waited for a reply, but none came, he knocked again and waited

but still nothing, one the third knock he open the door slightly taking

a peak at the room, but he couldn't see her, opening the door a little

further showed that she had changed and sat on the sofa and had

immediately fallen asleep. Cailean couldn't do much more than

chuckle to himself. He shook his head before gently picking her up

and carrying her to the bed before tucking her in under the plush

covers. It was very tempting for him to slide in next to her, the bed

did look very inviting, but his self-control took over him and he

settled on the sofa in his worn cotton trousers.

***

A bright flash appeared in front of Aerwyna making her shield her

eyes from the blinding light. As the light dimmed, she looked around,

she was walking through the forest again the bright pink forest that

she found both beautiful and terrifying at the same time, only this

time it was different she wasn't alone. Looking around she found

what she had now assumed were her mother and father standing

behind her talking to each other. She could see someone in front of

her, but she couldn't make out the person's face. She tried to move closer, but it seemed the closer she went the blurrier the person got. The dream changed her parents, and the others were no longer there, she was now in a walled garden that was covered in ivy and autumn leaves, some flowers seemed to be entwined within the ivy, the closer she got she realised they were Anemone. Both in the purest of white she had seen and the deepest pink similar to the forest of pink, she didn't know the name, so she had renamed it. As she walked further through the garden there was a metal gazebo standing towards the back. The roof pointed up with a small railing surrounding the table and two stairs that sat inside. Many flowers surrounded the gazebo, some of her favourites actually. There was Crocus, Helianthus, and Heather. She loved the smell of all the flowers out together, she wanted to linger around a little more, but the dream moved her on once more. She was still in the garden but the was at what looked like a pond on a lake, she couldn't see much so she couldn't be completely sure. There was something on the other side of the water, she moved closer to take a better look and when she did, she found that it wasn't on the other side of the water it was on the water. She walked closer, stepping into the water, she had to get a closer look. She must have slipped or taken a wrong step, but it wasn't long before she was under the water unable to break free of its watery hold. She thought she was going to drown; she couldn't get out, couldn't free herself, couldn't breathe. The water grew warm, and she stopped struggling, she knew that no matter what she did it wouldn't help she tried and tried but nothing worked, soon her eyes closed, and everything felt lighter. Until two small hands grabbed her around the waist pulling her up onto the small island in the middle of the water. Even though she wasn't moving she could still hear everything she heard someone shout that she wasn't breathing, and they didn't know what to do, they were calling for help. She heard two more people running over towards her. They spoke but she couldn't fully hear them enough to understand what they were saying. She felt a hand go behind her neck and lip touch hers breathing air into her before two hands pressed hard on her chest, this happened a couple of times before she coughed up all the water she swallowed. Her eyes slowly opened but everything was blurry. She couldn't see anyone's faces clearly, she couldn't see who had saved her, before long everything faded to black before a familiar face popped up in the darkness. She said everything she had heard before but this time there was something else, someone else standing behind her, somehow, they seemed similar. She saw long blonde hair standing behind the familiar face, the only person she sort of knew with long blonde hair was her. Father. When she woke up with a start crying in the bed she couldn't find her surroundings she couldn't breathe; everything was closing in on her the room was getting smaller, she started to panic. Two hands

took hold of her shoulders shaking her a little bringing her out of the

trance she was in, she could hear something, someone she trusted.

"na…wyna…Aerwyna……Aerwyna snap out of it, your fine breath

take a breath for me……please Aerwyna take a breath."

The hands took her quicker, shook her harder, she slowly came

around the tears streaming down her eyes blurred everything a little,

but she could make out Caileans silhouette.

"Cailean?"

She couldn't say any more than that before she leapt into his arms

throwing her arms around his neck pulling him as closer to her as she

could before she said through a quavering voice.

"m…my father was there. Standing behind her. When they shut me in

the tree."

***

Her father was there, he was there, and he didn't stop it from

happening, something wasn't right there had to be some reason why

he didn't stop it. He didn't know the fairy king personally, but he

must have loved his daughter. Mustn't he. The thoughts didn't matter

to him at that moment; all that mattered was trying to comfort

Aerwyna. She was what mattered the most at the moment, finding out

233

that the man who should have cared for her now was a part of the task to trap her in the tree would be devastating. He couldn't imagine what she was feeling at the moment. He sat there holding a sobbing Aerwyna in his arms, her shaking made him mad the very thought of it all annoyed him beyond all reason. But he settled down on the space next to her on the bed holding her close to him allowing her to know that he was there until she wanted him to move, but she made no move to move him away from her, if anything she brought him closer to her but wrapping her arms around his waist in theory trying to pull him closer to her. Cailean raised a hand placing it on her hair before running his finger through the enchanting strands as he hummed the lullaby of his mother's soothing her as best he could, it didn't take her long to join in with him by humming the Selkie lullaby, the sound of their voice together harmonised perfectly, the songs interconnected brilliantly creating a alluring soothing tune with sent them both of the land of dreams, he hoped that with him beside her, the dreams she experienced would be nicer ones.

***

As the sun streamed through the window it landed on Caileans eyes ripping him from his peaceful and comfortable sleep, why he was so comfortable he couldn't remember he was asleep on the sofa across the room. It wasn't until he opened his eyes and spotted the sofa that he realised he was on the oversized extremely comfortable bed, but if he was here then that meant. He tilted his head slightly to the side to find Aerwyna tucked very closely beside her, her night gown falling off her beautifully tempting pale shoulder, the sight of it tempting him to rest his lips there and see if he was as delicious as it looked, if she was as delicious as she looked. His thoughts returned to the kiss they shared in the foyer late last night. He removed his arm from underneath her head. He had to cool himself down or she would do something that he wouldn't regret but would put a massive wedge between them both and he didn't want that being near her was enough for him whether his body agreed with him or not. The slight movement caused Aerwyna to stir, causing Cailean to stop dead in his tracks at the side of the bed. He hoped that she wouldn't wake up; she couldn't see him like this, not now and not anywhere in the future. Even though he hoped that something was in their future he thought she wasn't ready for that definitely not ready yet. After a few minutes she settled back down, rolling over which caused the gown to drop a little further revealing her wings and her bare back. How he wanted to run his hands up her hand and into her hair and he pulled it back so he wouldn't be able to sample her neck running his tongue down towards. His thoughts stopped. He definitely needed a cold shower and a very cold shower. He turned and ran to the shower locking the door behind him. Unfortunately for him his senses must have been impaired to not find that Aerwyna was awake and smiling to herself knowing exactly what reactions she was bringing out from him. She sat up in bed as she heard the shower turn on which in turn resulted in a small yelp from Cailean as what she presumed was the cold water hit his bare body. All the images ran through Aerwyna's head. She could imagine Cailean from what she had felt when he held her close and what he was like when he protected her from anyone or anything that threatened her. She wondered what it would feel like to run her hands up his bare chest slowly circling around his neck pulling herself ever so close to him, she wondered if he had good control of himself or if she allowed herself to get close would he lose all control. The very thought made her smile; she couldn't picture him losing his control. The very thought was too tempting not to act upon. She slipped herself from the warmth of the bed approaching the door which held the bathroom and placed light knocks on the door. Which received her a surprised gasp from Cailean on the other side.

"I…I'll be out in a minute then you can use the bathroom."

The fact that his voice broke at the beginning of his sentence made her laugh. The temptation to try the door walked in and brush her hair and prepare for the day, but the door was locked, she heard him lock it moments after he shut the door. So instead, she stood just to the right brushing her hair in the mirror on the chest of drawers beside the door. Pulling the brush through her hair was therapeutic fairies' hair never seemed to have any knots or tangles so brushing it made it easy. Sometimes too easy, sometimes it would be nice for it to get a tangle then she could ask Cailean to brush it out for her, then she could feel his hands against her neck once more. The very thought made her blush, she hadn't reacted like this to anyone or that she knew of many of her memories where either after the incident or shortly before, nothing had resurfaced from two days prior to her going into the tree. She was ripped from her thoughts when the door to the bathroom opened to reveal a half-naked Cailean dressed only in a towel that covered his waist. Her eyes widened and her mouth fell open. All the images she had in her head were nothing compared to what stood before her. His clothes did well in hiding the well-defined muscles that lined his stomach. Two lines that created a v shape disappeared into the folds of the towel, below the towel two very well-defined legs held up the strong well-developed body that preceded it.

"Hey, eyes up here."

Her eyes snapped up from the legs and stomach to his eyes and what she saw in them made her blush intensely. The heat they seemed to radiate made her feel hot like there was nothing in this world that would cool her down. It was then she remembered that all that separated her body and his was a flimsy nightgown and a towel which could easily be removed. A blush covered her face when Cailean had decided to rest his arm above his head leaning against the door frame of the bathroom, making it that if she wanted to go through the only way was to past under his arm, where her thought told her that she could easily be trapped against him and the frame. Would she mind that though being stuck between all of him and something that made it impossible to move away. In the end it was what she wanted wasn't it, to torment him, make him seem so uncomfortable that he would do something, wouldn't this be the best way to do that.

***

Aerwyna raised her head to face him if she was going to do this, she wanted to turn her eyes from his, she was going to make him look at her the whole time, it was now a challenge, a challenge to see who would look away first. She squared her shoulders as she passed under him, his eyes following her each step of the way the smirk on his face only deepening.

"If you excuse me, I'm going to freshen up before we set off once more."

She pointed into the bathroom as she was ducking under his arm, that was before said arm dropped around her shouldering pulling her towards him quickly. A small gasp escaped her lips as he pulled her towards his bare chest, it was warm which surprised her, she thought that Kelpies would be cold considering they spent so much time next to or on the water. But the warmth was comforting. He lent down until his lips were next to her ear. His warmth breath caressed it so easily.

"You should know, your little challenges and torments are working but unless you're prepared for what follows I would stop, or my control that you so easily want to challenge will break and you will see how different a Kelpie is to a Fairies. We treat our lovers very differently and we've had complaints, everyone we have has always left…. With lack of a better word well served in their experience. So, my dear little caramel fairy I would be very, very, very careful with who you challenge. You may end up biting off more than you bargained for."

He gently let out a little breath which he blew against her ear causing her to shrink against him , the very action resulting in a smirk on his face as he removed himself from her vicinity entangling her with the cold air that now encircled her before she turned shutting and locking the bathroom door. Leaving him safely on the other side. She could smile from the other side of the door.

"Stubborn Kelpie."

"Naïve Fairy."

She turned towards the shower before sorting herself out for the day.

Heaven knew when they were going to sleep comfortably again for a

while. And with what happened today she had to keep her wits about

her on this adventure.

Chapter Twenty - Six

Ghillie Dhu

The journey to the Banshee valley was long and winding up around

small mountains and through blissful valleys filled with flowers, but

what made it seem even longer was the fact that all conversation had

ceased, which in turn made the journey feel ten times as long.

Aerwyna would take a glance towards Cailean but scare herself to a

stop when she remembered what he had said to her back at the inn.

Blush always coated her face when her memory drifted back there

which when Cailean looked down at her made him smile a little to

himself, it was nice to know that he could still unnerve someone

when he hadn't done it for years without using his powers. The very

thought made him feel proud, but at the same time he missed how

Aerwyna would get so excited about little things along the road and

point them out to him like they were something completely brand

new although to her they probably where, but to him she paint

everyday objects in a new and wonderful light, she described them in

way he hadn't thought of before, and now that she was quiet from

being too embarrassed by this morning, he realised how much he

missed it. He had to find a way to help her relax once more so she could be more like herself once more. Thankfully for him the fairy glen was approaching one thing he thought she would love and be able to tell him a little more about.

"Aerwyna, just over the next ridge is something the humans call a fairy glen, you want to stop and have a look. We can have our lunch there that the nice inn owner packed for us."

Aerwyna didn't say much but a slightly little nod of her head to acknowledge his statement. He hoped that something in this glen would bring her back out of her self-enclosed shell, it was like when she first came to him silent, little movement, just not lie herself in anyway.

"Okay."

Aerwyna's voice was so small, so quiet that if there was anyone else around, anyone else talking it would have masked the sound. How he loved that sound, but he needed to find a way to make it seem as lively as she normally was. He would find away even if it meant denying all that he said to her in the inn, denying all that his mind and body told him, if it meant denying himself of her until she was ready, if that's what it took to bring her back to her happy normal self then so be it, that would be what he would do. Standing upon the top of the ridge, a few houses could be seen in the distance. A few mountains dotted around the ridge they walked make the land seem very bumpy, almost like waves in the sea. The sunshine beat down on them as they approached the fairy glen, Aerwyna couldn't remember much but she didn't think there was a glen this close to humans, they always tried to keep their unused gateways fairly far from any human house even if they were far in the distance. She was sure there wouldn't be one this close, but she also knew that not all her memories had returned, so she couldn't rely on that.

***

The fairy ring itself was a man made version of the one the fairies actually used to transport themselves through, she didn't need her memories for that one, fairies always left a little of their magic behind when they created a fairies rings, even if was an ancient one that was created many, many years before she was born before even her parents and grandparents were born there was still trace magic left behind, this one had nothing, not traces of magic no magic overflowing so it wasn't newly made or even an ancient one made centuries ago, it was just there. Aerwyna turned her gaze to Cailean. His smile was magnificent; it seemed from her perspective that he truly thought this was a true fairy ring. The riddle reran through her head they told them to find a fairy ring and find the fairy sign at sunset to find the stone, she wondered if it could be this fairy ring,

243

they were meant to look for one through the Banshee valley. She turned in Caileans directions.

"Cailean the riddle told us to find the fairies rings and look for the fairy sign at sunset to find the stone, do you think this could be the fairies ring they meant."

Aerwyna had made a very valid point the riddle didn't specify which fairy ring it was or even if it was an actually fairy ring made by a fairy, for all they knew it could be a human made one like the one in front of them, he didn't know much about fairy rings but he knew that whenever a magical being made something trace amounts of magic were left behind, so it made it easier for other magical beings to tell which ones were safe to use and which ones were most likely used to entrap them. If this was the one, they needed then he had to be careful, he looked just like everyone else unless you looked at his eyes but Aerwyna, she had wings that they needed to be careful, some human like the ones from Lunaris used rings likes theses to trap them and there was no way he was letting that happen. There was really only one way they would be able to find out if this was the ring they needed and that was to spend the night here. It would be too late to continue their journey after sunset, so it didn't leave much of a choice.

"We'll stay here for today. Stay for the sunset to see if we can see the fairy sign then, if not then we can cross this fairy ring off the list. It will be too late to continue on after, so we'll have to camp here. But we'll have to be careful about your wings. Sometimes people use these to trap innocent fairies like you and enslave them as their wives or worse their servants where you'll have no choice but to follow their rules. We don't want that to happen so unfortunately, you'll have to sleep close to me, if you keep you back next to me then I can hide your wings from sight."

Once more Aerwyna couldn't say much but okay. She had to spend an entire night with her back pressed against his chest, she hoped that he wouldn't be able to hear how fast her heart would be beating with him that close. Cailean only prayed that nothing was hidden away out of their sights tonight. He didn't feel entirely comfortable being this out in the open.

***

Little to Caileans disappointment the fairy ring they found wasn't the one that would lead them to the Myrios stone, but he was thankful that they could watch on of the most beautiful the cloud aligned themselves to that when you tilted your head to the side it looked like a face with it hand to it mouth, and the closer the sunset to the earth the more it looked the sky was telling the earth a secret. The sunset

245

sky lit the sky behind the cloud creating it so that the cloud had the most beautiful scene that had slowly unfolded in front of them, but it couldn't mask the disappointment that this hadn't been the ring they were looking for. The next morning was very much the same as all the others, the sun rose casting the sky in an abundance of colours, the ground was covered in the dew of night and Aerwyna's back was warm with Cailean breath, the only thing that wasn't normal was the man covered in a in what looked like a cloak of the softest looking grass Aerwyna had ever seen. She didn't have much time to say anything before the stranger's hand was over her mouth and nose. He was carrying her away, away from safety, away for Cailean. He was the last thing she saw before everything went black from the darkness of the woods.

***

The darkness of the woods was all that surrounded her when she reopened her eyes, there wasn't even a speck of daylight, it was like nothing was able to breach the density of the woods around them. Then, there was someone with her, someone carrying her, someone who wasn't Cailean. Who was this person? Aerwyna struggled against the brutal strength that held her to this stranger's shoulder. His grip was like an iron lock keeping her firmly in place against him. When she realised struggling wasn't going to work, she tried to turn around to take a look at the strangers' face, but no luck the cloak he was wearing covered his face when the hood was up, all she could see were strands of woven dark black hair peeking out here and there. As much as she tried to turn herself around to take a look and Mr. Dark and possibly dangerous, everything she tried seemed to fail her. She thought to leave a trail for Cailean to follow but her bag was still at the campsite next to the lovely warmth of her companion. There wasn't much more she could think of to help herself; it was then she realised that if the stranger wanted to hurt her or cause her any harm at all then he would have done so already.

"Have you come to hurt me or help me?"

Aerwyna had to know. She had to know whether she could somewhat trust this stranger who from what she could see looked kind, but what kind of kind person stole a woman from her campsite when she was asleep let alone when there was another man lying next to her at said campsite.

"You are safe now my child, the Kelpie can no longer hurt you."

Safe? From the kelpie? Maybe he thought she was being held captive by Cailean, she knew it was known that kelpies often used to take people captive for what she didn't know.

"It's okay, that kelpie he's my friend, we are travelling together, if you can take me back to my companion I would be ever so grateful."

That caused men to look at her the best he could considering she was still slung over his shoulders.

"Kelpies don't have companions or friends, they have slaves and food. He has tricked your mind into thinking that he is your friend, but you cannot believe a word he said, he will drag you down until he owns you completely, by he will own you completely in the worst way possible my child, trust me child Kelpies cannot be trusted." Could it be so, she knew some Kelpies could captivate people, mostly women, to become anything they wanted, the majority becoming food for them, but from what she heard that hadn't happened in many centuries, they kind of breed it out of the genetic system of their race. It couldn't be possible that, that was all Cailean wanted her for, of that was the case why would he try and help her find the Myrios stone, if that was the case why had he helped her all this time since she emerged for the tree, if that was the case would that explain why she felt like she did towards him, were all her feeling made up for her to believe he care for her to make her bei8lve he cared for her, make her believe that he could possibly love her in any way, would he really do that to her.

"It's okay my child, you're safe, will get you some food and then I'll help you find your way home, home to where you are safe and away from the dangers of the outside world."

With that said he squeezed her just a tiny bit tighter than he should

have making her fall asleep against his shoulder.

"It's okay my child sleeps and when you wake all will be well."

***

When Aerwyna awoke after what must have been at least a couple of

hours, what faced her was one of the most beautiful scenery she

could ever remember herself seeing. She was in what looked like a

dilapidated church, five big arch ways surrounded a single white tree

in the centre, another tree surrounded it causing the area to shadow

only a small area was illuminated by the smaller tree. Moss and

leaves covered the area both on the ground and entwining up and

around the arches surrounding them. Little rivers and streams seem to

forge their way in and around the moss-covered ground. She raised

her head from the tree she rested against situated in front of the white

tree. The stranger was standing in front with a hand placed on the

trunk of the tree, it seemed that wherever he placed his hand the tree

glowed more in that area. Aerwyna couldn't figure out how she didn't

see him when she first opened her eyes, it was like he appeared out of

nowhere, sort of like a ghost, maybe he couldn't be a ghost of some

kind, it seemed to her that if her kind and other could exist then what

couldn't ghost exist. She tried to rise from where she rested but it

249

seemed like her legs were asleep still, the stranger somehow seemed to have sensed her movement as he turned to face her.

"Ah my child you have awakened once more, it seems like all is well if you have somewhat moved enough for me to sense you."

Aerwyna tried to move once more but nothing seemed to listen to her. Her limb seemed to have their own mind

"What did you do to me? Why can't I move?"

"It's fine my child the Gelsemium will wear off momentarily, it was only a little dose, you wouldn't stop moving around and I have to bring you to the safety of Tundra woods, only people that I permit may enter these woods to be your companion."

Aerwyna didn't like the way he said that she hoped that he wouldn't hurt him that was the last thing she needed, she needed to find a way to make him trust Cailean, maybe she couldn't make him see that he wasn't the bad kelpie he thought he was and then maybe he would return her to Cailean.

"Your companion wouldn't be able to find you here, I've enchanted the woods around us so that unless I let them in, they will walk around the woods forever never finding the exit or whoever lies within this enchanted area."

***

It took a while for the Gelsemium to wear off and for her to be able to move once more, when she couldn't she moved closer to the tree that seemed to glow brighter and brighter the closer she got to it.

"What about this tree, I've never seen a tree glow with such an ethereal light. "

The stranger moved closer to her peering down at her before placing a hand on the tree somewhat making him smile, his smile made him look human, even though she still couldn't see his face properly, his hood still concealed his identity from her. It didn't matter how much she tried to peer underneath the hood, he seemed to have counted on her doing that, so he always made sure that his hood was placed over his head and always made sure that he stayed where it was darker than the rest to hide his face from her.

"It's called the tree of truth. It's what I use to see what lies within someone's heart. It doesn't matter how much they try to hide the truth that always lies within someone's heart."

She looked up at him seeing a slight smile appear on his face, she wondered what he looked like and maybe if she convince him to let Cailean in here and he could touch the tree then he would be able to see that he only means well to her, that he doesn't meant to cause her any harm at all, that in fact he cares for her the way she cares for him.

"Maybe if you let my companion here, he could touch the tree and see that he means so much harm to anyone, he's different from the kelpies of the past. He wouldn't hurt anyone let alone me. If you let him in you'll see."

This seemed to hit some truth with the stranger she couldn't only tell as the small smile that decorated his lips grew bigger enhancing the already delicate feature that she could see.

"That is true my child, it seems that what you say has some merit to the truth, it seems that your companion has already found you somehow, maybe a connection that runs deeper than we can see or maybe he's drawn to you through the connection he made by controlling your mind. Shall we see?"

Aerwyna couldn't see how they couldn't find out other than having him here to touch the tree, was he already here? Had Cailean found her already? If so, she hoped that he didn't think that she abandoned him. The Stranger only smiled down at her worried appearance. A small laugh escaped his lips as the knelt down to the little pond that formed in front of them, whether it was there the whole time and she didn't see it or if he had somehow called upon it, she wasn't sure, all she was certain of was the once he touched the water she could see Cailean standing just the other side of the curtain of trees that separated her from his grasp.

"Ghillie Dhu, you bastard, she is not a lost child or one that has been taken. You have no right to take her from me. You grass covered bastard, you release her right now, before I get mad. We both know that I can get in there if I so wish too, but I'm being nice and asking politely."

Aerwyna laughed; she didn't know when swearing at someone and calling them a bastard counted as being polite, but it seemed very much like him. The stranger that was called ghillie Dhu according to Cailean just smiled at the water. She looked from Cailean to him trying to figure out what was going on there. They obviously had some kind of history, but whether it was good or bad she didn't know.

"I'll tell you what oh mighty prince, if you can find your way in her without travelling through the water and touch the tree of truth then maybe I'll let you have her back, if you don't or you prove to have lied at all to her or to me then I shall return her to her world sand you'll never see her again."

"That's not fair you bastard and you know it, this place is an impenetrable fortress if you make it so. You have to leave an opening somewhere otherwise it's an impossible task no matter what powers the others may have. You don't understand if you return her to her world then there is a high chance that she'll be in more danger there then anywhere else in this god forsaken world. You know yourself what the humans are like, we just made it out of Lunaris, you know

what they do to our kind there. Do you want her to go through that,

do you want her to go through what you had to."

This caused Aerwyna to look up at him. It was true though you could

see faint scars on his wrist where he had obviously been shackled or

bound for a very long time. What had the wicked human done to

him? How had he escaped? Did it explain why he kept himself

covered in moss and leaves to stay hidden away for the horrible

humans who would be out to torture her kind and other like her. She

saw when she walked through the village that many of her kind were

enslaved to work or trapped to be trophies of a kind. She placed a

gentle hand on his which caused him flinch at her gentle touch,

Aerwyna couldn't help but smile when a small blush crept its way up

his face, when was the last time anyone had shown him kindness,

when was the last time he was able to befriend anyone without having

to worry that they were going to see him out. She didn't know much

about the strange aloof fairy called Ghillie Dhu but what she did

know what that the protected children he was described as being kind

hearted and gentle which she could agree with, minus squeezing her

to hard to make her fall asleep he had never hurt her was always

gentle and had her best interests at heart, even now he was trying to

protect her as he thought Cailean meant to cause her harm. She raised her hands slowly as to not worry him as she slowly pushed the hood

of his cloak back revealing skin that was a lighter shade of green that

was she had expected, he was clothed in only a skirt with was

fashions out of leaves layered together to make it warmer the colder

months, he had fashions vines together intertwining them together to

create a ripe he used as a belt along with what looked like another blet

fashioned of branches intertwining themselves also. He was barefoot

but had leaves cascading down from his knees stopping just to rest on

the tops of his feet hiding his legs from view, with his cloak on he

was practically invisible to the naked eye of humans if he was hiding

within the trees and bushes of the wood and forests. His hair which

she thought was entwined together was actually braided several times

in tiny sections allowing him to change the style depending on the

season he could incorporate whatever he wished in between so easily,

tiny metal clasp hugged the certain braids at different points. She

assumed this was to reflect any light that would hit him when hiding.

His face was angular with a jawline that was sharp enough to cut

anything and everything she could think of. His eyes were green like

hers. She assumed that was because he was a fairy of some kind. She

didn't notice before, but small twigs stuck out of the arms and hood

of his cloak while autumn leaves decorated the hood to the left just

above his eyes while small vines and leaves rested against the bare subtly indented muscular chest. He was an attractive fairy and she could see why the children who got lost trust him.

"Please Ghillie Dhu believe me, he means me no harm, if anything he is trying to help me the best he can. For you see…."

It took Aerwyna a while to explain everything that happened up until now to Ghillie Dhu, but she persevered she had to try and gain his trust by any means possible and if this was the best way, so be it.

"I see, so he found you and is trying to help you find the Myrios stone that lies beyond the valley of the banshees. What I can't seem to figure out is why the Myrios stone, you need to find four separate stones to make the Myrios stone up."

"You know about the Myrios stone?"

Aerwyna's face beamed with delight any help that they could get would be wonderful but to get the help she would need to gain his trust and he would have to trust Cailean as well.

"Maybe we can talk about it, if you let Cailean in, we can all discuss this together."

Aerwyna tried and tried if she could just get them to talk to them maybe just maybe it could work.

"You know I'm still out here Ghillie and getting bloody freezing out here by the way, do you have a weather machine in there to change the temperature or something. Jeez hurry up and open the door you, green bastard and give me Back my girl."

Aerwyna's face blushed when he called her his girl, she hadn't ever been someone girl before, could she be counted as his, Cailean obviously thought so.

"Fine you waterlogged bugger, come in and get your tomato." Ghillie Dhu's obvious comment at her blushing just made her blush more, which resulted in her getting the comment of using her as a campfire if she got any redder. It seemed that these two whatever happened had some sort of friendship. What kind it was, well it seemed she was about to find out.

***

"Seriously Ghillie you left me out there knowing what i'm like."

"I had to check that your companion wasn't just using you for your talents."

"She doesn't even know my talents as you put it past being about to change into a horse and cleanse the waters."

The conversation between them both would have sounded like an argument to anyone who couldn't see them, but the smiles that decorated both their faces proved otherwise.

"so, you two know each other, and your friends, and you was checking me out to make sure I wasn't going to hurt him."

She pointed to Cailean who even sitting down next to her seemed to

tower over her.

"to make sure I wasn't going to hurt or use him,"

Ghillie just nodded at her brief understanding of the situation they

seemed to have found themselves in.

"Have you seen the bloody size of him? He could knock me out with

one flick of his finger or even worse he could probably kill me if he

wished to. Seriously you were worried that I. little old me was going

to hurt his giant of a Kelpie. Jeez I think you've been stuck in here far

too long if you think that it's possible, or you're just a little bit more

stupid than I originally thought."

Cailean and Ghillie just looked at each other; they knew they were a

peculiar friendship that wasn't seen that often but then again Kelpies

and fairies never seemed to get on in the past.

"She's a right little firecracker isn't she."

Ghillie Said holding his hand up in a mock surrender. Aerwyna

crossed her arms over her chest, these two could be as nice as they

wanted but she wasn't about to forgive them anytime soon for

deceiving her.

"So Ghillie…"

Caileans voice turned serious the moment he turned to Ghillie , it

seemed to Aerwyna that the time for fun had passed and now it was time for the more serious matter at hand to find the four presumed stones to make the Myrios stone.

"You said earlier that there are four stones that make up the Myrios stone. Is that true? Do you know anything about them? Anything would be helpful."

Ghillie's face turned serious as well as he spoke to him voice dropping to a deeper level than it already was.

"The last I knew there were four stones in total that if paired together corrected formed the Myrios stone."

He rose from where he was sitting to get a piece of browning parchment from a nook in a tree that seemed to house other pieces of parchment, which Aerwyna didn't know. Sitting himself back down, Ghillie unravelled the parchment revealing the locations of the four stones and the riddles that accompanied them.

"to the last of my knowledge the four stones that you need are the Stone of Misery, that's located in the valley of the banshee, you already have the riddle for that one which if you are this far you must have already solved. The Stone of Purity which I'm surprised you don't know about Cailean seeing as it is located in your world. "

This caused the smile to be wiped completely off of his face as he looked up from the parchment, his father never told him about hiding any stone and his mother was human so she wouldn't have known about any stones if there were any at all.

"the Stone of the Ocean which the last known location was the world of the Selkies "

Ghillie continued before Aerwyna looked over at Cailean in shock; they were there a couple of days ago if they had only thought of this before they could have asked Saoirse for help locating the stone with any need for the riddle itself.

"The Stone of Night, which was last located in the Brownies world, makes sense seeing as it's always nighttime in their world. And lastly the hardest to find isn't a stone at all but a place to combine the stones together as one, the sacred grounds of harmony. Where it is said they directions to combine the stone together lies within this riddle."

Ghillie stopped reading before handing the parchment over to Aerwyna to read the following riddle that would help merge the stones together.

"It's written in fairies' language but not one that I'm familiar with, I haven't ventured to the fairy's realm in a long time. I'm afraid I'm a bit rusty."

Aerwyna looked down at the parchment in her hand and read the riddle aloud for everyone to hear, she thought that maybe just maybe everyone would be able to figure it out together. She began .

" it says… sounds of the forest in sweet harmony, we give the gift of our song to the fairy, dancing a spiral we sing unaware, the fairy night wings our songs fill the air, our song in the night as we dance around the flame, the fairy nightsongs are never the same, the words from our lips as we sing for the night, impart to the fae pour hearts truest sight."

Once she finished reading the riddle it didn't take long for the darkness to overtake her mind as more memories flooded her mind. Memories of her mother, of her father, of places she didn't remember seeing. She saw her ancestors hide the stones in all their locations, but it wasn't clear enough to solve without the riddle. She could faintly hear both Ghillie and Cailean shouting to her to open her eyes but to her it seemed impossible as everything flooded all at once. Memories that weren't her flood back, face of people she had never meant she saw her mother as a young girl through the eyes of what she assumed was her grandmother, the grandmother she never meant.

"Now my sweet child you must remember that the stones must never be used for evil, you can never let anyone of evil intentions use the stones to extend their time, everything comes at a price and the price of using them is never worth it. They must one be used in dire circumstances, bringing them together with ill intention can get catastrophic. So, my child be sure to past down the stories of each to you children and so forward until the time when the stories as no longer needed."

Her grandmother smiled down at her small child before she looked directly at Aerwyna. She didn't think it was possible this was a memory she couldn't speak to her through a memory, could she?

"Oh, my dear granddaughter, how have you grown?"

Aerwyna looked behind her. There was no one there; she didn't know who her grandmother was talking to. But her father had told her once that her grandmother went insane with age and made up all kinds of tall tales about him and the imaginary stones.

"my dear this must be quick. You must be careful on your hunt for the stones. I fear your father may be trying to trick you into finding them. He knows that only people of our bloodline can find them. He tried the same thing with your mother but thankfully I was there quicker and erased the; locations from her mind before he could use her against everyone she cared about. You cannot allow him the chance to do the same to you. If you hunt the stone then so be, but be warned that the final ground that's hard to find, the sacred ground of harmony lies within your realm, it lies within the places and your father knows this, i'm afraid your father has been corrupted, I do not know by what or by whom, but he is not the same man you know he's not the same man you love. He's no longer your father. Keep Ghillie Dhu and Cailean close to you at all times. The tree was made for your protection. I didn't know it would erase all of your memories my dear. Elvina is not the evil person you believe her to be, she acts that way to stay close to your father to try and hinder his advancement on the stones. You can trust her my dear. Just as much as your trust you put in Cailean. Your meeting was a predestined event it was chosen to happen at that time and for you to reemerge at that point in time. Trust your instincts my dear, they can never lead you wrong."

"Aerwyna, can you hear me, if you can please open your eyes please come back to me."

Aerwyna could hear Caileans shouts through the darkness of the memories that flooded her mind.

"But grandmother, what if I'm not strong enough, what if I fail and father gets the stones and he turns everyone against me. What do I do then."

The older woman who was dressed in a gown similar to Aerwyna's green flora dress approached her, taking both hands in hers before placing them over her ears, tipping her head down to place a kiss on her forehead.

"my dear you would never fail, you have more power than you have discovered, this is just one of many you'll find you've inherited. Seeing past memories if a bloodline power much like your other you'll discover when the time deemed, they are needed. Until then remember to trust your instincts, stay closer to both those very cute I have to admit boys, the visions didn't show them that good looking."

"Grandmother"

Aerwyna placed her hands on her hips, she couldn't help but smile at her grandmother, she seemed just like her mother before she became aloof which she now knew was because she lost the memories of the stones.

"Sorry my dear but can't you blame me. Stay with them and you'll be fine, now my dear I must go. We can't keep this line open for long. It's very draining on the mind. You'll find you'll be very distorted when you wake, you may fall right back to sleep so let those yummy men take good care of you. Even though they'll most likely worry from what I can hear "

They hadn't stopped calling her name asking her to wake up and return to them which caused her grandmother winked causing her to blush. She wasn't ready for her grandmother to go yet but she didn't seem to have much choice before the older lady faded in the darkness and Ghillie and Cailean re appeared in the line of vision before all went to total darkness as she drifted off to sleep again the boys

yelling her name.

Chapter Twenty-Seven

Banshee Valley

Aerwyna lay sleeping in a bed made of moss and leaves Cortese of Ghillie. Nothing entered her mind, and nothing left. She could hear her grandmother's warnings over and over again, but she could also feel her love and trust that remained so eternally fixed. Although all was dark in her mind the songs of birds chipping away and the soft lullaby of a forest flute playing beside the gentle rippling waters of the little streams that Ghillie created. A slight scratching sound could be heard, but it seemed that using the power she didn't know existed controlled the healing of her body and by the feel of it, it wasn't going to let her awaken anytime soon.

***

Cailean never left Aerwyna's side, even though Ghillie said that she'll be okay once she's rested and well awakened at that time and not before, he found himself unable to remove himself from her presence. With nothing better to do he decided to borrow, even though he hadn't asked Ghillie's stationary yet, he thought it was about time to write out some of those letters he promised her, before magical stones and mystic powers or anything else that decided to raise its ugly head once more. Cailean looked up from the stationary he had perched on his knee looking at her laying there, he took a deep breath before putting pen to paper as he started to write.

My dearest Aerwyna,

Seeing you lying there was one of the hardest things I've ever seen in a long time. But if anything, it brought everything I've ever wanted to tell you to the surface, so I think I thank it for that and only that. So here goes anything, here's everything I've wanted to tell you since my last letter.

Cailean took a deep breath, peering over at the makeshift bed that Ghillie made which currently Held a sleeping Aerwyna. Cailean lent forward to gently brush a stray hair away tucking it behind her ear before gliding his fingers down her cheek. He brushed his thumb across her lips, remembering the kiss they shared in the inn only a couple of day ago prior to this dreaded day. So many things had happened in such a short time that he realised there was no point in hiding feeling away when life was short, and the time spent with the people you cared about was even shorter. He stood up placing a kiss on her brow before sitting down to continue his letter.

I do apologise my dear if this letter is rather long.

So many things have happened since the time of my last letter to you, since telling you the tale of my parents, after finding you you're a princess which I have to say made my day, that day on the beach was one of the best days knowing that I could stand a chance with someone as amazing as you. We had the wonderful trip to town which you brought the mysterious box which even to this day I have no idea what is in there, half of me hopes that maybe you brought something for me, but the other half hopes that it's something that will make you smile, it would be even better if it was both, but that would be an ideal world, wouldn't it my caramel fairy. The fireflies and meteors we saw that night ended the night perfectly even though my dear you didn't see much of the meteor shower, all of the walking and amazing new stuff you found in town it must have knackered you out, you poor little fairy. The highlight of that night was holding you close to me the entire way back home, I never knew that a person could fit so perfectly next to me. You felt so small, so light weight but at the same time I knew that if I gave you any leeway into my heart you could very easily destroy my being with a single word. That's how much power you hold over me and my heart, for you I would do anything. I would hurt and use my powers on anyone that hurt you or even thought to hurt you, that brings us to the next day with so-called heartthrob 'Prince Aelfdane' the douche of doucheville.

The next day after the most wonderful day, the trouble between us raised its ugly head. As soon as that letter came, stating that he changed his mind and wanted you back, after everything, I have to say I saw red, and it took every ounce of my strength not to disperse him right there and then. If you weren't a star and took my full attention to keep him away from you then with all my might help me, he wouldn't be in this world anymore. If I find out that he did anything to you in the past, then he will no longer be here. That is a promise. The hope that he never recognizes you is so huge that this realm cannot contain it, to be precise all the realms that exist cannot contain how much I wish he never knew who you are. When he was gone and we learnt of the Myrios stone and the riddles everything seems to happen all at once, with so much going on I feel that I neglected you a little we found we never had time together after that. And for that I apologise for that if you ever felt neglected then tell me and I'll do everything in my power to make it up to you, I'll do anything you ask of me, anything at all.

Lunaris had to be one of the scariest times of my life walking. You thought that village where human enslaved people of pout kinds and others for their own benefit was horrible. The things they must all go through just because they can't help and they have no choice at all as they'd been taken away from them much like their freedom, freedom

of choice, freedom to choice what they wanted to do even the freedom

to choice who they get married to, but the human took them away

sealed their wings stoles their skins, just to trap them. To think that if

we weren't careful that could have been you, they could have taken

you away from me much like what Ghillie did, but we won't get into

that, I'll make him pay for that later the little bastard. Sorry my dear

for the language but he deserves everything he's going to get.

But thankfully we made it through that awful town and found the most

beautiful of places, the inn we stayed was both amazing and

excruciating painful. I still think to this day that the little old lady

planned that to happen, that most wonderful most shocking thing to

ever happen in my life, when you kiss me in the foyer of that inn my

mind went blank, and I felt like my heart was going to burst. The very

thought that you would kiss me never crossed my mind. The torture I

felt when we got to that room and there was only the one bed when we

asked for two. The pain that I felt when I saw you sleeping in that bed

and I was on the sofa, the temptation I had to sneak over there and

hold you into my arms providing you with warmth and comfort. I

thought holding you close to me would help ease the beating of my

heart, but then you had that nightmare and didn't want me to leave holding you so close that I could smell how sweet you were and how small you were compared to me. You were so small and yet you radiated heat like anything, keeping me warm and comfortable that falling asleep next to you seemed natural. Then bloody Ghillie had to get involved and take you from me creating all kinds of different serious in my head, in wasn't sure if the villagers had come and taken you away, if you had left me, I thought the worse that you didn't care about me anymore and decided to either go back to your world or even go to the douche Aelfdane. But I'm not going to waste anymore of this letter on any of them. I found that over the past days that missing you has become my hobby caring for you has become my job and making you happy is now my duty while I've found falling in love you is now my life, seeing you happy everyday has become something that I need in life for you. I found my soulmate; I found my one true love. I found my one and forever and always and I feel that I've found that in you and I hope that one day you would have found the same in me and whenever that day comes then I'll give you the key to the geode. I can't give you the key to my heart as you've already won that over for now and always.

Your beautiful smile and your happy laughter attracted me to you, but your caring loving heart is the reason why I want to spend the rest of my life with you. I want to sit by your side and hold your hand, stare into your eyes and cuddle up with you every night keeping each other warm and sharing kisses with you every single day.

So, my love this ends my letter to you for now. My sweet caramel fairy. To you I promise that I'll make you feel wanted, loved and needed every single day .

You're forever the only Kelpie in your life.

Cailean.

Sealing the letter in the transparent envelope, a sound of movement on grass captured his attention. As he looked up from his sitting position, he could see that Aerwyna was stirring for her sleep. Dropping the notepad and envelope on the floor he rushed to her side grasping her hand in his need to feel her warmth.

"Aerwyna. My caramel fairy, can you hear me?"

Aerwyna rocked her head side to side trying hard to fight the urge to stay asleep, she could feel someone's hand holding hers, the pull of sleep was strong but whoever was calling her name seemed to be stronger than the draw of sleep that was trying to hold over her. Lifting her hand to her eyes she rubbed them trying to pull herself out of the last grip of sleep before opening her eyes and seeing Cailean for the first time in what seemed like forever.

"Cailean, is this a dream? Is that you or am I dreaming of you? If this is a dream then let me sleep forever with that look in your eyes as if i'm the only one for you in the world, holding my hand and giving me the look of love. I don't remember the last time someone looked at me with utter adoration."

Cailean couldn't help but smile kneeling down next to her as he placed his hand on the top of her head, running his fingers through the silken ends. Only she could think that him holding her hand and looking down at her with love that was unhidden would think that she was dreaming it all.

"My love you know this isn't a dream im here, i'm always here for you."

"Well, if this is true then let me die here now and forever live in this moment."

Cailean couldn't help but smile at that. He didn't think that she was as dramatic as she was. But then again now that her memories were returning more and more maybe this was her true personality. If that was the case then he couldn't have found her more attractive, it was like she turned into a little child when she was being dramatic, if that was the case well then, he supposed he would have to indulge her in that aspect.

"My dear I think that is a tad bit dramatic but oh well if you want to die in this moment then I my love shall join you there so that we may both live in this moment together forever."

The look on her face was all he needed to prove that the idea of them together moving closer to her pulling her gently into his embrace, his lips ever so close to her that if either of them moved just a hair their lips would touch. It only took one person to ruin that moment with.

"pl...ease you to need to get a room and stop with all the dramatics no one is going to die and moments like this may not last forever but that's good. I didn't want to see my lunch once more. I highly doubt it will look as nice coming back than it did before I ate it. "

Ghillie said leaning against the makeshift door frame of a tree that separated what he had told Cailean was his front room and bedroom. The look that Cailean gave him was one of such severity that if looks could kill then he estimated that Ghillie would have died about two thousand times since Aerwyna fell asleep.

"Seriously Ghillie you choose this moment to be annoying."

Ghillie couldn't help but laugh as he reminded them that it was about time to continue with what they were doing by looking for the stones to create the Myrios stone. Cailean rolled his head to look once more at Aerwyna before turning back to Ghillie who stood with a smug grin on his face knowing that he interrupted an important moment to Cailean between himself and Aerwyna.

"fine."

Was all he said before he took both of Aerwyna hands helping her to her feet once more be careful of her incase she felt dizzy at any point and fainted once more, he wanted to be the one there to catch her.

***

After Cailean and Aerwyna had returned to Ghillie's little makeshift front room after a few death glares for Cailean much to Ghillie's delight, they continued looking into the riddles that revealed the locations of the remaining stones.

"If I remember correctly the stones are actually semi-precious gemstones that are related to the stone name and not anything to do with the locations. For instance, the stone of the ocean is actually Aquamarine, which is connected to the moon and the ocean. The stone of misery is a black diamond which had acquired the reputation of being unlucky to the owner. The stone of purity is an opal that's been considered the gemstone of hope, purity and truth for thousands of years. And lastly the stone of night is a gemstone called Kunzite, it is a unique stone as it is normally called the evening stone. And it flashes from a light pink to an almost purple as it turns. When the stones all merge together it creates the gemstone imperial topaz which is one of the most powerful manifestations stones you can get your hands on, when the driving force behind all we do is awaken and it's fully activated, anything becomes possible."

Ghillie relayed all the information he knew about the stones and what they looked like. All this time both Cailean and Aerwyna thought the names were a clue to the locations, not gemstones that reminded the owners of the powers they held.

"The banshee valley holds the stone of misery, so the gemstone we're looking for is going to be a black diamond. That's going to be hard to find the valley of the banshee, the entire valley was shrouded in darkness, it was told that the banshee preferred it that way, that way they could lure in unexpecting people and lure them to their death, that and it gave their permissions a more morbid effect , if they were told in a miserably dark gloomy place. Or so I've overheard from people walking through the woods on their way back from there." That stopped all conversation. If they both thought if people had walked through these woods talking about the banshees, then it couldn't be that far away from here. They didn't know what to do if the valley was so close to them then they could have the misery stone by the end of the day, and they would be one step closer to having them all and stopping her father from ever hurting anyone again, if he had their powers on top of his own then no one would be safe.

"So, in theory we could get the misery stone today and bring her back to safety before the end of the day. Ghillie so I have that correct."

"In theory, yes, you're correct, but the banshee are devious; they will try anything in their powers to keep you there and lead you to your death. So, if we do go then we'll all have to be careful."

It was at that point that Cailean joined in the conversation , inserting himself in between Aerwyna and Ghillie, who had somehow come to stand next to each other.

"Excuse me. we'll? I think you'll find this is my and Aerwyna journey and we don't have any more room for anyone else, so I'm afraid my poor, poor ghillie you'll have to stay here in your forest and do what you do best."

"And what that's you, stubborn, jealous kelpie."

Before Cailean could answer Aerwyna step in between them, he had realised that since their little discussion was commencing, they were moving closer and closer to each other and the looks in their eyes weren't the happiest even he had to say.

"Alright calm down boys there is enough room on this journey for all of us, we all have our own unique abilities that may help us along this journey so in my opinion we should all go along on this together. Now do you both promise to get along with each other."

With a grimace on each of their faces they stood in front of the other taking a deep breath while they turned their head looking down at Aerwyna who stood with her hands on her hips trying her hardest to look intimidating which made them both smile. How she thought she could look intimidating to them when they stood so much taller than her. They looked at each other once more, both signing in unison a smiler etching it way onto their faces.

"Fine, he can come."

"Fine, I'll come along."

Both said in unison which made Aerwyna unable to stop smiling. Pulling them both into a hug they found it quite funny seeing her hands around their waists made them look down with their arms splayed around her.Looking at each other they shared a look which only they knew. It didn't take long for them to bend down and scoop her up, balancing her on the joined arms which rested on the other's shoulders placing their heads on her lap which was now within reach.

"You guys, this is going to be amazing."

In unison the boys spoke.

"Only you would think walking perilously into the banshee valley would be amazing."

"Why do I have a feeling you're going to be in trouble?"

Aerwyna couldn't help but smile more as she hugged the boys' heads, knowing they were beside her made her fearless, she knew that they both wouldn't let anything happen to her, if her grandmother was right then it was predestined to happen, she just hope that she could protect them as much as they were going to protect her. With all said and done they packed a small bag with a few essentials and left the safe confines of ghillie secluded woodland home to venture into the valley of the Banshees.

***

The walk to banshee valley was surprisingly beautiful. The trees were in full bloom as were the plants and bushes which filled in the gaps in between the trees which lined the path they walked upon. The path they walked upon was covered in fallen leaves and indents made by people walking and carts and wagons being driven along, even though they walked in the middle of the day there was no other being, being human or other anywhere near them. Small walls lined the trees in front made up of line rock and stones that were placed on top of each other, most grew in between the rocks some hiding the crevice other completely covering the rocks it lay upon. Aerwyna looked up at the two boys, not actually the two men that stood either side of her, and couldn't help but smile, Cailean carried the bag of supplies for them all and ghillie carried the map, checking it every so often

279

making sure that they were following the correct path. It didn't matter
how much she tried to carry things they both gave her a look which
made her think they were saying how dare you even try, which out
even saying anything so after three futile attempts she gave up.
Instead, she went along and plucked flowers along the way creating
two crowns one for each of them. When she completed each one she
gestured to Cailean to lower his head which resulted in a coy smile
from him, she didn't know what he was thinking but either way she
didn't think it was this. Placing the flower crown of his head was
surprising for her, she didn't think that she would have guessed the
size right the first time and it amazed her how the flowers
complemented his hair. She smiled and clapped her hands.
"I hope you have one for me as well my little Erinus Alpinus."
Ghillie lent his head down towards her and brought his lips closer to
her ear as he spoke, leaving tiny goosebumps along her skin. A huff
sounded behind her which she knew came from Cailean, she didn't
know that he could be so jealous, what he was jealous of she didn't
know.
"As a matter of fact, I do."
She reached up to place it on his head but realised halfway that he
still wore his hood.
"Ghillie your hood, its in the way."

A smile enchanted in his face as he reached up and lowered his hood

revealing his long black braided hair. It surprised her that the silver

bead he had at the front extended to the braids at the back.

"Ghillie your hair, it's so pretty, the little beads are beautiful , I

wonder how you made them."

Ghillie reached up to the braids at the front of his face. Take out the

silver beads that decorated them. Pulling one out from his braid

Aerwyna could see that it had an emerald dangling from the bottom

of the spiralled metal. Ghillie reached forwards grasping a small

section of Aerwyna hair pulling it towards him as he gently coiled the

section of hair around the base of the spiral before twisting the top in,

letting it hang there decorating the front of her hair with something of

his made him slightly proud. It made him more proud to see the

reaction it had on Cailean from what he could see, nothing of

Caileans was on her, which meant he hadn't yet marked her, so it left

her open for him as well as Cailean, it meant it left the choice up to

her.

"Oh, ghillie, it's beautiful. Cailean look how beautiful it is."

Cailean's face quickly mellowed as he looked at Aerwyna, as much as

he disliked the person it came from, he had to admit that it suited her,

he found that anything in an emerald green suited her, be it clothes or

jewellery.

"It looks beautiful, my caramel fairy; it suits you perfectly."

Cailean placed his hand on her head running his fingers through her hair. Aerwyna realised that they had stopped walking, looking around her she noticed that the lush green trees had started to lose their leaves, losing the vibrancy in them. Looking around Cailean she saw the impending darkness of the entrance to the valley of the banshees; the lush green faded away to murky waters raging against the sides of the path that seemed to float on the waters. Dark mountains parted leading to a dark cavernous tunnel with a rocking old sign at the front which half read vall the shee the sign was so old half of the letters had rubbed away from the harsh winds that battered the walls, water and the very path itself. Even the very sky itself darken the further in the tunnel they went. Although Aerwyna was scared she tried not to show it, it didn't last long when a massive crash sound of thunder, making her grasp Caileans arm tightly to her chest hiding her face in his clothes. The action itself made Cailean smugly look over at Ghillie who was scowling at him.

***

The further into the tunnel they walked the louder the music filtered into the enclosed space, the enchanting yet hypnotising sound led them closer and closer to the darkness that encompassed the entire space in front of them. The further they went, they didn't think it

282

could get any darker but somehow it did, they all held on tightly to
each other in fear that they would lose the others if they let go. It
wasn't long before something pulled Ghillie away, enchanting him
with the hypnotising sound leading him away before a deafening
shriek sounded as Cailean got pulled away too leaving only Aerwyna
in the middle of the long dark cold path that lead into the heart of the
valley. She stood there taking a deep breath before storming into the
heart to the valley, if anyone was going to save her friends then so be
it, it will be done by her and no one else.

Chapter Twenty-Eight

Capture

The dark cavern the banshees resided in was always hidden in plain sight in the heart of the valley. From the topside the entrance of the cavern was discreetly hidden between carved trees that bent and twisted over the top of the entrance blending the opening perfectly with the rest of the valley. Once inside stalagmites formed from both the ceiling and floor leaving whoever entered having to carefully walk around upon fear of impalement. Only the Banshees knew the way through the carven, anyone else who tried to find them would be lost within their winding paths leaving them lost within its walls forever. It was within the heart of this dark dingy cavern that four banshees held both Cailean and Ghillie Dhu chained to the far wall away from all prying eyes and any source of life or light.

***

the four Banshees that faced them were in their human forms their long hair flowing behind them, from what Cailean had read about banshees was that they could take the form of one of four different animals which if he remembered were either a crow, stoat, hare or a weasel, allowing them to sneak into villages and torment all who resided within. The four in front of them took the forms of crows allowing them to sneak up on them and drag them here in hopes of trapping Aerwyna and making her give up the stones.it seemed they though she had the others, and this was the last to collect to create the Myrios stone, he didn't know what they wanted it for, but he knew it wouldn't be good.

"It doesn't matter what you do. It won't work, Aerwyna she won't fall for this, and she's way more powerful than you and she'll destroy you all if given half the chance."

The Banshees looked over at him with their eyes boring into him. The smile that appeared on their faces then was one to strike fear into people's hearts. With a voice so hollow and high.

"It doesn't matter if she is powerful."

One said sneaking closer to the two men bound against the wall

"Once we have the stone the powerful will fall."

Another said creeping up from the left this one voice was high and shrieky. They were slowly surrounding them from all sides. Did they think that it was a scare tactic , if they thought that this was going to work then they were sorely mistaken.

"It's the same as the others, when we present them with the ones they love, they all try to save them.no matter what the alternative is. Be it death or sacrifice."

The last two approached, now they were fully surrounded by all four one to the left, one to the right and two in front, the two in front had yet to speak but Cailean knew that their voices were going to be the ear-splitting ones, the gave the shriek of death.

"The thing we do is take away the things you care about and luckily for us both of you care about the same someone."

They all said the last part in unison masking the last two banshees' high shrieking voices. How they knew they cared so deeply for Aerwyna. The smiles that coiled into their faces, didn't give any of their plans away other than what they had already told them.

"You know I didn't care about a lot of things before. Until I met a girl named Aerwyna. That's when I realised I care about so many things. So, it doesn't matter what you do, nothing about that is going to change. And if you dare to hurt her then so help me. I will track you down and kill every one of you."

Ghillie nodded in turn agreeing with what Cailean said. Cailean knew at that moment that if the worse came to pass then Ghillie had his back to the end of the world.

***

At the entrance to the cavern Aerwyna prepared herself to venture into the darkness that lied before her. She didn't know how far into the cavern they were being held but it didn't matter, she knew what she had to do, but finding them in the dark was going to be the problem. It was then that warmth radiated in the palms of her hands. Bring them into her line of sight, she saw a faint light glowing. Her grandmother did tell her that she had more powers that haven't surfaced yet, maybe glowing palms was one of them. Picking up her bag that Cailean had dropped when he got taken, she took a deep breath before her first step into the chasm.

***

"You know it's worthless keeping us here. She came and we told her ages ago to leave us if anything ever happened to us. So, you're wasting what little time you have. Cause once we're out of theses shackles your all dead anyway."

Cailean growled at them, the more restrained he was the more annoyed he was getting. He didn't know what made them think that these tiny shackles could hold him.

"She more powerful than even we know, she doesn't even have the stones yet and she'll have more than enough power to destroy you, in the only way can"

"Only one is able to destroy a Banshee, and only one has survived doing so. They call her Alya."

The shock that worked its way onto both Caileans and Ghillies faces was unmeasurable the tale of the Alya had been spread wide, a being of unmeasurable power of chlorokinesis, clairvoyance, healing, photokinesis, and the one that scared even the bravest of people was Electrokinesis.

"The Alya is a myth, a legend if you will. The last died hundreds of years ago."

Ghillie shouted if anyone would know it would be Ghillie he heard everything that happened, the humans themselves thought he was a myth, in fact the humans though everyone of the kind being Brownies, Kelpie, Selkies, and fairies were a myth they even though the Banshees were a myth and the ran from their screams a death. But then again if Ghillie the man the myth could be true, then why couldn't the Alya be true.

***

Walking through the winding turns in the dark cavern of the Banshees, Aerwyna lit her way around the rock formations and stalagmites. Her palms dimmed and glowed brighter when pointed in a certain direction. She wondered if it grew brighter when pointed in the direction of Cailean and Ghillie, she wondered if it was like a

288

homing beacon for them, it pointed her to what her heart desired. In the dark depths of the cavern the brighter the light grew the more hope she had. She knew that they were fine; she knew it within her heart that they were alive and perfectly fine if anything they were causing trouble for the Banshees, knowing that gave her the strength to continue into the darkness. The further in she ventured the louder the slightly muffled sounds became; she could hear high pitched voices and two deeper ones which she knew belonged to Cailean and Ghillie. Crouching down Aerwyna approached an overhang that provided her with the perfect vantage point to overhear all and any conversations that was made between that the men were having with the Banshees, left her blushing at certain points, she loved how much faith they had in he, but it also surprised her that they thought she was going to abandon them. It was then she remembered what her grandmother told her.

" You have all the power you need if you just dared look for it."

Taking a deep breath, she lifted herself up from her crouched position, aimed her hand at the one of the Banshees and willed the light from the inside that guided her here to help her save the two most important people to her right now.

"Hey, you ugly Banshees, let my friends go."

With a shout of her voice the light in her hand shot out hitting the Banshee to the left leaving her laying on the floor unmoving. The other Banshee stood there in shock looking at their unmoving acquaintance. The look on the guy's face was priceless and Aerwyna wished she had time to savour their shock, but the other Banshee were moving towards her quickly. One was climbing the wall the overhand tapped and the others were climbing the stairs all trying to get to her.

"How dare you kill our sister, for that you too shall die."

The closer they got to her the more the Cailean and ghillie struggled against the shackles that restrained them, leaving them feeling helpless to do anything.

"Aerwyna the Alya."

Ghillie said in shock which caused Cailean to glance at him briefly not wanting to take his eyes off Aerwyna, he may be bound but he could shout out to help her. She had his full attention until Ghillie said that. But it made sense she had just shot a beam of light from her hand and killed a Banshee in one blast. As the Banshees lunged for her, she shot more beams of light randomly at them not wanting to look behind her in dear of falling over and losing her advantage.

"What makes you say that? And why did you even think that at this time, when she is fighting for her life and possibly ours, because she a stupid fool who can't listen to instructions."

 A beam of light hit the shackles that joined them both together on the left causing both men to quickly jolt out of the way from where it struck, causing them both to look up at where Aerwyna was hanging off the overhang with one arm and aimed the other at them with a scowl on her face.

"I think my friend you may have pissed her off."

Ghillie looked at Cailean as he wrestled himself out of the remaining shackle.

"I think my friend you may be right. "

A look of worry appeared on Caileans face as he looked at Aerwyna jump from the overhang and land just in front of the dead fireplace. A glimmer of light radiated from the railing that surrounded the fireplace. Ignoring the light, Aerwyna turned her attention to the three remaining Banshee that followed her. She looked behind them and saw that both Ghillie and Cailean had now freed themselves from the restraints.

"Ghillie threw me a plant, a flower, anything alive and green."

Reaching up Ghillie broke off one on the twigs that decorated the hood of his cape, throwing it towards her open hand. Aerwyna clutched the twig in her hand and called on her grandmother for the power to do what she hoped she would be able to. Closing her eyes, she spoke.

"Grow big, grow strong, grow tall enough. Help me protect the ones I love. Grow big, grow strong, grow tall, help me protect the ones I love."

Caileans face dropped as small beads of green light fell from her hands and circles around the tiny branch that Aerwyna held. The green orbs entered the twig being absorbed by it, allowing the tiny twig to start to grow. Aerwyna knelt down in front of both Cailean and Ghillie protecting them from behind her. In a matter of second the twig grew to an immeasurable size sprouting smaller twigs from itself darting out in different direction aiming for the Banshees, even though she eyes were closed Aerwyna could see exactly were the branches were heading, as she aimed for the banshees. The twigs she controlled impaled the remaining Banshees, putting a stop to their advancement's. Having them pinned in place they were able to move freely around the chasm that they kept them hostage in.

***

Aerwyna moved back toward the fireplaces making sure to stay out of the Banshees reach. Kneeling down the small streams of light that radiated from her palms illuminated the fireplace once more, allowing the shining object to glimmer in the darkness. Reaching into the very back of the fireplace Aerwyna plucked the small black diamond from the wall. Bringing it into light she could see how people previously had missed the stones, they were tiny compared to her and seeing as she was a small fairy to start with that was saying something. Both Cailean and Ghillie leaned over her shoulders looking down at the tiny diamond that sat in the palm of her still glowing hand.

"So that's the stone of misery. That tiny thing."

Ghillie leaned further down and took a good look at the tiny diamond that was no bigger than an acorn that he would find in the woods. It was round in shape and pointed down at the bottom, Cailean had seen many of the style, human use dot put them in rings and present them to their lady loves. Their inspection of the stone was rudely interrupted by the Banshees.

"So, Ayla lives once more."

The hollow Banshee spoke looking at Aerwyna taking in her glowing palms.

"But sister it seems that she has yet to master the power, if she still needs to speak the words of growth and light. I bet she can't even control the dreaded power yet."

Aerwyna looked over at the boys trying to gauge their ideas on what to do next. Did they leave them here, did they get rid of them, she had no idea, the very thought of her powers still scared her immensely.

Wrapping their arms around her both Cailean and Ghillie pulled her

into a hug, relishing in knowing that she was once again safe from all

harm. Pulling away to look at her they saw the exhaustion that was

there. Giving them a small smile, she turned to the Banshees.

"I'm not going to kill you and I'm not going to free you either.im

going to leave you here trapped for all entirely, to slowly be driven

mad with wanting. Much like hoe you torment everyone else to the

point of insanity with your scream of death, worrying them until the

worse happens. That's what is going to happen to you right here, right

now you'll be driven mad as you see us leave the wretched place

while you're stuck here in the dark where no one will come looking

for you."

Turning quickly on her heels she turned to face the boys once more,

before she wobbled on her feet, feeling faint. Cailean reached under

her pulling her close to him as he held her against himself. Ghillie

returned from the overhang with the bag that held their supplies

before he tucked a section of Aerwyna hair behind her ear revealing

her sleeping face. Saving them must have drained her, using a power

she didn't know she had would be immense pressure on her mind let

alone using two for an extended period of time. Turning to walk up

the stairs the Banshees cried out one last time.

"she won't live long if she continues like that, not knowing the strength of her powers will rip her apart from the inside and shatter her mind. You have no way of saving her even if you collect all the stone, shell die in front of you and you'll have no way of stopping it." The Banshees laughed as the men retreated up the stairs and away from the darkness of the cavern.

***

Standing at the entrance of the cavern the boys looked at one another as they continued their walk through the Banshee valley, the thought that it was Banshee free now calmed them immensely. Reaching the end of the valley allowed them to let loose a sigh of relief, though the bare crooked tree and beyond the stairs was a portal that led them back to Ghillies forest, seeing the plush green field and sunset sky freed them from all the worry and pain that they just went through. "Home."

Ghillie sighed. Looking down at the sleeping Aerwyna. The exhaustion was still presented on her face. He could see that the powers were draining her and what the Banshees told them worried him. Was she in theory killing herself by using the powers that were bestowed upon her. Would there be a way to save her from that fate, he wasn't sure but by his life he would find a way to save her even if it meant his life. There had to be something in the library in his home,

295

something on the Ayla. Some kind of cure for the powers, anything if

there was something he would find. A hand dropped to his shoulder

as Cailean adjusted Aerwyna holding her and his shoulder all at once.

"Let's go back home. And see what we can find, while she

recuperates."

With a nod of his head all three of them walked through the portal

and back into the safety of the forest.

Chapter Twenty-Nine

Stone of Purity

Safely back in the confines of Caileans woodland home, Aerwyna lay

resting on the bed of moss once more, recuperating once more after

saving them from the clutches of the Banshees.

"There's got to be some information on Alya."

Cailean checked every book he could think of in Ghillies library

when they held no answers, he slammed them shit with one hand

before he threw them over his shoulder. One flew towards Ghillies

head if he didn't duck out of the way it would have collided with his

face.

"Okay, okay, I know you're stressed but please respect the books,

don't throw them on the ground, I know it is covered in moss but still

come on man."

Ghillie bent to pick up the scattered books, placing them back on the

shelves which at present were bare from Cailean throwing them

everywhere.

"I know I'm sorry, I know you care about your 'books' but there has to be something here. You have books on everything. Please if you have one with something in it, point me in the right direction."

Ghillie didn't like how he said 'books' like he didn't care. He knew he was stressed but to treat books like that was disgraceful. Ghillie stepped up the ladder beside him pulling down a dusty dark red book with golden edge caps and golden filigree design on the front. Blowing the dust of the front it revealed the name.

'The myths and tales of the Ayla'

"This is the only book that exists with any information on Ayla. There's not much as many of the Alya disappeared mysteriously or died young, but if there's anything we should I know it'll be in here. Hopefully it will hold something that we can use to save her."

***

Opening the book was a delicate operation, Cailean estimated it to be around 500 years old which would date back to the very first Ayla. Most of the back pages had crumbled and turned to dust, but the pages which held information seemed in perfect condition almost like they were enchanted to stay in a perfect condition, for future Ayla's. flicking through the pages it revealed chapters on the appearances of the past Ayla's, their powers and everything they could possibly need to know, it had all the information except what they wanted, which was a way in which to save her.

298

"Why doesn't it have anything on how to save her? There's got to be something, I can't let her go, Ghillie we've got to save her."

It hurt Ghillie to see Cailean, a proud Kelpie looking so dejected. There wasn't much that could be done, the information wasn't there, they couldn't magic it out of the thin air, they wanted anyone else around they could ask either. If it was as easy as purifying her then that would be easily done, all that required was Caileans blood.

It was then that a thought struck Ghillie, Aerwyna was fine before she stepped into the Banshee valley, could the darkness have polluted her soul and that was what was making her sleep, maybe if Cailean tried to purify her then maybe she would wake up. If anything, it was worth a try.

"Cailean, have you tried purification, maybe the darkness of the valley corrupted her, it could be an idea and we all know that Kelpies are the gods of purification, its basically in your blood, literally."

The look on Caileans face was one of acceptance, the thought of it working filled him with hope, he had to try and pray that it worked even a little bit. Not taking the time for the thought to process in his mind, he jumped off the ladder and ran towards the bedroom where a sleeping Aerwyna lay.

***

Kneeling down beside her, Cailean looked down at her sleeping face. Aerwyna's hair was splayed around the top of her head, her hands crossed over her stomach, and her dress floating around her legs, giving her an angelic appearance that Cailean loved. Tucking her hair behind her ear allowed him a better view of her face, he loved looking at her. Thinking about the purification he would normally drop a small bit of his blood on their tongue and that would work, but with Aerwyna being unconscious at the moment he didn't think that would work. I knew one other way that he could administer his blood to her but doing that when she was asleep and without her agreeing and joining in didn't feel right to him. The only other way that he thought of it was if he put his blood on his lips and kissed her, it would drip in her mouth that way and what he hoped would help her. Ghillie stood behind him leaning against the door jamb looking over at his once and hopefully once again friend and saw the anguish that presented itself on his face.

"You know she'll understand why you did it, she won't hold it against you if that's what you're worried about."

Ghillie said walking into the room kneeling down next to Cailean. Placing his hand on Caileans shoulder.

"It's the only thing we can think of, and I can tell you from what I've seen she is the most understanding person I've ever met. If this is all we could think of then we've got to try right."

All Cailean could offer was a small smile towards Ghillie, he knew he was trying his hardest, but would it truly work? Would she truly be okay with this, with him kissing her like this. It was then it hit him, The Stone of Purity. It was the purest stone said to be even purer than the Kelpies blood.

"The stone."

Was all Cailean said before he was up and running out of the room towards the map.

***

"What's the location of the stone of purity? If we find that, it should help her. I've heard it is more powerful than Kelpie blood."

The look on Ghillie's face told Cailean that he had heard the same thing. Both said in unison that if they retrieve the song then bring it back here to Aerwyna then one she would get her rest and then they could purify anything around her that was keeping her sleep.

Looking at the next riddle for the stone of purity was actually easier than what Cailean thought it would be. It read.

Stallions sleek that bray and bleat with voices fey and agenbite, my love, May think to snare your soul so fair that bobs upon the night.

301

So, sail to sleep on currents deep with blankets, bladderwrack and brine, my love, And all the beasts that haunt the seas wouldn't harm a babe of mine.

"Right grab me a pen and paper and let's decipher this riddle."

Both Caileans and Ghillie sat at the table looking at the riddle breaking it down into sections.

"Stallions sleek that bray and bleat with voices fey and agenbite, my love, this could mean me in my Kelpie form which is a stallion which is sleek and brays and bleats. But the 'my love' at the end has me confused.

So, sail to sleep on currents deep with blankets bladderwrack and brine, the sail along the river in the middle of the realm, it had both deep currents and blankets of bladderwrack that mean to a willow tree on the other side.

And all the beasts that haunt the seas wouldn't harm a babe of mine. This could mean Kelpies. They normally haunt the seas and rivers but don't mind if they are young or old, but my father married a human and had me which broke the laws which would mean I was their babe in a sense. Maybe I could be the tie to both the stallion and the unhurt babe.``

Cailean turned his head to see Ghillie nodding his head agreeing with him.

"That could be very plausible, it all matches up that for sure. All we need now is to find a way to the Kelpie realm, and find a way to make sure Aerwyna is safe here while we're away collecting this stone. I don't know why my father never told me about the stone, if it's hidden there why not tell me."

Once all said and done thy made their way around making sure everything was secure, Ghillie casted and enchantment which would lock the door to the bedroom so no one from the outside could get in but if Aerwyna were to awaken would be able to leave and the enchantment would be broken.

"Cailean, I know there is a place in the woods that hold doors in the trees themselves, im ninety nine percent sure there's a door to the Kelpie realm, we might have to go through the other to find the right one as the don't have name or labels above them, but we'll find them."

Packing the last few supplies, Cailean heaved up the bag onto his shoulder before turning towards the door and Ghillie.

"Right then, you're ready."

Ghillie nodded, heaving his bag onto his shoulders before they headed off towards the Kelpie realm.

***

Walking through the woods without Aerwyna felt both strange and unusual, Cailean had gotten so used to walking around with her at his side, and now that she wasn't here it was like a part of him was missing. Approaching a circle of tall broad oak trees both Cailean and Ghillie decided to each take one tree and see where it led that way they could narrow down the possibilities of finding the right tree.

"This place is going to be perfect for travelling around to find the stones if they lie in other realms, why didn't you tell us before."

"If it was a place that my parents told me about and they said it was special and needed to be protected, they said that if people found it, if humans found it then it would be dangerous for all of our kinds, so it needed to be protected."

Ghillie stood there with his hand and forehead resting against the tree while Cailean looked at him before lifting his head to look at the tall oaks that stood before him. Looking back at Ghillie he could see that this place meant a lot to him and showing Cailean who was as close to a friend as he thought he was, meant a lot, to the both of them for very different reasons. They tried four doors, Caileans too led to the Brownies and Selkies door, and Ghillies doors led to the human town of Llwyn and the fairy's realm so that only left one door.

"Well, this is the only one left so it must be this one."

Cailean took a deep breath before opening the door, he didn't have any idea of where this door was going to lead him in his world would it be close to where he lived like when Ghillie used to visit him, he would randomly show up in the gardens and disappear just as quickly, or would it lead him far away on the other side by the tree entrance, he didn't know but there was only one way to find out. Cailean felt a pressure on his shoulder causing him to turn his head, Ghillie stood there with the most stupid grin on his face making Cailean instantly relax.

"Come on buddy let's go save our girl."

Cailean placed his hand on Ghillie's shoulder as they both walked through the door and into the Kelpie realm.

***

Emerging from the door they were greeted by a sparkling lake that extended in front of them with the places far in the distance appearing just above the tops of the trees.

"So, this was how you snuck in to see me."

Ghillie just smiled in response, not needing to say anything, as he walked towards the lake, almost as if he could remember the way.

"Hey, do you know where you are going?"

"Yeah, it's just down the secret path your mother showed me."

That put a stop to Caileans movements, his mother had shown him a secret path that even he didn't know about. Was it a path he knew about but had forgotten he couldn't remember but either way it was a part of his mother he was going to rediscover.

"Of course, she showed you a secret path, she knew you were petrified of my father. Well then lead the way."

***

Approaching a dark seemingly innocent cavern that led under the lake they saw from the door both Cailean and Ghillie took another breath.

"You ready man. You know this means you've got to possibly face my father"

Cailean turned towards Ghillie who wore a look of terror, Cailean knew his father could be a scary person but the thought that an almighty woodland spirit like Ghillie would be scared was something else entirely. He hoped that with him being there would calm his father down, if only by a little bit.

"Well, I was younger and much smaller then so even you looked scary being as tall as you were. And your father was taller than you, so he was definitely intimidating."

Cailean slapped his hand on Ghillie's shoulder trying in some way to show some support before they both took a deep breath and ventured into the cavern.

***

Entering the cavernous passageway every single little stand of light dispersed the further in they walked. From what seemed like hours they were walking in pitch darkness feeling around for anything that could possibly injure them or stop them from reaching the other side. That was until in the far distance they saw a faint blue light radiate in front of them. Ghillie saw it first drawing Caileans attention in that direction.

"What the hell is that?"

"I don't know, let's take a closer look, we have to walk in that direction anyways."

Both Ghillie and Cailean looked at each other before walking towards the mysterious blue light. Approaching the light, it revealed that it was created by a numerous amount of crystals. They covered every single space that was available in the small cave within; they covered the ceiling, the ground, even the walls around them.

"What are they?"

Cailean took a step closer looking at the crystals a little bit closer, almost inspecting them. They were a mixture of purples and blue and white, almost like it was three different gemstones all together.

"Well, it looks like a mixture of three different stones"

Cailean pointed to the blue stones ``This one's Aquamarine. It evokes purity and crystal blue waters and relaxation. It's also associated with trusting and letting go. According to the human in ancient time it was believed to be the treasured gemstone of mermaids."

Moving onto the purple one, it made him smile, seeing the gemstone in its raw form. " This one's Alexandrite. It signifies luck, prosperity and intellect. It represents the balance between the physical and spiritual. It said it can bring balance to anyone who owns it. It was also one of the stones that my father included one the ring he gave my mother, seeing as he was allegedly a spiritual being to the humans and my mother was one of the physical humans from the world. Therefore, being spiritual and physical, he found it suited them both perfectly."

The last one that drew his eyes was one of pure white and crystal clear but also slightly blurred within the stone, it didn't take him long he would recognize this stone from miles away.

"Moonstone. Inner clarity and a connection to the feminine. It's a symbol of light and hope but also encourages people to embrace new beginnings. The humans associated it with fertility, balance, softness and intuition. Also, within my mother's ring. So, this was where the old fool got the gems. No wonder my mother found this place "

Looking around at the stones that surrounded them they could both feel her presence around them holding them close but urging them on as well. Ghillie smiled down at Cailean who knelt next to the biggest moonstone he had ever seen, before crouching down looking at the gemstone himself. Ghillie could see why his mother showed him this way it was calm and peaceful, secretive of a sort. It was then that small light floated down around them illuminating the area that little bit more.

"Fireflies."

Cailean raised his head seeing himself surrounded with fireflies once more brought memories back of the tree lined walkway, with bag from the shops In town with Aerwyna looking up at the surrounding them, it also reminded him of his mother he could remember her dancing around the garden with fireflies surrounding her, and it was then that he realised how similar his mother and Aerwyna were. A laugh escaped him, as the two images danced in his head, he could now see why his father loved Aerwyna so much, why he have his mother ring to her, it was because he saw so much of his late wife in her, in her personality in how much she cared for people, it made him more determined to find the stone, he had to get back to her back to his caramel fairy.

"Look over there. Is that your mot...."

Cailean looked over his shoulder at the far crystal encrusted wall to see. His mother was standing there looking at him.

***

Rising slowly with his mouth open, Cailean looked at his mother who he hadn't seen since he was a very young boy. He couldn't even remember how old she was when she passed, but here now she stood behind him smiling at him like no time had passed at all.

"Mot….Mother?"

Even Ghillie stood there with his mother open, he hadn't seen the woman in years, she hadn't changed one bit. She still wore a smile that could enchant anyone who stood within her present. Her hair was still as black as night and her eyes still as enchanting and as blue as the ocean. Now that they were both older, she could see why Caileans father wanted to steal her away and why he got so bewitched by her. She was beautiful inside and out. The smile on her face was definitely that of his mother but Cailean couldn't understand how she was here.

"My son, how you've grown."

The tears that threatened to fall stung his eyes, hearing her voice once more brought all the pain and hurt back into his soul. He remembered how much he missed her, missed her hugs, her voice, missed just being able to be near her and talk to her when something in his life didn't make sense, she was always the one who helped him find the

310

logical way at looking at things. The tears stung as he fell, turning everything in his line of sight blurry, blurring his mother in the process.

"Mother, please don't go stay where I can see you, Mother." Running at full speed towards where she was standing led him nowhere, she disappeared.

***

Ghillie placed his hand on Caileans shoulder, not knowing what to stay, could it have been a trick of the gems, both of them knowing that she was once here in this beautiful place, id that risk their minds or was she actually here, here in her spirit form leading them to the stone to help her son's lady love. Ghillie stood and looked around, he knew she wouldn't have just appeared then disappeared when her son was so close to her, she had to be around she wasn't a torment like that, she had to be leading them somewhere. That was when he saw her, standing but a small opening on the far-right side of the cave pointed at her finger and the entrance, with that cheeky smile she always had when she was causing trouble.

"Cailean over there."

Cailean looked up just in time to see his mother duck down into the opening.

311

"I think she's leading us to the stone, what else could be down here in a cave full of crystals. Maybe she knows where it is."

Only being able to nod his head Cailean agreed. Rising up to his full height, drying his eyes he looked at Ghillie who offered him a small smile, nodding his head in agreement as they both headed into the direction his mother had directed them.

***

Entering the small space was difficult, for the fact there were two fully grown males, and the space was obviously made for children. It made sense it would be the perfect place to hide the stone of purity, it was right under their noses. The crystals continued their way down the little cavern as well illuminating the surrounding area basking it in all manners of coloured lights.

"Aerwyna would love this."

Cailean said making a mental note that when this whole hair brained adventure was over, to bring her here and see her face light up, he could imagine the colours that the gems radiated would contract with her hair perfectly. Just imagining it made him want to get back to her as soon as possible.

"We need to hurry, we can't leave Aerwyna alone for too long."

Cailean looked around the small enclosed space seeing if he could either find his mothers spirit or and exit from this tiny space. But from what he could see there was nothing, no exit and not his mother.

"Where do we go from here, do you see any exit at all."

"No, nothing."

Cailean stood as tall as he could in the confined space looking around trying to see if he could see anything that would indicate where they should go, what direction they should head. They both looked to no Advil nothing, they could see nothing, no exit for other openings, no but crystals everywhere. Until one shone just slightly brighter than the others, and upon closer inspection it was a completely different gemstone to the other, this one was an opal just like the map had told them. When Cailean turned around to tell Ghillie he found that the stubborn woodland spirit had left the small cave leaving him and only him alone . he thought of the last line of the riddle *And all the beasts that haunt the seas wouldn't harm a babe of mine. He* needed to be alone for the stone to reveal its hiding spot. He smiled knowing that this small tiny opal would be the key to waking the fairy.

"So, you've found it at last."

 A voice so soft and gentle made the tears form in the back of his eyes once more.

"Mum."

Cailean turned around so quickly in fear that she would just disappear once more like she had before.

"My how you've grown."

It didn't take him long to run into her embrace, oh how he missed her, her embrace felt the same as when he was a child, secure and loving just like a mother's embrace should be. The sobs came hard and fast from him, and it felt like there was nothing he could do to stop them.

"And I'll love thee still my dear, till all the seas run dry my dear , and the rocks melt with the sun, and I will love thee still my dear, while sands of life shall run."

With only a few lines for the lullaby she used to sing, he claimed him immensely. Raising his head to look at her he saw her ocean blue eyes that his father fell for, and all his memories of her came running back. His mother bent her head placing a light kiss on the top of his head causing him to smile.

"How I've missed you. There's so much I want to tell you, so many people I want you to meet, there's not enough time for everything."

His mother only smiles and assured him that she saw everything he did, as she was never too far away, he saw the shop he took over from his father and how often he visited the shop she used to work at supporting everything subtly in the background. She told him how proud she was of him and how sorry she was for leaving him.

"But my child, do you know what the best thing I've seen is?"

Cailean could feel the tears starting to sting the back of his eyes once more. It felt like it was her final goodbye to him.

"I love how you've found the one person who would love you no matter what you could do. Who would fight for you, look after you when myself and your father can't be there. Someone who no matter how perilously the journey is, is happy that you are by her side. She may not tell you physically but my child her actions are there."

"How do you know mother, if someone cares for you without telling you."

The smile his mother gave him beamed at him with the most abundance of sunlight.

"Does she make you drinks and food? "he nodded

"Does she make sure you eat no matter how busy you get?" he nodded once more.

"Does she make sure that the workshop is clean and tidy, so you can't hurt yourself on anything?" He didn't nod this time, he just looked at his mother.

"Does she check on you when you try to sneak out at night without telling her, I think if you look out the window on that night, you will see a tiny face looking out at you, making sure that you make it safely back inside. I can assure you she cares about you deeply. More deeply than I think she knows, your father knows that stubborn old coot, that's why he gave her my ring, because he knew that her feelings for you were the purest one you could ever find, and he knew that you would be well looked after by her. And my son I can tell you one thing not because you need to hear it but because you want to. I approve of her greatly, she is perfect for you in every way my child, these crystals here can show you for certain, some hold magic that can show you what is meant to happen. If you want to look, look at the one on the right, and it will show you something that will ensure you happiness for the rest of the trailing journey."

Crystals that could show the future, did he want to look at a possible future without Aerwyna, would that be the case by what his mother told him.

***

 Releasing her waist, he looked at the stone, but nothing happened.

"Mother nothing happening, am I doing it wrong?"

She knelt down beside her silly son and placed his hands on the stone creating the images that appeared in front of him."

"Place your hands and watch, see what some of your life holds for you."

Cailean took a deep breath and looked into the images appearing on the stone in front of him.

316

The images revealed the shop on any other day the sky was casted in

sunset illuminating the shop in a gentle orange glow.

"Hey"

Aerwyna said quickly fumbling around with the ties on the back of her

dress as he walked in holding their little baby………… On his arms.

"Cailean ."

He quickly said, passing the child over to his other arms so he could

pull Aerwyna closer to him. As he did, she let go of the ties of her

dress allowing her wings to flow free.

"W-What?"

Aerwyna looked up at him quizzically, the blush very promoted on her

cheeks. Cailean looking down at her a playful smirk on his lips

"It's not 'Hey'"

Cailean used his one free arm to do air brackets making sure she

knew he was being sarcastic.

"But Cailean there's no way you don't know your own husband's

name right.?"

Cailean lowered his head with that playful smirk only growing

bigger as he lowered his head placing a loving kiss on her lips.

"Of course, didn't you think I would forget after all the temptation I

had to do to land you."

Aerwyna smiled playfully, slapping his chest before reaching for the little baby that currently resided in Caileans arms.

"Hey my little Eilonwy."

Aerwyna reached her finger out going to tickle the little baby when the images stopped, and the stone went black. Cailean looked at his mother who had a smile on her face, in a way she was seeing her granddaughter, even though she wouldn't be able to hold her it looked like she was content enough to see her. There was not a lot that either of them could say, at some point in the future he was going to marry Aerwyna and have a child with her which he would name after his mother in a roundabout way, her middle name was Eilonwy

"But when will that happen, he didn't look much older than we are now."

A smile plastered her face as he tucked stray hairs behind his ear.

"Soon my child soon, there is a light at the end of the tunnel, all this pain is worth the future. Now my son, take this stone and wake you love so that the future may continue."

"But mother, that would mean to leave you."

"I never left, I was always with you and always will be, you may not be able to see me, but I shall always be there for squillions and billions forever and ever. Just like before."

Cailean wrapped his arms around his mother once more trying to imprint her embrace on him. He knew this would be the last time he would see her for a long, long time.

"Goodbye mother, be well and be safe wherever you are."

"Goodbye my son, just for now, be happy, be safe and be kind to anyone you see. Just remember that love is in the actions more than the words."

With a tear in his eye, he turned to exit the small cave before taking one more look over his shoulder to find his mother had already gone. With a heavy heart he left the cave she loved to do much, all the more determined to wake Aerwyna so they could get one step closer to the future, the future they shared together.

Chapter Thirty

The Stone Of The Ocean

Seeing that Aerwyna hadn't moved was a wave of relief for both Ghillie and Cailean. It made Cailean laugh how even though she hadn't moved her hair had come to rest over her face once more, making him feel the need to tuck it back behind her ear once more. Revealing her most beautiful face, to them.

"Do you really think this'll work?"

Ghillie looked at Cailean who held the stone close to his chest he tried to hide the worry on his face, he hope that his nervousness wasn't shown on his face, but he didn't have any hope left, it was all on this, hoping that his stone would wake Aerwyna.

"If I'm being completely honest. I don't know."

They both took a deep breath before Cailean placed the stone over Aerwyna's heart, before he dropped a small drop of his blood on her lips, hoping to purify whatever was keeping her asleep.

"Now we just have to wait. Let go work out the next riddle, see if we can get a head start on the location of the stone. Maybe that will help her a bit when she wakes."

Standing at the doorway both peered over their shoulder looking at Aerwyna hoping that soon they would be blessed to see her striking greens eyes once more.

***

Aerwyna could hear people talking but could make out what they were saying, everything around her was shrouded in darkness and every sound was muffled. She tried to move her head, but it didn't work. It was like something was pinning her to the ground. She looked through the darkness trying to find a way out, a way back to the guys, she had to help them, she had to save them from the Banshees.

"Cailean? Ghillie? Where are you guys?"

After a few minutes she was able to move, she walked through the darkness calling after both Cailean and Ghillie, but with no luck they were nowhere to be seen. Aerwyna didn't find the guys, but she seemed to find every little bump and dip in the dark falling over everything hidden in front of her.

"How many little holes and rocks am I going to find? Trust me to find every little thing to trip over but I can't find two tall big men.

Cailean?

Ghillie? Where are you? Please if you're here please come out. I'm scared I don't know what to do. I miss you."

Aerwyna fell to the floor holding her head in her hands as the tears started to fall. As she curled herself into a small ball, it seemed that the darkness was closing in on her. What she couldn't see was a small light moving towards her reaching out to her.

"My dear, why do you cry?"

At the sound a gentle voice Aerwyna's head whipped up to look into eyes as blue as the ocean.

***

Looking at the map with all the locations they found that the stone of the ocean was located in the selkie realm. They should have figured that out considering it was the ocean stone. What they didn't know was where in the selkie realm it was.

"So, it's in the Selkie realm. How are we going to find that, we don't know anyone from that realm."

Cailean looked over at Ghillie who was scratching his head, Cailean himself knew that they could easily get to the selkie realm and ask Saoirse for help but find the stone that was a different story. If the stone was underwater, they didn't really have much luck as neither of them could breathe underwater, nor he was fairly sure that Aerwyna couldn't breath underwater either.

"That my friend is wrong. Both me and Aerwyna have a friend in that realm. To be honest she's the selkie princess but who is checking."

Cailean couldn't help but smile at the shock that was plainly displayed on Ghillie's face. Was it that shocking that he was friends with a selkie, or was it the fact she was a selkie princess that shocked him.

"How is it that in a few years you're surrounded with the most beautiful women in the realms. What next, you're going to tell me you know about the brownie king Anion and his sons Cas and Kano."

Cailean just looked at Ghillie who was now passing up and down his library rattling off names of people Cailean knew he knew but didn't have the heart to tell him. All he offered him was a smile and a shrug of the shoulders which to Ghillie was all but acknowledging that he knew them.

"You've got to be kidding me? Seriously."

Cailean nodded as he told them how they came to see him and help him clean the shop and now they had been so enamoured with Aerwyna that they gave her a whistle to use If she ever needed rescuing from him which made him laugh. Ghillie just could help but be lost for words as his friend re-illiterate all that had happened between the selkie princess and the king and princes of the Brownies and everything in between.

***

Aerwyna sat there looking at the most beautiful woman she had ever seen, her eyes the bluest she had ever seen and hair as black as night which curled slightly like someone else, she knew, and it made her miss him even more. The woman smiled and extended a hand to Aerwyna lifting her up, so she was once more standing.

"You know my dear life's not that scary even if we do find ourselves alone in the darkness, the people we love will always help light the way. See."

Just as she said that her grandmother, her mother, Cailean and Ghillie all appeared in the darkness each of them chasing the darkness from her illuminating the beautiful scenery that unfolded itself in front of them.

"See even if the people themselves are no longer here or are just far away, they are always with you, light the way. "

Aerwyna stood within the mystery woman's embrace watching as her family and friends illuminated the area revealing a beautiful field full of every flower, she could think of trees covering the outskirts of the field enclosing them within the safety of their self-made enclosure. Aerwyna looked around at the now bright area before looking at the woman once more, she thought she looked familiar but was having trouble locating why.

"How did you know that would work?"

The woman smiled, stroking her hair before tucking it behind her ear.

"It was something my mother once told me. She said that even in the darkest of times, when everything around you seems dark, scary and in all bad, the people that surround you love you to their heart's content and that will help to chase away any darkness that chases you. She said that even if you can't see them, they're there and will support you without you knowing, they will help light the path that you are going to take. And that in itself is as she said one of the truest forms of love. Someone who's there no matter how hard the situation is, no matter how scary the world is, no matter how much you push them away. They will always be there supporting you from the sidelines. And that my dear is what you have waiting for you when you wake up. You have two people who will fight the world for your happiness. Two people who haven't stopped worrying about you since the Banshees. One in particular who has constantly kept checking on you every ten minutes."

She laughed at that thought.

"He's just like his father, ever the worrier."

That's when it hit Aerwyna, she remembered where she saw this woman last. It was in a painting in the Kelpies realms in King Cain's palace. This woman was the Queen. Skye, the human woman who captured the king's heart and who was the mother of Cailean, the man who she cared deeply for, the man she loved.

***

Cailean sat once more beside Aerwyna who still lay sleeping on the bed of moss. Looking as beautiful as the first day he saw her.

"When will you wake up? There's so many things I haven't told you. Please. You've got to wake up."

Cailean picked up one of her hands bringing it to his lips placing a kiss on the back, before holding it there so he could be close to her.

***

Cailean mother placed her hand on the small of her back leading her to a tiny river that ran alongside the trees.

"My dear by now you would have figured out who I am, and I know that must be scary."

Aerwyna looked at the woman and smiled. Meeting the mother of the man she refused to tell her feelings to was most definitely one of the most nerve-wracking moments she could remember.

"It's not the scariest of moments."

Skye smiled down at her like she knew exactly what the scariest moment was for her, and she understood.

"My son, he is so like his father, it really shocked me really. But knowing what he's like I can tell that even if he doesn't tell you he

326

really cares about you. His father must obviously think so too seeing as he gave you the geode box. He must see in you what he saw in me."

At the mention of the geode, it raised all the questions about it to the forefront of Aerwyna's mind. Any questions she had about Cailean, his father and that mysterious geode box; this woman here was the best person to ask.

"Can I ask you a question?"

Skye nodded her head allowing Aerwyna to ask away.

"What's in that box? When Cain gave it to me, the look on Caileans face was one of fear and I'm worried that he may not want me to have whatever is within there. Do you think that's true?"

With a sign Skye confirmed that she was going to kill that boy. With a shake of her head, she told Aerwyna that it was his nerves, and she knew that he wanted her to have what was within the box just not right now.

"He's trying to find the right time and at the moment I'm afraid it is not, so no matter how curious you may be you'll have to wait my dear, the time will come. Sooner than you think."

"But how do you know?"

With another laugh and another shake of the head she revealed the same section of the future to Aerwyna that she had to Cailean in the crystal caves, but Aerwyna didn't know that. Skye thought that even though she wasn't here physically she could still cause a little bit of mayhem between them both. Maybe all they needed was a little spiritual push.

"But how can that happen? When he doesn't even lo…."

"Before you even finish that sentence the young lady thinks about everything that's happened, looks at the actions and takes a second guess at that, if I've learnt anything from his father it's that he won't say anything, but he'll show it with his actions. These Kelpie men are as stubborn as stubborn comes. And you'll have to remember that. " Aerwyna could do little more than nod, at what his mother was telling her, it was true his actions were telling her many things, like her tea and cookies even if they weren't the best, keeping her safe and taking her to the village. But most of all taking her to see the meteors and the fireflies. His actions were telling her a story, a story of him and his possible love for her. She could see it but she would have to keep an eye out on his actions in the future, that was when she was able to leave this place.

"But if that's the case I have to leave, I have to leave wherever this is and get back to them back to him. But I'm scared I don't know how to do that. What should I do?"

Skye just smiled and placed her hands on Aerwyna's shoulder and told her to take a deep breath.

"Okay my dear I need you to breathe. Take a deep breath for me. That's it, good girl. Now what I need you to do is wake up. Just wake up okay and give the man sitting next to you a hug for me okay. " Aerwyna nodded taking the deep breathes as she was instructed

"Good. Now wake up."

***

Cailean hadn't let go of her hand for the entire night, not sleeping a wink, until his head got too heavy, and he couldn't resist anymore, resting his head down beside Aerwyna hoping she wasn't going to wake up alone. Slowly Aerwyna blinked, adjusting her eyes to the light above her, she could feel her hand stuck in something arm held tight. Raising her head, she saw that Cailean had fallen asleep with her hand in his. Had he really not left her side the entire time. A smile etched it way onto her face and she used her free hand to edge her way up into a sitting position before she ran her fingers through his hair, enjoying the feel of the silken strands between them.

"You stubborn silly Kelpie."

Leaning down with a smile on her face she placed a kiss on his brow before she wriggled her hadn't out of his just before throwing the cover over him. Letting him sleep as she didn't know how much rest he had since the Banshees but by the look of him she didn't think it was much. Looking around the room she didn't see Ghillie, so she ventured off to find him, if anything major happened while she was sleeping.

"Ghillie? Ghillie Dhu? Are you here?"

At the sound of his name Ghillie popped his head out of the library door before dropping the books he was holding and running to pick up Aerwyna and swing her around in a tight hug.

"Oh, you're awake so much better. I'm so glad. Come, you must be hungry, let's get you some food."

Placing her gently back down on her feet he directed her towards what some would call a walk in, but Ghillie called his kitchen.

"Does Cailean know you're awake yet. He's going to be so overjoyed if he doesn't. you know he hasn't left your side since we got back from the crystal caves."

That caused an enormous amount of questions that Aerwyna was stockpiling for them both, if they left and did something dangerous, she was going to kill them. And she told Ghillie that was the case.

***

Waking up to find Aerwyna gone was one of Caileans worst fears, that was until he heard a laugh that chased away all amounts of fear

and filled his soul with life once more. How he loved that laugh that
the person that accompanied it.

"Stubborn fairy who said she could get up without waking me first."
Walking towards the sounds of laughter that seemed to be coming
from the library. Leaning against the door jam he saw both Ghillie
and Aerwyna who was presently wrapped with a moss blanket draped
around her shouldering, looking at the map with the riddles while
Ghillie filled Aerwyna in on what he and Cailean figured out about
the stone of the ocean.

"Ah there's my stubborn caramel fairy. What in the devil are you
doing here and not resting in the bed."

Aerwyna looked around and found Cailean immediately, the look she
had on her face was one of both one of love and one that made him
think he was in serious trouble.

"Why do I get the feeling I'm in trouble?"

Ghillie couldn't help but smile, he already had his ass chewed out for
leaving without her and putting himself in trouble and he didn't go as
far in the caves as Cailean did, so he was looking forward to what she
was going to say to him. Aerwyna got off the chair from which was
opposite Ghillie to head towards him, the look on her face getting
more serious the closer she got to him, for some reason he had the
feeling to sit down so she was taller than him.

"First of all, how silly can you be going off on your own, what in the devil made you think that was a good idea. I understand that you thought you would be fine because you were in your own realm but what if something happened like in the banshee valley, what would you have done if you both got caught. Hmm."

Cailean sat on the chair, his hands gripping the edge turning his knuckles white, he hadn't seen Aerwyna this made ever, was she truly worried for him or was she just giving them equal telling off so neither felt left out. Before he could even speak, he felt a slap on the back of his head making his place his hand there rubbing the offended area. In the process Aerwyna lunged forwards embracing Cailean in the little circle her arms made enveloping him.

"don't you ever dare do that to me again, do you know how worried I was. And when I woke you looked so exhausted. You need to take better care of yourself, okay?"

Cailean couldn't do more than smile as Aerwyna let him go and knocked him on the top of his head before turning to give him a smile that could outshine all others.

"right now, that you've both been thoroughly told off to a degree. Let's have a look at this riddle and see if we can find this blasted stone, shall we?"

She turned and offered her hand to him to bring him closer to her, at the same time they both thought that maybe his mother was right, and that the future wasn't as far away as they both thought it was.

***

Looking at the riddle Ghillie couldn't figure out what it meant because it was in Selkies native tongue.

"I have no idea what this means. All I can figure out is we need someone who speaks selkie to decipher this one."

Cailean rested his arms against the side of the table that the map currently rested upon, leaning over to look at the maps. It was then he finally recognized the writing that was the riddle.

"it's a song, we don't need a selkie, we just need Aerwyna."

At the sound of her name Aerwyna looked up at what little kitchen style room she was currently in preparing some lunch for them all when she heard her name.

"What do you need me for? I don't speak native selkie. I only know what Saoirse told me."

Cailean smiled.

"That's the exact reason why we need you, here come take a look."

Cailean had to help #Aerwyna backed up onto the chair she was sitting in when he entered the room, he forgot that everything he was Ghillie and his size and Aerwyna was much smaller than them, so

333

taking a seat was like a climbing battle first to reach the top. Peering down at the riddle it didn't take Aerwyna long to realise why Cailean said she'll be able to, it was a part of the lullaby Saoirse taught her when they were younger.

"Amhran Na Farraige."

"exactly."

Aerwyna looked up at Cailean and smiled because once she thought she would be helpful to them both, she could nearly translate this thanks to her friend. Grabbing a pencil and paper for her to write the translation on, Aerwyna set herself off to work deciphering the riddle for the non-selkie speakers.

"Idir gaoth is idir tonn, Idir tuile is idir tra, As an sliogan, Amhran na farraige, Suaimhneach na ciuin, Ag cuadru go damanta, Idir costa idir cloch, Idir bri is idir muir. So, the riddle translates into between wind and between wave, between flood and between beach, from the shell, a song from the sea, neither quiet nor calm, searching fiercely, between coast between stone, between sense and between sea."

Aerwyna translated the riddle and told them it was definitely in the selkie realm, and she thought it must have been close to either the beach or in the selkie place.

"Maybe we could take the map to Saoirse, and she could tell us?"

Both Cailean and Ghillie said at the same time making Aerwyna laugh at how in sync they were without even trying. Both glared at her laughing, but they couldn't stay mad for long before they were laughing along with her. Ghillie stood in his kitchen packing what little food he had left in a dark brown, very worn and patched satchel that he slung over his right shoulder so that bag rested on his left hip. "Right, I have the provisions ready for us, we don't have to go far but just in case."

All Aerwyna could do was roll her eyes at Ghillie , she was starting to learn that he was a worrier to outmatch all worriers. With a path on the shoulder, they all set off towards the place in the woods that Ghillie had previously shown Cailean to get to the Kelpie realm.

***

Approaching the part of the woods that held all the doors to the other realms, Aerwyna could help but be a bit drawn to the door that would take her back to her home, back to her own realm, back to her parents, back to a life that was already planned out for her.

"Do you think they would be waiting for me on the other side?" Aerwyna said to no one in particular but both Cailean and Ghillie answered her, assuring her that if they weren't waiting it was completely their loss. She couldn't help but smile a little bit, she found they always knew what to say to make her smile. The smile only lasted for a little while before the sadness of missing her family took over her once more, making her cast her eyes down to the leaf cover ground below. Both Cailean and Ghillie looked at each other trying to figure out what was best to do. Until. Cailean walked forward stopping just in front of her, bending at the knees so he could see under the curtain of hair that she had created, looking underneath he could see that the tears had started to form on the edges of her eyes. Cailean knew that wasn't good. It hurt him that people could make her feel so rubbish about herself just for not being there, he wasn't going to have it, he was going to bring a smile back to her face if it was the last thing he did. Rising back up to his full height he gently caressed her cheek and progressed to trace her lips with his fingertips, the exceptionally provocative gesture on his behalf caused her cheeks to flush bright red and Aerwyna automatic instinct was to cast her eyes back down to hide her embarrassment, but he held her chin pinning her there with the gentlest touch and forced her to look at him.

"It doesn't matter what people think or what people do, it matters what you do and what you think. You are the leader of your own future and only you can decide what hurts you. No one else can hurt you if you don't allow them to. And if they do, you've got brave strong men beside you."

Aerwyna couldn't help but laugh. She knew Cailean was trying to be serious but with the last sentence all the seriousness in the situation disappeared and she laughed. Cailean loved that he could make her laugh even if he didn't think what he said was funny, if it made her laugh then fine let it be funny. After the laugh session that commenced after Aerwyna infectious laugh, they walked through the selkie door in search of the selkie princess Saoirse.

***

Walking through the door smelling the sea air once more, brought all Aerwyna memories back that included Saoirse, one especially stuck out from the rest. Aerwyna remembered playing with Saoirse back when they were kids, and she could spend more time out of the water before the illness took over. She could remember that one time Saoirse mother came to the surface with her, and she was still wearing her tiara, how they both loved Saoirse mother tiara it was covered in freshwater pearls and diamonds, but I had a massive Aquamarine in the middle that the diamonds and pearls accentuated. Saoirse's mother called it the heart of the marine. Apparently, it had the power to temporarily transform a human into a selkie for a couple of hours. Whether that was actually the case they were about to find out.

"Look over there."

Ghillie pointed towards someone who was resting against the beach looking at the sky on the multitude of bioluminescent plankton that covered the sea and waves the gentle rippled around them.

"That's not Saoirse, it looks male, are there male selkies?"

Cailean looked over at the selkie who was resting in the distance, so he didn't see the look Aerwyna gave him at the question of male selkies. Not being able to help herself she asked in a sarcastic tone if there were any female Kelpies.

"Of course, there's a female Kel…."

He looked back over the figure resting in the distance and realised how stupid his questions sounded.

"Right of course my bad."

Aerwyna could help herself, she laughed a full belly laugh that caused the attention of the stranger resting in the distance.

"Who there, if you're not of this realm you should leave the royals don't like strangers here."

Walking closer Aerwyna raised her hands to where the stranger could see them in an attempt to appear harmless, when she was close to the stranger, she saw that in fact it was someone she recognized but he had changed a lot from the child he once was. Gone were his freckles and baby fat, it was replaced with strong muscle and gold bronze skin that glistened with the remaining water that held onto his skin from his rapid rising to focus his attention on the intruders. His hair was no longer the short self-cut hair style of spikes, what top his head was a cascade of long blonde hair that stopped at his waist, a few seashells decorated the surface showing him to be a member of the Selkie world.

"Tasi?"

"Maybe it depends on who is asking?"

"Tasi it's me Aerwyna, do you remember from when we were little." It took the man called Tasi a little while for the recollection to take root in his mind before he was running towards Aerwyna scooping her up in a hug swinging her around like old friends reunited. Cailean looked to Ghillie and Ghillie looked back to Cailean both men didn't know how to take the stranger called Tasi who by their books was fairly up on the scale of good looks holding their girl.

"How have you been for twenty years or so? So much must have happened. Wait....."

Tasi paused as if something came back to the forefront of his memories.

"There was someone here that told us you went missing, how can you be here now, and who are these bozos? Are they the ones who held you captive."

At that he threw Aerwyna behind hind pulling a small knife out from behind him, she remembered that since he was little, he always wore a sash made of sea kelp around him which he used to hide his knife, which he now used in an attempt to protect Aerwyna. At this both Cailean and Ghillie couldn't help but move forward in the most dominating way they could muster, no one took Aerwyna from them not even someone she knew and the fact the had a knife made the situation that all much more dangerous, if Aerwyna was behind him all it took was a slight miscalculation of distance for her to be hurt for her to be hurt, at that fact Cailean saw red.

***

"Get your slimy hands off her!"

Cailean all but marched up to Tasi grabbing his neck lifting him off the ground until his feet no longer touched the ground.

"How do I know you are not out to hurt her? How do I know you weren't the ones to keep her captured for years? At least I know her, and she knows me, who are you huh? What gives you the right!"

In Tasi's defence he was still speaking quite well for someone who was currently pinned in the air by only his neck. Ghillie ran over taking Aerwyna away from Tasi's side bringing her back closer to himself.

340

"Right Aerwyna I need you to stay here and not move, I've only seen him like this once and it didn't end pretty. So, I need to you do me a favour and stay here while I bring him back around okay?"

Aerwyna couldn't do much more but nod. She had never seen Cailean like this, she didn't know he even could get like this.

"Cailean!"

Aerwyna screamed trying to draw his attention back to her once more, so she could distract him while Ghillie pried Tasi out of his infamously strong grip.

"I'm over here, I'm safe. You can let go. Come to me, see im okay." It was at the sound of her voice which drew Cailean attention away from the inferior life in which he held in his hand. Looking at his shoulder proved that in fact she was safely back by Ghillie's side, who was at present trying to slowly make his way over the Cailean to attempt to release the poor selkie who had chosen his words very badly.

"Aerwyna?"

At that he dropped Tasi and strode toward Aerwyna enveloping her in his embrace when he was there just needing to feel and understand that she was safe. Cailean sunk to the ground at the realisation of what he had done of what he had shown her, but to Aerwyna all she did was run her hand through his hair humming her lullaby to him once more, effectively calming him down.

"What the hell do you think you're doing?"

Tasi coughed as the air assaulted his lungs once more. Standing up once more Cailean slowly raked his gaze along Aerwyna body, from the top of her head that was covered in his favourite caramel hair down to her tones which were covered in shoes small enough for a child, in fact he thought that he got them from the children's stall in the market because it was the only one that went small enough for her. Pulling her close with an unusual amount of strength for Aerwyna.

"Why were you touching my woman!"

"Your woman, please I think Aerwyna has much better taste that some stupid stubborn headed brutish Kelpie"

Aerwyna knew another fight was bound to happen, so she made the properly stupid mistake of standing in between the two rowing men, she knew she made a mistake when she looked over and saw Ghillie with his head in his hands, from looking at the scene which was unfolding presently.

"Tasi? Aerwyna? Cailean? What are you doing here?"

Aerwyna looked towards where the new but overly familiar voice sounded to see Saoirse appearing out of the water, her seal skin shedding into the brilliantly white dress which adorned her body the first time they arrived here, when she had little memories of anything.

"Saoirse. Thank god you're here, help me with these bone head men will you."

Saoirse looked between Cailean and Tasi and sighed, Aerwyna didn't even have to say anything to the Selkie for her to understand what had happened, the slight bruising around Tasi neck and the fury in Cailean eyes as he looked at Tasi said everything she needed to know.

"Boys. There's no helping them there."

Aerwyna just laughed as they all sat on the beach while everyone calmed down and Aerwyna explained to Saoirse everything that had happened since her last visit here.

***

"So let me get this right. You had to come here to find the stone of the ocean and all you have to go on is this riddle which is part of the lullaby I taught you when we were kids?"

Everyone nodded except Tasi who was currently healing his bruised neck with the ocean water. Ghillie wasn't entirely paying attention as he watched Tasi heal, he had said selkies fascinated him and now he had a male selkie and the selkie princess in front of him.

" And you think that the stone might be here on the beach from lines of the riddle that say beach and waves?"

343

Again, everyone nodded, Saoirse liked to drag things out making sure she had every single detail she could possibly need.

"And Tasi the idiot over here attacked the guys thinking they were the ones who had held you captive all these years, is that everything?"

"Pretty much minus the Banshees and some unexplainable things." Aerwyna said smiling over at Tasi who was mocking Saoirse by mimicking her, that was until she turned around, he smiled, it was nice to see that the dynamic between them hadn't changed even though Tasi feeling for Saoirse hadn't really changed since he was a lovestruck selkie boy seeing her for the first time. Remembering the time when they were kids was amusing for her, the very fact that she could remember was amazing but the fact it was the moment Tasi feel in love with Saoirse was a different story she could remember her trying for years to get them together, but nothing worked Saoirse was to stubborn. For that she felt slightly sorry for Tasi, but she was glad that he seemed to not have given up the chase.

"Well, it looks like we've got an underwater trip ahead of us."

"Underwater? How we're not selkies?"

Saoirse just smiled before she looked over at Tasi and quickly stopped mocking her to smile back causing Saoirse to have a curious look upon her face.

"Tasi wasn't always a selkie either. He started with a few visits when we were all kids and he fell in love with the culture, and we changed him."

"I bet he fell in love with the cultu……"

Cailean didn't have long to finish his sentence before Aerwyna elbowed him in the ribs silencing him very effectively, resulting in a glare from Cailean which didn't last long when she showed him her dazzling smile which he couldn't resist.

"Saoirse crown has a stone which can temporarily transform human or others into selkies for a short amount of time, or in the right hands transform them completely, as long as both the wearer and the recipient agree. It's quite amazing really, I remember Tasi's transformation was quite spectacular."

That little sentence caused many to look over into her direction which shocked faces.

"What?"

"Since when did you remember something from your childhood when you could even remember what happened a few weeks ago, when you visited me last a month ago."

It didn't occur to Aerwyna that her memories were slowly returning to her, starting with her childhood, if she remembered that she would eventually regain her full memoires. Would she want to regain them?

"I don't remember, maybe it could have been when I saw my grandmother?"

"But your grandmother has been gone for years. She passed when we were kids, to my knowledge you never met her, how could you have seen her?"

Both Saoirse and Tasi asked in complete unison, it seems that they didn't even realise what they had done except ask her.

"I don't remember exactly, but it was around the time of the banshees I think, when I got really tired light emanated from me. When I was saving Cailean and Ghillie."

The two looked at each other before turning back to Aerwyna who stood there looking at them as if everything was completely fine.

Both looked over her towards Cailean and Ghillie.

"Boys a word!"

The sound of Saoirse's voice set the boys on edge, she may be a tiny selkie woman, but they knew without a doubt that if needed she would be their worst enemy, and that was the last place they wanted to be.

***

"Did you forget to mention that on purpose or what?"

"It's or what section I think?"

The look on Saoirse's face told them both that she was extremely not

impressed, with Ghillie's attempt at humorizing this situation.

"We found out after she woke up for the first time. "

"The first time?"

Cailean signed as he said to Saoirse that she better take seat as this

was going to be a long explanation and one that was full of

unanswered questions that they still didn't know the answers to.

"We have this map which shows us the destinations of the stone

which when put together created the Myrios stone. The first riddle

was in fairies tongue, so we asked Aerwyna to translate the text for us

nothing more as we didn't want to worry her with anything that she

needn't worry about, but after she read it, she passed out for a while,

but eventually woke up and told us all that happened in her dream,

that was before we actually made it to the Banshee valley. When we

got there unfortunately, we were captured by a banshee and taken to

their lair with a lack of a better word. And Aerwyna saved us, but not

with weapons or anything that you could hold, she saved us with

light, Light that almost seemed to come from her. The Banshees told

us when we were in captivity that there used to be an all powerful

person called the Ayla. Supposedly the Alya had the powers of

chlorokinesis, clairvoyance, healing, photokinesis, Electrokinesis.

Ghillies heard tales of the Alya but to his knowledge the last one died

347

hundreds of years ago, but Aerwyna was able to kill a Banshee and

trap the others easily, without any help from either of us. So, when

we returned from there, we started researching the Alya but not much

came up, there not much known about the Ayla's, due to many dying

at a young age from the strain of their powers. So, we started to

research how to eradicate the powers but again nothing came up. But

after the fight Aerwyna fell in a deep sleep once more and when she

had awoken with the help of the stone of purity this time, we came

here hoping that maybe once all the stones are together and they

create the Myrios stone we might be able to eradicate her powers. But

we don't know much else other than that."

Saoirse just stood there mouth opened and head nodding as she took

in all the information that Cailean dealt out to her. Could her friend be

the mysterious Alya that they spoke of. But then again if she had met

her dead grandmother who died young and had somehow regained

her memories even if only a little, then maybe that was true. Even the

selkies had heard of the Alya's powers and it terrified them seeing as

they could easily destroy everything in their path. Taking a deep

breath, she turned looking over at Aerwyna who sat next to Tasi who

was laughing with her, were they talking about past memories, were

they talking about the past or the future. If Aerwyna was the Alya, would she even have a future. Would they be able to give her a future?

"Okay I'll help you, but I want to come with you, no exceptions."

The boys just looked to one another, could a selkie be dangerous on the journey they were taking or could she be helpful.

"Before you even think about denying me you don't get a choice, so you'll have to suck it up and deal with it."

With that she turned around, flicking her hair over her shoulder as she walked back towards where Aerwyna and Tasi sat.

Cailean and Ghillie couldn't help but smile, they were not only stuck with one head strong female but two and the two got on extremely well and they knew that if in doubt they would gang together against them. Laughing as they rounded their arms around the other they made their way back towards the group which was indefinitely growing bigger as they progressed.

***

"If you're going then i'm going, no exceptions."

Tasi stood hands on hips as he looked down at Aerwyna who was ticked closely next to Saoirse the boy took the safer option and sat behind the girls valuing their lives. Saoirse just looked up at Tasi who she had to admit had fill out nicely since his childhood, his small lanky body had now filled out pathing the was so slightly defined

349

abdominal muscles which must have seen from all the swimming,
even in their selkie forms the muscles got excised resulting in more
defined human bodies, but she had to admit out of everyone she had
seen in their human form none had filled out better than Tasi. Shaking
her head she cleared the thoughts from her head, it was not the time to
start noticing Tasi in that manner, hat was important how was helping
Aerwyna and hopefully eradicating her powers or at least keeping
them under control so that what happen to the other Alya's didn't
happen to her.

"Tasi, you know the king and queen would have a field day if you
left. So why don't you stay here and give them peace of mind,
yeah?"

Looking up at him with her softest smile her head tilted to the side
she hoped that would be enough to persuaded him, she knew how he
felt about her, how could she not he made it so obvious, she found it
sweet, but it wasn't the right time, it was never the right time.

"Their your parents, If anything the shits are going to hit the fan if I
let you go unaccompanied. Save me the trouble of explaining to them
that I just let you go, without even trying to persuade you. You
already know that if I say i'm going then you're more likely to be
allowed to go, you know princess, you're their most precious
daughter."

The cocky grin on Tasi face already told her that he knew that he had won that argument, she didn't even have to say anything for him to continue the conversation on with Cailean and Ghillie who were happily sat behind them leaving her to deal with her stubborn even a little cute overprotective bodyguard.

"Fine you win. Like always. And you wipe that smile off your face." Saoirse swivelled to look at Aerwyna who had a shit eating grin on her face, she was always able to read her mind by her expressions, Saoirse knew she would have to be careful on this journey or Aerwyna who temp Cailean and Ghillie into her matching making plans she was obviously planning in her head.

***

After planning their newly added companions into the journey Saoirse had left to retrieve her crown from her home so they would be able to start their search for the stone of the ocean.

"Tasi, you need to use a gentle approach with Saoirse, I don't think you'll succeed otherwise."

Cailean and Ghillie round him flanking him on either side, hanging their arms over his shoulders.

"I don't think that would work. Saoirse's quite strong headed I don't think a gentle subtle approach would work. I doubt she would even notice, If I did it that way."

351

"Has the strong headed direct approach worked for you so far? Hmmm."

Ghillie looked down at the love struck selkie, who was at present starting out at the sea waiting for his only little selkie to reappear before him.

"That's true but neither of you have girls so why should I take your advice?"

The boys' smiles faulted as their little selkie was right neither of them had a girl, they had Ghillie who to Caileans knowledge hadn't ever had a girlfriend and then you have Cailean who was still trying to woo Aerwyna.

"What are you guys talking about?"

A small voice sounded behind them causing them to quickly turn in hope of hiding what they were previously talking about.

"The guys were just telling m……."

Ghillie reached his had around and covered Tasi mouth before he would drop them in what he could imagine would be a lot of gossip between the girls and they didn't need that on the long journey they had planned, if both Tasi and Saoirse were coming with them it was already going to be an even longer journey than normal, they hadn't travelled with selkies before, so they didn't know how well they travelled. Aerwyna raises her eyebrow at the guys knowing that they couldn't be up to anything but mischief.

"Will you guys leave him alone, he's not as boisterous as you both, he's gentler, I would say you understand what i'm saying but I don't think you know what gentle is."

Aerwyna flipped her hair at them as she turned towards the beach once more just as Saoirse was leaving the water.

***

"So how does this work?"

Ghillie looked at the crown curiously not knowing what to expect.

"It's quite easy actually, I place the crown on top of your head, you wish to be a selkie temporarily, you have to remember to say that, or it doesn't work. And then once you step into the water, it surrounds you and changes you for three hours then you start the change back, so we will have to be quick."

Saoirse went around placing the crown on everyone's head but hers and Tsai's. Aerwyna struggled with this the most internally, the feeling of a crown or tiara back on her head chased her back to home where she thought everything was fine, but inside it wasn't. One by one they stepped into the ocean, Tasi stood just inside directing them on what to do. It wasn't long before all three stood in the ocean before the very ocean itself rose up and covered them in the water bubble with Saoirse and Tasi just outside in their selkie forms. The water wound its way around their legs encircling their waist before it covered their heads and they transformed.

***

Cailean was the first to leave the sea bubble as a selkie his fur a dark brown with small spots covering his upper body and fins. Stopping just in front of the other he looked at his fins in disbelief, he didn't think it would work, turning around he looked at the bubble waiting for the other to appear and join them. Ghillie was next; his fur seemed to have more of a green tinge to it, which they accepted seeing as he was a forest spirit. When he joined the club, he laughed at Cailean who had spits and #Caielan laughed at Ghillie who was green, both weren't funny, but Saoirse thought whatever floats their boat, she looked up at the bubble apprehensively as Aerwyna had yet to emerge. Sometimes the bubble took a long time on certain people, some people rejected the change and others rejected them. Finally, Aerwyna emerged a bit confused as she was facing the wrong direction, everyone was behind her, she seemed to panic when she didn't see anyone, but that didn't last long when Tasi appeared before her, revealing everyone else. What made them drop was the fact that her fur was very similar to Saoirse. It was pure white but hers seemed to have spots that sort of looked like small flowers that decorated her entire body. Once everyone was assembled Saoirse swan to the front as they started on their underwater journey to find the stone of the ocean.

Chapter Thirty- One

The Selkie Palace

Swimming through the ocean was a surreal experience for Cailean, Aerwyna and Ghillie, one that they would never be able to experience again, not without becoming Selkies permanently like Tasi had done. Saoirse led them though winding coral reefs which held every possible colour Aerwyna could think of small sea folk resided within every now and then poking their head out to take a peek at who was passing them.

"Where are we going?"

Saoirse stopped and turned looking at the group behind her taking in the shock of the two biggest men she knew being smaller seals than her, she knew that was because she was royalty but still, she found it funny that she and Aerwyna were bigger.

"We're heading to the castle to ask for permission first to search the area. Just in case we upset any locals."

Cailean and ghillie sighed and it shocked them that it didn't come out in a sound but in a bubble that when popped revealed the sigh.

Loudly by anyone's standards.

356

"Really signing isn't going to get us there any quicker. Tasi, can you keep the bored boys company please?"

Tasi just looked at Saoirse he knew that he was going to do anything she asked him to but the last time he was stuck with them they were talking about girls more importantly talking about Saoirse and he couldn't do that again no when she herself didn't even know his feeling for her it just didn't feel right.

"Of course."

He just smiled and swam back towards Cailean and Ghillie who both had shit eating grins, he knew this was going to be trouble.

***

Being a seal was the most inconvenient thing Cailean could think of , not only could he torment the small seal currently swimming next to him but he couldn't even hold him there so he couldn't escape the torment.

"So Tasi tells us what's going on with you and Saoirse. Does she know?"

"Or is it an unrequited love?"

Both Cailean and Ghillie swam as close to Tasi as they could without interrupting each other's swimming. Tasi looked between both, turning his head side to side.

357

"No, she doesn't know. I've never been able to tell her and personally I don't think I'll ever be able to tell her. Do you ever find that, are you guys able to tell people what you're thinking? Does it ever get easier?"

Tasi stopped swimming and looked to the ocean floor, Cailean thought he looked helpless but there wasn't anything he could do, he still had been able to tell Aerwyna what he was feeling, sure other things had happened, but he had actually told her anything.

"No I'm in the same boat, there's someone I'm in complete and total love with and I can't bring myself to out anyone else above her. But still to this day I haven't told her, and I can't bring myself to tell her yet either. So, I know what you feeling."

Patting a fin on Tasi back he tried his hardest to offer some kind of comfort even with fins and a snout covered in fur. Tasi couldn't help but smile at the form of encouragement that he offered. Cailean looked ahead to where the girls swam and smiled a sort of sad smile as he did.

"My father told me once when I was young that real men don't love the most beautiful girl in their world, they love the girl who can make their world the most beautiful. And the longer you're with someone the tougher it is to part ways. I'm positive that when the time is right, we will both be able to tell the respective holders of our heart what we feel, and on that day, everything will be right in the world and immense happiness will take over you. And you have no help but to smile all the time, anytime you're sad you think of them and smile and soon the world won't seem as dark and dim. It will be like they brought colour to your life all by themselves and that's when you'll know what to do."

"But how do you know if that relationship with that person is the right one for you?"

Cailean smiled and let out a little laugh, it reminded him of when he was a child and was asking his father about everything, maybe Tasi didn't have anyone he could ask. That seemed the most plausible reason seeing as he was a human originally, maybe his parents were still in the human world or maybe they had passed.

"Being in a relationship isn't about dates, romance kisses and showing them off, all thought that helps and is nice, being in a relationship it's about being with the person who makes you the happiest. Do that and you'll be the happiest man or selkie in the world."

Tasi smiled. Cailean was right, being happy in a relationship with the person you loved was the most important thing.

"Yeah, you're right, thank you, you love sick Kelpie."

Cailean blushed; he couldn't have been found out that easily, if he had then it was impossible that Aerwyna didn't already know. If she did know that then was ignoring them on purpose, no she's not that kind of person.

"I have no idea what you mean, you stupid selkie."

"Uh huh. Course not, you're totally not crushing on the fairer princess."

Cailean faces changed from red to crimson. He had been found out, which meant everyone knew.

"Nope not at all, now keep swimming. The girls are miles ahead of us and we're meant to protect them."

Cailean didn't stay around long enough to hear everyone answer before he swam as fast as his fins would allow him, leaving the awkward conversation.

"We're here."

Saoirse said as they rounded that last section of coral which covered a small hill, once over the hill the selkie place was revealed

***

Selkies place itself was surrounded by a small town which according to the sign posted outside was called Swancoast. Pieces of sea kelp, corals and anemones covered a small section of the paths that encircled the palace.

"This is beautiful, is the whole selkie realm like this?"

"It is. If you think this is beautiful then just wait till you see the palace."

Swimming through the town the palace slowly came into view. Its tall turrets which were topped with a spiral shell appeared first, and the closer they swam the more the turrets grew. Soon the shell topped turrets revealed abalone shell encrusted walls, smaller turrets surrounded the vacant space between the tall towers and the build itself. What impressed them all the most was the fact the palace was hovering in the water on a section of rock which had been dislodged from the ocean floor. A chain and anchor was connected to the earth the palace was situated on. Many variations of coral surrounded the palace hiding the hole it created from the obvious area it rose from. Small hallway with many open arch windows surrounded the exterior allowing much ocean sunlight to illuminate the interior. This was where Saoirse grew up and lived her life, this was now where Tasi lived. Her friends' parents help raise him the rest of the way, help him understand the ways of the selkie.

"Wow."

Cailean could agree with Aerwyna there wow was right; this place was spectacular just the abalone shell itself was beautiful he wondered if she would be able to find a jewellery stall that sold stuff made out of the same shell or if it was specified to the palace.

"Hey Saoirse, I've got a question?

She nodded acknowledging his question.

"That shell, can you buy it somewhere or is it only for the palace?"

Saoirse turned with a knowing smirk on her face. She knew what he wanted that shell for or more likely who he wanted to get that shell for.

"It's just for the place but I'm sure I could find a way for you to get your hands on some if you wished."

A blush just worked its way onto his face, looking at that smirk he knew she knew, and was enjoying his pain. You're a bully. Cailean whispered under his breath hoping that she couldn't hear.

"I heard that selkies have good hearing and the ocean helps to carry the sound."

Tasi smiled and patted his fin onto Cailean furry back.

"Oh, you shush as well."

***

Swimming up towards and into the place was amazing. Not only did the abalone shell cover the outside it also lined the inside walls covering the ceiling and floors in a multitude of colours.

"Sersh, what are you doing back so soon, I thought you were on the surface?"

"Mum"

Saoirse swam as quickly as her little fins would carry her twirling around her mum in a circle. Finally resting their heads on top of the others.

"Who have you brought with you? Your friends?"

Saoirse's mother swam down with Saoirse following closely behind. Her mother was very similar to Saoirse she was a pure white seal but their only different she could see what that she had a grey circle the encircled the entirety of her head, Aerwyna assumed that would be her crown, the very crown that in her memories contained a pure brilliant blue Aquamarine stone in its centre.

***

"Mum, you know one of these people."

Saoirse swam toward the two very impending seals who looked down at her. Taking a deep breath or a deep inhale of ocean water, she smiled up at them and introduced herself to the woman who raised her bestest friend in the world.

"Hello, I'm princess Aerwyna Colquhoun of the Foghar forest, it's a pleasure to meet you, my Queen."

She bowed as best she could in her seal body, hoping that it was enough, hoping it was low enough.

"It's a pleasure Aerwyna Colquhoun of the foghar forest, Im Queen of the selkies. My name is Aramoana. You may call me Ara. Forgive me if I'm rude but I remember you. You used to come here to play with Sersh, am I correct?"

Aerwyna just nodded, she had vague memories of the selkie queen none that she could pin down exactly but from what she could remember they were all happy memories.

She lent to the side peering over Aerwyna's shoulder looking at the two peculiar coloured selkies behind her.

"And who are these two strapping gentleselkies beside you Tasi?"

Tasi turned towards Cailean and Ghillie who were currently looking at each other with what looked like a small amount of fear in their eyes. It was true that most beings were scared of selkie, the selkies themselves didn't understand why but they cherished it as it provided them with the quietness and security to maintain their lives hidden away. You'll be fine, Tasi whispered before he told them to follow him, follow him toward the majestic Selkie Queen. Tasi gently pushed Cailean forward first, he had the next highest standing in the room, so it made sense that he was next. Again, like Aerwyna he bowed as best he could in his selkie body.

"It's a pleasure my Queen, my name's Cailean Dubhghlas. And I'm

the prince of the Kelpie realm. I'm honoured to be here, your

majesty."

Aramoana looked over at Aerwyna and Saoirse who were looking

down at the all-powerful kelpie who was now stripped of his powers

and placed into a selkie form, effectively hindering him from

anything his normal form would allow him. And what surprised her

was that it seemed like he didn't care, he just bowed as low as he

could at the fins of the selkie queen but his eyes, his eyes were what

softened her the most they were peering at Aerwyna with such love

and affection, that it reminded her of how she looked at her husband.

This powerful creature softened for a tiny fairy that he could destroy

in a single movement. He must have changed his form for a reason,

could it have been for her, for the little fairy who seemed to hold the

most powerful heart that she could ever possess.

"it's an honor prince Cailean Dubhghlas. If I may ask why an

all-powerful Kelpie prince has come to the selkie realm with a fairy

and what I can assume is someone who has a deep connection to the

forest looking at your fur my dear sir. You are sir?"

She leaned over looking at Ghillie who was currently trying to hide

behind a much smaller Tasi

"My name's Ghillie Dhu, your majesty. It's a pleasure."

Once more he bowed to the Selkie queen who just smiled down at him like she wasn't bothered by his sudden shyness. Turning her attention back to Cailean.

"So, my Prince, what brings you to the selkie realm? What brings you here to the Selkie palace."

***

"If it would please you, your majesty…."

"Please call me Aramoana."

"Okay … .Aramoana we're here looking for the stone of the ocean. We asked for assistance from your daughter, who changed us into selkies so we would be able to look, but we stopped by here first to ask for permission from ourselves before we started the search."

Aramoana nodded and smiled slightly, looking at how earnest the prince was she couldn't help but smile.

"And why my prince are you looking for the stone of the ocean?"

Cailean took a deep breath before looking at Aerwyna who at present was floating next to Saoirse and Tasi, he could imagine that if she had her hands, she would be giving him a thumbs up, but she didn't so he took courage from her eyes and the slight smile she had on her face.

"You see we're trying to find the stone to merge them together with the other to make the Myrios stone to create more time. You see Aerwyna betrothed resurfaced and is trying to take her away from me,

366

and her memories are slowly returning, form that she can remember
she can't go back there not yet, not until we find a way to keep her
safe, and to do that we need more time, if he figures out who she is
he'll take her back there and she'll be in danger and I don't want that,
I can't allow that. You see at present she lives with me which means I
have a responsibility to keep her safe, that's what it means to live
with someone. Please your majesty help me keep her safe."
Cailean bowed as low as he could and stayed there until he felt a
small dainty fin rest on top of his head. Quickly looking up she saw
kindness and caring in the queen's eyes. She was going to help him,
and he was so thankful for that.
"My prince, you don't have to leave to look. I have the stone here in
the palace. And I understand how you feel, it may be the most
dangerous course of action but I can see that your intentions behind
them are good and for that reason and that reason alone I will help
you. But you must promise me. "
Aramoana's voice dropped to a small whisper as she said the last
sentence.
"When you two get married due to this, be sure to invite us okay."
Cailean blushed and the queen laughed causing everyone to look over
and try to dissect what was said but the both of them were very good
at hiding it. When he gained his voice once more, he agreed.

"So, Mum about this stone, do you know where it is?"

The queen smiled down at her daughter with the most affectionate gaze Aerwyna had ever seen, the fact people could look at their daughter that way was shocking to her, it was more shocking that she couldn't remember either of her parents looking at her the same way. Her mother now understood why she didn't have half of her memories but her father, he was a completely different reason.

"Yes, my darling I do know and so do you. It is in my crown the one that helped change Tasi to a selkie in the first place, do you remember what I told you that day."

Saoirse nodded she could vaguely remember her mother telling her that to become a selkie you had to become one with the ocean itself. That the ocean couldn't be contain within one place within one person within on stone, that only the heart of the ocean was shared by everyone, and anyone who gave their heart to the ocean got the stone placed on their hearts and the stone glow absorbing their love for the ocean into itself therefore making them on with the ocean.

"So, the stone of the ocean is the heart of the ocean."

"Yes, my darling, that right the heart of the ocean is what you seek, and it is that heart that is here."

Aramoana reached up and grabbed the small grey ring that encircled her head. And a small crown materialised in her fins. The small circlet was made of entwined silver thin at the side before it formed two Celtic knots on either side holding the stone of the ocean within its grasp, Another Celtic knot held the bottom keeping it in place. The entire circlet was as dainty as it was massive.

"Here take it, but be careful it may look small but it's one of the most powerful stones. In the wrong hands it could endanger the entire Selkie race. So, my dear, when you've completed your task, please return this as soon as you can. I'm entrusting you with the Selkies' most precious belongings. To be sure that you complete your task to the best of your abilities I have a request and I would be so grateful if you would agree."

As Aramoana passed the tiara and placed it on Aerwyna head, a small grey ring encircled her head showing anyone that she held one of the most precious selkie belongings. Aerwyna raised her eyes to look at Aramoana.

"Of course, your majesty, anything you wish."

"Take Saoirse and Tasi with you on this journey, to appease my mind that you will all be safe, Selkies have powers that most are afraid of. Do this a favour for me?"

Aerwyna turned to look over her shoulder at everyone Saoirse was floating next to Tasi who was staring at her with utter adoration.

Cailean and Ghillie were talking most likely planning the next part of the journey with two new travellers.

"But don't you need them here where they could be safe?"

The queen just smiled.

"Yes, I can see why you would think that, but Saoirse is a free spirit and I think this would be good for her, let her travel, let her experience freedom. You see it won't be long before she'll have to start looking for a partner. And I want her to live her life as freely as possible until that time. you see the only people who can decide your path is yourself, let no one tell you otherwise, only you can choose what happens. And if this is what she chooses then I let her do that, let her be free until the time comes when duty comes into it, unfortunately this is the way of princesses, unfortunately you yourself will have to choose at some point. I hope that your parents let you choose for yourself who you pick. Did you have anyone in mind."

Aerwyna couldn't help herself when her eyes drifted towards Cailean who was laughing at whatever Ghillie had told him, when he stopped, he looked over at her and smiled, a smile that she had grown to love. A smile that brightens her day is the best way possible.

"Maybe, I'm not completely sure. I've never been in love, I don't know what to expect."

"My dear by the look on your face I think you are about two days off completely mindless falling in love with him."

With a blush on her face, she asked with who. She hoped she was obvious, if it was obvious did, he already knew.

"By the look on your face I think you're in love or nearly completely in love with the Kelpie prince. It hasn't been heard of before, but a Kelpie and a Fairy can be together. If you want it to happen, then just decide your own path and go for it. From what I can see when it comes to you, he has no composure."

"Is that a good thing?"

"Yes, my dear I think it might mean he might feel the same way about you. But I'm afraid there's only one way to find out."

"Okay, I will take Saoirse and Tasi. It'll be fun to have another girl on the adventure."

The queen smiled once more, placing a kiss on her head before they both swam over to the other to give them the news. Both Saoirse and Tasi were over the moon that they were being allowed to go, but worried about spending that much time out of the water. Aramoana reassured them that the spell she was going to place on there would be more that sufficient for them to be fine but if they were worried if they stepped in any water for any amount of time, they would be able to changed back to their selkie form and the spell would still be fine.

After both Saoirse and Tasi swam off the fastest they could pack

whatever belonging they could carry everyone made their way back

towards the surface.

***

Breaking through the surface was amazing. The feeling of cold air

mixed with the unusual warmth from the ocean wreaked havoc on

their senses.

"That feeling is strangely amazing."

Walking back onto the beach with legs it was almost like they had to

relearn how to walk once more, like when they were kids, and

everything was wobbly.

"You'll get used to it but yeah it does feel both amazing and strange."

After regaining the ability to walk they all settled down on the beach

for the night.

"We need to sleep, we have a long journey ahead of us."

Saoirse snuggled down next to Aerwyna while the boys sat around

the fire as they talked things through.

"Hey guys I have a question?"

Tasi looked straight into the fire as he spoke to both Cailean and

Ghillie.

"What's that?"

372

"If you were to ever be separated from the most important person in your life, what would you want from that person as a memento?"

Ghillie didn't answer as he couldn't think of anything at all. Cailean thought about it long and hard, what would he want from Aerwyna if they got separated, and at that point he couldn't think of anything. The very thought of being separated from her was an answer he was never going to be separated from he wasn't going to let that happen.

"If I had to choose, I would choose……"

After a long pause he answered.

"Something she wore."

Cailean looked over at the girls who laid resting facing them, they looked so peaceful, he would do whatever he could to keep that peaceful look on their faces. He just hoped that at the end of the hair brained adventure, that he would be able to do that.

"Right get some rest everyone tomorrow we travel to the Brownies realm. We'll get a good welcome there but it's still a long journey so get your rest."

Everyone sulked off to get some rest while Cailean looked out at the ocean, something big was happening he knew it but where he didn't know, how bad was another thing he didn't know. But whatever it was he was prepared for it, for the people who trusted him he would protect them with his life if needed.

Chapter Thirty-Two

The Brownies Realm

Walking through the Brownies door, it surprised them that the further they got the more they shrunk.

"Did we just get smaller or has everything grown bigger?"

Cailean laughed he had been to the Brownies realm numerous times before but by the looks of things it was the first time for everyone else.

"Have you ever seen a brownie?

At a shake of two heads, he laughed again, which did last long before three now low-pitched voices called their names.

"Your highness, Cailean. What a pleasure to see you here."

"Anion, Kano, Cas. It's so good to see you, when did you grow."

"We didn't grow, my lady, you shrunk down to our height."

Looking at the boys in shock she turned around looking around the exit, looking up to see massive brooms, buckets and chest of draws. What would normally be a small light looked ten times bigger.

Standing next to the bucket she placed her hand on the side before she spoke.

"So, this is how you see things, we must have been very imposing to you if this is what a bucket looks like."

Aerwyna turned her head looking at her Brownie friends, she apologised if she was at any point intimidating to them, in any way. Anion walked over to her placing his hand on her shoulder, he didn't have to say anything to get his point across. He could reassure her that every time they had seen her, she was the least imposing person they had met.

" You were probably one of the kindest people we met in that realm, others excluded."

Anion turned his head slowly looking over his shoulder at where the stubborn Kelpie had his arms crossed looking over at them with a look that could only be interpreted as a look of jealousy.

"Every time we've been in that world minus that shop which you made a home and a safe place. We got used by those humans to clean, to make sure that their home was the best it could be. We didn't mind doing it but there was no gratitude from any of them. But you my lady made us feel at home in a place that we already felt comfortable in, you included us, you made us a place, you made us cups and a teapot, by doing that you told us that you wanted us to stay, you didn't want us to just clean and leave."

Both Kano and Cas walked over, placing their hands on Aerwyna before they joined in with Anion.

"We could be more thankful for you truly. You gave us a second chance at happiness in a world that only showed us hostility. You gave us a ray of sunshine in a world that was shrouded in darkness. There is no way you could have been anything more than welcoming. So please don't think that you intimidated us at all. If anything, you welcomed us into your home into your heart, and we thank you for that."

Aerwyna's eyes started to well up as the boys were talking, they were saying such heartwarming things to her that she was sure she didn't deserve, but she was glad for them. Aerwyna pulled Anion, Kano and Cas into a hug thanking them with everything she owned, as well as telling them that once everything was sorted, they would welcome anything, the pot would always be on and there would always be a spot for them right next to her.

***

Anion and the boys directed everyone over to the castle of the Brownies. The castle itself was far away from the door the exited from, walking through the woods that surrounded castle were beautiful they surrounded a path which led up a small hill which had a big stone wall lined the side stopping people from accidently falling over the side but also allowing them to observe the beautiful lake that extended in front of them, a small isle was situated in the middle of the lake from where they were it was hard to see what was on the isle but from what she could see it was beautiful and she wanted to see more of it. The castle itself was amazing, a tall wall surrounded the castle so all that was visible from the path was the bright red turrets and roofs that descended over the top of the walls.

"Is that the castle?"

Kano smiled looking at Aerwyna as she raised her eyes to look at the brilliantly red roofs that were just visible over the wall.

"It is your highness, to you normally it would look no bigger than what the humans would call a doll's house, but here it is just as big as the ones in your realm."

"It's beautiful."

"You haven't seen most of it yet, that's only the roofs."

"Still, it's beautiful."

Rounding the last corner of the wall and through the arch way the castle slowly came into view. The tall walls fell away to reveal a three-building structured castle hiding within. The main part was what held all the rooms that the royal Brownies reside within. The other she couldn't decipher from the outside.

"See I was right, it's beautiful."

"Your highness, your compliment is gratefully accepted, please come
in."

***

Walking into the courtyard, had to be one of the most magical things
Aerwyna had seen in ages. Ivy grew up and around the windows that
face the interior of the courtyard, a few arched windows allow people
to see just inside the castle library, from what she could see there
were numerous books in there, maybe some that could help them on
their journey. The small turret that she could see from the other side
of the wall was small but had a smaller staircase that led inside where
it led, she didn't know, two arched windows were displayed on either
side and one circular was situated in the middle.

A small alcove was under the staircase with a small door, when she
was allowed to go exploring that was the first place she was going.

"If you're wondering about the alcove, it's just another staircase that
leads to the library."

With a blush on her face Aerwyna looked away, staring up at the sky
which was changing from the most brilliant blue to shades of orange
and red as the sunset before them.

***

"To welcome the presence of our esteemed Princess and her friends,
we're holding a ball in your honour."

"A ball?"

Aerwyna couldn't believe that she was hearing a ball in her honour, wouldn't that bring attention to her, would people be able to find her that way.

"Before you start to panic my princess it will only be who is here now and the brownies, no one from the outside will know and be notified that it's happening."

A smile appeared on her face, she could dance once more, dance with the people she cared about, she could let loose for the first time since this journey started.

"But guys we have nothing to wear."

Anion and his boys smiled like they knew something everyone else didn't. Anion directed Aerwyna to a room that would be hers for the entire time that she was here. Upon opening the door, the smell of mahogany filled her nose, the room was filled with dark mahogany furniture, her bed was carved. The headboard had a mother of pearl inlaid within. Small balls were lined around the inlaid pearl, three circles encircled the headboard. A small scallop seashell decorated the largest mother of pearls. The base board was carved just the same as the headboard three circles the same size and location as the others only if they were filled with wood instead of pearl. Two sea snail shells rested along the bottom by the feet of the bed which rested on a darked red and beige rug covering the oak floor, which matched the bedding which covered the frame. A chest of drawers with a vanity mirror decorated the left-hand side of the room while a massive wardrobe filled the other side with two off white paper films were the only decoration on the massive expanse of mahogany.

"Oh, Anion, this is beautiful. Is this really for me."

"That's right, everyone else is just down the hall. All the rooms are right next door to each other. So, you've got Saoirse next door to you then Cailean and Ghillie are in the room next door to her. "

"Hey, why are we the only one sharing a room!"

Both Ghillie and Cailean shouted in unison. Looking hurt in the process.

"We only have a set number of guest rooms in the castle, I'm sorry but its that or you sleep outside. Actually, you would probably like that."

"Don't think that just because I'm small doesn't mean I can't squash you like a bug."

Anion just laughed at Caileans statement before he turned and joined Kano and Cas out in the hall. He turned and bowed to Aerwyna before he showed everyone else to their room, ignoring Caileans protests in the process. Aerwyna just stood there in the middle of the room twirling around taking in everything it could offer. She opened the wardrobe and found numerous different dresses inside all her size.

She wondered if the guys filled the wardrobe for her when they first

visited her just in case she came for a visit.

"Oh, guys you are so sweet."

She said aloud even though there was no one near her she knew that

her appreciation was taken by them, they knew how thankful she was

to them, for everything they did.

***

Saoirse sat on the bed while Aerwyna stood in front of the wardrobe

trying to decide which dress she should wear for this ball Anion and

his sons were throwing for her.

"You know anyone you pick will look amazing on you. And

whichever you decide to do, Cailean is going to lose his mind."

"It is not like that with us, we are just friends you know, nothing

romantic, just friends."

Uh huh. Was all Saoirse said as she watched Aerwyna peruse the

wardrobe full of the most beautiful dresses she had seen; they ranged

from burnt orange all the way down to midnight blue and everything

in between.

"Things like this get confused. I've only ever worn green. I don't

know what suits me best. Any ideas."

Saoirse rose from the bed to stan in front of the wardrobe, she picked

up dresses of pale pink, and burnt orange and held them to her bring

her hair over the fabric so she could compare the colour against her

skin and hair, neither of those seemed to fit, so she threw those on the

bed with a nope resounded from her. The next she tried was the beige

and the red, but again they just didn't seem to match the red blended

too much with her hair and the beige washed her out.

"Nope, not these either."

"Saoirse these are the only two left, there's got to be something."

Saoirse pulled the last two dresses from the wardrobe. It didn't take

them long to decide on which one to choose.

"This perfect colour suits you amazingly. Choose this one please

choose this."

Aerwyna reached for the dress as she nodded her head in agreement

silently with Saoirse. This dress was perfect for the colour, the style

and the embellishments. Everything about it was perfect.

"I bet anything that he will choose the same colour."

"He would not, would he? Anyway, it's not like I care what he's

wearing."

Uh huh was all she got from Saoirse as she left the room to get herself

ready for the ball, she had already chosen her dress, it was the same

colour as the sea allowing her to bring a little bit of home with her.

Although she had chosen Aerwyna wondered what Tasi would be wearing, would he have anticipated her and chosen the same or something similar, maybe he had chosen something completely different, it wasn't long till the ball so she would find out soon whether she was right and whether Saoirse was right as well.

***

The ballroom was all set up and the piano sat on the right-hand side ready to play all the music to make this evening as magical as possible. The chandeliers were lit, illuminating the freshly varnished marble floor, pillars with golden filigree at the top held up small balconies that overlooked the dancefloor; it was designed so that people could still be involved when resting from dancing. Small alcoves were situated underneath the balconies allowing people to take a seat to the side. There were no platforms that excluded anyone from where everyone was dancing. The stairs that descended from the balconies splayed at the bottom leave a wide berth at the bottom allowing people to choose which way they went at the end, it was here that Cailean, Ghillie and Tasi stood waiting for the girls to join them.

"Do girls normally take this long to get ready?"

Ghillie was growing impatient, but he had never had to wait for girls,
the girls they had weren't normally the ones to take a long time caring
about their appearance, maybe they got lost.

"Not normally but I think it'll be worth the wait, don't you think?"
Ghillie signed and looked over at Tasi who was currently wringing
his hands like he was nervous. Cailean bumped his shoulder and told
him not to worry, the girls would be here soon, and everything would
be okay. Tasi just signed and looked at the stairs then his jaw went
slack.

At the top of the stairs the girls stood there holding the handrail
looking down at them with a smile on their faces. Aerwyna stood
there in a dark midnight blue dress that glowed like stars. The top half
of her dress was covered in crystals that cascaded down the dress
stopping and spreading themselves out as they reached the bottom,
the dress itself was strapless which showed off Aerwyna delicate
shoulders one which was covered with her caramel hair, from the
looks of it she had a small tiara which sat on top her head.

"Wow."

Saoirse stood beside her in an ocean blue dress that was all over
subtle glitter, in the front there was a deep plunge and a thigh high slit
that stopped mid-thigh showing off her long slender legs. Two thin
straps held the dress up as they crisscrossed at the back stopping at

her lower back, leaving a vast expanse of skin visible and able to touch.

"Wow is right."

As the girls started the descent down the stairs both Cailean and Tasi moved closer to the stairs holding out their hands for them. When they reached them everything else seemed to blur away, it was like they were the only people in the world. Tasi held out his hand for Saoirse and Cailean for Aerwyna.

"Can I have this dance?"

For once since they had joined both Cailean and Tasi spoke in sync with each other. The girls looked at each other and smiled before they placed their hands in theirs as they led them to the dance floor.

***

Anion had told them that the music they use for their balls they told her that at the moment they were currently obsessing over someone who died a long time ago but apparently his music was the most beautiful they had heard in a long time.

"Hey, Saoirse, can you remember what the music guy's name was again. Anion told me but I can't remember."

"Umm I think they said he was ko-sky maybe. Or maybe chi-ko-key. I'm not too sure, when we find them, we can ask again."

Either way Aerwyna found it didn't matter, all that mattered to her in that moment was the fact that she had finally gotten over the shock of seeing Cailean in the outfit she brought him back to Llwyn all that time ago.

"And where did you find that hmmm?"

Cailean looked down at her and shrugged before answering.

"I may or may not have found it under your bed and packed it before we left, just in case."

Aerwyna just laughed as she looked him up and down taking in the clothes on him. He was wearing the dark blue jacket that had the silver button running down either side holding it closed what made her laugh was the fact that he even had the puff sleeved top on underneath which she would see poking out from the sleeves of the jacket, as well as the dark grey trousers that disappeared into matching dark blue boots with silver tread running down the sides.

"What not a cloak?"

Cailean just smiled down at her as he placed his hand on her lower back pulling her closer to him as he grasped her hand in his as he raised them before starting to turn and move around the floor, sweeping her with him in every move. The band situated behind them started up using their many instruments most of which they hadn't seen before, but some they had like a harp and flutes. As they floated around the room everyone vanished, it was just the two of them dancing on clouds as they enjoyed the music and the feel of each other in their arms.

"May I cut in?"

Anion stood there with his hand open awaiting to accept Aerwyna's delicate hand. Cailean looked at his hand and begrudging allowed him to whisk her away from his embrace.

"Hey, Anion, what's the person's name again?"

Anion laughed as he told her it was a composer called Tchaikovsky. And it didn't take long for Aerwyna to shout over to Cailean and Saoirse with the name filling them in, which made them both smile. He told her that this particular one was called Waltz of the Flowers. Anino told her that he found it appropriate considering she was normally decked out in flower dresses covered in flowers. After a couple of turns around the floor it wasn't long before Cailean cut in once more, finding herself back in his embrace felt like home. Anion announced that the next song was for all the couples that were in the room. Many couple crowed the room including Saoirse and Tasi, Cailean and Aerwyna, even Ghillie, Kano and Cas had found a partner for the dance which made Aerwyna happy all her friends looked happy, she was happy, and she was going to dance and enjoy herself.

"Next up we have a compassion called Dance of the Prince Orgeat and the sugar plum fairy."

The band started up with their flutes and string instruments as the piece started. The first instrument to start was the harp, the delicate sound filtered into their ear as the other string instruments joined in creating a layer sound as the waltz around the floor dancing in each other's embrace. The music was amazing that the feeling it made people feel when the flutes joined in and added another layer was magical. But was surprised when more and more instruments joined, and the piece got multiple layers that they thought wouldn't work but did. Aerwyna looked up at Cailean who was already smiling down at her, making her smile more when he tilted his head toward one of the open doors which lead out to the gardens outside, giving them a bit of cool air after all the dancing. What they didn't expect was who was waiting for them in the garden. As the music hit its most dramatic turning point with increased violins and then what was called a trumpet and a drum join a voice sounded behind them hidden away in one of the many dark alcoves that decorated the outside of the castle.

"Hello Princess."

The voice caused them to turn around quickly, but they didn't see anyone there, whoever was hiding in the shadows moved away quickly allowing them a section of peace and quiet which didn't last long as they looked at railing that ran along the edge of the patio, their stood the person they all least expected to see.

"Prince Aelfdane. What are you doing here?"

As he rose from the railing a smirk appeared on his face as he spoke to them in a hushed voice.

"I've just come to reclaim what is mine."

Cailean instinctively moved in front of Aerwyna, placing her behind him and out of harm's way or so he thought. Soon he felt a pressure to his head as someone hit him with a blunt object all he could see before he black out was two men and the bastard dragging Aerwyna away just as the music calmed down again and every applauded the band for the song as they dragged her away from him out of sight out of his grasp out of his protection before everything went black.

Chapter Thirty-Three

Foghar Forest

When the music had finished Ghillie and the group decided to cool

down after all the dancing on the balcony, it was then that they saw

Cailean laying on the floor. Saoirse saw him first screaming his name

as she ran and bent down to him.

"Cailean are you okay? speak to me? Where is Aerwyna? what

happened?"

All Cailean could manage was a mumble Aelfdane before he blacked

out once more.

"He found her."

Saoirse turned looking at Ghillie and Anion and the boy who ran out

at the sound of her screaming.

"Who found her? Where is she? What's going to happen?"

Ghillie was starting to panic, no one was telling him anything and

everyone knew something he didn't. All he did know was that

someone bad had Aerwyna and they had to go save her right now.

Saoirse explained to Ghillie everything she knew about the bastard

Aelfdane. She filled him in on everything she knew about him, how

he was Aerwyna's betrothed but he was only with her to gain more of

390

the fairy realm for himself, how he helped her own father put her in that tree for reasons they didn't know yet. All Saoirse knew for sure was he wasn't right for her in any way possible and they needed to do anything in their power to save her, right now.

***

Laying Cailean on his bed was difficult for everyone, even though he was the same size as them, he was still much lanky than everyone else, which for some strange reason made it harder, but once he was there it was only a matter of time until he woke up and would well and truly be on the warpath.

"He's going to be devastated when he finds out."

Saoirse sat beside his bed placing a cold towel on Cailean's head. There wasn't much they could do until Cailean woke up.

"Wait, we can find the stone, the reason why we came here is if we find that the next place on the journey is the fairies realm to create the Myrios stone, so in order to help we should find the stone of night."

"We could do it but someone has to stay here with Cailean, we need to keep an eye on him. If he wakes up and no one's here, he will go storming off and probably get himself killed. Take Tasi and ask Anion for help. I'll stay here and look after him."

Ghillie turned to Tasi who was standing behind him trying his hardest to hide. Ghillie turned with a smile on his face which made Tasi feel even more nervous than he already felt.

"Come on, let's find that stone and get our girl back."

Ghillie tugged Tasi along pulling him from the room on their way\to find Anion and the stone that will help them find Aerwyna.

***

When Aerwyna opened her eyes, she didn't automatically recognize where she was. The ceiling was painted like a night sky. Millions of stars were dotted around clouds covering some other outshining everything. Beams were visible that arched up towards the light which dangled from the centre of the ceiling. The walls were painted like the forests that surround them: one wall was for the foghar, one for the Samhradh, one for the earrach and the last panel was for the Geamhradh. Raising out of the bed she looked around a small door to her left and a fireplace to the right. Small wardrobe and a chest of drawers which she sort of recognized were situated around the room.

"Where is this?"

Aerwyna was so engrossed at looking around the room that she didn't hear the door open, or anyone walk in.

"This is your room my dear."

"Fa….Father?"

392

"Welcome home my daughter."

***

Cailean rocked his head side to side as Saoirse tried to keep him cool with the flannel.

"Aerwyna, we've got to save her."

It hurt her that every now and then he flashed back to him taking her from him. They had to have had the upper hand to be able to jump him.

"Their looking Cailean, their looking for the stone and once we have it, we will get her back. Don't worry they'll find it and will find her."

Tasi and Ghillie walked down the long expanse of the corridor towards Anions rooms.

"Do you think you will be able to find the stone?"

"Is that doubt I hear?"

"No, just worry for Cailean. For Aerwyna."

"They will both be fine, we just have to hold up our end of this. Okay?"

Tasi just smiled up at Ghillie who placed a hand on his shoulder in the most reassuring way he knew possible.

"Come on, it can't be hard to find one little Brownie."

***

Aerwyna moved back until she reached the wall and couldn't back away any further. The man that stood in front of her she recognized as her father. But after she knew what he had done and what he made her grandmother do, she no longer saw him as her father, he was just a man who had trapped her, hurt her mother and now aided her kidnapper.

"What do you want?"

Her father moved closer into the room making the room feel smaller than it already was when she had been so used to living in the shop and staying at Ghillies woodland home.

"I'm here to see you, my daughter, you've been missing for years. It's amazing to see you again."

He walked towards her with his arms open trying to envelope her in a hug, but she turned away as quickly as she could avoiding his hug as best she could.

"I want to go home."

"My dear you are home. And soon you'll be in your new home. With your husband, and you'll be happy and make a home and you'll have children. Everything I'll be fine."

"My husband?"

She looked at her father curiously as he walked towards the door. Humming as he went. Before he quickly turned to her with a sadist smile on his face.

"Yes, your husband, Prince Aelfdane. You'll marry him in three days, and all will be well with the world again. You'll not remember that stupid kelpie or those brownies and tree spirit. And you'll never see that selkie again. You'll marry him and continue the line as that is all that you're useful for. You'll stay here in this room until them, servants will bring you food and drink and on the day of your wedding they will bring you your dress and escort you down to the chapel and then to the honeymoon suit where you and you husband will stay before heading to his castle where you will reside for the remainder of your life, do you understand me?"

Aerwyna sank to the floor as her father spoke telling her she would never see anyone again, not Cailean, not Saoirse and not Ghillie or the Brownies. She was to be sued to reproduce children and that was it. This was why she ran in the first place; this is why she tried to hide. She remembers then that she hid in the tree, but Elvina and her father found her and activated the tree, locking her in there in hope that she would change her mind, only that when they returned to the tree a few weeks later, she was gone. She was gone and they couldn't find her because she transferred to the tree in the human realm, into the tree where Cailean had found her. She knew then that she could either sit there and take what they were giving her, or she could stand up for herself and fight.

***

After searching for what seemed like hours Ghillie and Tasi found Anion and the boys in the ball room sitting on the chairs holding the stone of night in their hands.

"How did you find it so quickly?"

"All the brownies royalty have known of its location for centuries. And we have known about every Ayla as well."

At the mention of the Ayla Ghillie face dropped. The Brownies knew information about Ayla. Maybe they knew some way to help Aerwyna. Did they know that she was Ayla?

"Do you know any information about Ayla?"

Anion nodded as Kano revealed a book which he brought out from behind him, Ghillie was too far away to see the title, but he assumed it would be a book containing all the known information about the mysterious Ayla. Kano passed the book to Ghillie who immediately sank to the floor opening it to the last chapter, what shocked him was what was written in the last chapter.

"The book automatically updates whenever a new Ayla comes into their powers and unfortunately for us. Our dear princess is the new Ayla. And if her father and that low life prince know then help us all. They will use her for everything and anything they want. Especially if the best prize they can get is the Myrios stone."

"What exactly does this stone do? And why is everyone under this blasted sun trying to find it."

Anion signed as he signalled Ghillie and Tasi to take a seat near him. He told them he would explain all they needed to know about the Ayla powers and the powers of the Myrios stone.

"The Ayla powers are extensive as you already know. They have the powers of Photokinesis, the power to control light and nature. W3hich you already saw firsthand with the Banshees. These rays of light can change depending on the situation and the mood the Ayla is in. They can range from colours of blue all the way down to a beautiful golden. Electrokinesis is one many people are afraid of. The Ayla can control electrical currents and conjure up lighting from the palms of their hands. Chlorokinesis the ability to control plants; they can use any plant as a form of attack. The one that is a better form allowing them to communicate with other past Ayla's is clairvoyance. This is the favoured ability previous Ayla's can help them along in many ways we still don't understand."

"How is all that power contained in a little body like hers?"

"Combine the powers of the Ayla's and the power of the Myrios stone and you can practically enhance the power she holds tenfold. Combining the powers together isn't only dangerous for everyone around them but it's dangerous for the Ayla themselves. Combining the powers in a worst-case scenario can either permanently comatose them or worse kill them."

Ghillie looked at the book at the small image of Aerwyna with the list of powers underneath her, before he looked up at Anion, Kano and Cas who all had a solemn look on their faces on that very well matched his, a few tear rested on the lip of his eyes threatening to fall.

"So, if the evil bastards pair Aerwyna and the Myrios stone together she could die."

Anion just nodded in acknowledgement that he got it right. Ghillie told them that they couldn't let that happen, she couldn't die, not now not ever. She was happy she found love.

"love?"

Anion looked at Ghillie as if he just showed them a silver lining.

"Aerwyna in love?"

"Yes, if you look at how she looks at him it's easy to see."

"Is her love reciprocated?"

Ghillie nodded; he believed that the looks on Cailean's face whenever he saw her, how protective he was over her, and the way he danced with her at the ball, he had no doubt that he was head over heels for her. Whether he knew it himself or not.

"I believe so."

"Then we may have found a way to save our dear princess."

Ghillie smiled if there was any way of saving her then no matter what it was, they were going to try.

***

Aerwyna sat on the end of her bed, looking at the array of dresses multiple people had brought in for her. It sickened her with the amount of white that was currently in her room. She always thought that someone's wedding day was supposed to be the happiest day of their lives, but hers filled her with dread. The thought that her father, the evil bastard that he was, was making her marry someone she didn't even love for his own benefit hurt her immensely. Over the last couple of days, she had tried to escape in as many ways as possible but each time she got caught and the route was either boarded up or severely guarded. The door opened then revealing more servants who came with more dresses.

"I've told you many times before to stop bringing them. I'm not getting married, I'm not wearing a dress and I'm not going!"

399

The servants didn't listen and just hung up the other three dresses next to the other ten that already adorned the rack at the end of her room. Dresses of all length short, long ones with trains, and everything in between. But it didn't matter none of them were ever going to be worn unless it was someone else waiting for her at the end of the aisle. But she knew her father would make her even if he had to tie her hands up and inhibit her ability to speak. Either way, if her father had anything to do about it, she was going to get married to the worst excuse of a man she could think of tomorrow, and that thought itself worried her more than the wedding itself.

"You haven't tried your dresses my dear."

Aerwyna looked over her shoulder at the sorry excuse of a father who darkened the doorway.

"As I've told you numerous times before, I'm not getting married tomorrow, if you love him so much you marry him."

He laughed, he laughed at her, she knew she had no choice, but it didn't stop her from trying. Nothing would stop her from getting back to the real man she loved. It was then that she realised she hadn't ever told him how she felt, what she felt for him, how he made her feel, how much she actually loved him. The very thought made her cry, here she was stuck being forced to marry someone she didn't love when she hadn't even told the man she loved that she loved him. The very thought made her sink to the floor as her tears flowed freely.

"Aw my dear these are just pre wedding jitters, you'll get over them and you'll be happy. So, smile, you're getting married tomorrow."

The very thought made her tears come harder as she balled herself up trying to find the strength to continue. But everything seemed to darken around her. She was losing her hope, she had nothing left.

***

Ghillie ran back to the room where Saoirse sat with a still unconscious Caelian. Brushing through the door he caused Saoirse to shriek, stirring Cailean in the process.

"W-What's happening, who's screaming?"

Everyone looked down at Cailean who was stirred from sleep from the screams of Saoirse.

"Where's Aerwyna?"

Saoirse looked at Ghillie with the look of help in her eyes, what did they do? They couldn't tell him now he'd just woken up after two days, whatever they hit him with really scrambled him. They couldn't hide it from him though he had to know, she had already been gone for two days already, plus the information Ghillie just found out, they needed to put together a plan and they needed to get it together right now if they stood any chance.

401

Ghillie ran back to Anions' rooms and brought them all back. If they were going to tell Cailean everything that happened they needed everyone there. When Ghillie explained everything that happened everyone's faces dropped. Explaining the powers and what would happen if the powers merged together. Ghillie also told them what Anion's reaction was when he told him that she was in love.

"Aerwyna in love?"

Cailean voice echoed down the halls, could he have been that shocked that Aerwyna was in love.

"Whoever she's in love with is the luckiest guy in this world."

Ghillie looked to Anion and Saoirse, could he be in that much denial that he wasn't aware that she was in love with him, or was he just denying it himself so save him from pain.

"Anion, what is the big deal if she's in love with someone, what does that have to do with helping her."

"Well, it's said that when people are in complete love with each other they share one heart, one soul, one mind. The other Ayla's that feel completely in love. They shared everything."

Ghillie looked down at Cailean who he could see was slowly absorbing the meaning behind it.

"So, if they shared everything, one heart, one mind, one soul. Does that mean they can share the power as well?"

Cailean tried to clarify everything, which to his relief was confirmed with a nod from Anion. He thought if they found the person she was completely in love with they could share the power then her father wouldn't be able to use her and the Myrios stone together as it wouldn't be a complete power.

"We have to find him. How does it work? How can we get them to share the power?"

Anino told him that in order for them to share the power they one had to admit to the feeling that they shared and the magnitude of them as well. By admitting to the depth of the feeling, it somehow shared the powers between the two people. Anino said that even to this day they still weren't sure how it worked but they knew it had to be honest and pure. It was the only way that they knew worked and the only way that would save Aerwyna.

"So, the only problem we have is finding him. We don't know who he is. Do we?"

Everyone looked to Saoirse, she knew the best way to deal with him, they couldn't believe that he could be this dense. Did he truly not know the depth of her feelings for him? Saoirse just smiled at him.

"You know we all love you to a certain degree, but you can be the densest person I've ever met, you know that right."

Cailean just looked at Saoirse as she smiled and shook her head at him. Cailean loved that she always seemed to know what he didn't and was able to show him a different way of seeing it himself.

"What are you saying?"

"Look back at your time with her and see if you can see what I'm saying."

Cailean sat there and replayed everything in his head, how she acted around him. All the tea and the cookies looking after him making sure he ate during the day. How the first time he took her to the market the only thing she brought was something for him. The time at the inn, pretending to be married and kissing him in front of everyone. All the little actions added up and then it hit him.

"It's me isn't it. I'm the one she loves."

Saoirse just smiled before looking up at Ghillie and then to Anion, Kano and Cas who smiled back down at her. Before they all spoke.

"Took you long enough."

***

Aerwyna stood at her window looking out at the forest that lay before her, wondering if she'll ever be free once more. She looked at the

404

moon in the sky as she watched it slowly move across, shortening the amount of time she had left of her supposed freedom.

"Cailean, where are you? Why aren't you here? Why can't you be the one I marry?"

"My dear?"

At the sound of a different voice, one she didn't think she would hear again for a long, long time, tears started to fall.

"Mother?"

At seeing her mother standing in her doorway she ran grabbing the woman around the waist sinking to the floor, tears flowing freely. Her mother sat there with her stroking her finger through her hair humming a lullaby.

"Mum, I don't know what to do."

"I can't help you there my dear, there is only one who can help you, and i'm sure he'll be here and save you before any of this can happen.im sorry my dear for everything your father has done, you shouldn't have to live through this."

She assured her that she'll get her thoughts if it was the last thing she would do.

***

"How do I get to Foghar forest.? Tell me now!"

405

Cailean rose out of bed quickly dressing himself while everyone flapped around him trying to get him to slow down saying he should slow down after being asleep for a couple of days.

"I don't need to take it easy, I need to save her right now."

"You just need to go through this door, and it will take you there, but be careful, that king is as mad as mad people get. He'll try everything in his power to stop you reaching her. If he finds out, you too care so deeply about each other that you will help you all."

Cailean nodded and turned and continued to pack his bag. Nothing was going to stop him from saving her. Saoirse, Ghillie and even Anion and his boys packed bags with him, Aerwyna had friends and people that loved her, and they were going to save her right now.

***

After the bags were packed, they entered the room that Anion told them held doors to all the different realms, it was how they came and visited him and Aerwyna all those time back at the shop.

"Everyone ready?"

Cailean turned around and looked at everyone and everyone nodded back at him. They all had their bags, Anion, and the boys carried all the books they could possibly need with all the information on the Ayla, Saoirse and Tasi had packed all the preserves for the journey they didn't know how long they would be there, but they were

prepared. Ghillie and Cailean had the look of death on their faces,
those bastards stole their girl, and they were going to get her back.
Walking through the door the crunch of autumn leaves under foot, the
smell of winter in the air as it drew always closer but never came.
The forest was beautiful but unfortunately some of the people who
reside within spoiled its beauty. In the far distance they swathe tops of
the castle.

"That's where we need to go, that is where we will find her. Come on,
we don't have long till morning."

Cailean led the way as they all marched towards the castle on their
way to help Cailean save the love of his life.

Chapter Thirty-Four

Wedding

Approaching the castle was frightening. Seeing the guards posted at every entrance, some were situated at the windows. Maybe she had tried to escape and bring herself back to him but was caught, could he allow himself to think that. Maybe she loved him as much as he loved her.

"Do we know where she is in the palace?"

"if I know anything about the king of this place. He would probably put her up somewhere high. Somewhere it's hard for us to get to. Somewhere like there."

Ghillie pointed to the further top right window that the only way of accessing it from the outside was from the courtyard which was located through two walls lined with guards.

"Of course, she had to be in the further towers style window that they could possibly put her in. How are we going to reach her."

Anion looked over at Ghillie and Cailean with one of the most sarcastic looks Saoirse had ever seen.

"Okay guys little ones have an idea."

The annoyed look followed the sarcastic look as they all looked at her with disdain.

"Thanks. Guys think about it, we have a Kelpie, one of the most deadly and powerful water spirits and the Ghillie Dhu the most powerful woodland spirit. What do you think we can do with that and three Brownies who are small and can sneak in, and two selkies who can control water. Think about it."

Cailean looked at Anion and smiled. He may be a small Brownie, but he cared about Aerwyna just as much as he did and that would be a benefit for them.

"All right, let's make a plan."

***

Aerwyna stood in front of her floor mirror as the servant tied up the corset strings of her wedding dress. The dress itself was beautiful but the reason behind it wasn't. The dress was an ivory silk, floor length skirt, the corset style top enhanced its style with lace and ribbon sewn around the bottom up the centres covering the top enhancing the sweetheart neckline. Two sleeves held around her upper arms, the save lace and ribbons sewn around the band. The two sleeves extended down her arm hiding her fingers and they drifted to the floor alongside her skirt. A golden crown encircled her head as autumn leaves decorated the frame. Small pink pearls were beaded in and

409

around the leaves while four individual diamonds sat on her forehead. The crown was the only decorated jewellery she had that adored her body.

"You look beautiful, my daughter."

Aerwyna looked up in the mirror to see her father standing in the doorway. She couldn't even fake a smile as he walked in, grabbed her hand and spun her around taking in a good look of her in the dress he picked for her.

"Prince Aelfdane is going to be very pleased."

She couldn't say anything, she couldn't smile, couldn't object to anything at all. Her father had brought someone in the last time she tried to escape after her mothers visit, someone who froze her mind, froze her action and made her a dummy in her own body. Frozen from speaking and acting out just like he wanted, this way she wouldn't be able to object to what the minister said, she could object to if anyone knows of any reason why these two shall not be wed speak now or forever hold your peace. She didn't have that choice, she was stuck, she had to do whatever they wanted her to do.

"Just know if you try to act up, I'll bring him back and get him to wipe your memoirs of anyone you care about. You'll never know of them."

Aerwyna stood there blank faced. She couldn't speak, couldn't cry, couldn't do anything by standing there when on the inside she was crying.

***

As Cailean and Ghillie's back hugged the walls and they snuck past the guards that manned the outer walls as Anion, Kano and Cas climbed up being able to climb up undetected. Weaving their small fingers in between the grooves of the rock wall, climbing slowly but surely towards the guard who manned the door as well as held the keys they would need to infiltrate the castle. How they were going to do that without causing a massive disturbance and causing her insane father to speed whatever plans he had up Cailean didn't know. But he knew they had to try, and this was the only way he knew how. Anion gently climbed up the guard's trouser leg which he was able to do undetected due to his size and therefore he didn't weigh that much. Carefully he unlatched the keys from the holder placing them in his mouth as he carefully climbed back down the guards leg and down, he wall carefully not to move too quickly in case of making the keys jingle. Reaching Cailean shoulder, Anion sank down, so we were sitting while Kano and Cas repeated the same action on Ghillie's shoulder.

411

"Here I got the keys. Not sure which is which, but we'll just have to try."

"Right guys you all know your jobs right?"

Everyone nodded, Anion, Kano and Cas readied their weapon, Ghillie rolled his neck cracking it in preparation for the battle that was most likely going to happen. Cailean readied his sword which he made and solidified of water. It was one power he had as a Kelpie that he had never used, never had a reason to use until today.

"Right then, let's go get our girl."

***

Aerwyna was led down a flower lined corridor towards what she assumed would be where she would be getting married. So many thoughts ran through her head, but she could voice any of them, as she was led down the hall. When she eventually raised her head to see where she was going she saw her mother standing at the end of the hall, smiling at her. Everyone was happy for her but her.

"My dear you look beautiful."

Aerwyna tried to smile at her mother as she took her by the arm, her mother leading her the rest of the way to the waiting wing that was situated beside the chapel. Once the door was closed her mother's smile dropped.

"What has he done to you?"

Her mother ran her hands around her face looking for anything out of the ordinary, looking for anything he could have placed on her to hinder her ability to speak and move freely of her own choice. Then she found it, behind her right ear was a small circle. Pulling it away from her enabled her the ability to speak her mind once more. As soon as the inhibitor was off the tears, she held in all the time it was there and was let free.

"Mum."

***

Opening the door which was hidden behind the only section of the wall that was covered in ivy, Unlike the rest of the wall which was covered in unbloomed wisteria. Cailean thought that if anything ever happened between him and Aerwyna this would be one thing he would tell her about to improve, it made it too easy to find and he couldn't have that now when eventually it would be her safety at risk.

"Where do you think they would have her?"

Anion told them that when they were stealing the keys, he overheard the guards saying she was to be married today, which explained the increase of guards.

"They've probably taken her to the waiting chamber."

Cailean looked at Anion then, the Kelpies didn't have waiting chambers, theirs were the groom awaited at the end and the bride

413

walked in after them lead by someone of their choice, it was usually someone they were extremely close to, mostly it was the parents, but he didn't think Aerwyna would have either of her parents there, maybe her mother but definitely not her father.

"Where is that?"

"It will be beside the chapel. Over there."

Cailean looked in the direction that Anion pointed. He didn't believe that was their chapel, it looked more like a rundown storage outbuilding. He looked back at everyone and pointed at the chapel.

"That's the chapel?"

Anion nodded starting on his way towards the building. Cailean followed behind him making a promise. A promise that if Aerwyna married him he would make it the most beautiful, most memorable one she could ever have, as if she married him, she would only have one wedding, one partner and it would be with him.

***

Aerwyna sat on the sofa with her mother who was currently running her fingers through Aerwyna's hair being careful to avoid the crown that sat upon her head.

"What do I do mother? I don't want to marry him."

"I'm sorry my dear you know your father there is nothing I can say to change his mind."

414

Suddenly there was shouting outside the window that was situated just to the left of where they were sitting. Her mother looked at her daughter once more before getting up and walking towards the window. Once she was there a smile covered her face as she turned to look at Aerwyna who was looking down at the feet worrying about what was about to happen.

"My dear I don't think you have to worry. We're going to get you out of here."

"How."

"Don't you worry, leave that all to me. I just have to go out and grab something you're missing, something blue. Cant get married within the four items, something old , something blue, something borrowed, something new. Aerwyna looked around and her mother was right; she had three of the four. Aerwyna just nodded at her mother who was now beaming at the seam, unable to hide her joy.

"I'll be back soon."

Her mother said, placing a kiss on her head before she left the room.

***

"Everyone run!"

Cailean shouted behind him as the guards appeared from every corner of the courtyard. Running towards them with more weapons then they had ever seen.

415

"Cailean, you run towards the chapel, we'll hold them off, you stop
that wedding from happening."

Cailean clasped Ghillie's arm before he turned around leaving his
friends to face their combined enemy, before turning towards the
chapel trying to find an entrance. Upon finding the entrance which
was easily found he knew he would have to talk to Aerwyna about
that at a later date. The door was hidden behind an ivy wall which
stood out immensely against the unbloomed wisteria. He wasn't sure
which way to go when he entered the building, he knew he couldn't
risk alerting people to his position not with Aerwyna life on the line.
Hugging the wall as he walked around, he saw a woman calling him
over with her hands before running up the stairs. Did she want him to
follow her, he wasn't sure but any help he could get he was going to
take.

"This way."

A small voice whispered towards him, and he saw the woman once
more beckoning him down the corridor.

"Where are you leading me?"

The woman didn't answer, only waved him over to her as she hid in
the dark alcoves that lined the walls along the corridor.

"I'm just a friend. We have the same goal. You will finish her at the
end of the corridor but be aware the king knows of your plan, and I

wouldn't put it past him to have moved her. If that is the case then he would have already moved her to the chapel for the wedding, please you must get there before that happens. If they get their hands on her then all of us are lost."

The woman said nothing more before crouching down as running down the corridor towards a different room. Cailean was perplexed with the woman; she looked very similar to Aerwyna but her mother, according to what Aerwyna had told him, lost her memories due to her grandmother. But maybe that didn't stop her from trying to save her daughter, maybe she knew what her daughter was and knew how much she needed to be saved. Cailean took a deep breath in before he stood to his full height and kicked the door down.

***

Two guards entered the room that Aerwyna waited in dragging her from it telling her the wedding had been moved up due to reasons beyond her need to know.

"Let me go!"

Thanks to her mother removing the inhibitor Aerwyna slowly regained her ability to move as well as her speech, and she was going to try everything to get free and get back to Cailean and the others, back to her home, back to the shop, back to her life with Cailean away from her father away from Aelfdane away from all of it.

Unfortunately, upon entering the chapel she knew that wasn't going to happen. Her father and the prince stood at the end of the aisle waiting for her. By the look on her father's face, he knew she no longer was under his control, and he wasn't happy about it. The two guards that held her arms dragged her down closer to them just as the minister approached the altar.

"No this isn't going to happen; it will never happen."

Her father replaced the inhibitor to the back of her neck taking away her ability to speak and move once more. All she could do was look upon the face of her groom, and his sneer revealed everything he was going to do to her, to her family, to everyone she cared about. She looked at the minister hoping that he would be able to understand her reaction to the marriage with just a look from her, but as he started the vows, she knew that nothing was going to stop this wedding.

"If there is anyone who knows of any reason why these two shall not be wed speak now or forever hold your peace."

Just as the minister spoke the last line before he made them wed a massive crash sounded from behind the door.

"Hurry up, wed them now. Make it permanent."

"I cannot in case someone knows of a reason. I must follow the rules, my king."

Aerwyna's father didn't like what the minister told him, he knew there was someone who would object as that someone was possibly on his way here or already here.

"Marry them now, I don't care about the rules. Do it now!"

The minister from feeling threatened by the king, the look in his eyes told him many things many bad things would happen if he didn't continue and wed them now.

"I now pronounce......."

Before the minister could continue a sword landed just in front of him. The door to the chapel burst open and a sword made of water, one unlike he had ever seen before.

"With all due respect, minister, I think you should hold that right there. I know the reason why they shouldn't be wed. and that is because she's going to marry me."

The massive crash of the door breaking down moved everyone back which is Aerwyna's favour knocked of the inhibitor once more, allowing her the ability to run to Cailean who stood at the door hands on hip looking at her like she was his whole world and nothing and no one was going to stop that. Running into his arms she felt like she was home once more.

"Cailean! I knew you would come for me."

"I could only watch as that prince stole you away in front of my eyes. I'm so helplessly in love with you that I couldn't free myself from this feeling ... .So how are you going to repay me?"

Aerwyna just stood in Caileans arms, he just told her that he was helplessly in love with her like she was with him. Could she believe her ears? Did he really just say that?

"Did you just say……"

Cailean just nodded and asked her if she felt the same. Saying that if she did, they could share her powers and it would ruin all of her fathers plans. Aerwyna had no words as she looked up at him with tears in her eyes before she rose on her toes and placed her lips on his whispering 'I love you too' on his lips.

Chapter Thirty-Five

Powers

As Cailean and Aerwyna stood at the entrance of the chapel the

minister behind them finished his sentence.

"Man and wife."

The prince who was on the floor from the massive burst of Cailean

breaking through the door stood to his full height and laughed.

"You're too late, she's mine. mine too use mine to control all her

powers are mine. now release my bride you stupid inbred Kelpie."

Cailean regrettably relinquished Aerwyna's lips as he pushed her

gently behind him.

"First of all, how dare you insult her, insult me by all means but insult

her not a chance , second how would you like to die?"

Aelfdane stood there flabbergasted how insolent he thought someone

who was beneath him insulted him, and had his bride. This wasn't

going to happen, he had to get her back to use her powers to gain the

Myrios stone, then he would be the most powerful person in the

realms.

"Aerwyna my love you know the only man you should be bound to is

me."

Aerwyna clung to Cailean sleeve she knew she wasn't ever going to

go to him of her own free will never.

"You know my dear by law we are married. So, by law as well you

must listen to your husband."

Aerwyna looked up at Cailean who looked down at her his hand

around her holding her close to him protecting her as best he could.

Cailean bent down and whispered into her ear telling her what thy

had found about how she could share her powers with someone she

loved complete and truly with someone who loved her the same

whole heartedly

"Do you trust me?"

"Yes."

Cailean pushed her gently towards the prince and her father masking

his face into a scowl. He had to hope that this would work otherwise

he was sending her off for a life of servitude and torture. The prince

held out his hands, taking her in his bring them to his lips as he kissed

the hands of his new bride.

"My dear you made the correct decision this way you can stay a

princess for the rest of your day rather than be the whore of a Kelpie.

Guards!"

The prince hollered out for the guards to take Cailean away to the

dungeons, place him with the others the prince had said. Ghillie,

Anion, Kano and Cas had been caught, they were trapped. But he knew they had a back up plan. They still had Saoirse and Tasi. The prince led Aerwyna away taking her away to what Cailean knew would be their honeymoon suit before they travelled to his region of the forest, it was also where Caileans plan would commence.

***

Aerwyna shrunk herself down making herself look small. Cailean had told her that Saoirse and Tasi were waiting for her outside the honeymoon suite, and they would act before anything could happen, but it didn't stop her from worrying. She didn't know what would trigger her powers or what her powers would entail but if she could, she would avoid it by all mean, Cailean said that they could share her powers, but he had told her he didn't know how it happened whether it was just by confirming their love for each other or if there was something else, they needed to do.

"Aelfdane, when will we go to your region?"

Aelfdane looked down at her and smiled before telling her in what she thought was one of the slimiest voices she'd ever heard that they would leave first thing in the morning, and they wouldn't be coming back here for many years. Aerwyna just looked down at her feet as she continued to be led down the corridor to the room that would become her suit for the night with her husband, the very thought sent shivers down her spine and not in a good way.

***

Aelfdane opened the door to the suit which only held a bed, some clothes from both herself and Aelfdane and a station which held a small basin and cloth for washing, nothing much else lined the walls but one massive window which held a balcony overhanging the majestic moonlight filled forest.

"It's beautiful."

"Yes, you are."

Aelfdane approached her from behind placing his hands on her shoulders as he ran his lips down her neck stopping just at the base between her neck and her shoulder, before he spun them around, so he was facing the door and Aerwyna was facing the window allowing the moonlight to illuminate her facial feature to their best advantage.

"Your highness?"

Aelfdane walked them backwards until his legs reached the bed forcing him to take a seat pulling Aerwyna with him. It didn't last long before a small smile appeared on Aerwyna's face which Aelfdane just took as her enjoying what he was doing.

"Umm buddy I don't think she enjoys that, and women should enjoy time alone with their men."

"Tasi!"

Aerwyna couldn't help but smile as she saw her friend sitting on the railing of the balcony with Saoirse sitting beside him smirking at them both.

"Yeah, she doesn't enjoy that at all. I think she enjoys it more when she is alone."

The insults from both Tasi and Saoirse riled up Aelfdane to the point of bursting. It wasn't long before he threw Aerwyna off him and was crashing after the two Selkies who had thoroughly insulted him, leaving Aerwyna alone in the room.

***

Cailean sat on the floor of his cell with Ghillie, Anion, Kano and Cas sitting in the cell beside him.

"Do you think the Selkies did their part?"

Ghillie leaned against the bars that separated his cells and Caileans. He brought his knee to his chest resting his arm on it for support. Sitting in this cell away from any form of life was depressing for him.

"We'll find out soon, if they have distracted him, they should run past in three, two ,one…..."

"You can't catch us."

"You're too slow."

"Old man."

"If you can't catch us there, there is no way you can satisfy her."

Everyone laughed and they could hear Saoirse's and Tasi's continuous insults, as Aelfdane chased after them shouting back answers like i'm not old and yes, I will. Cailean knew that the little man couldn't even satisfy a tree let alone a woman.

"Right time to act, everyone ready?"

Ghillie just smiled as he stood and beckoned the guards forward under the impression that he was in immense pain in his stomach.

"What's wrong with you?"

Ghillie groaned as he sank to the floor holding his middle as he cried out in pain, his cries were so deafening that the guard ran into the cell to inspect the prisoner. The Guards knelt down beside Ghillie who was rocking in the foetal position. As the Guard knelt further to Ghillie inspecting him, Cailean could see that he was panicking, maybe the king had told him to keep them alive, maybe he had a plan for them to use them as leverage against Aerwyna. He knew one thing: he wasn't going to let that happen.

"Ghillie now!"

As the guard lent over Ghillie head to inspect him Ghillie quickly threw his head up hitting the guard square on the jaw knocking him flying leaving him unconscious. Ghillie lent forward grabbing the keys from the unconscious guards belt as he worked them into the lock freeing everyone.

"Let's go."

Cailean rushed out of the cell up the stairs and into the courtyard, where he was just in time to see Saoirse and Tasi jump over the roof of the far building with Aelfdane following them close behind.

"Right, he's left, let's go get her."

***

Aerwyna sat on the bed looking out the balcony where her friends and her new husband left. There wasn't much she could do, she tried to leave but there were guards stationed at the door, probably to let her father know whether they consummated the marriage.

"You know he's not here right, he left through the window."

They didn't answer her and didn't let her through either. It seemed that she was stuck here whether she liked it or not. With a huff she shut the door with a slam.

"Oooh, don't break the door."

Aerwyna spun around quickly to find Cailean laying on the bed behind her. How he got in without her hearing him she didn't know but at that point she didn't care as she ran towards the bed jumping into Cailean awaiting arms.

"What are you doing here?"

427

Cailean smiled as she rose herself up on her arms, looking down at him. Brushing her hair behind her ear

"I came to see you, to take you back home, back home with me."

Aerwyna placed her hand over his as small tears spilled over her eyes, she couldn't help but smile, he came for her risked her life to come here to get her, to bring her home, home with him.

"Now I have something to say, and I need you not to reply until I've finished. okay."

Aerwyna nodded as Cailean moved them around, so her back was against his chest as she nestled down in his arms, enjoying his embrace. It felt like ages since she had been in his embrace. Cailean asked if she was ready and at her nod, he took a deep breath before he started.

"It was like you brought colour to my life. You changed my life , all by yourself. Whether it's through illness, wrinkles, grey hair or even a weakened body. I would still want to be beside you, live this life with you, be a part of you, will you let me?"

Aerwyna could feel herself blush at Cailean words, what she didn't expect was it to be a full body blush that he would be able to feel.

"I loved you from the start; I couldn't help loving you. I can't help but want to completely devour you. That's why from now on I'll keep you by my side even more than before. I've decided to spend my life with you. I love you and I know the weight of those words; and I intend to express to you all the love I have with everything I possess. Right now, all I need is you."

Aerwyna couldn't help but try to turn around to face him, but Cailean grip was too tight. She told him that she needed to turn around to see him and his reply was if I move right now, you'll run away, right? I won't let you do that. She couldn't help but try but every time she did his grip tighten every so much more hindering her movements.

"Please let me go. I want to see you."

" It's dangerous when you say adorable things."

Aerwyna tried to move once more to move and Cailean grip loosen slightly allowing her to slightly move only enough to see his face and what she saw was so much love the feeling radiated off him filling her empty heart but its magnitude.

"Don't think you can get away from me"

Cailean whispered as he lowered his head and brushed a kiss to the sensitive area between her neck and ear, placing a kiss there which sent shivers down her spine. They were here together in the honeymoon suit under the protection of the guards out front, no one would come here and disturb them.

"If you don't hate me, kiss me over my heart."

Aerwyna was shocked at the bravery that came out of her as she spoke. Did she really just ask him that, did she want him to do that. The smile on his face proved that he wanted to do it. As he laid her down gently on the bed, he hovered over her looking down at her like she was the most precious thing he ever found in the world.

" I will always find you as beautiful as the first day I saw you." He spoke as he lowered his head, placing a gentle kiss over his rapidly beating heart.

"If people judge and scrutinise you, just ignore them and do whatever your heart tells you to do, do whatever you want to do."

Aerwyna placed her hand on Cailean cheek as she looked up at him smiling down at her. Unfortunately, the moment of bliss didn't last long as Cailean let out an ear-piercing scream as he fell down on top of her with a dagger sticking out of his back. Aerwyna screamed as she fretted over Cailean who let out laboured breaths, she turned her head quickly towards the door to see her father there smiling at his victory.

"Now there's one less Kelpie in the world, such a shame. Now come here you ungrateful child."

As Aerwyna stood over Cailean body as she stared down at her father she screamed and a multitude of different colour light erupted form her, frightening her father was now staring up at her with a frightened look.

"Now dear daughter, calm down, there's nothing wrong, he was only a Kelpie, nothing to worry about."

"How dare you hurt him. How dare you even look at him, how dare you feel you're important enough to even stand in his presents."

Her father walked back slowly as Aerwyna with eyes glowing and light radiating from her body moved towards him, the look on his face showed him that he saw his own death in his daughter's eyes that he was going to see the powers of the Ayla firsthand, and the fact frightened him immensely.

Chapter Thirty-Six

Future.

With the powers radiating through her the strength it created in her was immense. Moving to her father who was standing there cowering in the corner as she moved closer and closer to him with as much murderous intent in her eyes.

"You've hurt him. You could have killed him. Shall I show you how that feels."

As Aerwyna spread her hands open small bolts of lighting flew from her fingers towards her father scorching the floor where they hit.

"Calm down my daughter, all of this can be fixed."

"You don't get to call me your daughter."

Aerwyna's voice dropped a multitude of decimals as the power contained within her took over the body. As Aerwyna approached her miserable excuse of a father the lighting overtook her body shooting off in different directions.

"Electrokinesis? The most powerful of all the powers."

As the powers continued to overtake her, the lightning hit the roof causing it to fall down allowing her to float out of the building and into the courtyard. From where she was floating, she could see her father trying to escape the room.

"Don't you think that you can get away from me."

"I'm not escaping, I'm going to get medical attention for the Kelpie, which is currently bleeding out."

"A problem that you caused."

"I-I understand my daughter. But if nothing happens then he will die."

"That's exactly what I mean. Don't act as if nothing has happened." Aerwyna shot her hand forward aiming for her father who hugged to the wall in hope of not getting hit.

"What I want you to do is leave and never come back, leave all the realm every single one. Do you understand me."

Her father nodded in understanding, as he moved to exit the room but as he turned the corner, he slowly reached down to his boot pulling out a second dagger that was hidden within. As he quickly turned around Cailean was there with his hand around his throat pinning him to the wall.

"So why don't you prove it here right now. Leave and don't come back."

Cailean growled at her father who was hanging off the wall by his neck, his feet off the floor. With a glare in his eyes Cailean dropped her father on the floor and turned his back to the balcony where

Aerwyna was currently hovering. Another scream ripped from

Aerwyna's throat when her father plunged a second dagger into

Cailean side and twisted, ripping the skin and leaving Cailean on the

floor in a pool of blood.

***

The power that radiated in her exploded. Lighten shot out in different

directions and plants flew up to her and encircled around her middle

before also shooting off to capture her father bringing him closer to

her.

"You don't learn do you."

With one hand she encircled her father's throat the other she threw in

the direction of Caileans body she tried her hardest to help him I

away but he just stayed there lying completely still.

"you've killed him. Now I'm going to hurt you. Not kill you, that's a

far too easy escape. Im going to torture your mind, bring all the

nightmares of the people you've killed to your mind, so you'll never

be able to escape them, you'll only be able to live with them as they

drive you slowly insane."

With that said she placed her hand on his forehead as she used her

power of clairvoyance to flood his brain with the face and memories

of every single person he had killed, tortured and forced into a

situation they didn't want. With a blood curdling scream her father's eyes widened with the flood of faces and people screamed, as

Aerwyna lowered him back down the ground where he balled himself

up and rocked.

"Take him to a cell and make sure he never sees the light of day ever

again. Do you understand me."

The guards nodded as they hooked their arms under the previous

kings and escorted him into a cell where he would spend the

remainder of his life tortured within his own mind.

***

Aerwyna lowered herself to the Cailean side, rolling him over to face

her. He smiled up at her. It hurt her heart to see such a weak smile

upon his face.. His pale moonlight skin lightened to almost white any

joy that sat in his eyes faded. He was dying and she knew it, she knew

that there was nothing she could do as he laid there dying in her arms.

"Cailean?"

"Hey there my caramel fairy."

His voice was but a whisper as he tried his hardest to speak to her a

cough escaped his lips as blood removed itself from his airways.

"Shhh, don't try to speak."

Aerwyna brushed his midnight black hair away from his face as she

continued to look up at her. With any strength that he had he raised

his hand brushing her tears away from his face.

435

"Don't cry for me. I'm okay you'll see."

Another cough escaped him. Coating her dress speaks of blood.

Aerwyna tried her hardest not to cry, holding back as much as she could.

" I – I need you to do something for me okay."

Aerwyna just nodded not knowing where her voice went but it wasn't here with her now.

"I need you to go back to the shop, take it over for me. Care for it as if it was your own. When you're there in my room you'll find the box."

Aerwyna tears overflowed as she was losing her control over them as she looked down at his ever-paling face.

"In the draw beside it you'll find a key. Take that and open it for me. Okay. I'm just sad that I wont get to put it on you and marry you myself."

"You what?"

His smile widened at her shock. He didn't think it could have been that shocking considering all he told her and all his actions.

"So, what do you say, will you marry me?"

Aerwyna couldn't say anything; she didn't know if he was saying it because he was dying or if he really meant it. Either way it wasn't the right time to answer him. The only answer she had from him was as she lent down and placed a kiss upon his lips which sparked a reaction within them. The powers that surged out of her only a few moments before now dimly glowed around them. Just as it did Anion, Kano, Cas Saoirse and Tasi turned up with Aelfdane being dragged behind them in cuffs.

"What's happening?"

Aerwyna looked at her hand that was starting to glow once more similar to how it did in the Banshee valley.

"The green light."

Anion walked up kneeling beside Aerwyna who looked at her green glowing hand. What Cailean had told her was that there were different colours meaning different things. But he hadn't mentioned a green light.

"The healing light. It means you can share your power with him and heal him, but in doing so you're sacrificing half of your soul, half your power. Half of yourself. By doing this you will be together as easily as I can explain and share one heart. Be one person."

Aerwyna understood what Anion was telling her by sharing her powers in the language of the Ayla; they would be one person effectively married, and he was making sure that that was what she wanted, assuming there would be no turning back once she did it.

"Will it save him?"

Anion nodded before he turned around and joined everyone else who stood behind her, no one could make this decision but her and only her.

"Cailean, i'm going to heal you now okay."

Cailean eased himself up onto his elbows as he looked at her and told her he's not afraid to die. She wasn't going to have it as she hovered her hands over his wounds., Cailean hands rose to hers and he tried to stop her.

"This is my way of asking you to stay together with me forever. Will you say yes?"

With tears in his eyes, he smiled and nodded, and she lowered her hands to his wound as they started to radiate the same green as her hands. The longer she held her hands there the quicker his wounds healed but it was also the faster she could feel herself get more and more dizzy.

"Aerwyna stop. You need to stop, he's healed, you need to stop now." But Aerwyna didn't stop she didn't stop until she could see that his wounds were completely closed. When they were, the world spun as Ghillie ran towards her slipping behind her as she fainted into his arms.

***

When Aerwyna awoke in the white filled area, looking around her there wasn't anything that she could instantly recognize, as she walked through blindly trying to find something, someone..

"My dear."

  At the voice of her grandmother, she spun around quickly seeing her standing behind her smiling. Aerwyna ran to her grandmother with open arms.

"Where am I, what am I doing here?"

Her grandmother just smiled as she held her to the white benches that sat just to the side of them.

"My dear there is much to tell you, much you don't yet know. I'm sure you're not ready to know but I'm afraid you need to."

Aerwyna just looked at her grandmother and nodded, whatever she had to say by the look on her face it was going to be a long talk.

"The powers that you have inherited down the family line. Thankfully they were inherited from your mothers side, so your sister doesn't have the powers. "

"Wait, my sister?"

Her grandmother looked at her with shock, and no one told her about Elvinia.

"Yes, your sister. Elvinia. Didn't anyone tell you."

"Elvinia was my friend until I found out she put me in that tree. "

"She didn't put you in the tree on purpose; she put you there to save your life. Your father wanted to do what he tried to do years ago, she put you in there to save your life. And now you need to save her if you can."

"What do you mean if I can, what happened to her?"

Her grandmother sighed before she looked at Aerwyna once more. She told her that her father had an affair which resulted in Elvinia, and how he had tried numerous times to get rid of her, he didn't want her. She reminded him of a time he regretted and in the years that you were missing he tried numerous times to kill her, poison assassins. I wouldn't be surprised if he succeeded. But if he hasn't, they shall be on your side and will be one of the bestest friends you'll ever have.

"Where would she be if she was still alive."

"Knowing your father, he would have put her in the dungeon under the castle. Keep her within arm's length."

"Cailean and everyone else was there; they didn't see anyone else there."

Her grandmother looked down at the entwined hands. It looked like her Grandmother cared for her deeply. No words needed to be spoken as Aerwyna wrapped her arms around her grandmother pulling her into her embrace as her grandmother let out some quiet tears. After a while they got back up and walked around the beautiful serene white landscape as they spoke about anything and everything.

"So, what happens now?"

"You live, you live every day to your fullest, make it the best day you could ever have. Treat every day like it's the last day. Can you do that for me? What I need you to do for me when you wake up is find Cailean, tell him exactly what is on your mind and live a happy life, can you do that."

Aerwyna just nodded as she hugged her grandmother. She asked about her powers, the powers of the Ayla, to which her grandmother informed her that her powers had been shared, she didn't have any more than what a normal fairy would have. She had saved Cailean and given him half of herself.

"Now my dear do me a favour and wake up okay. I hope it will be many years until I see you again and I hope to hear numerous stories filled with love and joy and most importantly hope. You understand."

Aerwyna nodded embracing her grandmother for the last time for what she hope was for a long time, as everything in front of her started to fade before she disappeared, she asked her grandmother what her name was, and before she faded completely, she whispered it into her ear, smiling down at her granddaughter for the last time.

***

441

As Aerwyna opened her eyes she saw a room she recognized, she recognized the smells and the sounds. She was home. She was back in her room at the shop, back where she belonged. She bound out of bed looking around her, she didn't believe it she was finally home. "Cailean! Ghillie" Saoirse" Tasi" Anion" Kano! Cas! Everyone!" She ran out of the room checking Cailean room, and just like he told her back in the Fairy realm on the side rested the box his father had given her what felt like all those years ago. She ran for the draw beside it and found the key inside just like he said. Grabbing the key and the box she barreled down the stairs to see everyone sitting in by the fireplace drinking tea and laughing. She stood there for a little while taking everyone in Anion, Kano and Cas sat on the table drinking tea and eating fairy cookies looking at everyone. Ghillie faced the window taking in the little town that lay just beyond. Saoirse and Tasi looked at each other sitting closely beside each other, Tasi arm behind her head. Aerwyna noted that she would have to interrogate Saoirse on that later. The only person she could seem to find was Cailean. She rose on her toes looking over people's heads but no Advil she couldn't seem to find him. That was until two hands encircled their way around.

"So, my sleep beauty has finally awoken."

At the sound of Cailean voices behind them everyone spun to see Cailean locking Aerwyna in his firm embrace, placing a kiss on top of her head.

"Well now that she awoken it can start"

Saoirse practically squealed at Aerwyna as she grabbed the box and key from Aerwyna heads handing them to Cailean and she grabbed Aerwyna now empty hands and ran upstairs with her once more.

"Saoirse what's happening."

"Your wedding, that's what is happening."

"M-my wedding?"

Saoirse ran into Aerwyna's room, locking the door behind them.

***

After Saoirse explained what happened in the last couple of days, it had turned out Aerwyna was unconscious for four days and everyone had planned her wedding without her.

"Well after all the declaration of your love back in the fairy realm we all assumed that you would want to get married, did we get that wrong?"

"N-no you didn't I just thought it would be a couple of years away yet."

Saoirse laughed as she turned her back to Aerwyna and readied her dress, both herself and Aerwyna's.

"Why wait after everything that's happened, I think we've all learned that you only have one life, we should live it to the best we can. If you want to do something don't hold back if it's within your power to achieve it. Don't you agree."

Aerwyna thought back to what her grandmother told her 'live a happy life and tell Cailean what you feel. 'Aerwyna nodded at Saoirse when her mouth dropped open when she saw the dress that Saoirse pulled from the wardrobe.

***

Cailean stood at the end of the aisle with Ghillie and Tasi standing to the left.

"Are you nervous my friend?"

Ghillie patted his friend on his back, even if he denied he was nervous it was plain to see that he was sweating buckets. He had spoken of this day for the last four days, even before that slightly and now that It was happening, he was worried. As the piano started everyone around them stood as Cailean looked up the aisle to where Saoirse stood in a dark blue sweetheart neckline floor length satin dress, Cailean nudged Tasi who stood there with his mouth hanging open.

"Your turn next."

Cailean laughed as he turned his attention back to Saoirse walking down. Just beyond Saoirse, Cailean could see his bride as she waited at the exit from the shop, looking at him with tears streaming down her face as she stood there in the most beautiful dress he had ever seen. Aerwyna stood with purple and blue wildflowers in her hands provided by Ghillie, the dress was head to toe covered in lace depicting leaves and flowers that descended all the way to the floor. Her chest was covered with similar lace, stopping just below her collarbone in a sweetheart cut. Her veil displayed similar lace along the font all the way down to the floor leaving the back fully exposed with clear tulle. Leaving everyone able to see the open back her dress sported. As she started her descent down the aisle the cello that stood just to the back of Cailean next to the piano along the water's edge started. Cailean could feel the tear pickling behind his eyes as he watched her walk towards him, her hair flowing freely behind her he never thought she looked more beautiful that right at this moment. When she reached him for the first time in a long time he as at a loss for words. Taking her hand in his he placed a kiss upon the back as a tear join it beside leaving a small droplet on her hand. She took her hand and wiped away his tears as she smiled up at him. Looking around at the guest that joined them on the magical day. Cailean's father sat in the front row smiling up at her with tears in his eyes.

As the minister in front of them spoke the vows it got to the section where he asked for the rings, it was at this point that Saoirse approached with the box and the key on a silk pillow, with another ring bigger to fit Cailean hands.

"I think it's about time that you open this box."

Aerwyna smiled and reached for the key unlocking the box which had stayed in her room for days when she tried to break into it all the months ago when she first received it. Once she opened the lid of the geode, what she found was Cailean mother ring, new years struck her as she looked at Cain then back at Cailean as they both nodded their approval.

"She would want you to have this."

Cailean smiled as he placed the ring on her delicate finger. The image of the ring on her finger had haunted his mind for ages and now that it had come true, he couldn't think of anything more perfect than this moment.

"This ring is proof we are man and wife."

Aerwyna smiled up at him as she placed his ring on his finger looking at the two of them side by side before she spoke with a tear strained voice.

"Man and wife."

The minister continued with the vows until get got to you may now kiss the bride and Cailean had completed that task before the words had even left the minister's mouth. Pulling Aerwyna into his body wrapping his arms around the small of her back as he dipped her, deepening the kiss as much as he could when he felt Aerwyna wrap her arms around his neck pulling him closer to her as everyone around them cheered. As the happy couple walked up the aisle hand in hand as everyone threw confetti around them Tasi took Saoirse's arm following them up the aisle. With a smirk on his face, he lent into Saoirse to whisper in her ear.

" Sooner or later we'll have the same last name."

Saoirse face immediately went bright red as Tasi statement as she twisted her had looking up at him, after the whole adventure they went on she was starting to see Tasi in a new light, maybe it was time to act upon her feeling or just torment him some more to see where it would lead, she hadn't decided yet, wither way she knew it was going to be fun finding out.

***

As the day turned to night and everyone went home Cailean helped Aerwyna out of her dress undoing the button that sat just above her behind at the small of her back. While undoing the button he placed

447

chaste kisses along her spine causing her to get a shiver that ran down her spine.

"Don't"

"Did you say something?"

Aerwyna shook her head as Cailean walked them backwards until her legs hit the edge of the bed and she fell backwards laying down with Cailean propped above her.

"I've been holding back because I wanted you to sleep."

Aerwyna knew what he meant and lost her breath feeling the blood brushing to her face, she blushed furiously.

"Seriously you need to be more aware of your effect on me."

She could hear the joy of tormenting her in his voice. He was enjoying this, enjoying tormenting her as much as he could .

"T-that wasn't my intention."

"That's why I'm telling you to be aware of it"

Cailean smiled awkwardly resting his hands around the back of her neck, just like that he pulled her in for a kiss.

"Aerwyna."

Cailean hands crept up around her back, lightly trailing his fingers up and down her spine sending more shivers through her. She Immediately tried to pull his hands away, but he made a somewhat mischievous smile, and she couldn't stop him.

"C-Cailean."

"What is it?"

"Y- your hand…."

"Should I stop?"

He murmured next to her ear, sending shivers down her spine, increasing the blush which decorated her face illuminating it like a red light.

"N-not really."

Cailean chuckled as she averted her eyes and planted a kiss on her cheek.

"You've gone red again."

"S-stop it."

"Well, it's like they say."

Cailean hands stopped abruptly.

"Huh."

Aerwyna looked up at him curiously As she wondered what made him stop, he grabbed her firmly and pulled her close. Laying her on top of him, she was looking down at him caught in his embrace unable to escape.

"Maybe this will be more effective than singing songs."

"What will?"

"If a person is tired, they would sleep soundly, right?"

Aerwyna gasped, shooting a hand to cover her mouth. Cailean grinned, and she felt his lips against her ear.

"I'll tire you out."

She could hear the laughter in his voice as he spoke, and a devilish smile decorated his face.

"Cailean!"

Aerwyna tried grabbing the pillow which lay behind Cailean's head to whack him in the face, but he stopped her grabbing her hands. She instinctively tried to pull back, Cailean held her firmly in his arms.

"You brought this on yourself, Aerwyna."

"But…. ahh."

Aerwyna couldn't help but yelp as Cailean blew across her ear. Meanwhile his hands moved playfully across her body.

"I might not be able to sleep tonight, either…."

Aerwyna signed and smiled. surrendering herself, she wrapped her arms around him as every touch warmed her and she let the blissful feeling take over her senses.

Epilogue

*** One year later.***

"Cailean, can you get the door? I think Anion and the boys are here."

Cailean walked to the Brownie door with a towel thrown over his

shoulder as Anion and the boy walked in holding a multitude of tiny

wrapped presents.

"Where's my little girl, where are you hiding her?"

"Dads been talking about her since this morning, he won't speak

about anything else."

Cailean laughed as he looked at the three little Brownies who had

helped him more than he admitted.

"Aerwyna sorting her out now she'll be down soon, some take a seat."

Before he could even get Anion and the boy comfortable the Selkie

door opened revealing Saoirse and Tasi holding another boat load of

tiny wrapped presents.

"Before you ask, they'll be down soon Anion and the boys are

already here. Go join them."

Cailean laughed as he approached the Kelpie door opening it to find his father standing there with three servants following him each holding their own magnitude of presents.

"You know we've got to find room for these all yet, you all spill her too much."

"I think I'm allowed to spoil her. I have a right to as gra ... .there's my girl's."

Cailean turned around to see Aerwyna holding their little baby girl in her arms. Their baby was wrapped up in a pastel blue shawl, her tiny wings tuck gently behind her. Her raven black hair was brushed to the side finished with a tiny pink bow. Here cheek a radiant pink from just being fed.

"Cain, it's so nice to see you."

Aerwyna hugged her father - in- law as he cooed at his new granddaughter. As all four of them walked into what was now called the front room, as she sat down in her chair with everyone she loved surrounding her, she didn't think things could get much better than this.

"So, what is this darling little one's name?"

Aerwyna looked around at all her friends, her new family and smiled while a small tear fell down her cheek. Cailean knelt down beside her wiping the tears away as she rubbed his daughter's head and kissed his wife who he adored more than he admitted in front of his family

and friend. Aerwyna looked at Cailean as they spoke in union.

"Everyone, I'd like you to meet our little deer. This is Eilonwy Skye

Colquhoun Dubhghlas."

Everyone around smiled down at the little babe that nestled down in

Aerwyna arms. She was proof that love, and trust within yourself and

others really could help save the world.

THE END

454

Myth/Lore

Kelpie - Kel - Pee

Selkie - Sell - Key

Banshee - Ban - She

Ghillie Dhu - Gill - e -Dhu

Characters

Aerwyna - A -er - win - ya

Cailean - Kay - Lean

Saorise - Ser - sha

Tasi - Ta -Sigh

Aelfdane - Elf - Dane

Aramoana - Ara - mo - a- na

Ghillie Dhu - Gill - e - Dhu

Anion - An - e - on

Kano - Ka - No

Cas - Cash

Eilonwy - El - Lon - wen

Elivina - El - vina

Town/Currency

Llwyn - Lle - win

Saruna - sa- rune - na

Folklore/Mythology

Even though the characters of this story are based on Scottish and Irish Folklore and Mythology, they are my interpretation of them. It is by no means an accurate representation of them and as such hopefully does no cause offence to the culture. If this inspires you to learn more about them I have included the lore below.

Kelpie - Kelpie typically reside near water taking the form of a black horse, they will lure travellers to their death. Scotland is full of wonderful folklore but none got me more than the Kelpies. They are vengeful and beautiful creatures. I was told that they are the enemy of every creature and humans alike. They would normally appear quiet and peaceful in order to temp the weary traveller to come closer and ride them, once they did they would run to the deepest body of water and drag their victim below. Once I heard this tale I always wondered what it would be like if they were the good guys, and save the world rather than try and lure people to their death. So be careful if you see a dark black horse on the edge of water, it might just be a kelpie trying to trap you.

Selkies - Selkies are magically shape-shifters often found all over Scotland and Ireland, sometimes Iceland. I first heard about them on the Orkney islands. I was told they are often seen as seals but they can shed their skin to explore our world, but when they are wearing their seal hide it gives them the ability to explore the world. I was told that many of the sightings were on the night the moon was viable, and they would dance on the sandy beaches, but they had to be sure that they kept their skins close as if they lost them they would stay human forever. Most of the people i spoke to told me that selkies were beautiful, like ungodly so. The tale that hit me most was once where men would take a female selkie skin and hide it which would mean they would no longer be able to return to the sea then be trapped in a loveless human marriage. So when you're in Scotland or Ireland and you see and seal it could be a selkie just be sure not to take their skin.

Banshee - long hair women who call is heard mean death. Being in a different part of the country that you don't know and hearing that definitely makes you on the lookout for any deathly screams. Even though the person i spoke to told me they are a woman with long hair no one is entirely sure what they look like, all they know is when they scream or cry something bad is going to happen.

Ghillie Dhu - This was a strange one of my travels. Everyone seems to have a different option of the Ghillie Dhu, some said he was a small fairy, some said he was a tall man wrapped in green. When I heard that I sort of picture jack in the green. But e=what everyone seemed to agree on was that he helped lost children find their way home. So I thought adding him in to help both Aerwyna and Cailean find their way but also add in some rivealy with Cailean would be a funny addition to the story.

Brownies- I was told this story in a bar in Scotland by an old gentleman. He told me that brownies were little men that came into the house at night and helped to clean. They often like sweet things and one of the best ways to lead them out when they lose their way is sugar water, so if things end up cleaner than when you left them then maybe you have been visited by a brownie, maybe leave a glass of sugar water on the window seal as a thank you.

If you want to learn more about Scottish mythology then the best website I recommend is **folklorescotland.com** I found this very helpful in my research. So thank you to the writers of that website.

These are the songs that helped inspire some of my favourite scenes.

- My Love Is Like A Red Red Rose - Sung And Played By Josienne Clarke & Ben Walker

- Amhran Na Farraige - Sung By Lisa Hannigan From The Movie Song Of The Sea.

- Dance Of The Prince Orgeat Ad The Sugar Plum Fairy By Tchaikovsky

- Banshee By Caranua.

- Fairytale By Alexander Rybak

- Fictional By Khloe Rose

- A Dream Worth Keeping By Shenna Easton From The Movie Ferngully The Last Rainforest